Harbour Secrets

Port In A Storm
Ely North

Red Handed Print

To contact ely@elynorthcrimefiction.com

Author's website at https://elynorthcrimefiction.com

https://www.facebook.com/elynorthcrimefictionUK

Cover design by Cherie Chapman/Chapman & Wilder

Cover images © Jack Cousin / konradbak / Костянтин Дубенець / Passakorn
/ Adobe Stock Photos
Disclaimer: This is a work of fiction. Names, characters, businesses, places,
events, locales, and incidents are either the products of the author's
imagination or used in a fictitious manner. Any resemblance to actual persons,
living or dead, or actual events is purely coincidental.

Published by Red Handed Print

First Edition

Kindle e-book ISBN-13: 978-0-6459958-9-3

Paperback ISBN-13: 978-0-6459958-8-6

Also By Ely North – DCI Finnegan Series

Book 1: **Black Nab**

Book 2: **Jawbone Walk**

Book 3: **Vertigo Alley**

Book 4: **Whitby Toll**

Book 5: **House Arrest**

Book 6: **Gothic Fog**

Book 7: **Happy Camp**

Book 8: **Harbour Secrets**

Book 9: **Murder Mystery** – Pre-order (Dec 2024)

DCI Finnegan Series Boxset #1: **Books 1 – 3**

DCI Finnegan Series Boxset #2: **Books 4 – 6**

Prequel: **Aquaphobia** (Free ebook for newsletter subscribers)

*Note: All books are available from Amazon in ebook, paperback, and in **Kindle Unlimited** (excluding Aquaphobia). Paperbacks can be ordered from all good bookshops. **Boxset print editions are one book compiled from three books. They do not come in a box. *** Pre-orders only apply to ebooks.

.

North Yorkshire Moors

Wednesday 19th July

ROPE

Twisted strands of fibre spun tight and strong.

Since the dawn of humanity, it has been a silent companion to progress, binding the world together with its simple elegance. It has hoisted sails, secured tents against the wildest storms, and pulled the weight of nations. In the hands of explorers, it's scaled mountains; in the weathered hands of farmers, tethered livestock; in the dexterous fingers of craftswomen, woven baskets.

Rope is survival, resilience, innovation.

And yet, amidst its countless uses, there lingers a darker purpose.

Her feet are cold.

No, not just cold, they are numb.

She can no longer feel them. Not good when trying to keep one's balance.

Shifting her weight, the ice beneath her moves.

It's unforgiving, slick and treacherous. Each tiny movement is a gamble, where the stakes are life or death.

A shiver runs down her spine, and not because of the ice.

The wound in her thigh pulses, sharp and persistent, sending warm blood trickling down her leg. It meanders in lazy rivulets. Soaks into the fabric of her trousers.

Past the knee, it free falls and lands with a graceless splat on the plastic bags, merging with icy liquid.

The warmth is almost comforting.

Almost... apart from the fact it's a harsh reminder... time is running out.

She can hear them.

The men.

They're coming for her.

Distant, but drawing nearer. Their voices are rough, authoritative, barking orders she can't quite make out.

They'll be methodical, cautious. It's how they've been trained. Textbook. They don't cut corners.

Her breathing is laboured, coming in ragged gasps.

It's painful to swallow, so she doesn't.

The stringent aromatics of cannabis creeps under the door.

The reason she's here.

Seems so irrelevant now.

She tries to steady herself, to ignore the fire in her lungs and the pounding in her head.

But it's hard—so hard.

The knot has been placed off-centre, not pressing into her carotid artery as it should.

At first, she thinks it's a mistake.

Sloppy work.

But she knows *her* too well.

She doesn't make mistakes.

No, she's a stickler, precise, calculating.

This knot has been placed just so. She'd expect nothing less from *her*.

A cruel, sick twist, to prolong suffering.

Her blood still flows, her heart still beats, her lungs still wheeze, and the clock... still ticks.

A small sound escapes her lips—a whimper, perhaps, though it's hard to tell.

She tries to focus, to push the pain aside, and think of something—anything—other than the cold beneath her feet and the groan of straining fibres above.

Ice that turns to liquid, blood that drains from wound, knot that doesn't press where it should—each detail conspires to drag her closer to the inevitable.

The noise outside is closer, but still some distance away from the condemned cell.

Her thoughts are muddled, a smokescreen of reality and woozy dreams.

Sleep would be a blessing.

But one thing is as clear as day: she'll be *dead* before they reach her.

ROPE

The strands quiver, moan.

Louder.

The final warning.

With a sudden, brutal certainty, it happens.

Ice shifts.

Feet slip.

The world drops away.

Noose tightens.

Legs jerk, naked feet twitch.

Prisha's last conscious thought is a fleeting acknowledgement of the truth she's always known.

Rope is a silent and efficient executioner.

2

Twelve Days Earlier

Friday 7th July - 9:05 pm

The tanker, loaded with forty-thousand litres of diesel, pulls out of the gate, the glaring headlights illuminating spears of spindly rain in the gloom of a distinctly bleak summer night.

Gareth taps a button on the steering wheel and Classic FM immediately floods the comfortable cabin with the sound of Johann Sebastian Bach.

He yawns. 'I hate Bach and his harpsichord,' he grumbles as he mutes the music and hits the call button on his phone. It purrs three times before it's answered.

'Hi, love, how yer going?' The dulcet tones of his wife.

'Aye, not bad, Angie. Last delivery of the day. Should be home about elevenish, give or take.'

'No problem. I might be tucked up in bed by then, but your dinner is keeping warm in the oven.'

'What's on the menu?'

'Cottage pie. There are peas in the freezer. Throw them into a pan of boiling water. They'll only take a couple of minutes.'

'You're a bloody star. What would I do without you. Any news?'

'About what?'

'I don't know. Heard from the kids or my mother?'

'No. No news is good news, eh?' she adds, laughing.

'Righto, see you in a couple of hours or so. Love you, babe.'

'Love you.'

He taps at the music button on the steering wheel repeatedly. Radio stations flick past on his console until he settles on Smooth FM. Relaxing into his seat, as the gears automatically change, he hums along to Sade and "Your Love is King".

***

With his week's shift almost finished, and the petrol station only ten miles away, Gareth curses as he spots the temporary traffic lights and the sign which reads, "Road Ahead Closed". A black transit van in front slows and turns left, following the detour sign.

'Bloody wonderful. Just my luck.'

He turns off onto a minor road, hedged in by stone walls and overhanging trees. Driving on for another five minutes, the lane narrows, the rain intensifies, and the depressed daylight slowly succumbs to creeping darkness.

'Christ, I'm buggered if I meet another truck.' He slows and studies his GPS. 'Ah, I see where it's taking me. Another mile and I should be able to turn back onto the main road.'

Feeling relieved, he presses on the accelerator and the powerful engine reciprocates.

As the tanker rounds a bend, Gareth groans and hits the brakes hard. 'Bollocks! What now?'

The transit van has come to a halt as a worker wearing a hi-viz vest, hard-hat, and holding a red and white stop sign speaks to the van driver. Gareth hits a button, and the window slides down. Popping his head out, he waves at the worker, who nods and ambles towards him.

'What's the problem?' Gareth asks.

'A water pipe has burst,' the worker replies in a soft Irish brogue. 'That's why the main road was closed. The water has backed up and caused major subsidence up ahead. You'll have to turn around. There's no way through.'

Gareth is incredulous. 'Turn around! Have you seen the size of this rig? I've no bloody chance.'

The worker smiles. 'Don't pop a gasket, granddad. There's a farm gate twenty yards behind you. I'll open it up and help you reverse in,' he explains as another worker materialises from nowhere and joins him.

Gareth is already mentally figuring out an alternative route to his intended destination. 'Okay, thanks. It's gonna be a tight fit.' Shifting gears, the reversing camera flashes up on his console. He waits a moment as the first worker appears at the back of the tanker and motions with his hand. The vehicle creaks and groans in annoyance as it rolls back, warning bleeps piercing the surrounding sleepy countryside. The second worker walks alongside the cabin, muttering into his radio clipped to his safety vest.

'Keep coming, keep coming. Another twenty feet, then put a full left-lock on, but watch your front end.'

Gareth whispers under his breath, 'Only been driving tankers for thirty years. I think I know how to reverse into a field.'

'Okay! Hard left!' the second worker calls out, still escorting the cab.

Gareth pokes his head out of the window and glances behind. As he firmly turns the steering wheel, he looks down at the worker and is slightly bemused.

Odd... he's wearing shoes.

Peering intently into the console, studying the reversing camera, he notices the first worker is sporting trainers on his feet. The air brakes explode with a hiss like a bronchial dinosaur as the tanker shudders to a halt. Gareth removes his right hand from the steering wheel, leans forward slightly, and places his fingertips on the rectangular panic button located underneath the dashboard. One press and the window will roll up, cabin doors will automatically lock, the engine will be immobilised, and the anti-siphoning mechanism will engage, as a signal is transmitted to the main depot alerting them of his position. In thirty years, he's never had to use it, and he's aware it's a big deal. A specially trained mechanic will be required to disengage the protection mechanisms, which could take hours. But then again, with a cargo worth nearly fifty thousand pounds wholesale, he can't take chances.

He stares at the worker. 'What department did you say you work for?'

The man smiles. 'Redcar and Cleveland Borough Council Highways Department,' he replies in his lilting Irish accent.

Gareth frowns. 'Bit far out of your area, aren't you? Your boundary is twenty miles north. This is North Yorkshire County Council's responsibility.'

The man shuffles. 'We're the nighttime emergency crew. The North Yorkshire boys are dealing with another incident and asked for our help.'

'Is that right. Got any ID on you, mate? Not being funny, but you can't be too cautious these days.'

He blinks, then grins again. 'Sure thing. I understand.' He reaches under his jacket, then pulls himself up onto the cab step. 'Here you go, here's my ID,' he states as a pistol is placed against Gareth's forehead. 'Now, take your hand off the panic button, leave the engine running, and get out of the fecking truck, otherwise the inside of your cab will be re-decorated with your brains. Understand?'

'Aye, okay, calm down, lad.'

Cautiously, Gareth opens the door as the man drops to the ground, still pointing the pistol at his face. Placing one foot on the cabin step, he spins around, holds the handrail and lowers himself onto the damp bitumen.

'Now give me your mobile,' the man demands as his co-worker saunters up behind Gareth.

As his hand nervously fumbles inside his jacket for the phone, he remembers his training. Press the off button three times in rapid succession, and it will send an SOS back to the depot, along with a GPS marker. His indecision becomes irrelevant as the man behind pulls out a hammer from his jacket and brings it down onto the back of his head. Gareth grunts and collapses to the ground.

'You stupid fecking, eejit! What did you do that for? We're supposed to tie him up.'

The assailant smirks. 'You're too soft, Fergus. He could have hit the panic button on his mobile. We take no chances,' he says as he retrieves Gareth's phone from his jacket, pulls the back off, prises the battery loose, then drops it into his pocket.

'Christ, Cillian, you didn't have to hit him that hard. The aul fella looks to be in terrible trouble, so he does,' he says with concern as he drops to his knees and notices the bloodied gash on the back of Gareth's head.

'Quit your bitching and change the number plates. We've wasted enough time already. We still have work ahead of us. It's going to be a long night.'

'What are we to do with the old codger?'

'Nothing. Leave him there. There's bound to be a passing vehicle at some point.'

'He could get run over.'

Cillian pops a smoke into his mouth and lights up. 'Feck me, so what? One less Redcoat bastard to worry about. Now, the number plates!' he yells as he pulls himself up into the cab. Holding a power screwdriver, he deftly removes the screws from the console, identifies the GPS tracker and yanks it from its housing, snapping the wiring as he does so.

As Gareth slips into the twilight between awareness and oblivion, Sade's song swirls around his head - your love is king. His last thoughts are of the cottage pie in the oven, the frozen peas, and his loving wife sound asleep in bed.

3

Runswick Bay

Saturday 8th July - 11:33 pm

Declan Hughes exits the battered Lada Riva and slams the driver's door shut, unsuccessfully.

'Piece of crap,' he mutters, disgruntled. He places his hip against the panel and gives it a firm shove. The door closes with a click. Peering up at the glittering stars, he rolls a skinny spliff, half-tobacco, half-weed. Sparks up and inhales. With the roach dangling from his lips, he zips up the front of his black puffer jacket and stamps his feet.

'Come on, you prick. Where are you? Eleven o'clock on the dot, you said.'

He gazes around the empty car park at Runswick Bay, and the twinkling street lights from the small fishing village to the left of him. Checking his phone again, for new notifications, he's dismayed to see there are none. He knows not to message his supplier too often. The less contact between them, the better.

His gaze wanders out to the North Sea and another set of lights blinking on the horizon. Possibly a container ship churning its way to the Port of Tyne, or maybe further north up to Scotland.

The growl of thunder and occasional flash of sheet lightning tells him the predicted storm is behind schedule, but definitely on its way, taking its time as it rolls in over an agitated sea.

Tired and weary, after a long shift as a trainee chef, Declan curses the fact he still has to deal small amounts of weed to supplement his meagre income. A beam of light behind him, followed by the unmistakable whoosh of a distant engine, has him peering inland as he bites the inside of his cheek. His supplier always stops about a mile away and sends a message to make sure the coast is clear. Glancing again at his mobile, he feels a pang of anxiety at the lack of any new messages.

'Fuck,' he mutters.

He jumps back into the car, and wincing, as if it will reduce the noise, he starts the engine. Without the aid of headlights, he navigates the vehicle to the far end of the car park, next to some adjoining bushes. Exiting, he bumps the door shut and slinks into the shrubs and squats. Nervous, he mutes his phone as a splash of car headlights approach from the road above. He groans as the vehicle creeps into the car park.

'What are the chances of that?' he whispers. 'Four empty car parks to choose from and they pick this one.'

The car, which in the gloom looks like a small SUV, comes to a halt fifty feet away from Declan's hiding spot.

It also parks in the shadows.

He grins to himself. 'Some dirty buggers are up to no good. Cheating on their husband or wife. Let's hope they're quick. In, out, shake it all about.' The moment of relaxation is short-lived as three men emerge from the SUV and survey the scene with an unnerving disquiet. The tallest man nods to a colleague in the direction of the Lada. 'Oh, fuck it,' he murmurs, edging further back into a thicket.

The figure approaches, short and stocky, his hands thrust deep into the pockets of a bomber jacket. Occasionally, the beam from a streetlamp bounces off his bald crown. Stooping, he peers through the glass on the passenger side, then tries the handle. As it gives, he pokes his head inside and studies the interior before emerging.

'Empty,' he states to his associates, who are waiting, patience wearing thin. 'The thing's a fecking wreck. Probably been dumped here.' His soft Irish brogue hovers in the eerie stillness of the night, the calm before the storm.

The tall man offers instructions to the other lackey. 'Check the beach. Make sure it's not a couple down there having a quickie under the starry night.'

The short bald man edges towards the bushes, unzips his fly, pulls his cock out.

Declan grimaces as the occasional splash of piss sprays onto his jacket, the strident whiff of urine assaulting his nostrils. Pins and needles run up his calf and into his hamstrings, the initial numbness turning into a searing pain in his left buttock.

The rhythmical rapid click of a zip indicates the bald man has finished relieving himself. As he turns to walk away, Declan, now in agony, moves his leg forward an inch. Under normal circumstances, the sound of the twig snapping beneath his boot would have been almost inaudible, but tonight, to Declan, it sounds like the crack of a bullwhip.

The bald man halts and glances over his shoulder.

He turns and dips his hands inside the jacket, retrieving a torch in one hand, and a pistol in the other.

'What is it?' the leader of the trio calls out.

'Not sure. Something or someone skulking in the bushes.'

Declan has seen a couple of real guns in his short life, usually brandished by wannabe gangsters as a penis extension. But this gun is different. It has a long barrel. The only time he's seen anything similar is in films and TV shows. Unless he's very much mistaken, this particular weapon has a silencer attached to it.

He closes his eyes, pulls his woollen hat down as far as it will go, and sucks himself in, trying to become invisible. He thinks of his girlfriend laid out on the couch at home, probably watching a crappy American rom-com, as his baby son sleeps upstairs in his cot, warm and safe. With heart beating like a snare drum, and all senses elevated to critical levels, he can almost smell his little boy, a delicate scent of fresh milk and talcum powder. Swallowing hard, he prays to an invisible God that he'll see his son again.

Please, God!

He thinks about fessing up and walking out with his hands in the air. Whatever these three are up to, they're up to no good. Once he explains he's also up to no good, waiting for his weed supplier, they'll understand. Simply four shady characters whose paths happened to cross, going about their shady business in the middle of a very shady night. They'd all have a good laugh about it.

Then again…

People on the wrong side of the law aren't prone to forgiveness and understanding. They exist in a vortex of violence and suspicion, forever looking over their shoulders, trusting no one, suspecting everyone, paranoia on steroids. And men carrying pistols with silencers weren't the sort of characters who were out to impress the ladies. They were the sort of people who were out to kill silently, then slip away into the night.

The searing beam of the flashlight dances over his closed eyelids.

Please, God!

A sudden rustle to his left startles him, terror gripping his gut. A high-pitched scream follows as he fights to control his rapidly clenching sphincter.

'Fucking thing!' the bald man yells, followed by the muted "pfft, pfft, pfft" of three muffled shots. Another flash of sheet lightning briefly illuminates the car park, turning night into midday.

'What is it?' the tall man shouts.

'A bastard fox. Scared me half to bloody death. Fecking vermin. I've never heard them yelp like that before. It was almost human.'

'Come on, Cillain, you stupid prick. Put the gun away and let's get on with it. I reckon we have an hour at most before the storm hits.'

Warily, the bald man slips the pistol back inside his jacket and rejoins the other man.

Declan swallows hard and dares to breathe again, overcome with exhaustion.

Thank you, God!

4

Whitby

Sunday 9th July

Frank enters his allotment hut and settles into his familiar chair, the worn leather creaking under his weight. He retrieves the diary from his satchel, uncaps the fountain pen, and makes himself comfortable at his desk. For a brief second, the nib hovers above the paper. Then he begins.

> What does everyone hold, but seldom keep?
> Give up?
> SECRETS.
>
> It's not one of mine. I'm not that profound.
> I got it from inside a Christmas cracker one year.
> Cheesy, I know. At least, that's what I thought, initially. But it has remained in my

memory for many a year, because that little aphorism, or adage, contains more than a grain of truth.

There's a contract which comes with knowing things others don't. If broken, it can unleash devastating consequences.

The next-door neighbour who knows the husband is cheating on his wife.

The killers who buried the body in the woods.

The young lass who had an abortion without telling her devout parents.

The man who has been handed the prognosis from his doctor... six months, if you're lucky. He keeps it from his wife and children.

Secrets are merely vessels which carry truths. And truths can be good or bad. A secret isn't just a whisper in the dark or a thought kept under lock and key. It's a burden, a living, breathing thing that can twist itself around your soul, tightening its grip with each passing day.

People think of secrets as hidden treasures, tucked away in the recesses of the mind, but they're more like debts you hide from the world. And debts accrue interest, compounding in silence, until the cost of keeping them outweighs the price of letting them go.

The tricky part is deciding which secrets are worth keeping and which ones are too dangerous to hold close. It's a balancing act—knowing when to speak and when to stay silent. A poorly kept secret can unravel everything, while a well-guarded one may protect not just you, but those you care about. The skill lies in knowing the difference.

In my line of work, I've seen secrets destroy lives and save them in equal measure. I've heard a single word, spoken at the wrong time, bring down corrupt drug empires. I've witnessed silence preserve the innocence of those who deserve a chance at happiness.

But all secrets have a way of slipping out, regardless of how tightly we hold them. They seep through the cracks of our resolve, whispering to confidants, or bursting forth to the throng in an unguarded drunken moment.

You can seal your lips and lock the door, but the truth has a nasty habit of finding its way out, one way or another.

Secrets are shields and weapons at the same time. Some protect, some kill. But eventually, shields get heavy, and weapons have but one purpose. If you bear a secret, be mindful of why you hold it, and be watchful of letting it go.

When will your secret be revealed, and by whom?

A cold sea breeze, partnered with the distant murmur of breakers, drifts through the open doorway of the hut as Frank closes his diary, drops it into the satchel, and fastens the leather straps. After placing the cap on his pen, he pours a shot of whisky into a grubby glass, leans back in his chair, lights a cigarette, and takes a long drag, watching the smoke curl upwards, lost in reflection. Breathing out, his gaze falls upon his bountiful allotment. In this rare moment of solitude, he allows himself a peaceful release. Whispering his fears and doubts into the fleeting tentacles of bluish-white smoke, he sets them free to dissipate into the salty air. It's a small ritual, but one that lightens the load, if only for a brief moment.

Taking a last drag on the cigarette, he turns to the faded photograph on the wall—a snapshot of a happier time, with his daughter on his shoulders, smiling brightly, as radiant as the summer sun. A sharp pang of loss encircles his heart, reminding him of the reason he continues to fight, endure... and weep.

Hope and despair—opposites on the same coin—make uneasy bedfellows.

Footsteps, accompanied by a familiar hacking cough, break his reverie. Strolling from his dusty hut, he emerges into the bright light of a cool summer's day. He smiles benignly at the old man approaching.

'Eh up, Frank. I see you're back.'

'Aye. Arrived home yesterday morning, Arthur.'

The old man pulls a smouldering cigarette butt from his cracked lips. 'How was it then, Greece?'

'Very enjoyable, although a touch too warm for my liking. But plenty of little taverns to escape into while Meera lay baking on the beach.'

Arthur chuckles. 'A few refreshing ales then?'

'One or two.'

'Never fancied going abroad, meself. Foreign food has never agreed wi' me, and they don't speak English. And I heard they drive on the wrong side of the road. Is it true?'

Now it's Frank's turn to laugh. 'True enough, Arthur. But they're a friendly bunch, the Greeks.' He pops back inside the hut and returns clutching a brown paper bag. 'Here you go, Arthur, a small token of my appreciation for tending to my allotment while I was away.'

The old man takes it warily and pulls the bottle from the bag. He fumbles his spectacles on and reads the label.

'Ouzo. What the bloody hell's that when it's at home?'

'It's a Greek liqueur. Aniseed flavour. Mix it with a quarter glass of water and it turns milky white. It's typically drunk as an apéritif.'

Arthur removes his flat cap and scratches his mottled bald head. 'A pair of teeth?' he quizzes, completely befuddled.

'Apéritif, an appetiser, you know... a small drink to go along with nibbles.' Frank pulls the hut door shut and locks up.

'Has it got a kick?'

Frank pats him on the back. 'Aye, Arthur. It will put the hair back on your head.' As he ambles towards the gate, he half-turns and calls out. 'Unless this bloody summer finally arrives, I don't think we're going to get much of a tomato crop this year.'

'Nay lad... nay. Bloody British summers.'

5

Monday 10th July

There's a crisp sharpness to the morning air despite the sun making an early appearance. A couple of trawlers chug slowly towards the harbour entrance, the throb of their diesel engines bouncing over dull waves.

On Tate Hill Sands, wedged between Whitby's East pier and the river, mother and daughter are nearing the midpoint of their customary morning walk. With the demands of everyday life, they don't often spend much time together to simply enjoy one another's company.

'Mam, I've been invited to a party on Friday night.'

The mother masks her concern with a spirited, 'Oh, yes. Whose party, and where?'

'It's Charlotte Mackenzie's fourteenth birthday.'

'She lives in Sandsend, right?'

'Yeah.'

'Will it be supervised?' She's already imagining alcohol, cigarettes, maybe even drugs.

The girl focuses on Baxter, their four-year-old golden Labrador, as it bounds into the sea up to its chest.

'Her parents are going out, but they'll be back by eleven. Charlotte asked me and some other girls to sleep over.'

The mother's anxiety rises. 'Will there be boys?' Damn boys, the rising threat. She knew this day would come, but why did it have to arrive so quickly?

'A couple,' she replies coyly, not as adept at subterfuge as her mother.

'Do I know them?'

'No.'

'These *two* boys, are they sleeping over?'

'As if.' Her response is too quick and flippant. 'So, can I sleep over?'

The mother stops walking and peers at her daughter. 'I don't see why not.'

The teenage girl's smile could lift the weariest of hearts, a dead giveaway she's been frugal with the truth.

'Yay! Thanks, mam.'

'Of course, I'll need the phone number of Charlotte's mother. I'll give her a quick call to make sure everything's above board.'

The smile evaporates, replaced by horror. 'What?'

Baxter leaps from the water, rolls around in the sand, stands bolt upright, tail erect, his black nose twitching as he savours the air.

'You heard.'

'No! You cannot do that. It will make me look like a right loser. Forget it. I won't bother going.'

The mother becomes distracted as her attention shifts to Baxter as he circles a clump of seaweed.

'Don't be so petulant. Why will it make you look like a loser?' She violently thrusts the dog lead into her daughter's arms. 'Quick! Get Baxter on the lead. He must have sniffed out another dead fish. The last time he ate one, it cost me two hundred bloody quid at the vets.'

'Why don't you put him on the lead?'

'Because you're younger and faster than me,' she replies, shoving her daughter gently on the shoulder.

'Fine!' She stomps off across the damp sand in an exaggerated display of petulance only teenagers can pull off with such aplomb.

'Hurry!'

'I am hurrying.'

The mother's phone pings as she resists a smile at her offspring's theatrics. 'Half girl, half woman,' she mutters. Retrieving the phone from her coat pocket, she reads the message from her husband, a banal morsel of life in sharp contrast to the niggling worry about her daughter's burgeoning social life.

> *Be home a bit later tonight. Catching up with the boys for a couple of jars at the brewery. See you about six. Love you. X*

She's about to reply with a thumbs up and a heart emoji when the tranquillity shatters. A piercing shriek slices the morning calm and scuds across the harbour. The phone slips from her fingers and lands without a sound on the sand as a primal force awakens within her. She sprints towards her little girl, as her maternal instincts surge.

6

Detective Inspector Prisha Kumar hurries down the slope towards the police barrier tape on the beach. In the distance, the all too familiar sight of the forensic tent covering the crime scene, and the bunny-suited swarm of forensics officers calmly carrying out their duties. DS Zac Stoker ambles towards her and ducks under the tape, his feet already clothed in protective wear.

'I came as soon as I heard,' Prisha states. 'Dead body?'

Zac nods. 'Aye. At least I think so. There's only part of a leg sticking out from the sand. Definitely an adult male, though.'

'How do you know?'

'Large foot, and there are hairs on the knuckle of the big toe.'

Prisha slips into her shoe coverings as she rests one hand on Zac's shoulder for balance.

'Have there been any reports of people missing at sea recently?'

A shake of the head. 'No. Last one was about three months back. A surfer near Robin Hood's Bay went missing. No body recovered yet.'

'What state is the leg in?'

'It's seen better days. Tip of the pinky toe is missing, probably fish food. And other scarring to the foot and some loose skin.'

'Sounds relatively recent, not three months old.'

'And Robin Hood's Bay is south. Typically, the coastal flow is north to south, although we did have that big storm that blew through late Saturday night.'

Prisha gazes around at the scene, her eyes resting on a middle-aged woman and young teenage girl sitting on a bench a hundred yards away.

'Who discovered the body?'

'Mother and daughter, over there,' he says, his foot pointing in the direction of the bench. 'The mother is Rebecca Foster, the daughter, Ruby Foster. It was their dog, Baxter, who alerted them to the leg at around seven this morning.'

'Where's the dog now?'

'Why? Do you want to get a statement from him?'

'Very amusing.'

'The husband arrived and collected the dog. They live up on Green Lane, behind the Abbey. The beach is their half-way point on their morning walk, then they head back the way they came. The young lass is a bit shook up.'

'Not surprised. It's enough to put you off your cornflakes. What about Doctor Whipple?'

'He could put anyone off their cornflakes.'

Prisha grins. 'Oh, I see. It's going to be one of those days, is it? Is Whipple on his way?'

'Unfortunately, yes. He didn't sound too pleased.'

'If he won the lottery, I doubt he'd crack a smile.'

Zac throws her a knowing glance. 'You know Whipple's views on gambling.' He drops into his sublime impersonation of the good doctor. 'A most nefarious scourge upon humanity. A vile machination preying upon the feeble of mind and witless, engendering nought but despair and ruination.'

Prisha chuckles as she notices lead forensics, Charlene Marsden, emerging from the tent. Charlene raises her hand and beckons them over.

Zac frowns. 'That's bloody quick. They've only been here thirty minutes.'

They slip under the barrier tape and stride over to the crime scene. Charlene lowers her face mask and smiles.

'Ah, Prisha, how are you on this fine July morning?'

'Feeling suitably refreshed, actually. I ran a half-marathon on Saturday, and yesterday Adam took me out for a lovely lunch at The Pheasant Hotel in Harome.'

'Lucky for some.'

'So, what have you got for us?'

Charlene pulls the flap back on the tent. 'Not much.'

Prisha stares at the dismembered leg. 'Is that it?'

'Yes, so far. The leg has been severed about six inches below the pelvis. As you can see, it's a jagged cut, possibly from a boat propeller. We'll use probing rods to scour the beach for the rest of the body, and if that doesn't work, we'll bring in cadaver dogs.'

Zac rubs his short-cropped beard. 'If a boat prop hit the body, then it's quite possible the rest of the body is still in the water?'

Charlene nods in the affirmative. 'Yes, I agree. But due diligence and all that.'

'Any idea how long it may have been here?'

Charlene frowns. 'Hard to say. The leg is in good condition, but the wet sand would have protected it from the elements. But it definitely hasn't been here for years.'

Zac rolls his eyes. 'That narrows it down.'

Charlene detects the heavy sarcasm. 'Sorry, Zac. It's the best I can do.' She glances out of the tent and chuckles. 'Maybe Doctor Whipple will be able to narrow down the time-frame for you.'

Prisha groans as the hulking frame of Whipple lumbers ungainly across the beach.

She turns to Zac. 'Please don't wind him up. He's insufferable at the best of times.'

Zac pulls a hurt expression. 'Me? I don't know what you mean.'

'Ah, morning Doctor Whipple,' Prisha declares as he approaches.

'Indeed, it is morning, Inspector Kumar. A morning that has been rudely interrupted. Mrs Whipple had just served up my breakfast. A veritable delight of devilled kidneys in a spicy mustard sauce, when the call came in. Needless to say, I had to abandon my morning glory.'

Zac snorts. 'Christ, no man should ever abandon his morning glory.'

Unaccustomed to smutty British humour, Zac's inference is lost in translation.

'Stand aside, stand aside!' the doctor bellows as he bumbles into the tent and stares incredulously at the severed limb. 'What is this?'

Zac can't help himself. 'Call it a hunch, Doc, but I'd say it's a leg.'

Whipple's eyes narrow as he glares at Zac. 'I can see it's a leg, Sergeant Stoker!' he retorts. 'Where is the rest of the body?'

'That's what the leg would like to know.'

Whipple's eyes close as he mumbles something in his native language. 'Am I to ascertain the limb is cast adrift?' he asks wearily.

Charlene tilts her head to the side. 'It looks that way. We're about to conduct a search along the beach. I'll yell out if we find any other body parts,' she replies, exiting the tent.

He turns to Prisha. 'I am an extremely busy man, inspector. My time cannot be squandered willy nilly on arbitrary limbs that surface in your locale.'

As he makes to leave, Prisha launches a charm offensive. 'I apologise profusely, Doctor Whipple, but as there was only the foot protruding from the sand, we weren't to know it was detached from the body. Since you're here, I'd be grateful if you could give us your valuable and esteemed professional opinion on the limb. Your razor sharp intellect may shed some light on the matter that mere mortals, like myself and Sergeant Stoker, could only dream of.'

'Arse licker,' Zac murmurs under his breath.

Whipple pulls his palm over his face and sighs. 'Very well, now I am here, I may as well give you the benefit of my unique wisdom. Let us commence with the examination of this unfortunate limb.' As he bends down to inspect the leg, his knees creak and crack like breaking twigs. Pulling a pair of latex gloves on, he gently touches the appendage. 'This leg belonged to an adult male of robust constitution, perhaps betwixt the ages of twenty and fifty years, abruptly truncated a mere six inches below the hip. The flesh, marred and macerated, bears the unmistakable hallmark of a maritime mishap. Indeed, such a fate befits only the most lamentable of circumstances. Observe, dear colleagues, the macabre artistry of this grievous wound. The epidermis and underlying musculature have been rent asunder with a ferocity befitting Neptune's own wrath. The severance, whilst jagged, evinces a pattern consistent with the merciless rotation of marine propellers. Pray, take note of the absence of significant decomposition; the sanguineous effusion remains relatively fresh, suggesting the dismemberment transpired but hours hence.'

Zac grimaces. 'Are you saying the leg was severed recently while the body was still fresh, or had the body been dead a while and it's merely the leg which was chopped off but hours hence?'

Prisha scrunches her nose up and whispers, 'But hours hence?'

Zac shrugs as Whipple glowers up at him. 'Maybe you should furnish me with a warrant card and I can do your job as well as my own, sergeant.'

'I'm sure it could be arranged.'

Prisha taps Zac on the shin with her boot. 'Shut up,' she hisses.

The doctor's attention is diverted as he peers intently at the knee. 'Ah, observe here, a most conspicuous cicatrix near the patella, no doubt the vestige of an anterior cruciate ligament reconstruction, a testament to some erstwhile affliction and subsequent surgical intervention this unfortunate soul once endured.'

'You mean an ACL scar?' Zac probes.

'That is what I said. Now, unless you have any further banal, moribund questions, I shall return to my kidneys.' As he attempts to rise, he groans and clutches his lower back.

'Are you in pain, doctor?' Prisha enquires.

'Not in pain, inspector. I am in exquisite agony.'

'Oh dear, how did that happen?'

As he stretches to his full, towering height, he winces. 'The origin of this affliction lies in a fateful encounter when Mrs Whipple, in what I suspect was a deliberate act of matrimonial malice, did propel a shopping trolley into my person, thus consigning me to this perpetual torment in the vicinity of my sacroiliac joint.'

'I'm sorry to hear that, but I'm sure it must have been an accident,' Prisha states, resisting the urge to laugh.

'Hmm... your condolences are graciously received, inspector. Alas, I must confess my scepticism regarding the purported so-called accident. In my extensive observations of the mature female, I have discerned a peculiar penchant for subtle vindictiveness, a quality most intriguing and, I daresay, conspicuously absent in the male of the species. It is a trait that adds a certain piquancy to the conjugal dance, though, regrettably, it has left me with this most persistent lumbar malady.'

Zac grins. 'Not sure you'll be doing much conjugal dancing with that back, Doc. What you need is a good massage. I can highly recommend Mandy's Massage Parlour down one of the alleys off Grape Street. Mandy will put you right. She has healing hands and a velvet touch.'

Whipple stares at him briefly. 'You can vouch for her efficacy?'

'I certainly can. Used her for years.'

Whipple pulls the flap of the tent back and plods away. 'I may take up your recommendation, sergeant. Good day.'

They watch on as he trudges laboriously across the beach. 'You bastard,' Prisha says with a chuckle.

'What?'

'You know what. Mandy's Massage Parlour is the local rub and tug shop.'

'So? It will do him good. When a man is as perpetually grumpy as he is, it points to only one thing.'

'What?'

'He's not getting any. Mrs Whipple has turned the tap off.' He pauses, then smirks. 'Does Adam ever get grumpy?'

Prisha's eyes twinkle. 'No, never. He's perpetually cheerful.'

'Lucky bugger.' He gazes down at the leg. 'Right, so we have an adult male aged twenty to fifty. Fit and active, well, until recently. An ACL scar, and if I understand Raspberry correctly, and I'm not sure I do, this leg was recently walking around.'

'Agreed. Double check with the coastguard to see if anyone has gone overboard during the night and I'll get Dinkel to chase up Missing Persons. It will be a few days until we have results back from forensics, but if we're in luck, we may get a DNA match on the system.'

Zac checks his watch. 'You hungry?'

'Famished.'

'Good. I've arranged to meet Frank at Miserly Joe's at eight.'

'Christ! I forgot he was back today. Is it really eight weeks since he had his pacemaker fitted?'

'It certainly is. I caught up with him on Saturday afternoon for a couple of pints. He'd just returned from a fortnight in Corfu.'

'Talking shop, no doubt.'

'No. He asked if you were safe and if MI5 had caught the Russian, and that was all. Said everything else could wait until today.'

'And how is he?'

'Firing on all cylinders. He has a spring in his step and is straining at the leash to get back to work. Daft old sod.'

7

Frank is in fine fettle as he orders the breakfasts. 'Morning, Jenny, love.'

'Hello, stranger. I hardly recognised you, with a suntan. You certainly didn't get that from sunbathing on Whitby Beach, and you've lost weight.'

Frank chuckles as he pats his stomach and winks at Prisha and Zac. 'Been on a Mediterranean diet for the last two bloody months. Shed eight kilo. I'm as fit as a butcher's dog.'

'Good for you. What can I get you?'

'Two full English breakfasts for me and Zac and a bacon butty for Prisha. Oh, and throw a couple of extra slices of fried bread and black pudding on my plate, and we'll have three mugs of tea, please.'

'Back on the North Sea diet, are we?'

'Aye. I've been hanging out for this,' he says, handing cash over.

'Be with you in a jiffy.'

The three officers take up seats around a battered Formica table. 'So,' Frank begins, 'get me up to speed with what's been going on?'

Prisha and Zac exchange a bemused glance. 'Been quiet to be honest with you, Frank,' Prisha states. 'A severed leg was discovered on Tate Hill Sands this morning. Adult male. It appears to have been cut off by a boat prop. No other body parts on the beach when we left forensics earlier.'

Zac taps at the table with his index finger. 'I went undercover for a couple of weeks as part of a County Lines drugs bust. A meth lab positioned slap bang in the middle of nowhere, not far from Malton. Got the bastards.'

'Good lad.'

'And we bust an illegal tobacco syndicate,' Prisha adds.

'Chop chop?' Frank asks.

Prisha nods. 'Yep. Plus the usual car thefts, breaking and entering, and dealers hanging around the amusement arcades selling gear to kids.'

Jenny arrives with the breakfasts on a tray. 'Here we go. I'll be back with your tea in a moment.'

'Thanks, Jenny.' Frank stares down at his plate in a state of orgasmic surrender. 'I love my wife dearly. She's my best pal, but we've been joined at the hip for two weeks, twenty-four-seven. You can have too much of a good thing. For the last fortnight, my breakfasts have consisted of Greek yogurt, mixed berries, and honey. Very nice... occasionally. But I've been dreaming of a big fry-up and today's the day. I need to put a lining on my stomach.' After liberally squirting HP sauce over everything, he attacks a rasher of bacon, stabs at a fried mushroom and dips the morsels into egg yolk, then takes a voracious bite of his fried bread. He relaxes back in his chair, eyes closed, munching.

Zac smiles, pleased to have his old boss back. 'Don't disturb him, Prisha. At his age he needs to savour every erection. They don't come around too often.'

'Oh, please. I'm eating here,' she replies, suppressing a giggle.

Frank's eyes spring open as he sets to work on his heart-attack on a plate. 'What about the Russian, Kira Volkov? When I left, you were apparently in imminent danger, Prisha?'

Jenny arrives with the tea and deftly dispenses the drinks. 'Storm in a teacup, pardon the pun,' she says, taking a sip of tea. 'It's all gone quiet. It wasn't made public, but I heard on the grapevine the security services had to deal with a big terrorist threat in London. Kira seems to have disappeared off their radar.'

'Have you still got security?'

'No. It lasted two weeks, thank god. I'm a big girl, Frank. I can take care of myself.'

'And what about this sharpshooter from MI5... what's his name?'

'Magnus Crawley.'

'Aye, that's the guy. Has he been in town?'

'No. Not a trace of him has been seen.'

'Hmm... I don't like it. Not one little bit.'

'Chillax, Frank. Look at the facts. If Kira is still in the country, she's up to no good. Whether that be stealing state secrets or being involved in some clandestine organised crime gang. She's hardly likely to blow her cover to come after a police officer over a petty grievance. She's a lot smarter than that.'

Frank devours his egg and the rest of his bacon in three ravenous mouthfuls, briefly chews, and washes it down with a slug of tea. 'Magic. And how's Superintendent Banks been?'

Zac mops up his baked bean juice with a slice of white bread, before answering. 'Pain in the freckle for the first two weeks. Analysing our overtime and expenses. She eased off once Chief Constable Critchley announced his retirement date. She's been very circumspect the last fortnight.'

Prisha nods her agreement. 'The chief constable's final day is this coming Friday. He's going to spend the week visiting all the stations to thank everyone and say goodbye.'

'Aye. I'd heard as much,' Frank replies nonchalantly, more concerned with the food on his plate.

'Rumour has it, Martin Overland will get his job.'

'Always on the cards. Deputies usually move into the top jobs.'

Prisha and Zac eyeball each other. Zac broaches the subject. 'Another rumour, Frank. We think Superintendent Banks has thrown her hat in the ring for the deputy chief constable's job. Last couple of weeks she's seemed distracted. Suddenly disappears with nothing in her online calendar.'

Frank mops up the residue of egg yolk, bacon fat, and HP sauce from his plate. 'She's coveted that position for many a year. And to be honest with you, there's no better person for the job. She's experienced, knows the system and is great with the media.'

Zac detects a hint of doubt. 'And yet?'

Frank deposits the last of the soaked bread into his mouth, then takes a swig of tea. 'She ain't got a cat in hell's chance.'

'Why?'

'Because Martin Overland will have a say in who he wants as his deputy. He's a new broom, and Anne Banks is a threat. If he stuffs up, it would be easy to supplant him with Anne. Overland has always been political. A shite copper in his day, but a schmoozer. He'll pull in an under-qualified lackey. That's how these guys operate.' He pushes his plate away and swigs the last of his tea. 'Anything else?'

Prisha cracks a large smile. 'Yes, PC Kylie Pembroke has been seconded to CID for three months. She sits her detective's exam in September. I had a word with Superintendent Banks and Kylie's sergeant and they both thought it was a good way for her to obtain on-the-job experience.'

'Excellent! She's a star in the making is Kylie. When does she start?'

'She started last Friday, but spent the day filling in paperwork and watching OH&S videos.'

'And how's Dinkel progressing?'

Prisha nods. 'Coming along. Give him data to analyse and he's great.'

Zac groans. 'But still a liability in the field. And he's still whistling and breaking things.' He half stops and chortles. 'Eh, Frank, the lad's got a girlfriend.'

'Really.'

'Very mysterious. Bumped into him one night with a right beauty. Her name's Trixy. That's all we know about her.' Zac spots his chance. 'I was thinking, Frank...'

'About?'

'I've been partnered with Dinkel for quite a while now. I thought maybe I could partner up with Kylie, you know, show her the ropes.'

Frank picks up a napkin and wipes his lips, then leans across and pats Zac on the shoulder. 'No, that wouldn't do at all, son. A pretty young lass like Kylie? It would put you off your game.'

Zac bristles. 'What does that mean? I'm a police officer of the highest integrity. I don't view my colleagues in anything but a professional manner, regardless of colour, gender, sexuality, or political views.'

'Sorry, Zac. You can't help yourself, you're a man.'

'So are you.'

'We're not talking about me!' Frank shouts, before regaining his composure. 'Those... thoughts, ideas, are long gone. I have nearly thirty years on you.'

'I swear, Frank. I'm a married man. I need a break from Dinkel, that's all. He's twisting my melon. I promise there'll be no shenanigans on my watch.'

'Aye. Tell it to the priest at confessional. No, definitely not. There's no point in change for change's sake. You stick with Dinkel. Prisha can partner Kylie.'

Prisha sniggers. 'Nice try, Zac,' she whispers.

Frank rises from the table and pats his stomach again. 'Christ, I could have eaten that twice over,' he says, loosening a notch on his belt. 'Right, jump to it. Let's get to work. We have snivelling, lowlife to put behind bars. I tell you what, since I had my pacemaker fitted, I feel twenty years younger. I reckon I might get back in the gym. Brush up on my boxing skills. You up for a bit of sparring, Zac, like the old days?'

'Possibly,' he replies sullenly. 'I'd like to knock your bloody block off,' he mutters under his breath.

Zac and Prisha follow Frank outside. As they struggle to catch up with him, he briefly stops and turns to them, concerned.

'By the way, if you should bump into Meera, say nowt about the full English breakfast. I had jam on toast if she asks. Got it?' They nod their understanding. 'Good. Come on then, look lively. Upwards and onwards!'

8

Frank peers out of his office window as Superintendent Banks strides confidently across the incident room.

'Welcome back, Frank!' she declares as she bustles into his office.

'Thank you, Anne. It's good to be back.'

She takes her jacket off and flops into a chair opposite him. 'And how's the pacemaker?'

Frank grins and relaxes in his seat, arms folded across his chest. 'Purring like a new Lamborghini.'

'I'm glad to hear it.'

'I've never felt better, Anne. Wish I'd had one fitted years ago. I ran up those steps like a bloody whippet. And how have you been? I hear Chief Constable Critchley is stepping down at the end of the week.'

'Yes. It's been on the cards for quite some time. Not a well-kept secret. He'll be paying us a whistle-stop visit tomorrow lunchtime to offer us his farewells.'

Frank picks a pen up and gently taps it on the desk. 'Any news about his successor?'

Anne rolls her eyes. 'Don't play coy, Frank. You know as well as I do, Martin Overland has been groomed for the position. It's a mere formality.'

'And the d*eputy* chief constable's position?'

Anne glances over her shoulder, failing to mask a whisper of a smile. 'Between you and me, I've had three interviews for the position over the last four weeks.'

'Really? Sounds promising.'

'Yes. During my last interview, I gave a short presentation on my ideas for moving forward and streamlining red tape. It was very well received.'

'I wish you all the best, Anne, but I'll hate to see you go.'

Anne emits a scoffing laugh and rises. 'Don't soft-soap me, Frank. We're chalk and cheese. Our relationship, at times, could best be described as fractious.'

He nods sagely. 'True. But it doesn't mean I won't miss you. We go back a long way, and despite butting heads on numerous occasions, you've always backed me up when push came to shove. I don't forget things like that.'

Anne eyes him suspiciously momentarily before softening. 'Yes, I suppose there has been a sense of loyalty to our relationship. Anyway, I won't be going far. Northallerton is hardly Timbuktu.' She appears impatient. 'Everything here has been running smoothly in your absence.'

'So I hear.'

'Prisha and Zac make a good team. Right, apologies for the fleeting visit, but I have a lot on. I'm escorting the chief constable this week on his farewell tour.'

'You make him sound like Rod Stewart.'

Immune to humour, she collects her jacket, then pauses. 'Oh, a couple of things on an operational front. You may recall that over the last two years, three people went missing at different times on the North Yorkshire Moors. There's been a recent campaign by some of the relatives to heighten public awareness. There was a veiled inference in some of their media interviews that the police haven't been doing enough. Certain quarters of the press have gone to town on the story and are labelling the moors the Northern Bermuda Triangle. All sorts of nonsense about Fylingdales, alien spaceships, and even werewolves. The chief constable asked me to re-investigate the disappearances before these wild conspiracy theories gain too much traction. We must be seen to be proactive. Can I leave it with you?'

'That's a Missing Persons case, not CID. Without any evidence of foul play, we really don't have a lot to go on.'

Pursing her lips, she throws him a severe frown. 'You missed the most salient point of my last sentence... we must be *seen* to be proactive. Public confidence is everything, Frank. Put Zac and Dinkel on the case for a couple of weeks and let me know how you progress. I want to get a media release out by Friday.'

'Oh, I see. So it's not about actually finding these missing souls. It's a public relations exercise to make the police look good. And meanwhile, I have two of my officers gallivanting about the moors on a wild, bloody goose chase.'

'Just do it, Frank,' she snaps.

He sighs. 'Very well.' As she pulls at the door, he calls out. 'You said two things?'

'Ah, yes. You may remember MI5 were due to send an officer up from London to investigate the Kira Volkov and Tiffany Butler case?'

'Yes.'

'I had a brief chat with the deputy director of MI5 last week. He apologised for the delay but said the arrival of his officer, Magnus Crawley, was imminent.'

Frank puffs out air in frustration. 'Strike a light. His arrival is imminent? They live in some fantasy world those guys. Is he going to arrive on the back of a jet-ski, hand a box of chocolates over and say—all because the lady loves Black Magic.'

'Don't be facetious. And it was Milk Tray, actually, not Black Magic.'

'I stand corrected, and look forward to the imminent arrival of Magnus Crawley, aka James Bond.'

She shakes her head in weary annoyance. 'Try to make a good impression, Frank. And offer him all the assistance he needs. Although, I've heard he's a bit of a maverick and likes to work solo. If he needs space to work, he can use my office. I'm going to be out and about for most of the week.'

'Roger that.' He offers her a weak smile as she turns to leave. 'Anne, about the deputy chief constable position...'

'What about it?'

'If it doesn't fall your way, it isn't the end of the world. Remember that,' he adds, gently.

Her eyes narrow momentarily. 'Hmm... I'll see you tomorrow around midday when the chief constable visits. Make sure everyone is here. Good to have you back, Frank.'

As the door closes, he rubs a hand over his greying locks. 'I hope you're wrong, Frank, old lad. I hope you're bloody wrong.' Glancing into the incident room, he notices Prisha beckon him and mouth the words "morning briefing".

He ambles into the room as Prisha claps her hands together and calls the team round.

'Right everyone, listen up. You've all heard about the leg washed up on Tate Hill Sands. According to forensics, they didn't locate any other body parts on the beach. We have a patrol boat out searching the harbour, and a team of uniformed officers are scouring the local beaches. I've asked forensics to expedite the DNA sample from the leg and I'm hoping we'll have something by tomorrow. On other news, a diesel tanker was stolen on Friday night, somewhere near Danby, with a full load worth close to fifty thousand pounds.'

Zac frowns. 'I thought those trucks were fitted with panic buttons and GPS tracking?'

'They are.'

'Ah. Possibly an inside job, then. The driver?'

Prisha shakes her head. 'Definitely not the driver. He's in intensive care at Scarborough Hospital with a fractured skull. I spoke with a nurse earlier and he's stable and had something to eat this morning. Zac, can you and Dinkel pay him a visit and see if he's up to making a statement? Make sure you obtain consent from the head nurse and the blessing of his wife, who's with him at the moment.'

'No can do, Prisha. Me and Dinkel are leading the raid on the iPhone Kid's house this morning... Milo Popescu. This is my third attempt to nab the bastard, but I'll get the skinny prick this time.'

Prisha winces. 'Oh, yes. Sorry, forgot about that.' She throws a glance at PC Kylie Pembroke, who is beaming like the cat who got the cream. 'Well then, me and Kylie will pay a visit to Gareth Atkin, see if we can get any more details on this hijack.' Her eyes fall onto Dinkel, who has his arms folded and his eyes half-closed. She kicks his chair. 'Oi! Wake up, Rip Van Winkle.'

Alarmed, he jolts back into his seat. 'Sorry, ma'am. I *was* listening.'

Prisha sighs, then continues. 'Right, anyone got anything else?'

Frank straightens and adjusts his tie. 'Yes, I have. I've had a word with the Super. In recent years, you may recall three people went missing, supposedly whilst visiting the North Yorkshire Moors. Some of their friends and relatives have started a campaign to heighten public awareness about their missing loved ones. For reasons beyond me, certain media sites are kicking up a storm with sensational headlines about the moors being akin to the Bermuda Triangle. The Super wants two officers to re-examine the disappearances.'

Prisha's eyes narrow. 'That's Missing Persons jurisdiction, not ours. Without any indication of...'

Frank interrupts. 'Yes, without any indication of foul play, we don't have a lot to go on. Nevertheless, this has come from the very top—the chief constable himself. Although, why he should care at this juncture is a conundrum I'm yet to solve. Anyway, when you can find time, I want two officers to at least begin a re-examination of the case. As you know, the chief constable is visiting our little station tomorrow at midday. I want to be able to tell him we're all over it like a cheap suit, should he ask. Oh, and make sure you're all here when he does call in.'

Prisha shrugs and acquiesces. 'Okay, fair enough.' She turns to Zac. 'Can you and Dinkel get onto it once you've nabbed this Milo character?'

'Yep. Not a problem.'

Prisha pushes herself up from the table. 'Righto, ladies and gents. Let's get to work.'

9

Zac pulls on the handbrake and parks up a street away from the suspect's house. Checking his watch, he grabs the police radio transmitter.

'Delta One to Foxtrot Two, come in, over,' he states as he watches in the rear-view mirror as the police van silently pulls up behind him.

'Foxtrot Two, here. Go ahead, Delta One, over.'

'Prepare for entry at 15 Maple Street. We execute the warrant at exactly 10:30. Team One, led by me, will take the front entrance. Team Two, led by DC Dinkel, will cover the rear of the house. Be ready to move on my signal, over.'

'Understood. Awaiting your signal to move, over.'

Zac places the radio transmitter back in its holster and turns to Dinkel, grinning in anticipation. 'Five minutes and the party begins, Dinkel, my little furry pheasant plucker.'

Dinkel appears less enthusiastic. 'Can you run it by me once again?'

'For fuck's sake,' he curses. 'Ever since you got yourself a girlfriend, you've been off with the fairies.'

'I'm sorry, but I had a bad night's sleep.'

Zac smirks. 'Oh, aye,' he says, raising one anticipatory eyebrow. 'Demanding, is she?'

'What? No, I didn't even see her last night.'

'Then why the bad night's sleep?'

'Reflux.'

'Christ,' he hisses. 'I thought it was only bairns who got reflux. Right, once more for the record. The suspect is thirty-year-old Milo Popescu, a Romanian refugee, also known as the iPhone Kid. He's like a modern day Fagin except his rendition of You've Got to Pick a Pocket or Two is sadly devoid of even a spark of musical ability.'

'What?'

'For god's sake! The musical... Oliver?'

Dinkel screws his face up. 'I'm sorry, but I haven't got the foggiest what you're talking about.'

'Have you no references to past cultural markers? Forget it. Milo Popescu uses a bunch of young lads in their early twenties to swarm the nightclubs in the Northeast on a weekend. They wait until late in the evening when most of the ladies are pissed, then they nick their mobile phones from their handbags, specifically iPhones. Milo takes the phones and wipes them clean and resets them, then he uses his runners to sell the phones on the street and in clubs and pubs. Now, as you know, although maybe you don't, the latest iPhone can cost anywhere from eight-hundred to twelve-hundred quid a pop. Our friend Milo knocks them out at half price and disables the location feature whereby people can detect where their stolen phone is. We've tried nicking him twice before, but he must have had a tip-off and got rid of the evidence before we arrived. This time, I know for a fact he has phones in the house with him.'

'Is he dangerous?'

Zac shrugs. 'He's unlikely to stab or shoot you, but he's handy with his fists, so watch out. If he tries escaping via the back door, or climbing out of the window, issue him with one warning, then Taser the fucker. He's a long, tall streak of rat piss, but he's got a mean left hook. Right, are you ready?'

Dinkel's face, contorted with anxiety, replies, 'I suppose.'

'Cheer up, Dinkel. This is the best part of the job. Busting down doors, ducking punches, cracking a few ribs. It's what gets me out of bed in the morning. Imagine you're in the Sweeney and I'm Jack Regan and you're George Carter.'

'Who?'

He shakes his head dismissively. 'You're a lost cause, man. Come on, let's go.'

With Dinkel and two uniformed officers positioned at the rear of the house, Zac and three other uniforms walk briskly up the garden path, one officer carrying the red "enforcer" battering ram. Standing on the doorstep, Zac rubs his hands together in excitement. 'Hey, I bet you a tenner you can't bust the door down with one hit?'

The officer grins back. 'You're on, sergeant. Get your money ready.'

Zac throws a flurry of shadow punches and cracks his neck from side to side. 'Okay, constable. Strut your stuff.'

The officer takes one step back, then swings the enforcer into the lock of the door whilst another officer yells, 'Police! Stand back from the door!'

The sound of splintering wood echoes out, but it takes another two almighty thwacks from the battering ram before the door bursts open. Zac is first in and immediately rushes up the stairs as two officers fly into the living room. As Zac approaches the landing, a bedroom door slams shut, hurried movement coming from within. Without waiting for back-up, he lifts his boot and crunches the heel into the door, taking it completely off its hinges as the officer who wielded the enforcer joins him outside the bedroom. He bursts into the room and spots the suspect, dressed only in a pair of faded denim jeans, struggle in vain with a window.

'Avon calling,' Zac says, sporting a wicked grin.

Milo, on spotting the officers down below in the back garden, tries a different escape route. Turning, he sidesteps Zac, then throws a haymaker at his head. Zac deftly ducks and returns fire with an uppercut, catching Milo a glancing blow on the jaw, sending him sprawling into a wardrobe. Sliding down the door in slow motion, he groans and slumps to the floor.

'You bastard! That's police brutality. I'll have you for that.'

Zac chuckles. 'It was merely a defensive parry, wouldn't you agree, constable?'

'Oh, aye. Definitely a defensive parry, sergeant.'

'Put the cuffs on him, constable, and read the emaciated stick insect his rights.'

As Milo is cuffed and read his rights, Zac unzips a large suitcase, conspicuous in a corner.

'Well, well, well. There must be at least eighty iPhones in this suitcase.' He turns to Milo. 'Let me guess—you've got a new job as a sales rep for Apple?'

'Piss off, Stoker, you Scottish twat. I found the suitcase on the street,' he grizzles in a peculiar accent, which is half Eastern European, half broad Yorkshire.

'Of course you did. Not sure a jury will believe you, though. Eighty phones at four hundred quid a throw on the black-market. That's some serious dough.'

'It's not all profit. I have overheads.'

'All small businesses do, Milo. I'm sure your accountant can offer you some tax minimisation schemes. Oops, silly me. You'll be going directly to jail. Do not pass go.' He stares at him for a moment as the officer leads him towards the doorway. 'You need to put a bit of weight on, sunshine. You're beginning to resemble a stick of desiccated spaghetti.'

'Fuck you. Haggis shagger.'

Zac's ears prick up as he hears shuffling from the adjoining room. 'Wait here a moment,' he orders the constable. 'And by the way, you owe me a tenner.' Pulling his telescopic baton from his jacket, he tentatively walks along the landing and quietly opens the bedroom door as Dinkel hurries up the stairs. Zac turns to him and puts a finger to his lips. 'Shush.'

A single bed, a chest of drawers, a wooden chair, and an old-fashioned wardrobe stand forlornly on a threadbare carpet.

'Hmm...'

He half turns to leave, then stops. His eyes fall onto the wardrobe as it imperceptibly creaks. Tiptoeing over, he raises his baton and pulls at the door, grabs the intruder by the collar, and yanks him out into the light of the room.

'Spank my blue arse! Declan Hughes. What the fuck are you doing in the wardrobe? Searching for woodworm?'

'Morning, Mr Stoker,' he replies sheepishly.

10

'Wait for me outside,' Zac says to Dinkel, who dutifully scurries down the stairs.

Zac closes the bedroom door and stares disappointedly at Declan Hughes, who is sitting on the bed wringing his hands. Zac holds the small plastic bag of weed up in the air and swings it from side to side.

'How long ago was it since we last met? Eighteen months ago, if my memory serves me correctly. And that time you gave me the big sob story about your girlfriend being up the plum duff and how you were struggling to make ends meet, how you wanted to be a world-class chef, maybe one day own a chain of restaurants, a Michelin star or two, maybe even reach celebrity status. And big dopey me, believed you, again. Sergeant Stoker, the soft touch. You've fucked up, Declan. You made me a promise you wouldn't deal again. What have you got to say for yourself, and why are you hanging around stagnant pond life like Milo Popescu?'

'It's not how it looks, Mr Stoker.'

'Enlighten me.'

'I'm struggling financially. I work upwards of fifty hours a week. Sometimes more. As a trainee chef, they pay me a pittance. It's not by the hour, and there's no overtime. It's a set salary per month. And they can insist on more hours as and when needed. Last orders are supposed to be nine-thirty, but sometimes, if they get a big party in, it can be ten-thirty, eleven. Some nights I don't get home until the small hours.'

'Where are you working?'

'Kindlewood Hall Hotel, near Easington.'

Zac arches his eyebrows, pulls up a rickety chair, spins it around, and straddles it. 'I took the wife there for her birthday six months back. Cost me an arm and a leg.'

'What did you order?'

'Half a dozen oysters for starters, then we both had the salmon fillet with new baby potatoes and garden greens.'

'With the lemon butter and saffron drizzle?'

'Aye, that's the one.'

Declan grins. 'That's one of mine. How was it?'

'Bloody outstanding. Then we had the passion fruit sorbet for dessert.'

Declan inches forward, invigorated. 'The secret there is the finely grated lime zest and the merest dash of ground nutmeg. It adds a real piquancy, don't you think?'

'Yes, it was excellent, a real palate cleanser.' Zac's benign smile fades to a scowl. 'Hang on a minute, this isn't a fucking MasterChef audition. We've crossed paths twice before and each time I've let you go with a boot up the backside and a flea in your ear. Now we're here again. I can't turn a blind eye for a third time, Declan.'

His enthusiasm evaporates. 'Please, Mr Stoker, give me another chance.'

'Why should I?'

'Because things are about to change for me. Six weeks ago, the celebrity chef, Pascal Verne, stayed at the hotel. After his meal, he took me aside and offered me a job at his restaurant in London, once I finish my apprenticeship in September.'

Zac screws his eyes up. 'Pascal Verne? Is he the French guy who looks like a meerkat in a blender?'

'That's him.'

'And he offered *you* a job?'

'Yes. In this game, good chefs are always being poached.'

'Is that a pun?'

'What?'

'Never mind. Carry on.'

'I'll be on six months' probation and if I fit in, he'll take me on permanently. It's four times the amount of money I'm on now.'

'You'll need it living in London. Not cheap.'

'I realise that, but my aunty and uncle have a house in Putney. They rent out a room. A guy is moving out at the end of August, and they've said it's mine if I want it. Offered me a good deal as well.'

'And what about this girlfriend of yours who had a bun in the oven?'

He smiles and sighs. 'We're still together. I'm a dad now, Mr Stoker. Baby boy, Charlie. Twelve months old. He's my life.'

Zac softens. 'I don't know...' he says, rubbing his beard thoughtfully. 'You haven't explained what you're doing here?'

'Milo is a long-term customer of mine. I drop him a bag of weed off every fortnight. Honest to god, I know about his phone scam but have nothing to do with it. I happened to be in the wrong place at the wrong time. And I swear on my lad's life, a small amount of weed is all I deal. Same customers each fortnight, just to earn enough to supplement my wage. Do you know how much it costs to bring up a kid? Rent, electricity, gas, council tax. Then there's milk formula, and baby food, which costs a bloody fortune. Nappies, toys. They grow out of their clothes every few months. The missus works mornings at the local Sainsbury's Supermarket while I look after Charlie. Then we change shifts, and I go to work. The dealing... it's low-level stuff.'

'Hmm… it's a tricky one.' He rises, picks up the chair and places it at the back of the room. 'Okay. Final chance. I'll turn a blind eye for the last time. And I'll give you a grace period until September when you start your new job. But you need to give me something.'

'What?'

'You heard. No such thing as a free meal, you should know that. Give me something. Who's your supplier?'

Declan shakes his head. 'I don't know.'

'Bullshit. Who is he?'

'I swear. I only know him as Bo-Bo.'

'Fuck me backwards up against a wall… Bo-Bo? Does he moonlight as a children's entertainer at the weekend?'

'He's a decent enough guy, not a heavy. A middle man. He buys it wholesale, sells it to me, and I sell it to my customer base. We both have a small mark-up. It's business.'

'Illegal business.'

'It's weed.'

'Still illegal.'

'Speeding is illegal. Doesn't stop it from happening.'

'And who does this Bo-Bo buy it from?'

Declan holds his hands out. 'Honest, I don't know and I don't ask.'

'Local or imported?'

'Local… I think, but I don't really know.'

'You don't know much, do you?'

'Look, it's a big operation, with some serious dudes running it. Ask no questions, and all that.'

Zac grimaces and shakes his head. 'Not good enough, Declan. I want more. I have bosses to answer to. They'll want to know why I let you off the hook and unless I have some good intel, then I'm as screwed as you. We all have masters to serve. I don't want to nick small fry like you. I want the sharks.'

'That's all I know. I swear.'

'Fine. Give me something else, then.'

Declan drops his head, and lowers his voice 'Okay, listen, I do have something, but you must promise to keep my name out of it,' he pleads.

'No promises, sunshine. But try me. It's your only option.'

Declan points at the bag of weed, still in Zac's hand. 'Can I roll a spliff first?'

Zac cackles, amused at the lad's audacity. 'Are you taking the piss? Of course you can't roll a fucking spliff. What do you think this is?'

Declan swallows hard. 'Saturday night, I was supposed to meet my supplier, Bo-Bo. You know Runswick Bay?'

'Aye.'

'There are four car parks. I was parked in the bottom one. Bo-Bo was supposed to turn up at eleven, but he was a no-show. I noticed a car heading my way. I moved my car to the far end and hid in a bush. I thought it might have been a police patrol or something. The car pulls up, parks in the shadows, and three guys pile out. One comes to inspect my car, then takes a leak. Got his stinking piss all over me. As he's finishing up, I get cramp and move slightly, breaking a twig. And then…'

'What?'

'The guy pulls out a torch and a pistol with a silencer on the end. I mean, how many people carry guns and how many have a fucking silencer on the end? This wasn't for show. This guy's a killer. I thought I was done for. Then a bloody fox lets out a yelp, and the guy heads back to the car.'

'Description?'

'Short, stocky, well-built. Bald head. Southern Irish accent.'

'Then what?'

'One guy returns from the beach. The tall guy had sent him to check it out. They go to the boot of the car and pull out a tarpaulin, or blanket, or some such thing. But I could tell there was something wrapped in it.'

'Such as?'

'A body… I think. It was body shaped. Long, elongated, and it took the three of them to carry it down to the beach, to the right, away from the village. By that stage, I've already pissed my pants and am in danger of shitting myself as well. I swear, Mr Stoker, this is way above my paygrade.'

'Then what?'

'I couldn't leave in my fucked up car. They'd have heard it. The exhaust is blowing, and it has a top speed of forty miles an hour. I knew I'd have to hunker down and wait until they left. I crept through the bushes and watched them as they carried the tarp towards the sea. There was a small rubber dinghy anchored up near the beach. They threw the tarp aboard, then two of the men jumped in and fired the outboard motor. The tall guy said something like—two miles out should do it. I'll pick you up at the boat ramp.'

'Which boat ramp?'

'He didn't say.'

'And?'

'The tall guy makes his way back to the car park, jumps in the car and fucks off. I waited ten minutes, then climbed into my car and got out of there, sharpish. I reckon I dodged a bullet that night, I can tell you.'

'Names?'

A shake of the head. 'Didn't hear any names. Oh, wait, yes, I did. The guy with the gun was called Cillian.'

'Descriptions of the other guys?'

Puffs out air. 'The taller one was in charge. Maybe a touch over six feet. Same accent. The other two, slightly smaller, I guess. The one with the gun had a bald head. But honestly, they were all in darkness and fifty feet away.'

Zac considers him for a moment. 'Okay, listen up Declan, because this is what's going to happen.'

ll

The first thing that hits Prisha is the disinfectant. The second thing is the noise and bustle of the hospital corridors. A place of respite and recovery… supposedly.

Their heels click clack on the hard sterile surface as they move briskly along.

She turns to Kylie. 'You're going to get lockjaw if you keep that smile up any longer.'

She mutes a laugh. 'Sorry. I'm just so excited. I can't believe I'm actually in civvies working with you. It's my dream come true.'

Prisha pushes at a door which swings open, then follows the signs to intensive care. 'Well, I'd bottle that smile because you'll need it one day. And a piece of friendly advice; it's maybe not the best idea to walk in there with a grin as wide as Whitby Harbour, considering the circumstances.'

'Oops, yes. Sorry.'

She speaks with the woman at reception and is pointed to a room down another corridor. A nurse exits the ward as the officers approach. Prisha pulls her warrant card out and performs introductions.

'Is Mr Atkin awake?'

'Yes. But he's very weak and his speech is slurred. We had to operate on his brain. He had internal bleeding and severe swelling. Basically, the same effects as a major stroke.'

'Is he well enough to answer a few questions?'

The nurse pauses. 'Yes, but no more than five minutes, please.'

Prisha nods her understanding and tentatively pushes at the door and pops her head inside. A woman in her late fifties to early sixties is sitting at the side of the bed, holding the hand of a chubby faced man with a bandage around his head. His eyes flicker open, and the woman instinctively turns.

'Police?' she asks.

Prisha nods and discreetly enters the room, along with Kylie. 'I'm DI Kumar and this is DC Pembroke. Whitby police.'

'I'm Gareth's wife. Angie.'

'Do you think your husband is fit enough to answer a few questions?'

The woman nods, reluctantly, and rises from the chair. 'I'm not sure you'll get much out of him. He's mumbling and hard to understand. I'll wait outside.'

Kylie pulls up a chair as Prisha slides into the abandoned one.

'Mr Atkin, Gareth, I'm DI Kumar from the police. I'm here to ask you a few questions about the robbery on Friday night. If you can understand me, please nod.' Her voice is slow, measured, soft.

Gareth's head offers the faintest of nods.

'Can you remember anything that happened?'

His eyes spring open, alarmed at his recollections. 'Hit... hit... on.' His right hand trembles as he feebly points to his bandage.

'Hit on the head?'

'Yesh. On head.'

'Can you describe your attackers?'

'N... noise. N... no.'

Prisha frowns and glances at Kylie, who is leaning forward attentively. 'Noise? There was a noise?'

A shake of the head. 'No... voi...voice,' he stammers.

'You heard a voice?'

He becomes clearly frustrated and tries to sit up, but the effort is too much.

Kylie whispers to Prisha. 'Can I have a go? My dad had a stroke ten years back and his speech was very similar to Gareth's. I built up a good idea of what he was trying to say. It's a bit like charades.'

Prisha shrugs. 'Be my guest.'

Kylie takes Gareth's hand. 'Gareth, your attackers, were they men?'

He nods.

'How many men?'

He holds up two fingers.

'Two. Young, old, middle-aged?'

'Fir...first.'

'Young?'

'Yes.'

'Twenties, thirties, forties?'

'Three.'

'Thirties.'

'Yes.'

'What colour were they?'

'Purple....' He grimaces, annoyed with himself. 'No, purple, blue, black... wh... white.'

'So, two men in their thirties, both white. Did they have an accent?'

Nods. 'Yes. It was... it was... it was... Wel...Welsh.'

'Welsh?'

His face contorts in pain. 'No. Eats, eats... no.'

'East?'

'Aye. Eats. No, other way.'

Kylie's eyes flicker to Prisha, who is busy taking notes, then back to Gareth. 'Do you mean West?'

'That's the one.'

'West Wales?'

'Nay. Further.'

'West *of* Wales?'

Licks his lips. Eyes clam shut. 'That's it.'

'Were the two men Irish?'

Head trembles up and down. 'Aye.'

'Gareth, were their accents Southern Irish or Northern Irish?'

'Down.'

'Southern?'

'Yes.'

Kylie squeezes his hand, gently. 'Gareth, you're doing great, really great. Now, can you recall how they managed to get you out of your cab?'

Staring into the distance, he tries to formulate his words. 'What's his name? Treasure…. you know, island. Dickens. No, not Dickens. Other one.'

Prisha prompts him. 'Robert Louis Stevenson?'

'That's her.'

Both officers blink incomprehensibly. This abstract clue even has Kylie flapping about in the dark. 'Treasure Island? Robert Louis Stevenson?'

'Cheese man.'

Giving up on that particular cul-de-sac, Kylie takes a new tack. 'Anything else you can recall about the two men?'

He points at his head again. 'Hats. Stop, stop, thingy.'

The door gently opens and the nurse bobs her head in. 'I think that's long enough, inspector. We don't want to exhaust him.'

Prisha hides her disappointment and offers her a smile.

'Thanks Gareth. You've been very helpful,' Kylie says, rising as Prisha folds her notebook away and moves towards the doorway.

'Van!' Gareth's husky voice barks.

They both stop and look at him. 'There was a van?' Kylie prompts.

'Blue... blue... no, black. Tran... tan.'

'A black transit van?'

He lets out a huge sigh, sporting a scared and bewildered expression. 'That's right. Lights. Green, red, orange.'

'Traffic lights?'

'No. I mean... yes. Bloody roadworks. Water. But no water.' He falls silent as his eyelids shut.

The officers exit the room and face Angie Atkin.

'How was he? Much use?' she enquires dolefully.

Prisha rests a hand on her shoulder. 'He's a very strong and brave man. He helped enormously. You look shattered. Have you any family or friends to stay with you? If not, I can arrange for a Family Liaison Officer to visit.'

'My son should be arriving in the next thirty minutes. He's driving up from North Wales. And my daughter is flying in from Lisbon, so I'll be fine, thanks.'

'Have you spoken with the surgeon yet?'

'No. He was supposed to see me three hours ago. I guess he's busy.' She hesitates, mired in her private hell. 'I'm not sure how we're going to survive with him not working. We have a modest amount in savings, but we still have a mortgage to pay every month.'

Prisha is puzzled. 'He'll receive sick pay, Mrs Atkin, and compensation.'

She shakes her head vigorously. 'No, he won't. He's worked for the same company for the last thirteen years but he's contract. He earns a little extra per hour, but he doesn't receive sick or holiday pay.'

'I'm sure the contracting firm will have some sort of scheme.'

'No. He's a sole trader, contracting to the contract company. As far as I'm aware, he'll get nothing.'

She sucks in a deep intake of breath. 'Believe me, there will be some safeguard that will come into play.' She sounds convincing, and it seems to alleviate Angie's pain, but Prisha has no belief in her own words. 'Once you've gathered yourself, I'd seek professional advice from a solicitor or injuries lawyer. You husband went to work fit and healthy. It is the employer's responsibility to ensure he returns home safe and well each day. Maybe your son or daughter could look into it?'

She smiles weakly. 'Thank you inspector,' she says, as she shuffles back inside the ward.

Prisha prods at the vending machine and a cup drops, followed by the tinkling of black coffee. She takes the cup and hands it to Kylie, before repeating the process. As they exit the hospital, Prisha smiles at her.

'Well done! Two white males, Southern Irish, in their thirties. And that stuff about traffic lights...'

'A fake diversion, perhaps?'

'Sounds like it. He was very annoyed when he blurted it out. What about the water?'

'Don't know. Maybe they used water over the road as a reason for the diversion?'

'You might be right. And the hat and stop, stop... perhaps the men were dressed as road workers with a stop sign?'

Prisha clicks the fob and the car beeps and clicks as they approach. 'At least we've got a start. Back at the station, I want you to check the PNC for any similar fuel thefts over the last eighteen months. Ever since the explosion of petrol and diesel prices due to the war in Ukraine, there's been an exponential increase in hijacking fuel tankers. Let's see if these guys are newcomers chancing their arm for a quick quid, or are they a serious outfit who do this for a living. Liaise with the fingerprint guys. They gave the truck the once over earlier this morning. See if they got anything, although I doubt they have. Even chancers know to wear gloves these days. Once you've done that, pay a visit to the haulage company - Northern Fuel Logistics. They're on Teesside docks. Be professional, but don't be nicey, nicey. You want records of the tachometers, shift patterns, hours worked. And they have GPS tracking on their vehicles, so they must have a record of where the tanker was stopped. I want that location. Find out if they've received any threats, or have disgruntled employees... sorry, contractors. And don't be fobbed off with a secretary or office boy. You need to speak to the person who has their finger on the pulse, *not* a senior manager. You want the person who runs the office. They're the kingpins. Also, before you leave, very subtly infer there could be civil, or even criminal proceedings arising from the attack on Gareth Atkin.'

They step into the car and fasten their seatbelts, as Kylie puzzles over Prisha's last instruction. 'Why the subtle inferences?'

'Because shonky operators are more likely to be forthcoming when they have a loaded gun pointed at their head. Aboveboard businesses do everything within their power to avoid shit like this. Cowboys and fly-by-nights are a different matter. That should keep you busy for the rest of the day.'

Kylie's smile returns. 'I love it!' she yells. 'I was born for this. I've always been ultra suspicious and inquisitive. Now I get paid for it.'

Prisha laughs, invigorated by her enthusiasm. She knows it won't last forever, but for the moment, she'll soak up her vibrant energy.

'Any idea about the Treasure Island thing?'

Kylie stares out of the window, her mind focused. 'No. That one has me beat.'

'Hmm, me too. For the moment, at least,' she says, flashing her a toothy grin. 'And make sure you're back at the station by six.'

'Why?'

'Because that's when we all knock off for the day and head to the White House Inn for a few refreshing drinks. Every Monday and Friday, and occasionally in between. That's if you're up for it?'

'Does the Pope shit in the woods?'

'Correct answer. Welcome to the team. You'll fit in well.' She presses the ignition start button, releases the handbrake, pushes the gear stick into position, then slaps her foot on the brake.

'What's the matter?'

Prisha's face hardens. 'I've figured it out.'

'What?'

'Treasure Island! The character who helped Jim Hawkins find the treasure was called Ben Gunn. He had a craving for cheese. That's what Gareth was trying to tell us—his attackers were armed.'

12

Prisha takes a late lunch and saunters down to the bandstand next to the West Pier. Finding an empty bench, she peels back the wrapper from the box and tucks into the prawn mayo sandwich in wholemeal bread. Despite a million and one things to attend to, and the constant demands on her time, she has developed a routine where she takes time out during the day to clear her mind, relax, and feel nature's elements on her face. It's a brief respite from a profession that often jangles the nerves, like a fingernail scratching down a blackboard.

The town is particularly busy due to the school summer holiday break. It's nearly two years since she relocated to the ancient fishing port, but she already has sympathies with some of the local Whitbyites.

She understands the tourists bring in a huge amount of income to the small town and provide a good living for many, but the truth is, they irritate her. Moping around like extras from a zombie apocalypse film, they clog up the roads and the narrow streets as they devour fish and chips, ice creams, and doughnuts. Families with unruly children, old people in wheelchairs, overweight people on mobility scooters, excursions, the homeless begging for money, the addicts looking for their next fix. And the damned seagulls, which seem to grow in size, and number, *and* ferocity every week. The town has a timeless charm despite all this, but Saint-Tropez, it is not.

She discards the wrapper in a nearby bin, sits back down and sips on a velvety cappuccino. She watches idly on as the Black Pearl pirate boat chugs across the harbour heading to open waters, carrying passengers as a Jack Sparrow lookalike entertains them. The image is not lost on her. Most people in the world are decent, honest, and hardworking, simply getting by and looking for a good time when and if they can afford it. And yet, she spends all her working life dealing with murderers, rapists, thieves, scam artists, violent offenders, and drug dealers. She enjoys the cut and thrust this brings, but occasionally she wonders if there's a better life for her, a simpler life. Her mind wanders to Adam as she paints a mental picture of him lifting hay bales from a trailer, pulling a pregnant ewe from a ditch, then sitting on the open fells eating a Cornish pasty and sipping hot tea from a thermos flask as a cool wind ruffles his hair. She imagines herself in the old farmhouse redecorating, preparing meals, hanging washing out, helping out at lambing season. It does seem idyllic. The rose-tinted image grows more vivid each time she replays it in her head.

Never one to dwell on things too long, her daydreaming is cut short as her eyes fall upon a woman near the railings, gazing out across the harbour. Her presence is incongruous to the setting. About Prisha's height, with a blonde shoulder-length bob, she is smartly dressed in what appear to be designer clothes and has an air of sophistication about her. She appears lost in a trance herself.

It's not uncommon for people to scatter the ashes of loved ones in the harbour entrance. Maybe that's it, Prisha thinks.

Checking her phone for messages, she notices one from Frank, which simply reads;

Can u get back to station asap, thanks

She slips her mobile away and notices the woman is now staring at her, the watery sun reflected in her large, round sunglasses. Prisha offers her a friendly smile, which is warmly reciprocated.

'No rest for the wicked,' Prisha says, with a playful shrug of the shoulders. She turns on her heels and strides briskly away.

As Prisha deftly sidesteps and weaves past holidaymakers, the woman watches on. Once there's a safe distance between them... she sets off and follows behind.

13

Entering the incident room, Prisha spots Zac on his mobile, obviously talking to his wife, Kelly.

'Yes, I should be home around seven. No, I won't forget to pick the boys up from the cinema. What? No, I haven't forgotten about the pizzas. I'll collect them once I've collected the lads. Aye, okay. Love you. Bye.' He hangs up and shakes his head. 'Sex and drugs and rock and roll, eh?' he says to Prisha.

Prisha glances through the Venetian blinds into Frank's office. She can make out his stout frame sitting behind his desk, talking animatedly to a man with his back to the window.

'Who's in with Frank?'

He shrugs. 'Not sure. He was in there when I arrived back about an hour ago. What's the latest with the hijacking?'

'Managed to get a few leads,' she replies, distracted by the newcomer.

'How's the driver?'

'Bewildered and confused, but I got the impression he's a fighter. I'm hoping he'll make a full recovery, but time will tell. How'd you go with the raid?'

'Caught the bastard red handed. Eighty-five mobiles in a suitcase, the majority of them iPhones. Quite the haul. I interviewed him an hour ago once the duty solicitor arrived. Milo was as predictable as ever - no comment. I can put that one to bed until the trial. He'll probably get two years. Out in twelve months, then set up shop in a new location and start again.'

'Hmm... sometimes we seem to go round and around, don't we?' she replies, her attention once again directed towards the stranger in Frank's office.

Zac scans the room. 'Hey, where's Kylie?'

'I sent her up to Teesside Docks to get some intel on the haulage company.'

'You've cut her loose already?' he asks, suitably surprised and impressed.

She smiles. 'Yes, as Frank would say, she's as wick as, that one.'

'Lucky for you. I'm still wet-nursing Dinkel. He's as green as he is cabbage looking. He should have become a criminal analyst instead of transferring to CID.'

'We all have different strengths, Zac. Where is he?'

'On his way to Northallerton to liaise with the Missing Persons Unit about the mysterious disappearances on the moors.'

'Couldn't he have done that over Zoom?'

'He could have, but I thought a little trip would do him good.'

'You mean, do *you* good?' She chuckles. 'Coming for drinks after work?'

'Aye, why not. Nice evening for a drink. What time you going?'

Prisha doesn't get a chance to answer as Frank appears on the threshold of his door and beckons her.

'Prisha, if I could have a moment, please.'

Feeling decidedly uneasy, she makes her way into his office. 'Frank?' she questions as her eyes fall upon the stranger.

'This is Magnus Crawley, compliance officer with MI5.'

Her uneasiness takes a turn for the worse as the man rises from his seat. Tall and skinny, his lank, black hair, and pointed features, remind her of a Dickensian character. In his mid to late forties, he sports a long leather overcoat which Prisha has only ever seen in music videos worn by pop-stars in the 1980s. His skin is oily, and the white flakes on his shoulders indicate a serious bout of dandruff.

He holds his hand out. 'Ah, Inspector Kumar. My pleasure.' His voice is deep, yet brittle and scratchy.

Prisha takes a step forward and shakes his hand as she catches a whiff of bad breath. She stops herself from recoiling and drops the limp hand.

'Likewise,' she says without conviction. 'We were expecting you weeks ago, Mr Crawley.'

He bares yellowing teeth in an attempt at a smile. 'Ah, yes. The machinations of a terror cell in the Capital meant all hands on deck. It couldn't be helped, I'm afraid, but I do extend my sincerest apologies for the delay.'

'Take a seat,' Frank says, gesticulating to both of them.

Magnus half turns to her. 'I've been going over the rudimentary facts of the kidnapping and ransom case involving Mark Bridges and Tiffany Butler, which also led to the assassination of one of our field operatives. I spent last night studying the reports and various witness statements. I shall let those facts percolate for a while before I drill down into them.'

Frank steeples his fingers together. 'Prisha is working on a number of cases at the moment, but I'm sure she'll be able to find an hour or two should you require clarification on any matter.'

A smarmy grin spreads across the face of Magnus Crawley as he focuses on Prisha, exploring her. 'Yes, I will require her assistance at some point.' His words, at face value, are innocuous enough.

But not to Prisha.

She can read a closed book.

'And how long do you intend staying in Whitby, Mr Crawley?' she enquires.

He throws his arms up. 'Oh, as long as it takes. Could be two days, two weeks, two months, who knows. My investigation will guide me.' He leans in towards her. 'And please, call me Magnus.' Prisha resists the urge to vomit. He rises from his seat. 'Now, it was a long, tiring drive up from London. I shall return to my hotel room and go over my notes from there. But rest assured I will get to the bottom of this case and find out the whereabouts of Tiffany Butler and the Russian, Kira Volkov, be they be dead or alive.'

'I don't wish to interfere in your investigation, Mr Crawley, but Miss Butler was only ever a suspect in the kidnapping case. She was not actually charged with anything.'

The ghastly smile reappears. 'You arrested her for using a false passport as she was sitting on a plane on the runway at Manchester Airport.'

'Arrested, yes. But not charged.'

'Hardly surprising, considering she escaped your custody before being interrogated.'

Prisha riles at this. 'Under extenuating circumstances, may I add. I was seriously incapacitated and under extreme duress considering I'd been threatened with rape and murder by a ruthless killer three times the size of me. And by the way, we don't interrogate suspects. We interview them.'

His puzzlement, false, parades itself. 'It wasn't an accusation of incompetence, inspector. I was merely pointing out the obvious fact she wasn't charged because she escaped. From what I understand, the late Mark Bridges, Tiffany's alleged accomplice, hardly possessed the wherewithal to hatch such a devious kidnap and ransom plot. Tiffany Butler, on the other hand, comes across as extremely intelligent, manipulative, and cunning.' The smile returns, the voice softens. 'And please forgive my faux pas regarding interrogation and interviewing. Different departments, different shades of grey. Nevertheless, rest assured, inspector, people like Miss Butler always overestimate their abilities. Hubris is their downfall. Somewhere along the convoluted trail of destruction she created, she *will* have left a vital clue behind. And... I will find it.' He finishes with a flourish, his arms spreadeagled.

'Shouldn't you be more concerned with catching Kira Volkov and bringing her to justice? After all, she has blood on her hands?'

His hooded eyes narrow to slits. 'I like to pick the low hanging fruit first. If Kira Volkov is still at large, I will use Tiffany Butler as my honey trap and entice the Russian out into the open.' He half bows to Prisha, then nods in deference to Frank. 'Right, if you'll excuse me, I really need to eat and take a shower.'

Frank escorts him to the door. 'Which hotel are you staying at, Magnus?'

'The Royal. I'm on the third-floor with magnificent views over the harbour and across to the abbey. This is my first visit to North Yorkshire and from what I've seen so far, I've been missing out on some of the finest countryside in the land. I have to admit, I'm already smitten with the place.'

'It's a well-kept secret, and that's the way we like it. Don't want all you southerners flocking up here buying up holiday homes.'

Magnus laughs. 'Indeed. My lips are sealed. I may return tomorrow at some point. I have my security clearance and tag.'

'No problem. And remember, you're free to use Superintendent Banks' office, as she won't be around much for the rest of the week.'

'I thank you for your gracious hospitality, Chief Inspector Finnegan.'

Frank watches him depart, then quietly closes the door and gazes down at Prisha.

She senses his eyes boring into her. 'What?' she finally snaps, throwing him a piercing glare.

'What in all buggeration has got into you?'

Her reply is terse. 'I don't know what you mean.'

'Since when did you become Tiffany Butler's bloody defence barrister?'

'Don't talk wet. I was merely highlighting the point that Kira is a killer—fact. Whereas Tiffany is only under suspicion of kidnapping and ransom. I think his priorities are wrong, that's all.'

'Only kidnapping and ransom?' he replies with an element of incredulity. He mellows. 'You certainly got off to a good start with Crawley. Don't rock the boat, Prisha. This guy has a lot of power and clout. Way more than you can imagine. Keep him sweet. His title may be compliance officer, but that's a euphemism for a sharpshooter. From what I've heard, his success rate is nearly one hundred per cent.'

'He makes my skin crawl,' she hisses, her distaste obvious.

Frank drops into his chair, the cushion expelling a loud rush of air. 'Now, now, Prisha. Be professional. I agree, he's not the most pleasant man I've ever met. There's an air of...'

'Sinister malevolence wrapped in an oily veneer of obsequious punctiliousness.' Her voice rises towards the end, seeking validation.

Frank puffs his cheeks out and pushes back and forth in the chair, testing the integrity of the springs. 'Not the words I'd have chosen, but yes, pretty close to the mark.' He sits upright and leans across the desk, hands clasped. 'Listen up, lass—don't get personal,' he says, the fatherly undertone reassuring, yet commanding at the same time. 'Do I make myself clear?'

She nods, slightly contrite. 'Yes, Frank.'

'Good.' He relaxes back. 'Right. Care to update me on the tanker hijacking?'

14

Frank navigates to the side entrance carrying the tray of drinks, drops his shoulder and pushes open the door. He takes a quick glance around the beer garden of the White House Inn, and spots his team sitting in prime position around a large wooden table opposite the golf course, engaged in animated conversation.

'Ah, there they are,' he murmurs.

The warm breeze, scented with sea salt and freshly cut grass, gently tousles his hair. The golden shores of Sandsend glint in the distance to the left, while the bustling Whitby Harbour and the stark silhouettes of St Mary's Church and the ancient abbey command the right. The soft hum of insects mingles with the murmur of conversation and the clinking of glasses. The refreshing aroma of beer beckons, promising a crisp taste to match the golden glow of the evening. As he reaches the table, the laughter of his team resonates, embodying the essence of a perfect summer's evening.

Zac looks up and grins. 'About bloody time. Did you brew it yourself?'

'Very funny. The bar was chockers,' he says placing the tray down and dispensing the drinks. 'Pint of Guinness for Zac. A bottle of Heineken for Prisha and Kylie, a pint of Theakston's bitter for me and, last but not least, a glass of Crabbies ginger beer for Dinkel.'

'Watch you don't get drunk on that, Dinkel. Don't want to be carrying you home tonight,' Zac quips as he takes a hefty quaff of his cold stout.

Frank holds his glass aloft. 'Cheers, everyone. I don't want to speak too soon, but I think summer may have finally arrived.' As a round of good-natured cheers resonates, Frank relaxes, feeling happy. His first day back on the job after eight weeks away, and how he's missed it. He takes a seat and chuckles. 'Now, my wife, Meera, thinks these get togethers at the pub a couple of times a week after work are simply an excuse to have a few beers.'

'She'd be right, wouldn't she?' Prisha says, smiling.

Frank holds his hand aloft. 'Hang on, hang on. The alcohol is merely for lubrication.'

Zac doesn't miss his chance. 'No wonder Meera's always wearing a pained expression. I'd try KY Jelly if I were you, Frank.'

Laughter rings out as Prisha shakes her head. 'He's been like this all day. Even when we found the leg this morning.'

Frank continues unabated. 'What I'm trying to say is, these after work confabulations are essential to the smooth running of a team. A time to air grievances, discuss cases, get things off your chest and unwind.'

'Confabulation?' Zac queries. 'Have you been spending time with Whipple on the sly?'

Kylie's ears prick up. 'Hey, talking of Doctor Whipple, guess what I heard on the grapevine today?'

Her question has everyone leaning forward in anticipation.

'What?' Dinkel encourages, taking a sip of ginger beer.

'He's part owner of a racehorse.'

Her statement is met with a chorus of disapproval and scepticism.

'No way!' Zac declares. 'He's vehemently against any form of gambling, or enjoyment, for that matter.'

'It's true. I was speaking to my old shift partner earlier today. He went to Thirsk races at the weekend and spotted Whipple in the Owners and Trainers Enclosure.'

'That doesn't mean anything. He might have a friend who's an owner.'

'No. My mate said he was listed as part owner in the Racing Post form guide.'

'Did you get the name of the horse?'

Kylie scrunches her nose up. 'He did mention it, but I've forgotten. Some weird name.'

More banter ensues as the fluid in the glasses inexorably dwindles.

Zac returns with refills as the laughter dies away, and the conversation turns to work.

Prisha glances at Kylie. 'How'd you go at Northern Fuel Logistics?'

She pulls out her notepad and flicks through the pages. 'I was able to identify the spot where the tanker deviated from the main road. After about ten minutes, it came to a halt for exactly seven minutes, then disappeared from the GPS.'

'The same spot where Gareth Atkin was discovered on the road?'

'Yes.'

'Good. So that's our hijack point—Danby. We now know he wasn't dumped there. We'll pay a visit tomorrow.' Throwing a handful of peanuts into her mouth, she munches then washes them down with a mouthful of crisp, refreshing lager. 'What about Northern Fuel Logistics? Are they legit?'

Kylie winces. 'Definitely legit. But all their workers are contract. I also visited the contract company in regard to any assistance they can offer Gareth.'

'And?'

She pouts. 'They've had a whip round and raised a hundred and fifty-three quid.'

'Bastards.'

Frank, attuned to such conversations, intervenes. 'We're not here to solve the world's problems, Prisha. We can only tackle the crimes we're tasked with.'

'I know, but it's so unfair. A hardworking, honest guy, doing his job, clobbered over the head by some ruthless bastards, and what is he going to come out of it with? Nothing. Northern Fuel Logistics will be insured for the loss of their diesel and damage to their vehicle. The contracting company will simply recruit a new driver. Life goes on for them as normal. Not for Gareth and Angie Atkin.'

'Something else,' Kylie says. 'I went on the PNC and there have been three diesel tanker hijackings during the last year, within what I'd consider close range. North Yorkshire, Northumberland, and Teesside.'

'Similar MO?'

Her brow furrows. 'Yes, sort of. The first two drivers were tied up and left in a field. All the tankers were stolen on the last shift of the night. But the diversion tactics were slightly different. '

'How so?'

'We think with Gareth, they used a false roadwork diversion. The one in Northumberland was an apparent motorbike accident blocking the road. And the Teesside one was a dead cow in the middle of the road. But in each instance the driver recalls seeing a black transit van and two, sometimes three men.'

'Irish accents?'

She nods. 'Yes.'

'It's the same gang,' Prisha states with clear conviction.

Zac, who has been busily replying to a text message from his wife, suddenly takes an interest. 'What did you say?'

Prisha frowns. 'About?'

'That last bit... Irish.'

'Oh. We think the tanker hijackers are Southern Irish. Why?'

'The raid today, on the iPhone Kid. I found a guy hiding in a bedroom. I know him from the past. He's a low-level weed dealer. A good kid in a spot of financial hardship. On Saturday night, he was supposed to meet his supplier at Runswick Bay. The supplier never showed, but three guys turned up in a car, removed a suspicious-looking tarp from the boot and headed to the beach. Threw it into a motorised dinghy and took off out to sea. My guy thought it could have been a body.'

Prisha focuses her attention. 'Possibly the source of the missing leg?'

'Aye. But here's the interesting thing. There was one guy he heard speak clearly.'

'And?'

'He was called Cillian and had a Southern Irish accent.'

'Get out of here!'

'True. Could be a coincidence. But there were three of them.'

Frank taps at the table. 'This is exactly why we have these drinks. You're all working different cases, running around, ships that pass in the night. And now we possibly have a connection between the severed leg, a possible body in a tarp, and three diesel tanker hijackings. And what connects them all?'

'A Southern Irish accent?' Prisha says, gazing out to sea.

15

Tuesday 11th July

Kylie holds her phone skywards and spins around under the dark canopy of the overhanging trees.

'Well?' Prisha asks.

'Hang on. Trying to get a decent signal. Ah, yes, this is the spot where the tanker's last known position was.'

Prisha bends and inspects the road. 'Can't see any tyre marks.' She rises and scans the narrow country lane. 'Perfect place for an ambush. Poor bugger wouldn't have stood a chance.'

'The guy from Northern Fuel Logistics said all their vehicles are fitted with panic buttons. He was wondering why Gareth didn't use it.'

'Did you tell him he probably had a gun pointed in his face?'

'Yes.'

'And what did he say to that?'

'Not much. He went white and gripped the edge of his desk. I think he was inferring Gareth may have been in on it.'

'Prick. With that vicious bang to the head, his brain would have resembled day-old porridge. I've heard of method acting, but that's ridiculous.' She bites down on her lip and studies the crime scene. 'The question is, we know diesel is worth a small fortune, but who would they sell forty-thousand litres to?'

'What about farmers?'

Prisha scowls. 'Nah, I don't think so. Farmers already get tax relief on fuel. A red dye is added to it and it's highly regulated. They can be randomly tested. A lot of risk in buying black-market fuel to save a few quid that they already get cheaper.'

'What about a dirty bomb? Maybe a terrorist group?'

Prisha considers the idea for about three seconds. 'No. I don't think so. Diesel has a high ignition point and low volatility. If you wanted a dirty bomb, you'd go with petrol.'

'Sorry, you've lost me.'

'Diesel is more difficult to ignite and produces far fewer volatile fumes compared to petrol. Petrol would create a massive explosion. Diesel would probably just burn once it was alight. Let's say diesel would not be the preferred choice of terrorists to wreak havoc.'

'Sorry.'

'Don't be sorry. You have to learn. That's what I'm here for. I wasn't born with this knowledge. So, thinking cap back on.'

Trying to make amends, Kylie says, 'What about an independent petrol station? They could fill up their underground tanks with cheap diesel, then undercut the opposition by twenty pence per litre and pull in all the traffic.'

Prisha feels bad, but in this job you need a thick skin. 'No. Again, petrol stations are highly regulated. It wouldn't be worth the risk. Most stations make their money from all the crap they sell inside; inflated prices for chocolate, milk, bread, coke, water, sausage rolls. The fuel only makes a few pence per litre.'

Slightly put out, Kylie shrugs. 'I give up then.'

Prisha smiles at her. 'Never give up. Keep it bouncing around your head and when you're least expecting it, the answer may jump out at you. And when that happens, it's the best feeling in the world.'

'Better than sex?'

'That depends on who you're having sex with,' she says with a coy smile, checking her watch. 'Come on, we better shake a leg. It's nearly eleven and the chief constable is due in the station at twelve for his farewell goodbyes. We don't want to miss it, otherwise Superintendent Banks will wet her knickers.'

'I take it you don't like her,' Kylie says as she heads to the driver's side of the car.

'Not really. She's devoid of any empathy and is obsessed with what I'd call the fluff.'

'Fluff?'

'Yes,' she replies, fastening her seatbelt. 'Paperwork, KPIs, benchmarks, press releases. That's not the job. That's not what the public care about. They want scumbags off the streets. And that's why we're here.'

Kylie giggles. 'You remind me of Frank.'

Prisha scowls and slaps her on the shoulder. 'Don't say that. I am not Frank bloody Finnegan! Right, when we get back to Whitby, drop me off at the end of my street, and I'll see you back at the station for canapes and a cuppa.'

'Why the end of your street?'

'I put a full load in the washing machine this morning, and as the weather's nice, I thought I'd hang it out in instead of using the tumble dryer. Cut down on my electricity bill.'

'I thought you lived in a third-floor flat?'

'I do. We share a communal back garden.'

———◦———

The car pulls up and Prisha quickly hops out and waves goodbye to Kylie.

Strolling up the short concrete path to the entrance to the flats, she fumbles in her pocket for the key to the door. As she inserts the key and turns the handle, a woman's voice, with a distinctive foreign accent, calls her name.

'Prisha.'

She turns and peers at the woman, instinctively recognising her from yesterday. It's the attractive female who was staring across the harbour, near the bandstand. Prisha smiles at her, bemused, her interest piqued.

'Yes. Do I know you?'

'Don't you recognise me?'

Prisha focuses on the round sunglasses, mirroring her own reflection.

'No. Should I?'

The woman removes her shades and smiles. 'It's me.'

Prisha's heart skips a beat. 'My god,' she whispers. 'Tiffany Butler.'

16

Zac enters the incident room, which is uncannily quiet apart from the discordant whistling emanating from the kitchenette. He silently curses Dinkel, then wanders over to the junior officer's desk and picks up a manilla folder. Flicking through the documents inside, duplicates from the Missing Persons Unit, he studies the police flyers handed out to the public, three different cases in all, and the detailed police report, along with photographs. Dinkel saunters into the office, sipping on a coffee.

Zac throws him a jaded glance. 'Dinkel, my little caber tosser, grab your coat.'

'Where are we going?'

He holds the file up in the air and waggles it back and forth. 'To show suitable concern and convince the poor relatives the police are doing everything in their power to locate their missing loved ones.'

Dinkel places his cup down on a table, a concerned frown sprinting across his face. 'Reading between the lines, I gather you have no intention of trying to find these people?'

'How very perceptive of you, sunshine. As the proctologist said to his patient, sometimes we just have to go through the motions.' He throws Dinkel the car keys. 'You drive. I need to get my head around the details of each report.'

'Shouldn't we ring ahead to make sure someone's home?'

'Already done it.'

They clatter down the steps of the station and out into the car park. Men without a mission, on a mission.

'I've been doing some research,' Dinkel says as he fumbles with the fob and drops it.

'Good for you.'

'Would you like to hear it?' he asks, bending down to retrieve the key.

'Not really.'

The car beeps and flashes its lights. Zac hops into the passenger seat, as Dinkel occupies the driver's side and fiddles with the seat, pushing it back and forth with his backside.

'Lights. Seat belt. Indicators working. Wing mirrors positioned correctly. Fuel tank - three quarters full. Start the engine. Handbrake on... handbrake off. Hang on... handbrake back on.' Again, he adjusts the seat backwards, then forward, then backwards as Zac taps his knee and bites his tongue. 'Rear-view mirror. Wipers working correctly.'

'FOR FUCK'S SAKE! Just drive the goddamned car, would you!'

Dinkel is suitably offended. 'This is the routine as taught by the defensive driving programme.'

'I don't care if it's the routine as taught by the British Defence League. Hand me the keys!'

'No.'

'I said, give me the keys.'

'No. I will not give you the keys.'

'I'm warning you, Dinkel, if you don't hand me the keys you're going to get a punch up the gullet.'

'And we're off.'

Zac rubs at his beard, agitated, as the car hops up the slope to the entrance of the car park.

'Why me, Frank?' he whispers mournfully. He opens the folder and glances at the names. 'Right, first stop, Glaisdale. Mrs Beth Sykes. Wife of missing man, John Sykes, aged sixty-six. Set off from Glaisdale on November 4th, 2022, for a day's hike heading towards Hutton-le-Hole. Seen hide nor hair of him since. Probably had a heart-attack in the back of beyond off the beaten track. There'll be nothing left of him now apart from a skeleton and some extremely loose fitting clothing.'

'I must say, I find your attitude to be flippant in the extreme. We're talking about missing people.'

'No, we're not. We're talking about dead people who came a cropper. It's unfortunate, but it happens all the time. Life is a lottery, Dinkel. When your number's up, it's up.'

'You don't suspect anything sinister?'

'No. There's no connection between the three people. They have nothing in common apart from the fact they're all adult males.'

'That's not true. They do have something in common.'
'What?'

'They all went missing on the North Yorkshire Moors within a couple years of each other.'

'Do you know how big the moors are?'

'Quite big.'

'Aye, quite big. Five-hundred-and-fifty-five square miles of quite fucking big. Covered in heather and woodland, rocks, and caves, hidden mineshafts, potholes, old quarries, quagmires, rivers, lakes. One of the biggest open spaces in the country. You could lose an army in there and never find them. When you go into the wilderness, there's always the possibility you won't return.'

———◦———

"You have arrived at your destination" the posh sat-nav lady informs them.

Dinkel parks outside a quaint stone cottage in the rustic village of Glaisdale, as Zac reorganises the folder, placing the details of John Sykes to the top.

'Remember, reassurance, kindly words, and the occasional concerned sincere frown. We want to be in and out within twenty minutes. Got it?'

'Got it.'

They walk up the brick-paved path which carves a swathe through a well-manicured garden in full bloom. It's overcast but humid, and both Zac and Dinkel, in blue cotton shirts, loosen their ties as they approach the door.

Zac knocks and winks at Dinkel. 'Who knows, we may even get lucky and be offered a cuppa tea and a slice of cake.' Zac detects a slight truculence from his colleague. 'Are you sulking?'

Dinkel doesn't answer as the door creaks open. A slender woman, about mid-sixties, confronts them.

'Sergeant Stoker?' she asks, worry lines circling her eyes.

'That's right. Beth Sykes?' he says, flashing his warrant card.

The woman nods and opens the door wider. 'Yes. Do come in and make yourself comfortable in the front room. The kettle's boiled. I'll bring us tea and cake.'

Zac elbows Dinkel in the ribs and grins. 'Oh, that would be just the ticket. By the way, this is my colleague, DC Dinkel.'

The woman offers Dinkel a warm, if brief, smile and heads to the kitchen.

The officers make their way into a comfortable living room overlooking the immaculate garden. Zac drops into a chair as Dinkel peruses the various pictures and photographs adorning the walls. He picks up one photo frame from the mantel and studies it.

'This is John Sykes,' he says, holding it aloft for Zac to look at. The image captures a healthy-looking man in his sixties, walking gear on, along with backpack. In the distance are rolling moorlands.

'Put it down before you drop it,' Zac says as Beth enters carrying a wooden tray. She places it down on a coffee table.

'Help yourself. There's milk and sugar and two slices of orange cake. I baked it today.'

Zac wastes no time in helping himself to the refreshments.

'It's a nice place you have here, Mrs Sykes,' he says, attempting small talk.

'Yes. We've lived here since we were married. Brought our family up here. John loved the place,' she adds wistfully as Dinkel takes a seat.

Zac leans forward, his face a picture of serious concern. 'We are doing everything in our power to find your husband, Mrs Sykes. Even though we don't have much to go on, it is still an active investigation.'

'Have you any updates?'

'I'm afraid not.'

'Then why the visit?' she asks sternly.

The question catches Zac off-guard. 'Well... we thought...'

Dinkel interrupts. 'Mrs Sykes, we know you've given a detailed statement to the Missing Persons Unit when your husband failed to return home, but we're here to go over everything again. Sometimes people recall small things which slipped by them the first time around.'

His words mildly surprise and visibly hearten her. 'Oh, well. Yes. I'm happy to go over everything again.'

Zac throws daggers Dinkel's way and grits his teeth. 'Aye. A brief recap. In your own time, Mrs Sykes.'

She takes a sip of tea, then places the cup down on a saucer. 'It was a Thursday morning, the 4th November, 2022. A cool but calm day. John had only recently retired and was looking forward to spending more time indulging in his passion.'

'Walking?' Dinkel suggests.

'Yes. He was a keen on orienteering, and experienced. He could read maps and knew how to use a compass. He set off early on that Thursday. I'd say about seven-thirty. I'd made him a pack-up; sandwiches, biscuits, an apple, a banana, and a flask of sweet tea. He also had two water bottles with him. Plus, all the usual paraphernalia; torch, box of matches, binoculars, mobile phone, and gloves and a hat.'

'He was well prepared,' Dinkel says, steadily taking notes.

'Yes. He was meticulous. He didn't specifically tell me the route he intended to take. He never did. All he said was he was heading towards Hutton-le-Hole, and from there, a short walk to Gillamore and the Royal Oak Inn. He'd done the walk a few times before. He'd have a couple of pints at the pub, then ring for a taxi to bring him home. It's only a thirty-minute drive.'

Dinkel taps the pen on the pages. 'I've done some research and there is no direct path or bridleway from Glaisdale to Hutton-le-Hole.'

Beth laughs. 'That didn't worry, John. In fact, he liked to follow his own route. He enjoyed his own company and the solitude.'

'Reading the report, it states that John never arrived at the Royal Oak?'

'No, he didn't.'

'And no one saw him after he left the house.'

'That's correct.'

'So, you were the last person to see him?'

'I suppose so, yes. The moors can be very isolated. And as it was November, I'm guessing there wouldn't have been as many hikers out and about.'

'You said he'd done the walk before. How long did it usually take him?'

'At a steady pace, about four to five hours.'

'If he left here at seven-thirty, he should have arrived at the pub by twelve-thirty, one o'clock at the latest?'

'Yes.'

'The report also says his mobile phone wasn't used that day and although the telco tried to ping his location, there was no signal from the phone.'

'That's correct.'

'And you raised the alarm at five-thirty that evening?'

'Yes. He was normally home by about three. I became concerned around four, four-thirty. I called my son to see if he'd heard from him, but he hadn't.'

'And John didn't have any pre-existing medical conditions?'

'No. He was as fit as a lop.'

Dinkel involuntarily twitches. He has no idea what a lop is, but he assumes that whatever it is, it must be fit.

'I see. Can you think of anything else, no matter how insignificant?'

'Well, only about the cave.'

Both officers frown as Zac flicks over the case notes. 'Cave?' he asks.

'Yes. I did mention it to the interviewing officer at the time… or at least I think I did.'

'What about the cave?'

'John had mentioned it once or twice in the past. On one of his previous walks, he'd come across a cave. It was fenced off with a sign warning not to enter. Apparently, it was unsafe. Prone to rockfalls or something.'

Zac nods. 'It's not out of the ordinary to stumble across such caves on the moors, Mrs Sykes.'

'No, but this one was different.'

'In what way?'

'John said it wasn't marked on the ordnance survey map. He found it odd.'

'Was your husband a cave explorer or potholer?'

She emits a false laugh. 'Good lord, no. To be honest, I think he may have suffered from a mild form of claustrophobia. Hated any form of confined spaces. Couldn't even get him on an aeroplane.'

'It's unlikely he'd have ventured into the cave?'

She hesitates and glances out into the garden. 'Yes. Or at least that's what I've told myself since his disappearance.'

'There's an element of doubt in your voice, Mrs Sykes,' Dinkel notes.

'Yes. I was thinking about him the other day while I was dead-heading some roses. If there was one word to sum up John's personality, it would have been inquisitive. He couldn't let things go. Always had to get to the bottom of a problem. I wondered if maybe he did enter the cave and had an accident. It's a terrible thought,' she adds, wringing her hands.

Zac slyly glances at his watch. 'There were four extensive searches conducted on the moors, and no sign of your husband or any of his possessions was ever found.' He pauses briefly as he thinks of the correct words to use. 'Mrs Sykes, Beth, I'm sure you've been asked this question before, but is there any possibility, however remote, your husband was in a relationship with someone else and simply disappeared to start a new life?'

Her face hardens as she sits upright. 'No. Definitely not. He'd never do that. My husband was faithful.'

Zac snatches the keys from Dinkel, jumps into the driver's seat, and fires the engine. 'That took a lot longer than I anticipated,' he grizzles as Dinkel gets in. 'We've another two people to interview and the morning is slipping away from us, thanks to you driving like an octogenarian three-toed sloth to get here.'

'What's the rush?'

'The chief constable is bidding us all a fond farewell at midday, or had you forgotten?'

'Oh, yes. So, what are your thoughts about John Sykes?'

'It's either misadventure, as I suspect, or the randy old git has set up a new life with someone. She was a little too quick at refuting that suggestion, in my opinion.'

'What about the cave?'

'A false lead. You heard what she said. A person who is afraid of confined spaces would not have ventured into a dangerous cave, especially one that had a warning sign about rockfalls.'

'Intriguing it isn't listed on the ordnance map.'

As the car pulls away, Zac turns to Dinkel. 'Of course, there is one other possibility.'

'What?'

'She was the last person to see him alive. Maybe he never left the house to go on the walk in the first place. We only have her word for it.'

17

Prisha manhandles Tiffany up the stairs into her flat and slams the door shut.

In a wild temper, she glares at her. 'What in hell's name are you playing at? Do you know the predicament you've put me in? I told you I never wanted to see you again for the rest of my life. That was the deal for me letting you go and covering for you.'

Tiffany pulls a false hurt expression. 'Come on, Prisha, admit it; you've missed me.'

Prisha grabs her by the arm and drags her into the living room. Pacing back and forth, clearly agitated, she lets her have it with both barrels.

'You're a loose cannon. If anyone recognises you, then we're both done for. This is completely reckless. What are you doing here, anyway? I thought you were in Argentina? Oh, and by the way—great timing. Yesterday I met some hot-shot bounty-hunter from MI5 who is re-investigating your case. Your timing is impeccable. My god! What were you thinking?'

'Prisha, you always sweat the small stuff,' Tiffany replies, in a blasé manner which further infuriates her.

'And what's with the foreign accent you used outside?'

'I've learnt Spanish, or at least Rioplatense; River Plate Spanish, which is slightly different.'

'Really,' Prisha replies, still seething.

'Yes. Want to hear some?'

'Not really.'

'Pienso en vos todos los días y todas las noches. Somos almas gemelas. Amame como yo te amo y podemos pasar el resto de la eternidad juntos.'

'Very clever,' she snarls with contempt. 'And what does that mean?'

'It means I think about you every day and every night. We are soulmates. Love me as I love you and we can spend the rest of eternity together.'

Tiffany moves closer and slides the back of her index finger down Prisha's cheek.

Prisha flinches. 'Wait, hang on...'

'There's plenty of time for recriminations later, Prisha. For the moment, can't we rejoice in each other's company? After all, we did make a good couple.' She leans in, her lips plump and wet.

Prisha pulls back and lifts her hand aloft. 'Whoa! Step off, girl. I think you've formed the wrong impression about me. I'm not gay. I have a boyfriend.'

Tiffany chuckles. 'Likewise. In fact, I have two. A well-to-do Buenos Aires banker, sophisticated and rich. Owns his own yacht, thirty thousand acres of land, and a couple of mansions. And a twenty-three-year-old gaucho, all taut muscle, dripping in testosterone—as poor as dirt. I like them both.' She kisses her own finger and places it on Prisha's lips. 'Sexuality is not always black and white, Prisha. There's overlap. Don't fight it. Go with the flow. You might surprise yourself.'

Inextricably drawn together, like two magnets, they inch towards each other.

Prisha's heartbeat is at levels she only experiences during a ten-mile power-run.

Silken lips briefly touch as the rattle of the front door has both women instinctively stepping away from each other.

'Yoo-hoo! Anyone home? It's only me.'

'Damn,' Prisha hisses.

Adam enters the room and stops dead in his tracks, slightly surprised. 'Oops, sorry. Didn't mean to intrude. I was in town collecting supplies for the farm and I bought some fillet steak for tonight's tea.' His eyes flit back and forth between both women. 'I thought I better get it in the fridge.'

There's a moment of uneasy silence until Tiffany grabs the initiative. 'Prisha, aren't you going to introduce me to this hunk?'

'Yes, sorry. Ahem, Adam, this is an old school friend of mine who I bumped into. We haven't seen each other for years.'

Adam reaches out his hand. 'Adam Rushford, pleased to meet you,' he says, all politeness and charm.

'Michelle Gervais,' Tiffany replies, pulling another pseudonym out of thin air. 'Prisha's a lucky girl. She's been extolling your many virtues.'

Adam grins and blushes slightly. 'Has she?'

'Yes, she has. And I mean *all* your virtues... and vices,' Tiffany says, flirting outrageously with him as she flicks at her hair and flutters her eyelashes.

Embarrassed, he turns and heads to the kitchen. 'Right, I best put this steak in the fridge.' The door closes behind him.

Tiffany turns back to Prisha. 'He's a catch. But a farmer? Considering your profession, that's a marriage made in hell. You work late and he starts early. You'll never see each other.'

'We get on really well, for your information,' she replies curtly, annoyed that Tiffany not only flirted with her boyfriend but also that Adam should be so moronically gullible as to fall for her obvious charms.

Adam re-enters the room. 'What time do you think you'll knock off tonight, love?'

Prisha eyeballs him coolly. 'No later than six-thirty.'

'Great. I'll have dinner ready by six-forty-five, and a glass of chilled white wine waiting for you. I can't sleep over as I need to get fifty lambs to market by six. Need to be up by five at the latest. Must dash as I left the engine running and I'm parked on a double yellow.' He leans in and pecks her on the cheek.

Prisha responds without much enthusiasm. 'Bye.'

'Nice to meet you, Michelle. I'm sure we'll meet again.'

'I'm certain of it. I'm leaving too. I'll walk down the stairs with you. Prisha and I have exchanged phone numbers and we'll catch up another time. Isn't that right, Prisha?'

Prisha exudes a false smile. 'Yes, that's right.'

Tiffany and Adam exit together as Prisha not only fights with her twisted emotions, but the enormity of Tiffany's presence back in Whitby.

Her life has become a convoluted mess which she fears could spiral out of control.

But as for the present... she doesn't trust Tiffany as far as she could throw her. The woman is a shameless, on-heat vixen, and she's now with her boyfriend.

'It wouldn't surprise me if she starts shagging him in the back of his Land Rover,' she mutters, edging towards the window. She gazes down onto the street from her high vantage point. To her relief, Adam and Tiffany exchange tentative waves. Tiffany heads up the street to North Terrace, and Adam jumps into his vehicle and drives away in the opposite direction.

Prisha flops onto her settee and cradles her head.

'This is bad. Really, really bad.'

18

Prisha tiptoes into the incident room, hoping to be invisible as Chief Constable Critchley nears the end of his speech.

'And so, for the last time, I'd like to say it gives me great comfort to leave the force in better shape than when I took over. Overall, morale is up, and our arrest and conviction rates have risen consistently year on year, despite being somewhat hamstrung by budget cuts. Some of you I know very well, having worked closely with you in the past,' he adds as his gaze drifts to Frank and Superintendent Banks. 'Others, I may not know as well personally, but believe me, I always keep abreast of the continued development of my officers. It is with mixed emotions that I bid you all farewell today. It's sad to say goodbye, but the golf course beckons, and my wife has all sorts of adventures planned for us both. Life in the force can take a heavy toll on our loved ones. Now it's my turn to focus on my relationships outside of work. Thank you for your unwavering loyalty and dedication to the job. I wish you all the best for the future. And remember, I'll be keeping an eye on you all... from the nineteenth hole!'

As applause mixed with cheers echoes out, Superintendent Banks slips to the front of the room and raises her hands.

'Please help yourself to nibbles and refreshments on the table. Chief Constable Critchley is on a tight schedule, so he must leave in ten minutes. If you'd like to wish him all the best, then you better be quick.'

As the throng of uniformed, plain-clothed officers, and civvies head to the table, Prisha sidles up to Zac.

He looks at her disparagingly. 'Nice of you to join us.'

'Did I miss much?'

He shrugs. 'Nah. Frank said a few words, then the Super, then the big man himself. You didn't miss the Gettysburg Address, that's for sure.' On noticing her demeanour, he says, 'Are you alright? You look like you've seen a ghost.'

Wearily, she shakes her head. 'I have, in a roundabout way.'

'Do you want to talk about it?'

'No, except to say, it's something from the past that has come back to bite me on the arse.'

'Oh, one of them. Well, when you're ready, you know where to find me.'

Standing to the side of Superintendent Banks, Frank gazes upon the table of food with utter contempt.

'What miserable, miserly, misanthrope ordered the food?' he grumbles.

Anne Banks scowls back. 'I did. What's wrong with it?'

'What's bloody right with it? A fruit platter, vegetable crudites, whole grain crackers, dips, and mini peppers stuffed with brown rice.'

'Wild rice, actually.'

'This is the sort of crap I'd expect at a vegetarian orgy. Where's the sausage rolls, party pies, and deep-fried chicken wings?'

'There are a lot of officers who are vegetarian and vegan these days.'

'Tough titty. Throw them an apple. Where are the sandwiches?'

'Allergies, Frank, allergies. People can suffer from Celiac disease, or have gluten sensitivity, not to mention nut allergies.'

'And where's the cans of pop?'

'Carbonated sugar drinks have been linked to an exponential increase in obesity and diabetes. It's the twenty-first-century, Frank. Time you opened the door and walked through it. There's mineral water. That will hydrate you,' she says with a half-smile, feeling confident and in an exceptionally good mood, not that anyone but the most astute observer would notice.

As she wanders off, Frank is joined by the chief constable.

'Well, Frank, don't be a stranger. You know where I live and if you ever fancy taking up golf, then I can nominate you as a member at my club. I'm the president, so there won't be any trouble getting you in despite the long waiting list.'

Frank, still slightly shell-shocked by the lack of anything unhealthy to eat, grunts. 'Thanks for the offer, Gordon. But I tried golf once. A good way to ruin an enjoyable walk, in my opinion. But yes, we must keep in touch, maybe go for a few beers now and again.'

'I take it you and Meera will be attending my farewell dinner at Kindlewood Hall later this month?'

'Wouldn't miss it for the world, Gordon,' he replies, masking the lie. Frank recalls the old days when an officer's retirement do meant a good old knees-up in a back room of a working men's club. The air swirling with blue cigarette smoke, fat cigars, foul language, and dirty jokes told by a politically incorrect northern comedian. And that was before the arrival of the strippers. Those were the days.

'Excellent. It's a three-course meal. A few speeches, then some entertainment.'

'What sort of entertainment?' he asks eyeing a carrot stick suspiciously.

'A four-piece string quartet. I believe they'll be playing Beethoven, Schubert, and, of course, Mozart.'

'I take it there'll be no Status Quo, then.'

The chief constable laughs. 'I know what you mean. It is all a bit highbrow and stuffy. But times have changed, Frank. We must move on.'

Frank is beginning to feel like a fossil. 'Aye, so I've been told.'

'Now, one of my last edicts was to tell Anne to put a couple of officers onto the missing hikers last seen on the moors. The media are whipping themselves up into a frenzy about it. Before too long, we'll have YouTubers and amateur sleuths swarming up here with their conspiracy theories and crackpot ideas.'

'Onto it already, Gordon. I have two of my best officers on it at the moment. We'll pull something together to release to the public by the end of the week.'

'Excellent. I knew I could rely on you.'

They eyeball each other in silence before Frank discreetly touches the chief constable's arm.

Glancing around furtively, he whispers, 'I know the official announcement isn't until Friday, but can I take it Martin Overland has got the top job?'

Appearing as decidedly shady as Frank, he taps his nose and replies, 'Between you and me, yes. A safe pair of hands. Although, I'm not enamoured with some of his plans for the future. He's always been an overly ambitious man.'

'Hmm... beware the ambitious man is my motto. And any idea who will step into his shoes?'

The chief constable is less forthcoming on this matter. 'Can't really say. A bit too close to home, if you know what I mean.' His eyes flit onto Superintendent Banks, who is chatting happily with Kylie and Dinkel.

Frank follows his gaze. 'Is Anne in with a chance?'

He doesn't reply, as more furrows than a ploughed field run across his brow. 'As I said... now, I really must mingle for a few minutes.'

Frank sighs deeply as Zac joins him. 'I see trouble ahead, Zac.'

'The Super?'

'Aye.'

'Oh. I take it she hasn't got the deputy job?'

'I fear not.' His attention refocuses on the display of rabbit food. 'I've eaten enough of this crap for the last eight weeks. A man can only take so much. Fancy fish and chips on the prom?'

Zac grins. 'Is the Tin Man's cock made of sheet metal?'

19

Zac emerges from Trenchers takeaway fish and chip shop carrying two bundles wrapped in white butcher's paper. He hands one to Frank.

'Ah, bloody champion. Let's find a pew on the harbour front. They always taste better in the fresh air. What did you order?' Frank quizzes as they set off at a brisk pace towards the swing bridge.

'Same as you; cod, chips, mushy peas.'

'Scraps?'

Zac winks at him. 'Of course.'

They find a bench seat on the promenade overlooking the East Pier, peel back the wrapping and attack their food with vigour.

'Oh, this is ambrosia. Food of the gods,' Frank declares as he drops a golden morsel of battered fish into his mouth.

'Aye. Simple pleasures.'

'So, this Declan Hughes you caught hiding in the wardrobe? What's the story?'

'I gave him a free pass on dealing weed on the proviso he helps us out.'

'With what?'

'He's going to arrange another drop off with his supplier later this week, late at night. We'll have two unmarked cars in the vicinity. Once the drop has been made, we'll follow the dealer, get his plates and hopefully his address. Declan is going to tell him he has a mate who wants two kilos of weed, and that he is to be the intermediary. We keep surveillance on the supplier and hopefully he will lead us to the head-honchos. According to Declan, he seems to think this is a serious outfit and a big operation. It's not some local scrags growing the stuff in their back room.'

'Hmm... sounds like a plan. And this supposed body in the boot. Where are you going with that?'

'There's not much we can do until we a get a positive ID on the severed leg. Dinkel was with the Mispers unit yesterday. They have a list as long as my arm of missing adult males. New ones daily. Most turn up safe and well. But others... you know the score.'

Frank scoops a slurry of mushy peas onto a chip and drops it into his mouth. 'You have a witness who thinks he saw a body being put into a boat late Saturday night. A severed leg turns up on the beach Monday morning. To me, they're obviously connected.'

'Not anymore,' Zac says with a chuckle.

'Very droll. If they're dumping bodies at sea, then they sound ruthless and professional. But surely, they'd have weighted it down?' he says, slightly distracted as he gazes down the road at the throng of holidaymakers buzzing to and fro.

'You'd have thought so. But we did get that storm late Saturday, early Sunday morning. It's possible it disturbed the body, and it rose to the surface, then got hit by a trawler or boat.'

'Hmm... plausible. Oh, shit the bloody bed!' Frank declares in a mild panic as he jumps from his seat.

'What's wrong?'

He nods down the road. 'Bloody Meera, heading this way. If she catches me with fish and chips, she'll have my guts for garters.' In a state of discombobulation, he turns one way, then the next, before spotting an overflowing council rubbish bin. He hurriedly re-wraps his food and deposits it in the top of the bin, then resumes his seat as Meera approaches.

'Yoo-hoo, Frank!' she calls out.

Frank rises and wipes his chin on the back of his coat sleeve. 'Ah, Meera, my love. What are you doing here?'

She ambles up and pecks him on the cheek. 'I live here.'

Frank emits a false belly laugh. 'Yes, I know that. I meant what brings you along the harbour front at this time of day?'

'I've taken an extended lunch break. I'm heading to the chemist to stock up on vitamins. There's a sale on.' Her eyes fall onto Zac, who is nonchalantly enjoying his fish and chips. 'Hello, Zac. How are Kelly and the boys?'

'Hi, Meera. Yeah, all good. How was your trip to Corfu?'

'Oh, it was absolute bliss. I told Frank we should holiday there once a year.'

'Weather must have been good. I see you've picked up a tan.'

She pouts, then smiles. 'Ha, ha. Very funny. We had a wonderful relaxing time, didn't we, Frank?'

'Oh, aye. Stunning scenery.'

Meera scoffs. 'How would you know? You spent most of your time in that tavern on top of the cliff drinking beer and reading the British newspapers. So, what are you two boys up to?' she asks, her eyes belatedly falling onto the wrapper in Zac's lap.

'Having a bite to eat and talking shop,' Zac replies.

The smile drops from her face as she peers at Frank, then Zac, then back to Frank. 'Not eating, Frank?' The question is loaded with meaning.

'What? Me?'

'Is there another Frank?'

'Ahem, no. I'm not eating. Definitely not... eating.'

'Didn't fancy fish and chips?'

'Ha, ha. No. You know very well it's not on our diet plan.'

'I'm glad to hear it. Still, it must be tempting, watching Zac.'

Frank's sad gaze falls onto the fish and chips as he inadvertently licks his lips. 'To be honest, Meera, love, the very sight of them turns my stomach. All that batter, dripping in saturated fat. I've told Zac he needs to start looking after himself. He's heading for an early grave if he keeps this up. His arteries will be clogged up to buggery.'

Zac raises his head and deposits a fat juicy chip into his mouth. 'Worse ways to go, though, eh, Frank?' he says with a wink.

Meera eyes both men suspiciously. 'Have you not eaten yet?' she questions her husband.

'No, not yet. Thought I'd get something on the way back to the station.'

'Really? I tell you what, if you're going to be here for the next ten minutes, I can bring you something back from that health-food cafe near the chemists. An alfalfa sprout salad, perhaps? Or what about wholegrain couscous with broccolini and chopped walnuts?'

'Sounds wonderful, Meera, and my mouth's salivating at the very thought. But me and Zac were about to head back. We've got a lot on. Isn't that right, Zac?'

'What?' he says, stuffing a succulent morsel of tender white flesh into his gob. 'Oh, aye. That's right. A lot on.'

Frank spots a vicious-looking seagull the size of a small dog circling the rubbish bin. Waving his arms in the air, he cries, 'Shoo! Get out of it, you big, ugly bastard.' The bird backs off in a belligerent manner, already circling for a second attack.

'Right, I'll leave you boys to it. Give my love to Kelly when you see her, Zac. We really must have you both round for dinner one weekend. It's been a while.'

Zac mumbles an incoherent reply as he shovels mushy peas into his mouth with a wooden fork. Frank watches on until his wife turns the corner and disappears from sight.

'Strike a bloody light. Am I blessed or what?' He scrabbles about in the rubbish bin and retrieves his hastily discarded ambrosia as a young girl with a pained expression watches on.

She tugs at her mother's sleeve. 'Mammy, is that man homeless?' she enquires in blissful innocence.

The woman gives Frank a derisory and cursory once over. 'I don't know. Why?'

'He's eating old food out of the rubbish bin.'

The woman drags the child away as Frank sits down and unwraps the fish and chips.

Chewing thoughtfully, Zac stares out over the water. 'You've got a problem, Frank. A big problem. You can't keep this charade up forever,' he states, with not an ounce of sympathy.

'Tell me about it.' He picks the whole fish up and takes a humongous bite, then closes his eyes and chomps contentedly.

20

The car rolls down the main high street in the charming market town of Guisborough.

'Next left, then second right,' Prisha instructs as Kylie dutifully flicks the indicator.

'How are we going to play this?'

'What do you mean?'

Kylie appears concerned. 'Usually, when we've identified a dead body, we inform the next of kin first, before anyone else. It's a strict protocol. Speaking with his business partner first could land us in trouble.'

'Firstly, we don't know conclusively if Jake Hill is dead. And secondly, we don't know who his next of kin is. His ex-wife disappeared off the radar five years ago. Which leaves a few possibilities. Either she's dead and her body has never been found or identified, or she may have left the country. I've contacted Border Security and put in a request.'

'Jake Hill must be dead. We found his leg on the beach.'

'And that's where we need to tread carefully, no pun intended. A body part is not conclusive proof of death. It's classed as a missing person under suspicious circumstances.'

'Suspicious being the operative word. I think I'll let you do the talking. I'm scared I might put my foot in it... no pun intended, either.'

Prisha points ahead. 'Here we are. Pull up on the forecourt and let's see if Mr Nick Prescott can shed any light on the matter.'

The unmarked Skoda Octavia pulls up outside a small commercial building with signage that reads, 'Prescott & Hill Electrical Services - For All Your Domestic Needs.'

The roller door is up and a man in his early forties is loading equipment into the back of a Mercedes-Benz Sprinter van.

Prisha hands Kylie a brown envelope and they exit the vehicle and saunter up to the entrance, Prisha holding her warrant card out.

'Excuse me, I'm DI Kumar and this is DC Pembroke, CID. Are you Nick Prescott?'

The man pauses, then nods guardedly. 'Aye, that's me. What can I do for you, inspector?'

'Your business partner, Jake Hill, can you tell me the last time you saw or spoke with him?'

Prescott drops a roll of electrical cable into the van, then pulls out a packet of smokes and lights up. 'About five weeks back. Why?' he questions, blowing out a plume of grey smoke into the air.

'Five weeks. That's a long time, especially for a business partner. Can you tell us where he is?'

A thin smile curls his lips. 'Aye. He's in New Zealand.'

'Really? And he left five weeks ago?'

'That's right.'

'Is he on holiday?'

Prescott's eyes swivel back and forth between the two officers. 'No. He's gone to see his young lad. Apparently, he was involved in an accident. It sounded serious, so Jake hopped on a plane to go see him.'

'What sort of accident?'

'He was on his push-bike.'

'Is his ex-wife in New Zealand?'

'Yes. Jake and Zoe split up about six years back. She remarried a Kiwi. Zoe got custody. Been there ever since.'

'Can you remember the surname of the man Zoe married?'

'Nay. Can I hell.'

It's always been a dilemma for Prisha since relocating to Yorkshire. Typically, when someone is hiding something, they offer very little information. They appear reticent, evasive. To her it's a sign they're not telling the truth. But she's found that Yorkshire men, in particular, are like that by nature. Guilty or innocent, they keep things close to their chest. No one could ever accuse them of verbosity.

'I see,' she says, throwing Kylie a thwarted expression.

He spits something from the corner of his mouth. 'Look, what's all the fuss about?'

'Has he not been in touch since he left for New Zealand?'

'No.'

She grimaces. 'Bit odd, isn't it? You being partners and he hasn't let you know how his son is faring?'

'We may be partners on paper, but it's a marriage of convenience,' he states, as he wanders into the lock-up and scrabbles around in a large cardboard box full of plugs and sockets.

'Sorry, I don't understand.'

He wearily lifts his head from inside the box. 'He has his customers. I have mine. We share the running costs on the building, and split any advertising bills equally. But that's as far as it goes. Occasionally, I may help him out on a big job, and vice versa. But we're not buddies or nowt. And you still haven't told me what all this is about.'

Prisha nods to Kylie, who pulls a photo from the envelope and hands it to Prescott.

'What the bloody hell!' he exclaims, disgust zipping across his face.

'The severed leg was found on Tate Hill Sands, Whitby, on Monday morning. A DNA sample was matched with a person on our database. The leg belonged to Jake Hill, your business associate.'

Prescott thrusts the photo back into Kylie's hands. 'I don't know what to say. I presume he's dead?'

Prisha's eyebrows arch. 'We don't know. But it doesn't look promising. Do you know if Jake had any financial issues or was being threatened by anyone?'

He becomes distant, eyes glazed over. 'Nah, not that I'm aware. The business always keeps a healthy bank balance, you know, for stock and what not. I mean, he was a very private person, subdued a lot of the time. I suppose it is possible he took his own life. It's so hard to spot, isn't it, depression?'

'Apart from his wife and son in New Zealand, do you know of any other close relatives who are still alive?'

A shake of the head. 'I couldn't tell yer. Like I say, we weren't buddies or anything.'

'Right. Well thank you for your time, Mr Prescott. We'll be in touch if we have any further questions, and we'll keep you informed of our progress.'

'Thanks.'

The officers turn to walk away, then Prisha stops. 'Oh, Mr Prescott, you said you last spoke with Jake five weeks ago.'

'Aye.'

'Where *exactly* did you speak with him?'

His weight shifts from his right to left side. 'I didn't speak to him as such. He sent me a text message.'

'Can I see it?'

He pulls his mobile out and scrolls the screen. 'Here you go.'

> *Hi Nick, bad news. My lad is in a serious condition in hospital. I've booked my flight to New Zealand. Not sure when I'll be back. See you when I see you.*

Prisha mentally notes the time and date and hands the phone back. 'And that's the only contact you had with him regarding his son's accident?'

'That's right.'

'Good day, Mr Prescott.'

The Skoda pulls away as Prescott continues to load his van.

'What do you think?' Kylie asks. 'He seems legit.'

'He's a lying toerag.'

'How do you know?'

'Jake's text message said his son was in a serious condition in hospital, and he'd booked his flight to New Zealand. And that was it.'

Kylie shrugs. 'So? That tallies with what Prescott told us.'

Prisha turns to her and grins. 'It's always the little things, Kylie.'

'Go on, what am I missing?'

'There was no mention of Jake's son being involved in a cycling accident.'

'Then why didn't you pull him up on it?'

'And let him know we're onto him? No. It's strategic. We need to maintain the upper hand and not give away our suspicions while we gather more evidence. It's called playing the long game. Right, I want you to obtain a search warrant for Jake's house. Interview the neighbours and locate his vehicle. We need to find out exactly the last time anyone saw Jake Hill alive.'

Nick Prescott watches from the workshop until the car disappears from view. He pulls his phone out and taps at a contact.

21

Prisha knocks on the office door of Superintendent Banks. Without waiting for a reply, she enters. Magnus Crawley keeps his head down as he meticulously writes in a journal.

'Take a seat, Inspector Kumar. I was expecting you,' he states in an officious tone.

Prisha is already seething at the summons. *Who the hell does this reptilian slime-ball think he is?*

Finally, he closes the journal, clicks the top of his pen and carefully places it down at the side of the notebook, adjusting it so it lies perfectly adjacent. He clasps his hands together, rests them on the desk, and smiles across at Prisha, his eyes darting back and forth over her poker-faced expression.

'You have a most impressive record, inspector. Arrest rates, convictions. You've caught some big fish in your short time here.'

'That's what they pay me for.'

'Hmm... indeed.' His eyes drop onto a folder on the desk. He taps at it. 'I've acquainted myself of all the facts regarding the Tiffany Butler case, and the Russian agents, Kira Volkov, and Maxim Lenokov.'

'Good.' The word is dry, perfunctory.

Hooded eyes clamp shut, then spring open, as deep lines announce themselves on his brow. 'Your official statement, after your ordeal with the Russians in the Hawsker Lighthouse...' A long pause, as if deep in thought.

'What about it?'

'A few things puzzle me.'

'Such as?'

He unclasps his hands, drops his head and pinches his thin elongated nose between thumb and forefinger, as if trying to shake off a migraine. Prisha is nothing, if not an expert in body language. His performance is designed to rattle her.

'Let me see if I've interpreted all the facts correctly. Please stop me if I'm wrong.'

'Don't worry. I will.'

Her reply momentarily alerts him, and they eyeball each other intensely for a brief moment. He relaxes. 'You arrested Miss Butler on a plane at Manchester Airport for using a forged passport.'

'That's right. We, myself, and an MI5 operative, tracked her down to Keswick in Cumbria. She'd hired a car from there, then driven almost to the airport, but had stopped off at the motorway services. We sent a patrol to intercept her, but she eluded us. On a hunch we raced to the airport and once I'd shown security her photograph, we ascertained what flight she was on.'

Magnus Crawley shuffles restlessly in his seat. 'Yes. I am aware of that. However, I want to jump forward a little.'

'Sorry. Go on.'

'You and Miss Butler were being held hostage in the lantern room of the lighthouse. Kira Volkov had left to prepare the dinghy used in her escape.'

'A rigid hulled inflatable boat. Yes.'

'Maxim had been left behind in the room with you and Miss Butler. Apparently, he intended to rape you before slitting your throat.'

'There's no "apparently" about it. Kira had said as much, and Maxim definitely intended to carry out both atrocities.'

His face creases as he forms a fist. 'If you *could* let me finish, inspector, before your interjections.'

A nonchalant shrug. 'Fine.'

'Prior to Maxim arriving in the lantern room, you had cut the cable ties binding your wrists using a paring knife you'd picked up from a farmhouse you'd stayed in while trying to avoid capture. You also freed Miss Butler's wrists at the same time. You then devised a plan with Miss Butler. When Maxim returned and began to paw at you...'

'Sexually assault me, you mean? Pawing makes him sound like a kitten.'

'My apologies, inspector. I didn't mean to understate his reprehensible actions. When Maxim enacted his sexual assault upon your person, you brought the knife down into the back of his neck. He staggered away, nearly falling down the spiral steps. You slammed the iron door shut on him, severing several fingers. Maxim tumbled down the steps and was knocked unconscious, although you assumed he was dead when you and Miss Butler descended the stairs. It was at this point Miss Butler saw her chance and took flight, escaping via the main entrance and bearing right. As you were incapacitated with a severely swollen knee, you didn't give chase.'

'At that point, I couldn't care less about Tiffany. I wanted to get the hell out of there as fast as possible and save my own skin.'

Eyes widen in surprise. 'Intriguing,' he declares.

'What is?'

'You called her Tiffany, rather than Miss Butler.'

'So?'

'I find it odd you'd refer to a suspected kidnapper in such a familiar manner.'

'If you'd read my report correctly, I did say Tiffany, Miss Butler, had saved my life on two occasions.'

'I noted that. Would you say you'd formed a bond during your ordeal?'

'Who wouldn't have? We were both in the same predicament, trying to evade death. But if you're inferring I let her escape as some sort of payback, you're wrong.'

'Hmm... may I continue?'

'Please.'

'Before you had a chance to make good your escape, Maxim regained consciousness and grabbed your ankle as Kira returned. You ignited a flare to create a smokescreen diversion and at that point your colleagues arrived on the scene, as Kira now made good her escape. Would you say I have grasped the salient points, inspector?'

'Pretty much.'

'Good. Now to my...' his head waggles from side to side, jettisoning a flurry of dandruff onto his black shirt as he seemingly struggles with a conundrum. 'I was going to say - concerns. But that's rather a strong word. Reservations would be a more suitable word choice. Yes, reservations.' He appears pleased with himself. 'Going back to Miss Butler's escape. You said she exited the door and turned right.'

'Correct.'

He leans back in his chair, a thin smile on his lips. 'I took the liberty of walking to the lighthouse yesterday. A very pleasant stroll indeed, if a little long. Magnificent views. If you turn right, heading out of the lighthouse, then you are confronted by a wall. On the other side is a very long drop to the rocks below. And the Russians' boat was further down the coast, in the direction of Robin Hood's Bay, only accessible by a rope ladder.'

'Your point being?'

'Why would Miss Butler have turned right, knowing full well she'd have probably run straight into Kira Volkov?'

Another shrug. 'Who knows? It all happened quickly, and she wouldn't have been familiar with the layout. She maybe hid and waited until Kira arrived back then made her escape.'

He nods thoughtfully. 'Yes. Perhaps she did.' His eyes, for nothing more than a fleeting moment, fall onto Prisha's chest. He quickly looks away and flicks open the folder on his desk.

Prisha glances down and notices the two top buttons on her blouse are undone, revealing a small amount of cleavage. Feeling queasy and vulnerable at the same time, she quickly fastens the buttons.

'Are we done?'

'Not quite, my dear,' he purrs. 'Your statement ends abruptly.'

'What do you mean?'

'Frank and his team arrive - *the* end.'

'So? There's nothing else to say.'

He purses his lips and steeples his fingers together. 'What happened after the arrival of your colleagues? Did you spend the night in the hospital?'

'No. Frank drove me to the station where I waited for a doctor. She gave me the once over and stabilised my knee. Then handed me painkillers and some sedatives to help me sleep. Frank drove me back to my flat, and I went to bed.'

'And what time would that have been when you arrived back at your flat?'

'Is it relevant?'

'Nothing is relevant until it is. The time, inspector?'

'I can't be certain, but I'd say twelve to twelve-thirty.'

'In the morning?'

Her anger, which she's managed to bridle, is on the rise. 'Of course in the bloody morning!'

'I see,' he adds, picking his pen up and jotting something down in his journal. 'And you definitely didn't leave your flat until the following day?'

Her temper boils over. 'Look, what is this? I feel like I'm on trial here. I was the victim in all this. It was one of your officers, a high-ranking officer, may I add, who was the mole, a traitor, in cahoots with the Russians. It was he who was responsible for the death of one of your men, and an innocent woman, Shirley Fox. It was he who set all this up and nearly got me and Tiffany killed. What's happened to him? Where's he disappeared to? Why hasn't he been put on trial?'

He stares blankly at her. Eyelids occasionally flutter like a chameleon lazing on a rock beneath the sun. 'We cannot have a public trial when it involves state secrets and national security. Even you must be aware of that?'

She hisses her reply. 'So, you sweep your grubby dirt under the carpet and move on. Answerable to no one?'

Magnus is not used to people standing up to him. He feels his ascendancy is on the wane. 'I think that will do for today, inspector.'

Prisha violently pushes her chair back, sending it toppling. 'For today? If you want to speak to me again, then it will be in front of Frank, and HR, *and* I want it recorded. If you're going to treat me like a criminal, then I want the same safeguards they're afforded.'

The door is slammed shut with such force it reverberates around the top floor. She briefly pauses in the corridor, breathing hard.

'You bloody fool,' she whispers to herself, before storming off.

22

Wednesday 12th July

Pounding rhythm. Legs burning, muscles searing with lactic acid.

She sprints along the Cleveland Way, racing against the pale, ascending sun. The imposing gothic silhouette of Whitby Abbey inches closer, rising from the misty sea air like a guardian of the past—unyielding and eternal.

Her heart hammers in her chest, each breath a sharp needle to her lungs.

Waterlogged shoes drum an unrelenting beat on the ancient soil, the earth beneath her feet a silent crypt, keeper of a million forgotten secrets.

A lone figure.

Solitary.

Alone.

Because we are always alone, even in the midst of those we love and cherish.

There is freedom in pain.

And pain in freedom.

Pain is a constant—past, present, and future. Inextinguishable. Everlasting. Immutable.

Freedom is a different matter.

Normally, when reaching the abbey, she takes the path that leads down by St Mary's, bounds down the 199 Steps, and heads across the old town to the swing bridge. Today she extends her run for as long as possible, wanting to experience pain, hoping it will flush her mind of unwelcome thoughts.

Hanging left, she jogs by the abbey and the brewery, barely noticing the approaching car.

It slows as it nears, the heavily tinted windows obscuring the driver.

As it passes by, Prisha's training and heightened senses kick in.

Black BMW M4 Convertible. Registration plate LR21 CBA.

She races on, refusing to slow her pace.

At last, pain arrives, smothering the thoughts she's trying to outrun.

The purr of an engine.

A quick glance over her shoulder, and she moves to the left to allow the car to pass, unobstructed.

The same car that just passed her.

Holidaymakers. Taken the wrong turn or looking for free parking, she thinks.

Again, the vehicle slows, moves to the right, overtakes, and leaves her behind.

Head down, she ploughs on, pushing, enduring.

Her eyes rise from the bitumen to see the BMW, thirty yards ahead, parked on the opposite side of the road, brake lights on.

For the first time, she suspects something's amiss.

Odd. Stopped to ask for directions? Or is it some recently released weirdo I put behind bars who's come to exact revenge?

She slows to a gentle jog, quickly scanning the area.

Not a soul in sight.

Her energy is almost spent.

She's pushed too hard.

Coffee and a croissant, followed by a robust breakfast, will refuel her—but that's some way off.

To her left, open fields.

Behind her, a long empty road back to the brewery and deserted abbey.

To her right, another smaller field leading to a housing estate. If push comes to shove, that's her escape route.

Her jog slows to a walk as she pulls the phone from her bumbag and pretends to check for messages. Instead, she surreptitiously snaps a photo of the car's number plate and sends it to her email.

A clue for her colleagues, lest she die.

She nears the car.

Sucks oxygen into her lungs, readying for a sudden sprint.

The passenger window slides down.

Curiosity killed the cat.

She turns her head to the right and peers into the vehicle.

Her heart thumps hard against her chest, a fluttering sparrow trapped in a bony cage.

'Oh, fuck.'

She cannot run.

23

A crisp crack resonates as the knife strikes with lethal precision, the blade slicing through the hard exterior with ease, halting shy of completely severing the crown. With one determined thrust, it accomplishes its objective, taking the top clean off and exposing the soft, vulnerable interior. Thick, viscous fluid oozes out, glacial. Holding the knife aloft, his tongue darts forward and licks the glutinous residue from the blade.

'Hmm... you taste good, my little beauty,' he murmurs, experiencing the familiar, delicious taste.

He leans in closer, eyes narrowing as he studies the exposed surface. There's a moment of stillness, a pause, as if he's contemplating his next move. His grip tightens around the handle, fingers flexing in anticipation. Satisfied with the result, he sets the knife aside and reaches for a spoon, ready to scoop out the gloopy flesh.

A moment's hesitation.

Has he forgotten something?

Frank takes a pinch of pepper from his plate and sprinkles it over the glistening, rich yellow yolk, then picks up a slice of toast, cut into soldiers, and dips it into the egg. He savours a bite as Meera enters the kitchen holding an envelope.

Frank looks up. 'Morning love. There are two eggs in the pan for you. I put them in a couple of minutes after mine, so they should be about done. Fresh brew in the teapot. Bread in the toaster.'

'Thanks,' she murmurs.

'When did you say Emily was due up next?'

'Who?'

The spoon hovers mid-air as Frank turns to his wife, puzzled. 'Who? Our bloody niece, Emily.'

'Oh, sorry. Erm, week on Saturday. But you know what teenage girls are like. If something more interesting pops up on the horizon, she's likely to change her plans.'

'No, she won't. She'll want to see her Uncle Frank,' he replies with a chuckle. 'Are you getting those eggs or what? They'll be hard-boiled if you leave them in much longer.'

'What? Oh. I'm not hungry,' she mutters, gazing out of the kitchen window into the garden.

'Fair enough. Leave them on and I'll have hard-boiled eggs for my mid-morning snack.'

'Frank?'

'Yes, love,' he replies, scooping the last of the white from the bottom of the shell.

'There's something I've been meaning to tell you.'

Frank frowns, sensing bad news on the domestic front. 'Please don't tell me Sandra's invited us round for dinner again? That last roast she cooked was barely edible. I had lockjaw for a week after, and the veggies were boiled to death.'

She turns sharply, clutching the envelope to her chest. 'Can you please bloody-well shut up for once!' she snaps, her voice cracking.

Frank bolts upright and stares at his wife, for the first time noticing her trembling hands and pale face. He stands and walks over to her.

'Hey, love, what's the matter?' he asks gently, his gaze falling onto the brown envelope crumpled in her hand.

'I should have told you earlier. I've kept it a secret.'

'What secret?'

'You remember about a month ago I went for my routine mammogram?'

He certainly can't remember, but errs on the side of caution. 'Aye, of course I do.'

'They found a lump.'

'Oh.'

'They took a biopsy before we left for Corfu.'

'And?'

She thrusts the envelope into his hand. 'The specialist wants me to come in to discuss the results.'

Frank pulls the letter out and reads the brief, official notice. 'That doesn't necessarily mean it's bad news. He might want to explain things in person, maybe to give you the all-clear.'

'Or he might not. I know how it works. If you're clear, they ring and tell you. Anything else and they ask you to come into the surgery. My mother and grandmother both died of breast cancer. It runs in the family.' Tears well up, then spill over, streaming down her cheeks.

Frank gently grasps her by the shoulders, then pulls out a handkerchief to dab at the tears. 'Hey, there, there, love. Don't jump to conclusions before you know the facts.'

'I don't know if I can go through it all, Frank. Chemotherapy, radiotherapy... I've seen too much of it working at the hospice these past ten years. It's pitiful.'

Frank guides her to a chair, then pours a cup of tea. 'Here you go, sweetheart. Get this down you. It will make you feel better.' He kneels beside her, one hand resting on her thigh, the other gently smoothing the hair back from her face. He doesn't speak, doesn't rush her. Simply lets her be. His presence, a quiet anchor in a storm of emotions.

The kitchen is hushed, save for the soft ticking of the clock on the wall. Meera wipes at her face, her fingers brushing away the lingering tears, but her eyes remain downcast.

'I'm not ready, Frank. I'm scared.'

He nods, understanding the words left unsaid. The fear of the unknown, the dread of what might come, the memories of the women in her family who'd faced the same battle. His heart aches for her, for the woman who's always been the bedrock of his life, now faced with something so terrifyingly uncertain.

He takes her hand in his. 'You don't have to be ready,' he murmurs. 'Not yet. One step at a time, yeah?'

She nods, squeezing his hand. It's always been like this—when one falters, the other stands firm. They've weathered storms before, but this one feels different, darker.

Meera takes a deep breath, and for a moment, the tension in her body seems to ease. She looks up at Frank, her eyes softening, a hint of a smile playing on her lips.

'I don't know what I'd do without you,' she whispers, the vulnerability in her voice raw.

He vibrates his lips in scorn. 'Without me? Ha! I'm the lucky one, not you. Come here, you daft 'apeth.' He pulls her into his chest. 'Now listen to me; don't go getting all mithered until you know what it's all about. Hopefully, it will be the all-clear. And if it's anything different, then we'll tackle it together, right? Strength in unity.'

They embrace silently for a few moments until Meera pulls away. She straightens, brushing a hand over her hair.

'I'd better take a shower and get ready for work.'

Frank nods. He watches intently as she gathers herself, the brave mask slipping back into place.

As she leaves the kitchen, he saunters to the window, staring out at the morning light filtering through the varied plants in full bloom. The house feels silent now. As if it's witnessed a ghastly play and dare not speak.

He sighs. 'Secrets,' he mutters under his breath.

24

A pair of seagulls glide overhead, their screeching mews carried away on a stiffening breeze.

'I'm damp and sweaty. I'll ruin your seats,' Prisha states, hovering at the passenger door.

Tiffany smiles. 'It's a hire car. What do I care? Anyway, they're leather. They'll wipe down. Hop in.'

'Pull over to the other side of the road. If a patrol car happens to drive past, they may find it odd the way you've parked.' She reluctantly climbs into the car, still breathing hard. 'You've got to stop this. It's not fair,' she adds as Tiffany manoeuvres the vehicle to the opposite side of the lane.

'What's not fair?'

'You, doing this, coming back into my life. You're putting everything I've worked so hard for in jeopardy. What are you doing here? Why are you back?'

Tiffany presses a button to activate the handbrake. 'You sound like you hate me.'

'I do,' she snaps, instantly regretting her words as she glances across at Tiffany, who stares wistfully ahead. 'I didn't mean that. I don't hate you,' she murmurs. 'You don't understand the possible consequences. There's still a warrant out for your arrest, and that MI5 officer I told you about is big trouble. He's already interrogated me. You need to go back to Argentina and never return, for both our sakes.'

Tiffany nods thoughtfully. 'I do understand. I'm not stupid. And that's why I make meticulous plans backed up with contingencies. Always expect the unexpected. I'm leaving for London shortly, and in a few days I'll be boarding a plane to Mexico. A quick change of costume and passport, and I'll be on a flight to Argentina.'

'You still haven't explained why you're back here? Surely it wasn't just to see me?'

'No, it wasn't.'

For some reason, her words sting Prisha and she inadvertently lets out a crestfallen, 'Oh.'

Tiffany reaches out and places her hand on top of Prisha's. 'Not *just* to see you. That was one reason. But I also have unfinished business to take care of. Tidy up some loose ends. And now that's nearly done, I'll depart this septic isle and never return.'

Prisha half-smiles. 'It's sceptred isle, not septic. It's from Shakespeare.'

'I'm fully aware of the origin and the correct quotation, but I think you'll find septic isle is a far better way to describe this country.'

'Oh, very clever.'

'Anyway, I have something for you.' Tiffany reaches into her pocket and pulls out a keyring in the shape of a bagel with a key attached. She dangles it in the air, then hands it to Prisha.

'What's this?'

'The key to my house... in Whitby. You should receive a large envelope tomorrow delivered by registered mail.'

Prisha shakes her head and frowns. 'Why, and from whom, and more importantly, what's inside it, and why the house key?'

'The envelope is from my solicitors, Dooley and Hargreaves. Inside the envelope are the deeds to my house. I'm transferring my house across to you. It's yours—my gift. All you need to do is sign the paperwork and return it. My solicitor will take care of the rest.'

Prisha's eyes widen as she drops her head into her hands. 'You bloody, stupid idiot,' she groans. 'It's the worst thing you could have done. Now there is a direct link between us. This will finish me. I'll go to prison. Perverting the cause of justice, bribery, and corruption, misconduct in public office, conspiracy to defraud. And that's just off the top of my head. I'll be looking at twenty years, minimum.'

Tiffany pouts like an annoyed mother. 'Calm down, Prisha. You can be so melodramatic sometimes.'

'Melodramatic!' she screams, throwing the key back at her. 'You're detached from reality. A fucking airhead who lives in some parallel fantasy world. You've ruined me, completely ruined me. I let you escape because you saved my life. And this is how you repay me?' Her anger subsides as another realisation dawns on her. 'Oh, I see. It's all been a ruse, hasn't it? You don't love me, you hate me. Always have. This is your perverse, convoluted form of retribution. To discredit me and obliterate my reputation.'

'My, my, this is a real hissy fit. Most people who were handed a house worth upwards of four-hundred-thousand pounds, fully furnished in exquisite taste, may I add, would be jumping for joy. I wasn't expecting cartwheels along the promenade, but a little gratitude would have been nice.'

Prisha pulls at the handle of the door. 'I'm out of here. I'm going straight to Frank and Superintendent Banks and coming completely clean. I also have your number plate, so you won't get far.' She half steps from the car.

Tiffany emits a weary sigh. 'Prisha, get back in and let me explain. I'm not out to ruin you. And you're wrong, I do love you. Even if it's unrequited. Come on, please. Give me five minutes and hear me out. Then if you're not convinced, I'll come with you to the police station and hand myself in. Promise.'

Prisha wavers, then slips back into her seat and closes the door. 'Five minutes. Go on.'

'First of all, let's go back to the beginning: the kidnapping and ransom case. You had not one shred of evidence against me. All you had was the testimony of Mark Bridges, who is dead. And dead men cannot testify in court. There may be a warrant out for my arrest, but so what? That doesn't mean I'm guilty.'

'But you are guilty.'

She shrugs, contritely. 'True, but you're missing the point. I'm innocent until proven guilty, and without evidence, you cannot prove my guilt. The ransom money was transferred into privacy-focused cryptocurrencies a long time ago, which already makes finding it extremely difficult. And with the addition of a dubious mixing service, it's practically untraceable. The only reason you arrested me at Manchester Airport was to bring me back for questioning in the forlorn hope I would break down under intimidation, cajoling, or by appealing to my sense of decency. I can assure you, *that* would never have happened. I am not Mark Bridges.'

Prisha glares at her. 'You really are insane, aren't you?'

'To quote Oscar Levant, there's a fine line between genius and insanity.'

Prisha snorts. 'My god. That creep was right.'

'Who?'

'Magnus Crawley. Hubris, he said. Hubris would be your downfall.' Her eyes lazily drift to a distant figure walking towards them.

After an awkward petulant silence from both of them, Tiffany breaks the impasse. 'I take it you don't want my house then?'

Prisha stares at her. 'Read my lips—no. And instruct your solicitor *today* to destroy any documents that contain my name and obliterate any record of the paper-trail you had discussing it. I have a good life here. This place, Whitby, North Yorkshire, I love it. I excel in my job. I have a flat that I love and a boyfriend I'm... very fond of.'

Tiffany sniggers. 'You don't love him, do you?'

'What?'

'You love Whitby and your poky little flat, but you don't love Adam.'

'Yes, I do!' she snaps.

'Then why didn't you use the word—love—instead of fond?'

'Shut up! It has nothing to do with you.'

'Pardon me for breathing.'

'And my flat is not poky.'

'My apologies. It's clean and tastefully decorated... I suppose.'

'Yes, well, we don't all have twenty million pounds in ransom money lying around, do we?' Staring out of the windscreen, she finally focuses on the figure approaching. 'Oh, shit,' she whispers.

'What?'

'It's him. Magnus Crawley. He's heading this way. If he sees us, we're both finished,' she says, slipping from the seat into the footwell.

Tiffany studies him as he nears. 'Oh, my word, I see what you mean, Prisha. He's like a walking dung beetle... but slimmer, and not as attractive.'

'Shut up and get down.'

Tiffany cackles with laughter. 'He can't see us. The windows are tinted. He's obviously out for an early morning stroll. Why would he be interested in a random car parked up?'

'I told you; he's a lizard, a snake. He seems to have this ability to know the truth without even knowing it. A sixth sense.'

'Your paranoia is getting the better of you. He's passed us by. You can come out of hiding now.'

'No. Drive on and take the next right. I'll jump out there.'

As the car pulls away, Prisha dares to squint in the wing mirror and witness the diminishing figure of Crawley. He glances back over his shoulder as he crosses the road.

Tiffany hangs a right and parks up adjacent to the allotments. She pulls a small, cheap mobile phone out and hands it to Prisha, who finally extricates herself from the footwell.

'What's this?' she asks.

'To say you're a detective, you're a bit slow on the uptake. It's a phone. There's only one number in contacts—mine. If you want to talk, ring three times, then hang up and I'll call you back.'

'I don't want it.'

'Take it. We can keep in touch.'

She reluctantly slips the phone into her bumbag, then opens the door. 'Right, I guess this is it then.'

'Yes. I hate goodbyes. And please don't worry, Prisha. I'm very thorough and cover my tracks. I'll speak with my solicitor this morning and instruct him to destroy all documents with your name on.'

Prisha places one foot on the pavement. 'Bye, Tiffany.'

She leans across and places a tender kiss on her lips. 'Bye, Prisha. I'll miss you.'

Prisha silently nods, and with an aching heart, exits the car. 'Take care.' She ends with a half-hearted wave.

Tiffany grins. 'You've got to admit it, Prisha, there's never a dull moment when we're together. It's a chemistry.'

As the car takes off, Prisha squats and drops her head between her knees. 'What just happened?' she whimpers.

25

The incident room is a hubbub of affable activity as Frank enters, wrestling with unwanted thoughts. Ever the professional, he puts his own inner turmoil to one side and calls the team together.

'Okay everyone, let's have a debrief. Zac, you're first up. How are you coming along with the missing persons? Have you done enough legwork for us to issue a press release by Friday?'

Zac jumps from his seat and mans the interactive whiteboard. 'Aye, me and Dinkel did some preliminary work yesterday, enough to get our heads around the cases.'

With everyone gathered around, Frank takes a prime seat in front of the board.

'Let the cameras roll,' he says, without much joy.

Zac taps at the board and a bullet-pointed report splashes onto the screen.

- ```
  John Sykes. Aged 66. Wife –
  Beth Sykes. Lived at Glaisdale.
  Set off at 7:30 am on November
  ```
  ```

4th, 2022, heading towards Hutton-le-Hole - never arrived. Last person to see him was his wife.

- Oliver 'Ollie' Hargreaves. Aged 24. Lived near Goathland with his mother - Anita Hargreaves. Set off on his trail bike at around 3:15 pm, June 22nd, 2023, to meet a friend whose father owns a farm at Low Mill, around 18 km away as the crow flies. Never arrived.

- James Wakefield. Aged 39. Lived at Fryup. Wife - Jacinta Wakefield. Set off at 9:30 am, October 5th, 2023, for a day's hike to the village of Cropton, 17 km away. Intended to stay at a bed and breakfast and return the next day via a different route. Never arrived at the B&B.

'None of the missing men knew each other. The weather conditions on the days they disappeared were good. Searches were launched the day after they were reported missing, involving police, mountain rescue teams, and members of the public, along with family members. Rescue dogs were deployed, and four flyovers by the National Police Air Service, using helicopters fitted with thermal imaging cameras, were conducted, as well as drones. All came up with sweet FA. Not a backpack, an item of clothing, or even a discarded drinks bottle was ever found.'

'What about the lad on the motorbike? No sign of it?'

'No, Frank. We provided their telcos with authorisation to ping their phones using cell tower triangulation and GPS, but they got no hits. Hardly surprising considering the remote area, and those pings weren't sent until nearly forty-eight hours after they were first reported missing. It's possible the batteries on their respective phones were dead.'

'Why the delay in trying to locate the whereabouts of the phones?'

'Usual bureaucracy.'

Frank rubs his nose and huffs. 'I see. Any skeletons in the cupboards? You know secret affairs, debts, or what about mental health issues?'

'Not that we've discovered. Their bank accounts haven't been accessed. All were physically active and fit with no known health or mental issues.'

'Eyewitness sightings?'

'We double checked with a couple who made a statement regarding Ollie Hargreaves, the lad on the trail bike. Mr and Mrs Boisdale, from Newcastle. They said they saw a young man who fitted Ollie's description at around 5 pm, June 22nd. In fact, Mr Boisdale had words with him. Challenged him about riding a motorbike on the bridleway. The lad in question gave him a mouthful and rode off.'

'Which direction?'

'Towards Rosedale Abbey, approximately four kilometres away.'

'Anything else?'

'That's all for now, Frank. We have been a little busy.'

'Aye, I know you have. Okay, put together a summary and email it to Superintendent Banks and she can handball it to the Media Relations Department. Right, what's the latest with this Declan Hughes and his dealer?'

'It's happening tonight. Declan has organised a time with his dealer, Bo-Bo. We'll position two undercover vehicles in the area to trail him once he's finished the transaction with Declan.'

'Good,' he says, turning to Prisha. 'Okay, Prisha. Let's hear your latest.'

Zac and Prisha exchange places. She disregards the whiteboard, as due to external events she has not had the clarity of thought to update it with the latest intel.

'The severed leg discovered on Tate Hill Sands belongs to a white male, forty-four-year-old, Jake Hill, a local electrician from Guisborough. We got a match on the DNA database. Jake was arrested, charged, and convicted of drink driving five years ago when he was involved in a traffic accident. Luckily, no one was injured. He received a two grand fine and a twelve month driving ban, as it was his first run-in with the law, and he was only slightly over the limit. He's a partner in Prescott and Hill Domestic Electrical, again based in Guisborough. Me and Kylie paid a visit to his business partner yesterday, a Nick Prescott. He said he hadn't seen or heard from Jake in over five weeks. Said the last time he had contact with him, Jake said he had to make an urgent trip to see his son in New Zealand, who'd been injured in a bicycle accident. According to Prescott, Jake's ex-wife, Zoe, and son moved to New Zealand five years ago. I'm chasing that up at the moment and have been in touch with the New Zealand Police. When I quizzed Prescott again about his last contact with Jake, he showed me a text message, purportedly sent from Jake. Interestingly, the text message did say he was heading to New Zealand, but there was no mention of his son being involved in a bike accident.'

Frank folds his arms. 'Fishy. Did you eyeball the number on the text message?'

'Yes, boss. It tallies with the number that Jake gave when he was arrested for drink driving.'

Kylie raises her hand. 'I've been thinking about that,' she says tentatively.

Prisha smiles and nods her approval. 'Go on.'

'The text message may have originated from Jake Hill's phone, but not necessarily from his hand.'

'Good point,' Prisha replies, turning back to Frank. 'I also gave Doctor Whipple a call.'

'You're brave,' Frank says with a chuckle.

Prisha rolls her eyes. 'Yes, he wasn't impressed. I asked him for a definitive time-frame on when the leg had been separated from the body. He said it was recent. When I pointed out the word "recent" is subjective, I think he cursed in Nigerian, then said, no longer than a week.'

Frank puckers his lips. 'Hmm... so what are your theories?'

'Nick Prescott is lying. The reason for which, I'm not yet certain. I'm due at the magistrates in an hour to request warrants to search the premises of Prescott and Hill, get access to Jake's house, phone records from his provider, and access the business bank account. Prescott said the business was in a healthy state. I want to check that out.'

'And what about the leg? If Whipple says it was attached to the body no more than a week ago, but the last contact with Jake was five weeks ago, then where has he been since?'

Prisha's eyebrows arch. 'That's the puzzle, Frank. It is possible he was being held against his will.'

'It all ties in with Zac's witness, Declan Hughes, who said he was sure a body was removed from a vehicle at Runswick Bay on Saturday night and taken to a boat.'

'And there's the Irish accent connection, Frank. Two of the men at Runswick Bay had a southern Irish accent, and the guys who hijacked the oil tanker on Friday night had southern Irish accents. Could be a coincidence, I know, but...'

Frank rises wearily from his seat. 'No such thing as coincidence, Prisha. You should know that by now. Every event, every action has a cause and effect. If you think something's a coincidence, it means you're not looking hard enough. Patterns, evidence, connections, Prisha. When they align, then you have the truth.' He offers everyone a pained smile. 'Well done, team. Things are progressing nicely. That's what I like to see.'

As he strides towards his office, Zac sidles up behind Prisha and performs his Frank impersonation in an overly broad Yorkshire accent.

'No such thing as coincidence, lass. Patterns, evidence, connections. You're not looking hard enough. Do I make myself clear, inspector?'

'Piss off,' she says, annoyed, yet grinning.

26

Magnus Crawley saunters into the yard of Keswick Car Hire, his eyes taking in every little detail. He stops in the compound and performs a slow three-sixty as he evaluates the vehicles for rent.

'Hmm... a parochial little business,' he mutters as he sets off towards the portable cabin acting as the main office.

He enters, a bell above the door announcing his arrival. The older gentleman behind the counter wearily peers over his spectacles at the potential customer. He places his newspaper on the counter and rises.

'Morning, sir. After a car, are we?'

Crawley pulls out his ID. 'No, I'm not. The name is Magnus Crawley and I'm a compliance officer with MI5.'

The old man blinks rapidly and frowns. 'Oh, aye?' he notes suspiciously.

Crawley detects the hardened demeanour and immediately acts to get the man on side. 'My investigation has nothing to do with you, or your business, I can assure you,' he says with a warm, slippery smile.

The man relaxes a little. 'Okay. Then how can I help?'

'If you could cast your mind back almost two years to Saturday, September 5th.'

'Hell, you'll be lucky.'

'Bear with me while I jog your memory. A young, dare I say attractive woman, hired a BMW Mini Cooper from you. Her name was Tiffany Butler.'

The man straightens. 'Aye, I remember the lass. Bit of a rogue, by all accounts. Gave me some cock and bull story about needing to get up to Scotland to visit her dying father. Then abandoned my car near Manchester in a service station. The police visited a few hours after she'd left, and we were soon onto her as I fit my more expensive vehicles with tracking devices. Did they ever catch her?'

'No. She escaped.'

'Oh, I see. It never was explained to me what she'd actually done.'

'She was wanted for kidnap and ransom.'

'Bugger me. And to look at her, butter wouldn't melt in her mouth.'

'Indeed. The officer that visited you that day. Can you remember her name?'

He grimaces and slowly shakes his head from side to side. 'Nah. Coloured lass, you know, Indian or Pakistani. Had quite a sharp manner. Bonny looker, though.'

'Inspector Prisha Kumar?' he prompts.

'Aye, I think that was her name.'

Crawley feels he's wasting his time. 'Can you tell me anything else about the incident?'

'Such as?'

He pulls a photograph of Tiffany Butler from his jacket and hands it to the man. 'And this was definitely the young woman who hired the Mini Cooper?'

The man studies it intently. 'Positive. Couldn't forget a face like that. A real stunner. That's definitely her.'

Crawley taps at the counter, slightly annoyed with himself. The visit to Keswick was always a fishing expedition, but he was hoping something, no matter how small, may have reared its head.

He was wrong.

'Right, well thank you for your time, Mr...'

'Morris. Brian Morris.'

'Mr Morris.' He turns and pulls at the door.

'Hang on a mo.'

Crawley turns, noting the confused tone in the man's voice. 'Yes?'

'When you walked in, you said her name was Tiffany Butler?'

'That's right.'

'Nay, lad. That's not what she was called.'

Crawley purposefully closes the door. 'Really?'

'Certain. She had a fancy foreign name. Spanish sounding. Erm, let me think a moment.' He rubs at his chin with eyes tightly closed. His eyes spring open. 'Fernandez Dolores, or Dolores Fernandez, somat like that.'

A smirk sidles across Crawley's face. 'Are you certain?' he says, licking his lips.

'Aye. That was the name on her credit card and licence. It stuck in my mind because she didn't look Spanish.'

'I know the incident took place nearly two years ago, but would you still have documentation with her name on it?'

Morris purses his lips and sighs. 'Christ, I wish I'd kept me big gob shut. Yes, I'll have a record somewhere. It'll be out the back. Wait here.'

'I do appreciate your effort, Mr Morris,' Crawley gushes in his most unctuous manner, as he also congratulates himself on his astute instincts.

———◦———

Gazing from the hotel room, hooded eyes focus on the ancient abbey perched on the headland. The imposing gothic structure fails to hold his attention. Nor does the constant screech of seagulls distract him. The ceaseless rhythmic crash of waves against the shore, and the roiling hiss of sand, also fails to penetrate his deep preoccupation.

No, the shrewd, calculating mind of Magnus Crawley is... troubled.

A large bluebottle constantly climbs up and down the window, buzzing, agitated.

A lesson in futility. It has no concept of entrapment.

It can see the outside world. It's there on the other side of the glass, but freedom is unattainable.

Magnus places his thumb in position and, with a quick jab, squashes the fly against the pane. A smile creeps across his face at the sharp, satisfying crunch. He nonchalantly smears the fly's remains on his trousers, then brushes it off with the back of his bony hand.

Rising from his desk, he paces back and forth across the room.

He knows Prisha is hiding something. His intuition tells him so, and his intuition is never wrong. Via his contacts, he's already hacked into her banking details and found nothing untoward.

He'd formed a theory, a sound theory, that there may have been a financial pact between Tiffany Butler and Prisha. In return for her freedom, and the inspector acting oblique on certain recollections, Tiffany would deposit money into Prisha's bank. A lot of money.

But it's not the case. There was no lump sum that magically appeared.

Some large payments were paid out by Prisha when she first relocated to Whitby, but these were to builders; a new kitchen and bathroom. That money had been accrued over a number of years in a savings account. There were other expenses too; carpets, dining suite, chairs, a settee, a television. To be expected when moving into a new home. But apart from that, the detective inspector lived well within her means and her savings were modest. There were no expensive holidays. Her car was over fifteen years old. Her outlay on clothing, moderate. Perfume and jewellery from cheap high street shops.

Marie Antoinette, she is not.

All in all, no smoking gun.

But Magnus is nothing, if not thorough.

Again, through his connections, he confirmed Prisha only used one institution for all her financial transactions.

She was clean.

Apparently.

There were no hidden accounts... unless it was in an offshore haven.

But even if that were the case, there was nothing about her lifestyle to suggest she'd accessed the funds.

Two years since Tiffany Butler may have been the architect behind the kidnapping of two teenage girls.

Two years since the ransom of twenty million pounds was deposited into an offshore account in the Cayman Islands.

Two years since the trail, which was never hot, went ice cold.

If Prisha had been paid a handsome kickback, would she have been able to resist delving into it for two years?

No one could resist that long. The temptation would be too great.

And that's why the mind of Magnus Crawley is troubled.

Virtuous facts undermine his theory, his sound theory.

However, he does have some weapons in his armoury, but they are not incontrovertible facts.

Inspector Kumar, in her report, made no mention of the alias Tiffany had used to hire a car in Keswick.

Dolores Fernandez is not the sort of name one could forget in a hurry.

But forget, she did.

Her signed statements do not once mention that unforgettable name.

However, this anomaly is easily explained away by the traumatic circumstances Prisha endured.

She underwent months of counselling after the tumultuous events, and PTSD could easily account for her lapse in memory.

Magnus does not believe that for one second. He's an excellent judge of character.

Prisha Kumar is resilient, as tough as nails, unflinching. She does not suffer mental aberrations, no matter what trauma she undergoes. She is a respected officer with an unblemished record.

But it doesn't matter what he believes. Her superiors would believe it. Yes, the memory lapse, whilst out of character, is not the noose to slip, and tighten, around that slender, delicate neck.

The neck he aches to kiss.

Even if he were to parade his suspicions to *his* superiors, how would the powers-that-be view him after he presents his findings?

Unfavourably, at best.

He can see, and hear, their fierce rebukes and chastisement, as if they were standing before him right now.

Crawley, you were supposed to be on the trail of Tiffany Butler, and specifically, the Russian, Kira Volkov! Why in hell's bloody name have you been wasting your time delving into one of our own?

Magnus understands Prisha's immediate boss, DCI Finnegan, is another officer held in high regard. Apparently, he has the ear of the chief constable. And the chief constable has the ear of those in power.

Magnus understands the potential pitfalls he could face. Once before, he made a similar mistake, when he was young, naïve. If he were to present his theories to *her* superiors, he knows how they'd react.

The inner circle would corral their wagons around Inspector Kumar and send billowing smoke signals to those higher up the food chain.

Then Magnus would become the whipping boy.

Overzealous; beyond his remit; a witch hunt; off-piste; gone rogue.

Instead of Prisha facing a disciplinary hearing and further investigation, it could be him staring down the barrel.

And that's why his mind is troubled.

Not just because of his weak evidence. But also because of his yearning, an itch that must be scratched.

'Come along, Magnus. Think laterally. Go back to basics. Stop focusing on Prisha and think about Tiffany Butler.'

He resumes pacing back and forth, his brain aching with the effort to find the smallest breach in the dam wall.

Mentally exhausted, he takes a seat and surfs the internet on his laptop. Absentmindedly, he finds himself looking at houses and flats for sale in and around the Whitby area. He's amazed at how cheap they are compared to London prices.

'I could live in a palace with a sea view for the same price as my shoe-box in Fulham,' he murmurs.

He freezes. Smiles. The niggling thought on the carousel comes to a jarring halt.

'Of course. Why didn't I think of it before?'

27

Declan Hughes chain smokes rollies, as he paces up and down the side of his Lada. He usually enjoys his day off, spending more time with his son, pushing him in the pram along the harbour front, up cobbled streets, down hidden ginnels and snickets. Stopping off for a coffee, a doughnut, occasionally, a pint of ale in a relaxing beer garden in one of the quieter pubs.

But today, he's not enjoying himself.

He checks his phone for the fifth time—10:42 pm.

He's already having second, and third and fourth thoughts. Caught by the short and curlies, he's a pawn in someone else's game.

It's the story of his life.

He can't survive on his meagre trainee's wage, not with a young kid to raise.

His employer doesn't give a damn... why should he?

And now he's an extra with a walk-on part in DS Stoker's little stage-play. Once again, on the receiving end of other people's decisions.

Controlling his own destiny seems to be a pipe dream.

Feeling trapped, alone and vulnerable, he swears that come September everything will change.

His mobile pings. He reads the message from his supplier, Bo-Bo.

> *A mile away? You still on?*

He types his reply.

> *Yep. Usual spot. Coast is clear. See you in 5.*

Hits the send button. 'There's no going back now,' he mutters.

Types a message to DS Stoker.

> *Should be here in next few minutes. Usually drives old BMW. Dark blue or black, I think.*

Stoker has promised him that neither Declan nor Bo-Bo will be arrested. Said he was fishing for sharks, not minnows. His assurances don't help Declan's unease. Basically, he's buggered whichever way it plays out. If his name is mentioned, then he'll have some seriously pissed off drug gang after him. If they get busted, then Bo-Bo has lost his regular supplier, which in turn means so has Declan.

'Just a fucking pawn,' he moans, stubbing his ciggy out on the bitumen and immediately rolling another.

As he sparks up, a car engine grows louder. He watches on as the lights flash, disappear, then return as the car rolls quietly down the steep incline to the bottom car park. It circumnavigates the Lada and comes to a stop facing the entrance.

Bo-Bo steps out and offers a big Jamaican smile that, metaphorically, could light up the entire village of Runswick Bay.

'Sorry about the other night, Declan, my man. Girlfriend trouble, if you know what I mean.'

He holds his hand in the air and both men hi-five then fist bump.

'Don't worry about it. These things happen,' Declan replies.

'Usual?' he asks, the smile replaced with a businesslike expression.

'Yeah, four ounces.'

'You're in luck because I'm just about dry. I need to visit my men for a reload.' He pulls out a plastic snap-lock bag from his jacket and hands it over.

Declan stuffs a roll of notes into Bo-Bo's hand. 'Three-fifty, yeah?'

'Cool, brother. Always a pleasure doing business with you. See you in a fortnight.' He turns to head back to his car.

'Hang on, Bo-Bo, almost forgot. I have a mate who's heading down to London. He wants to take a big bag of weed with him to sell.'

'How big?'

'Two kilos.'

Bo-Bo sucks his teeth, making a clicking sound. 'That's going to be five big ones. Is he good for that sort of dough?'

'Yeah, he's good.'

Bo-Bo ambles forward, suspicion plastered over his face. 'I don't like dealing large amounts in one hit, especially to someone I don't know. Who is this guy? I'll need to check him out first.'

Declan laughs, trying to diffuse the air of mistrust. 'No, you misunderstand. You deliver to me as usual. And I pass it onto my mate... for a little mark-up, of course.'

His eyes blink before his welcoming smile returns. 'Okay, my man. When do you need it by?'

'As soon as.'

'Leave it with me. I'll be in touch. Keep it sweet, bro.'

Waiting a moment, he watches on as the car's rear lights head up the hill, turn a corner and disappear. Twenty seconds later, a second car's headlights appear and follow in the same direction as the BMW.

Declan clambers into the car and gently bangs his forehead against the steering wheel.

'Fuck. What have I done?'

28

Zac speaks quietly into the mobile. 'Okay, Dinkel. Me and Prisha have him. You and Kylie can knock off for the night.'

'Roger Whitaker, that. Night, Zac, night P...'

Zac cuts him off, ending the call. 'Dickhead,' he mutters.

'You're too hard on him. Try a little encouragement now and then,' Prisha says as she navigates the car around a tight corner, deliberately dropping further back from the BMW in front.

'Fuck that.' Yawning, he stretches his long frame out in the passenger seat. 'I hope this Bo-Bo doesn't live too far away. I'm ready for the sack. It's been a long day.'

'Tell me about it. I had a meeting with that weasel from MI5 yesterday afternoon.'

'Oh, aye.'

'I say meeting, it was more like being in the headmaster's office. Gave me a right grilling. And I caught the sleaze looking at my tits.'

'Can't blame him for that.'

She slaps him on the thigh. 'Dirty old perv,' she says, grinning.

'Oi, less of the old, if you don't mind. What did this Crawley fella quiz you about?'

'Kept going over the details of when me and Tiffany were held in the lighthouse. I think he's onto me.'

'Don't talk daft.'

'I'm not. He's so hard to read, and he's fixated on how Tiffany escaped. It's almost like he knows I gave her my house keys and credit card to get away.'

'You're letting your imagination run away with you. There's only three people who know the truth. Me—and I know nothing. You—and you're not going to say anything. And Tiffany, who is living it up in Argentina.'

'She's not.'

'What?'

'She's not in Argentina.'

'Then where is she?'

'Whitby.'

'You're pulling my pisser?'

'She collared me yesterday outside my flat. Just turned up out of the blue. Then I saw her again this morning while I was out jogging.'

'What the hell is she doing back here?'

'Tidying up loose ends, so she says. She was in the process of transferring her house deeds into my name, as a gift.'

'This gets worse. I hope you declined?'

'Of course I did.'

'Christ, her timing is lousy.'

'I've got a bad feeling about it all.'

'Have you told Adam?'

'Have I hell. I rarely, if ever, discuss my work with him. There has to be a boundary. A time to switch off and forget about all the crap.'

'Secrets aren't a good thing in a relationship.'

She turns to him, annoyed. 'And have you told Kelly about throwing Wayne Barber off the cliff behind St Mary's?'

'Fair point.'

'I often wonder about that. Does it ever keep you awake at night, you know, killing a man?'

He chuckles. 'Nah. I sleep like a babe. I did the world a favour. Hang on, slow down. He's coming to a junction. Shit, he's pulled over. You'll have to drive past, otherwise he'll be onto us.'

She eases off the accelerator, passes the BMW and takes a left at the junction. 'I think we're safe. It looked like he was on his phone.' Navigating the car onto a narrow side road, she performs a three-point-turn and kills the lights. A few seconds later, the BMW passes by.

Zac peers out of the windscreen. 'Give him some distance. It's a long, straight road for the next few miles. I'm not sure where he's heading, but he must live in a secluded spot.'

'Unless we're in luck and he's arranged to meet *his* supplier.'

'Aye. You could be right. He did make a call.'

They drive cautiously on for another fifteen minutes, entering deeper into the wilds, shadows creeping out from every corner. The car ahead slows, then hangs a right. Prisha parks up, as they both watch the red taillights climb a rocky gravel lane. The car reaches the crest of the hill and disappears over the other side.

Zac huffs. 'Not ideal. We don't want to get over the top of the hill and run straight into him and his bloody drugs gang.'

'No. How about we park up just before the crest and take a look on foot?'

'Aye. Sounds like a plan.'

Prisha turns off the main headlights, leaving only the parking lights on, which offer barely any illumination at all. The moon provides a modicum of light, but it's intermittent due to the clouds rolling by. Slowing to a crawl, she hunches over the steering wheel, staring out at the dusty gravel track. Zac fumbles under his seat and pulls out a pair of binoculars.

Prisha spots a small passing-area at the side of a drystone wall, pulls in and turns the engine and lights off.

Zac stares at the GPS on his phone. 'We are truly in the middle of nowhere. Right, you stay here. I'll take a peep.'

Exiting the car, he gingerly scales the wall and drops to the other side clutching the binoculars. He turns and gives Prisha the thumbs up and a cheeky grin before bobbing down and scurrying along.

Prisha peers around at the blanket of darkness. A small wood to her right, hills to the distant left. The occasional bleat of sheep is the only sound to puncture the air.

Her sense of unease grows.

Zac positions himself at the crest of the hill and steadies his arms on the wall as he focuses the field glasses. At the bottom of the hill is a compound, fenced off, and with a large double gate at the front. Inside are three large sheds, various items of work machinery, and a portable workers' hut in the far corner. Floodlights illuminate the area. The BMW slowly comes to a stop outside the main gates and the tall Jamaican exits his car.

'Come on, sunshine, play ball for Uncle Zac,' he whispers. He spots sudden movement as a man emerges from the hut and scampers across the compound carrying something. Zac slowly spins the focus dial, zooming in on the action.

The two men seem to exchange words before the man from the compound tosses a bag over the gate as Bo-Bo pushes something through the fence. He picks the bag up, half waves, and climbs back into the BMW.

'Shit!' Before pulling away, Zac focuses on the signage out the front, then turns and hurriedly follows the contours of the wall.

'Come on, Zac, where are you?' Prisha murmurs. A shard of light hits her eyes, heartbeat immediately accelerating. She stares horrified into the rear-view mirror. 'Damn!'

A vehicle has turned off the main road and is heading up the steep track. The bang on the side of the car makes her jump as Zac slides back into the passenger seat.

'We have visitors.'

'What shall we do?'

'Good question.'

As the headlights slowly bear down upon them, he turns to her. 'Kiss me!'

'What?'

'You heard. Snog me!' He throws his arms around her as they both engage in a false kiss, which quickly morphs into something much more passionate.

The vehicle behind turns its full beam on as it nears, highlighting the kissing couple inside. Zac lifts one hand up and gives the two-fingered salute. It briefly stops before the full beam disappears and it slowly drives alongside the car.

A man's voice yells out in jocular fashion, 'Oi, get a room, you randy bastards!'

The kissing continues until the vehicle traverses the peak of the hill and disappears.

They pull away slowly and stare at each other before coming to their senses. They jolt back from one another as Prisha starts the engine.

'Ahem, that was, I mean...' Zac struggles to make sense.

'Yes. Of course it was.'

'Operational reasons. There was nothing in it.'

'No. Nothing in it at all. Had to be done.'

'No point mentioning it to anyone.'

'Definitely not. It will remain a secret.'

'Aye. To take to the grave. Right, we better get out of here, sharpish.'

Prisha swiftly spins the car around and heads off at speed down the track, her emotions a mixture of fear... and tingling excitement.

'What did you see?'

'A mushroom farm in a compound. A small Asian guy tossed something over the fence, I assume two kilos of weed, then Bo-Bo handed something through the gate. Probably payment.'

'A mushroom farm? Good cover for growing weed. What's it called?'

'Top Moor Mushroom Farm.'

The thought hits Prisha like a lightning bolt. 'That guy who called out as he passed the car...'

'What about him?'

'Did you detect the accent?'

'No... hang on, yes, it was Irish. Southern Irish.'

29

Thursday 13th July

The two early morning hikers appear innocuous enough as they meander across the North Yorkshire Moors. Their gear is typical for a day out in the English countryside; waterproof trail-hiking shoes, lightweight pants with more pockets than a kleptomaniac could fill, summer fleece tops, hooded wind jackets, and the ubiquitous backpacks. They look like any other walkers enjoying a day in the English summer sun – if only the reluctant sun would agree to make an appearance.

And yet...

Their choice of attire, both dressed in jet black, casts a subtle but unmistakable air of paramilitary menace.

But still, from a distance they look like a harmless couple, husband and wife, girlfriend and boyfriend, perhaps, taking in the grandeur of the wilderness.

But if they were to pass a fellow walker, their appearance may raise, not concern, but possibly, curiosity.

The young man stands at six-five, muscular, with a harsh angularity to his features, topped with a thatch of close-cropped blonde hair. A slight slant to his eyes, and a vicious-looking scar on his neck. The female is a striking figure with a tall, lithe, powerful build. Shiny black hair pulled into a sharp ponytail, contrasting with her flawless ivory skin. Green eyes and full red lips exude confidence and authority, while her subtle Baltic lineage is a signpost to a fierce temperament that lies but millimetres beneath her goddess-like features.

The man pulls a map from his jacket and studies it. 'Not far to go.'

Unfastening her backpack, the woman retrieves a pair of micro-binoculars, small but extremely powerful, and scans the horizon. 'I'd say another three brisk miles. We'll take a break here and keep watch.'

The man spins three-sixty, slightly bemused at her command. 'We are the only ones here, Kira. Us and a few sheep and bison.'

She lowers the binoculars and glowers at him. 'Imbecile. There are no bison over here. You mean cows. And just because your eyes see nothing, does not mean we are alone. Did you learn nothing from your time in Spetsnaz, Viktor? Now drink, eat and be silent.'

The man drops to the spongy heather, unzips a pocket and pulls out a walnut. He places it between his biceps and flexes, cracking the shell open. Despite his thick powerful fingers, he nimbly picks at the fruit inside and places it gently in his mouth.

Kira watches on with barely concealed contempt. 'On Stalin's grave,' she curses. 'Just like your brother. Always with the walnuts.'

'They are natures multivitamin, Kira,' he declares in a slow baritone.

'They are natures multivitamin, Kira,' she repeats in a deep, mocking voice, mimicking him.

Viktor gazes at the never-ending landscape. 'I don't understand. If we are business partners with these men, then why are we creeping up on them? Why not simply make contact and arrange a rendezvous?'

Kira sucks air through her teeth, creating a whistling sound. 'Have you ever been to the theatre, Viktor?'

'No.'

'No, of course not. When you go to see a play, and take your seat to witness a performance, the actors know their lines, the props are in place, the music comes in on cue. However, if you were to go backstage before the play began, you would observe the chaos, the petty squabbles, the jealousies, the realities.'

Viktor's creased brow telegraphs his confused thoughts, as he watches a rabbit materialise from a burrow fifteen feet away, and nibble contentedly on young shoots of grass.

'I don't understand.'

Kira huffs. 'If we tell them of our arrival, then they can make everything look perfect. Catch them unawares and we will see them in the raw. Sergei has invested a considerable amount of money into this venture, and it is my task to ensure he makes a handsome return on his investment. We must always keep the boss happy.'

'I see.' Pulling an apple from his pack, he slips a small hunting knife from its sheath attached to his belt and methodically peels the fruit. 'When will I avenge my brother's death?'

Kira turns to him, her harsh demeanour for once softening. 'All in good time, Viktor. We have work to do. Once we have completed our tasks, the hunt begins.'

The razor-sharp knife slices a cheek off the apple. He pops it into his mouth and chews. Tossing the knife in the air, he catches it by the blade, then, like a sling shot, releases it. A dull thwack resonates as the rabbit's back legs twitch in a death throe, the blade embedded deep within its skull.

'And when we do, Inspector Kumar will wish she had never been born.'

30

They approach the cave tentatively, every step measured and slow. Rusty fencing, no longer fit for purpose, confronts them. The decrepit signage is in danger of collapsing altogether.

Viktor stares at the sign, the words incomprehensible. 'What does it say, Kira?'

'Danger. Do not enter. Cave prone to rockfalls.'

'The letters are weird.'

'Russia uses the Cyrillic alphabet. Britain uses the Latin alphabet. It takes a while to adjust.'

'The cave sounds dangerous. What should we do?'

She tut tuts, and casts him a dismissive glance. 'It is a ruse, that's all. The cave is safe.'

'Then why the sign?'

Her chest heaves in frustration. 'Like your brother, you have brawn and killing skills, but your brain is the size of one of the walnuts you continually eat. The escape route from the nuclear bunker is in the cave. The signage is used to scare off the public. Potholers, rock-climbers, busy-bodies. Years ago, this would have belonged to the M.O.D.'

'M.O.D?' he repeats.

'Ministry of Defence. In Russian, the Minoborony Rossii.'

He ponders her response before a light-bulb moment. 'Ya ponimayu.'

Her glower hardens. 'When in England, speak English. How many times do I have to tell you!'

'Sorry. I meant to say, yes, I understand.'

A false smile is offered. 'Good.' She moves towards the fence and inspects a rusty chain and ancient padlock, defiantly trying to protect a gate. 'Now, it's time for your brawn, Viktor. God knows I need to get some use out of you. Open the gate.'

He smiles, cockily. 'Sometimes brain is mightier than brawn, Kira.' Reaching into his jacket pocket, he pulls out a small leather pouch, opens it and removes a four-inch tension wrench and a slightly longer hook pick with a slender, curved tip. Inserting the wrench into the bottom of the keyhole, he applies gentle pressure and carefully probes the pins with the hook pick. The lock clicks open, the tools leaving no trace of their work.

Kira is moderately impressed. 'Nice work,' she says as she pulls open the creaky gate and creeps through.

Viktor follows behind. 'Should I re-lock it, Kira?'

Puckering her lips, she stares at the padlock and chain. 'No. Not for the moment.'

'Why?'

'Because we don't know what the future holds. Slide the chain back into position, but do not lock it.'

She gazes up at the cave and the overhang above, then pulls out a flashlight. Cautiously, they enter the narrow opening to the cave, the torch illuminating a slender passage. The distant sound of water can be heard ahead. They scramble over rocks and boulders and along a passage, ducking their heads from overhead obstructions. The tunnel takes a sharp left and brings them out into a large cavern.

The gurgling water is louder as Kira shines the torch onto the rocky ground. She notices a steel grating over a round hole, just large enough to fit a body through. She peers down into the abyss, and the huge drop.

'What is it?' Viktor asks.

'It's a pothole.' He blinks, uncomprehending. 'An underground tunnel created by running water over thousands of years. North Yorkshire is riddled with them due to the limestone. Some imbeciles even consider it a sport to navigate them.'

'It sounds dangerous.'

'Imbeciles are impervious to danger, but thankfully, not immune from it.'

'Where do the tunnels lead to?'

'To lakes or caves, many miles away. Others lead nowhere.'

'I don't like them.'

'For such a giant of a man, you sometimes act like a kitten.' She tires of the conversation and casts the torchlight over the rest of the cave until she spots something in a corner. 'Aha!'

They clamber over more rocks, as drips of water fall from glistening stalactites. Standing in front of a concrete structure with a dark green door, Kira chuckles.

'I have a very good feeling about this, Viktor. This underground bunker is perfect for our operation.'

'How do we get in?'

'I'm sure our associates employ motion sensors, but just in case they don't...' She hammers on the huge steel plated, reinforced concrete door with the butt of the torch, the clanking noise ricocheting off the hard walls creating a deafening echo.

Movement can be heard from behind the impenetrable structure. Levers, and bolts screech against metal, as finally, the huge door rumbles outwards.

Eamon Murphy struts forward carrying a shotgun and stares at the intruders.

He suddenly grins and laughs. 'Kira, we were expecting you weeks ago, so we were. I see you've come via the tradesman's entrance. You like to make things hard for yourself.' He turns and heads back inside the bunker. 'Follow me and I'll give you a guided tour of our humble abode, then we'll share a vodka or two and talk business.'

'How did you know we were here?' she enquires.

'We have sensors on the outside of the bunker. Picks up anything larger than a dog.'

Kira throws Viktor a cocky smile as they follow Eamon into the bunker. He presses a large red button and the door swings shut, accompanied by the whirring sound of hydraulics at work.

Kira is impressed with the operation as Eamon leads her and Viktor around the myriad of underground corridors and rooms.

Eamon walks ahead. As he passes each door, he slaps it with his hand. 'These five rooms are the cultivation rooms. I won't open the doors, otherwise the whole place will reek of cannabis. We have a staggered rotation, so we have a constant supply. My son Fergus is in charge of the crops.'

'That's a lot of work for one man.'

Eamon chuckles. 'It is. That's why we have outside help.'

Kira frowns. 'Outside help?'

'Illegal migrants. Three Vietnamese gentlemen. Bloody hard workers and easy to keep in line.'

'Do you pay them?'

'No. Let's say they're working off the cost of their transportation to get here. My other son, Cillian, he's in charge of distribution. We don't do any direct dealing ourselves. We sell to middlemen who sell it on to the pushers. Lot less hassle that way and less chance of getting caught. Come on, we'll have a nip of vodka in the kitchen and talk business. After all, that's why you're here.'

'Yes. And did you get me the intel I requested?'

'I did. I have an envelope in the kitchen for you.' They turn around and head back along the corridor. 'And how is Sergei?'

'Sergei is well. But unhappy.'

'Oh. Why's that?'

'He invested a large amount of money in this operation and your repayments for the last six months have been short.'

Eamon leads the way into a huge kitchen—dining area and pours three shots of vodka. 'Is that the reason for your visit?' he says, handing the drinks out.

'It's not my only reason. Sergei wanted me to check out your facility and make sure everything was running smoothly. So, care to explain the shortfall in payments?'

'It's simple, really; it's your lots fault.'

'My lot?'

'Yes. Invading Ukraine played havoc with the fuel prices, especially diesel. A twenty-five per cent increase altogether. But that's all been taken care of now. We are far less reliant on diesel than we used to be.'

'How so?'

'We've tapped into an overhead power line. During the day, the operation is powered by electricity. We only use the diesel generators on a nighttime. It's taken a few months to fine tune and iron out some minor issues, but we're firing on all cylinders now.'

'Clever. So we can expect to see your repayments return to normal?'

'As of next month, Kira.' He raises the vodka glass. 'Here's to our continued success.'

'Za uspekh!' Kira and Viktor reply as they clink glasses and throw the shots down.

Eamon stares at Viktor. 'Doesn't say much, does he?'

'He's not here to talk. He's here to do.'

Eamon picks up an envelope from the bench and passes it to her. 'As requested.'

Kira places the glass down and slowly pulls out the photograph. She studies it intently. 'When was this taken?'

'Last Tuesday—two days ago.'

Nodding thoughtfully, she appears distracted as she slips the photo back in the envelope. 'I will take care of this tomorrow. Have you a vehicle I can borrow?'

'Of course.'

'Good. Right, please introduce me to your sons.'

31

Magnus Crawley leans against the counter, ogling the receptionist as she lifts the receiver. He picks a business card from a dispenser and studies it—Dooley and Hargreaves Solicitors.

'Mr Dooley,' the receptionist says, 'a Magnus Crawley from MI5 to see you. No, he didn't specify what it was about. Said it was urgent and confidential. Yes, okay.' She replaces the receiver and stares at the stranger, who, for reasons she can't quite fathom, gives her the creeps. 'Mr Dooley will see you now, sir. Third door on the left,' she explains, pointing down the corridor.

Crawley nods politely. 'Thank you, my dear.'

Walking down the corridor, he takes out his phone, swipes across, opens the app, then taps the record button. He knocks on the door and enters.

Mr Dooley rises and extends his arm. 'Mr Crawley, please take a seat and tell me how I can help you.'

They shake hands as Crawley slides into a chair, pulling out his ID, flashing it in front of Dooley. 'Compliance

Officer—MI5. I do appreciate you taking the time to see me on such short notice, Mr Dooley. I can see you're a very busy man, so I'll be brief.'

'Not a problem. What's this about?' Dooley asks, slightly bemused, and a little unnerved by the visit.

Crawley adjusts the collar on his jacket, crosses his legs, then flicks fluff from his trousers. 'A delicate matter regarding one of your clients.'

'Oh, I see. Well, I'll help as far as I can, but I must warn you I am a strict adherent to the client confidentiality ethos, and although I can answer general questions about clients, I cannot divulge sensitive legal information. Do we understand one another, Mr Crawley?'

Magnus smiles, flashing his jagged yellow teeth. 'Of course, and I fully respect your ethics.'

'Good. Because client confidentiality is my castle.'

'Noble sentiments, I'm sure.'

'Okay, fire away, Mr Crawley,' Dooley states, relaxing back in his chair, confident he's marked his boundaries.

'I'm investigating Miss Tiffany Butler in relation to a number of matters.'

'Hang on. Why do you assume the woman mentioned is one of my clients?'

'I checked with the Land Registry Office and you were listed as the solicitor who dealt with the property she bought a number of years ago.'

Dooley sits upright and grimaces, already on his guard. 'As far as I'm aware, the Land Registry Office doesn't record who the solicitor was for a property.'

'Then your awareness is in need of an update, Mr Dooley,' Crawley lies. 'You may recall Miss Butler was a suspect in the kidnap and ransom demand of a pair of young schoolgirls a couple of years ago.'

'It was a rumour around town, that's all. She was never charged.'

'Quite. She was never charged because she evaded capture during her transportation to the police station. Are you aware there is still a warrant out for her arrest?'

Dooley shuffles uncomfortably and coughs. 'No, I wasn't aware of that. However, I can still act on behalf of a client, whether they've been convicted of a crime or not. It's a right protected under law to ensure all individuals, regardless of their criminal history, or current status, have access to legal representation.'

Crawley nods, accepting the fact. 'Indeed you can.' He offers another ghastly smile. 'At least we've established the fact she is one of your clients. However, I've done a little research. It would have been remiss of me not to. Most of your business is conveyancing, is it not?'

'Yes. That's right.' He frowns and twiddles with a pen. 'Mr Crawley, can you get to the point?'

'Of course. This is a matter of *national* security.'

'As far as I'm aware, what Miss Butler did or didn't do is a police matter. A domestic affair.'

Magnus sticks his tongue under his top teeth and makes a sucking noise. 'Technically speaking, that's correct. However, as well as the suspicions against Miss Butler regarding the kidnapping case, it transpires she may also have been involved in espionage activities involving foreign actors. As serious as the former allegations are, it pales into insignificance compared to national security.'

Dooley becomes impatient. 'What exactly is it you want from me, Mr Crawley?'

'Have you had recent contact with Miss Butler?'

He squirms uneasily. 'I may have.'

'I may have,' he repeats under his breath, glancing out of the window. 'And during this contact that you *may* have had, was it in person?'

'No.'

'I see. Therefore, if it wasn't in person, it leaves only two other possibilities; communication by voice, or communication by written means.'

Dooley shrugs. 'Possibly.'

'Which one?'

'The latter.'

'By electronic means. Email?'

Dooley nods. 'Yes.'

'May I ask what these communications were about?'

'I'll refer you to my earlier statement about client confidentiality.'

'You do realise I have similar powers to police officers?' he lies again.

'I'm not really sure what powers you have.'

'Well, believe me, I do. And do you also realise I have almost *unlimited* powers if I believe national security is under threat?'

'No. I wasn't aware of that.'

'For instance, if I believed a certain Whitby solicitor was complicit in selling state secrets to our enemies then it is within my remit to request the police to arrest and detain the suspect and have a team of digital forensic officers from MI5, descend upon their premises and go through every client portfolio, every transaction, and every email ever sent to and from their premises.'

'Are you threatening me, Mr Crawley, because it sounds like a threat?' Dooley replies, raising his voice.

'You're very perceptive, Mr Dooley. Yes, it is a threat. A real threat I intend to carry out if you refuse to engage. A forensic audit would ruin your reputation. After all, I'm sure your business is built upon trust. Such a hard thing to earn, such an easy thing to lose.'

Dooley's face hardens, muscles tense. 'I'd like you to leave, Mr Crawley.'

He rises, slowly. 'Very well. You leave me with no other choice.' Crawley is playing a game of bluff. Without hard evidence, his superiors would never sanction such actions. But he's assuming Dooley, an ordinary man who deals in conveyancing for much of his livelihood, doesn't know that. 'Good day, Mr Dooley. You'll be seeing me again, very soon, under very different circumstances.' He pulls at the door handle.

Dominic Dooley is processing faster than a supercomputer.

He has a wife and two young daughters. He plays badminton once a week—mixed doubles. On Friday nights, he catches up with a few old school friends for a couple of pints. Saturday mornings, he takes his girls to the local park. In the afternoon he watches a Premier League football match on Fox Sports, followed by a takeaway Chinese meal for the family dinner. He has a good life. The business is doing well. He makes a comfortable living. National security, police raids, and shady foreign actors are not of his world.

Like the Walls of Jericho, his client confidentiality ethos tumbles brick by brick.

'Wait.'

Magnus Crawley half turns, but stares at the carpet. 'Yes?'

Squirming uncomfortably, he asks, 'Hypothetically, if I were to answer your questions, would it be confidential? My name wouldn't be recorded anywhere?'

Crawley offers him a reassuring smile. 'I offer you my assurances, Mr Dooley. I can see you're an honest man. The last thing I want is to ruin a good reputation. I'm after bad, not good people. Unfortunately, sometimes in life, good people cross paths with the bad without even knowing it.'

'I see. Please take a seat, Mr Crawley. Let's start afresh.'

32

The door to the incident room doesn't creak as it usually does when opened.

Footsteps go unheard.

As Prisha taps at the keyboard, a cold chill runs down her spine. Even though she's alone in the room... she senses a presence. Spinning around on the swivel chair, she stares up into the hooded slash of Magnus Crawley's eyes.

'Christ! You scared me half to death.'

He does not move one iota, save for his tongue, which snakes out to slick his lips. The action reminds Prisha of a lizard, cold, calculating as it tastes the air, searching for its next meal.

'Didn't mean to startle you, inspector. Old habits die hard. I wasn't always a compliance officer. Many moons ago, I worked in the field as an operative. Rubber-soled shoes and stealth are a great asset.'

Silence ensues between them as one leers, and one squirms in disgust.

Prisha is the first to break the impasse. 'Well, if you don't mind, I have to...'

'Of course.' His eyes flick to the whiteboard, where information relating to the severed leg is laid out for any self-respecting investigator to digest in seconds. 'Hmm... I see. Interesting. Progress?' he asks, his hungry eyes returning to Prisha.

'Slow. But we're getting there.'

The reptilian smile returns. 'If you need my help, you only need ask,' he states, attempting a charm offensive. 'My ability at finding the truth is a gift.'

Prisha resists the urge to scratch her face off... or his. 'Thanks. If we hit a brick wall, and you're still around, I may run a few things past you.' *Like hell!*

His eyes blink in slow motion.

Hesitation.

'My mind,' he murmurs in a low, scratchy drawl, 'once a thought, a little niggle, worms its way in, it circles endlessly. Like a child, wide-eyed and alone, trapped on a carousel, its parents a mere memory. Round and round, without end, always spiralling back to the same haunting spot. It's a sign I'm missing something. The mind is alerting me to this fact. Do you ever experience that, Detective Inspector Kumar?'

'Sometimes. What exactly is your thought about?' she enquires, finally turning back to face her monitor and finish up for the day.

'Tiffany Butler.'

Her cheeks flush. She acts nonchalant. 'What about her?'

'Oh... like how she's managed to evade capture for so long? It's nearly two years since your little adventure with her.'

'It wasn't an adventure.'

He gazes out at the bobbing boats moored at the marina. 'I use the term figuratively. If the Russian, Kira Volkov, had killed her, I'm sure Tiffany's mutilated body would have turned up by now. After all, our Russian friend seemed to take great delight in parading her kills in the most gruesome of public fashion. And yet... no body.'

'Who knows? I'm not investigating her—you are.'

'Indeed, I am.'

Prisha hits the Shut Down button and pauses as the screen flickers. She slams the lid shut on the laptop and rises.

'Right. That's me done for the day.'

'Not quite. I'd like to probe you a little longer.'

Having worked in a male-dominated environment for many years, she can tell the difference between jocular banter and predatory innuendo.

She boils with anger. 'Let's get this fucking straight! There'll be no probing from you, not tonight, not ever. I am a detective inspector of North Yorkshire Police, and I have as much power as you. I am not answerable to anyone but my superiors, and believe me, you are not my superior. Now, if you'll excuse me, it's been a long day.' She grabs her bag and marches towards the door.

'Keswick,' he calls out after her. One simple word, a place name, a market town in Cumbria. It has the desired effect, as Prisha halts.

She spins around and glares at him. 'Pardon?'

Smugness, a regular visitor, rests on his face. 'Keswick Car Hire. A rather tired and dreary little business. Tiffany Butler hired a car from there when she was on the run, remember?'

'Of course I remember.'

'Except she hired it, not under the name Tiffany Butler, but using an alias; Dolores Fernandez.'

Her pulse quickens. She needs to think fast. Her eyes narrow, brow creases, as if juggling with a complex mathematical equation.

'Dolores Fernandez,' she repeats slowly.

'The name never made it into your report, inspector. Bit of a faux pas. It seems Tiffany used a number of aliases. But if you *had* mentioned the name *Dolores Fernandez* on the night she escaped from your custody, at Hawsker

Lighthouse, then your colleagues would have alerted all port authorities to the name. And that way, she would have been picked up at passport control at Manchester Airport. Instead, she boarded a plane to Mexico, after which, she simply vanished.'

'Yes, I do remember the name. It must have slipped my mind due to the traumatic events.'

He nods thoughtfully. 'Yes, I came to the same conclusion. After all you underwent, it's hardly surprising some facts were forgotten or overlooked. You stared death in the face and episodes like that can leave debilitating consequences.'

'I'll need to inform Frank and update my statement.'

'Yes, that would be prudent. I mean, that has to be it...' he trails off, as he taps a bony finger against his lips.

'You have an element of doubt in your voice, Mr Crawley. Are you questioning my sincerity?' she says, raising her voice.

He feigns surprise. 'No, of course not. You would have taken the Police Oath when you first joined the force. If I remember correctly, I think there's something in there about integrity and diligence.' He emits a raucous laugh and leans forward, arms splayed out. 'After all, it had to be memory loss caused by the trauma. What other possible explanation could you have for omitting such a significant detail from your report and not mentioning it to your colleagues?'

'Have you finished?'

'Yes... for tonight. Sleep well, my dear.'

Prisha hurries for the exit. The door slams shut with a resounding bang. In its echo, Magnus Crawley collapses into a seat with a graceless thud. He nonchalantly hoists his feet onto Prisha's chair opposite, lounging in a pose of arrogant confidence. Fishing a toothpick from his inside pocket, he idly jabs at his yellow-stained teeth, his attention ensnared by the meticulous weaving of his next calculated move. Gradually, a supercilious smirk unfurls.

'Step into my web, little fly.'

33

Friday 14th July

Magnus Crawley peers out at the early afternoon sun. Its golden rays eagerly absorbed by the crowds of holidaymakers on the streets below. His attention drifts onto a group of teenagers who are taking selfies in front of Whalebone Arch. Sighing heavily, he rubs at his face, then flicks the kettle on and glances around the hotel room.

It's become an obsession—the Tiffany Butler, Prisha Kumar conundrum.

'Could I be wrong? Is she innocent? Am I so consumed with desire it's clouding my judgement?'

He makes a coffee and returns to staring outside but sees nothing.

'Go back to basics, Magnus. You have a lot of experience. You've seen it all before and then some. What are the two biggest motivating factors for criminals? That's easy; greed, and emotion. They act for financial gain, or they act out of emotion—hate, fear, pride, revenge. Yet Prisha has not gained financially. So that leaves emotion, but which emotion? She has no reason to fear Tiffany. Her life is not in jeopardy. And none of the other emotions apply to her.'

His heavy lids close as a thought flits like a butterfly around his mind. Eyes snap open. A smile creeps across wet lips. Tongue darts out and just as quickly retreats into the dark hole of his mouth.

'Silly, Magnus.' He chuckles to himself. 'You're getting careless in your old age. Blindingly obvious. The most powerful emotion of them all and you overlooked it. Prisha didn't help Tiffany escape for financial gain. She works on a much higher moral level. Tiffany escaped because... Prisha loves her.'

The pleasure of a small breakthrough soon dissipates. He may have identified the motivating factor behind Prisha's actions, but it has no impact upon the sketchy evidence he's accumulated. To enact his master-plan, he needs something concrete, undeniable, irrefutable. A fact that even the inspector's most ardent, one-eyed supporter would throw their hands up in the air and say, "the game's up, governor."

He spends the next hour sitting on the bed trawling over the case notes for the umpteenth time.

Witness statements, Prisha's statement, dates, times, photographic evidence, but nothing jumps out or even raises an arm and says, "please sir, take a closer look at me."

Dispirited and tired, he returns to his desk and gazes down upon two years' worth of bank and credit card statements.

'There must be something that connects Tiffany to Prisha,' he mutters as he pours himself a small tumbler of scotch.

He begins the task again, painstakingly checking every transaction on Prisha's debit account, checking the amounts, dates and trying to decipher what was bought.

After a fruitless hour, he's on the verge of throwing the towel in. He's already spent way too much time on Tiffany Butler. The parting words from his boss at MI5 play out in his mind.

"We are not particularly interested in Tiffany Butler, Magnus. But she could be the lightning rod to Kira Volkov. However, don't get sidetracked. It is the Russian we must locate. She is the one who was privy to state secrets, and we must find out what those secrets were at any cost. Do I make myself clear, Magnus? Focus on the Russian."

He drifts out of his reverie and finishes his whisky as another buzzing bluebottle zips around the window, desperate for release. He places his empty glass over the fly, then slips a coaster between the tumbler and window.

He positions the glass prison on the windowsill, in direct sunlight, and watches the trapped insect for a moment, mesmerised by its inability to comprehend it will soon be dead.

'If you had any brains, you'd play possum and pretend to be dead. I'd remove the coaster, and you'd be free again. If you were really smart, you'd hide. And when I leave the room, you'd silently hitch a lift on my back until I was outside. But you're not smart, are you? Hard-wired to act by instinct. Your only purpose is survival and procreation.' He gazes dismissively down upon the hordes of holidaymakers on the street below, like a swarm of ants, seemingly without purpose. 'You're not much different from that lot, are you?'

He soon tires of the fly and his attention reluctantly falls onto Prisha's credit card statements, which are hardly worth giving a second glance. She is fiscally responsible and barely touches the card.

Twenty-four statements and most are blank. On the rare occasions she used it, she'd allow twenty-nine days to pass before paying it off in full, thereby avoiding any interest charges.

'Finish the job, Magnus, finish the job.'

He flicks through the statements with disdain as he studies the purchases.

Three hundred and ninety-nine pounds paid to Argos, a high street electrical retailer. Possibly a new washing machine or tumble dryer. A purchase from Amazon for less than a hundred pounds, for sports apparel. Wearily, and with waning interest, he casts his eye over the remainder.

The last time the card was used is almost two years ago; A taxi fare to Manchester Airport.

Must have been a red-eye flight to a holiday destination. He idly wonders where she went, then imagines her in a bikini lying on a sun-kissed beach, as his own vision drifts onto the sands of West Beach directly opposite him.

Angry voices from the street divert his attention. An overweight, middle-aged man, accompanied by a dour woman, are remonstrating with a taxi driver. The driver lifts two suitcases from the boot and thumps them onto the pavement.

After a flurry of wild gesticulations, the driver jumps into the cab and speeds off.

The carousel in his mind spins as his eyes return to the credit card statement and the taxi fare.

Two-hundred-and-eighty pounds. Not cheap, but it was late at night.

The date lifts from the page and hits him between the eyes.

Sunday, 6th September

A surge of euphoria floods his body.

Scampering to the bed, he picks up the official report again.

Finds the sheet he's looking for and stares in satisfaction at the date, hands quivering in excitement.

Grins.

Pours a fresh tot of whisky and resumes his seat at the desk. 'I knew it. I bloody-well knew it. You see, Magnus, you are *never* wrong.'

Spinning the trapped fly around and around in the glass, he cackles.

'Got you, my dear.'

34

Zac looks at his watch. 'How long are we going to be here?'

Prisha continues to update the interactive whiteboard with the latest case details. 'Not long. Another thirty to forty minutes.'

'I'm bloody ravenous. I've barely eaten all day.'

'Yeah, me too.'

'Tell you what, why don't I nip out and get us a snack? '

Prisha curtails her work and glances at him. 'Good idea. Something light. Adam's due at my place later with a takeaway, so I don't want to ruin my appetite.'

'A few sushi rolls?' Zac says, heading briskly towards the door.

'Perfect.'

As he departs, muffled voices echo in the corridor, followed by the door creaking open.

She pops her head around the whiteboard and groans. 'Oh, gawd. Give me strength,' she murmurs, then quickly returns to her tasks.

He ghosts around the corner like Uriah Heep. His smile, sickly sweet, does not resonate from genuine empathy; it was yanked, caesarean style, from a black heart.

'You appear to be making good progress, inspector,' Magnus states, viperous eyes disseminating the updated investigation board.

'Yep.' She responds, perfunctory, cold.

'I see you're following old-school philosophy.'

'Sorry?'

'Eliminate everyone who couldn't have committed the crime until you are left with the killer.'

She has no wish to interact. 'Something like that.'

'Excellent. Except for the obvious flaw.'

The comment piques her interest. 'Which is?' she replies, still facing the board.

Licking his lips, he shuffles a step closer. 'A scheming villain always has a watertight alibi. Just like Tiffany Butler had.'

She glances at him before returning her attention back to the severed leg, and missing man, Jake Hill. 'Like Tiffany Butler *has,* Mr Crawley. Now, if you don't mind, I need to focus.'

'Of course. I'm distracting you.' He half turns as if to leave. 'Oh, forgot to mention. Over the last few days, I've had some breakthroughs.'

'Good.'

He stares at the carpet, hands stuck deep into his long, black leather coat. 'Yes. My noose is tightening around Tiffany. I did say at the start, hubris is the downfall of many a clever criminal. They may think they've picked up their dirty washing along the way, but they always leave a smelly stray sock behind.'

She sighs, tired of his mind games. If he has something to say, then damn well say it. 'You're obviously not going to leave me alone until you've articulated how brilliant you are, and I flutter my eyelashes in admiration. Be my guest, get it off your chest,' she replies, finally turning to peer into the pools of black ink.

Feigns surprise, then relents. 'I'm merely keeping you abreast...' he lets the word linger in the air. '... inspector. I wasn't getting anywhere in tracing the whereabouts of Miss Butler until I was surfing the net looking at estate agent websites. You see, since arriving in North Yorkshire, I've been mesmerised by the rugged, unspoilt beauty. Out of curiosity, I idly wondered what a modest three-bedroom house would cost in Whitby.' He laughs. 'Compared to London, they are a steal.' His face creases. 'And that's when it hit me.'

The pause for dramatic effect is so long Prisha eventually has to prompt him, which is exactly what he desires.

'What hit you?'

'Tiffany's house, right here in Whitby, less than a few minutes' brisk walk from this very station. I checked with the Land Registry and it's still under Miss Butler's name.' He taps his lips with a spindly finger. 'Serendipity at work again.'

For the first time, Prisha feels a rising disquiet. 'And?'

'Who pays the council taxes, the utilities? The upkeep of the garden. Maintenance if it should arise? In another moment of curiosity, I paid a visit to her abode. Very nice indeed. A conservative estimate would value the house at four-hundred-thousand plus.'

'I'm not sure where you're heading with this, but Tiffany is not a convicted criminal. The proceeds of crime act would not kick in until after a conviction, and only if her house purchase was proved to be funded by criminal activity. As I recall, when first questioning Tiffany at her home, she indicated she'd paid off the house some years ago.'

Magnus frowns. 'Yes, I garnered that information from the Land Registry. If you'd allow me to finish, my dear.'

'Go on. Get on with it.'

'Back to the costs of running a house. I'm actually a little embarrassed about this next part. It could hardly be classed as cutting-edge detective work, but nevertheless, the old ways can still pay dividends. Back at my hotel room, I made some enquiries and found out who Miss Butler's solicitor was when she purchased the house. To cut a long story short, I paid a visit to Dooley and Hargreaves Solicitors and had an interesting chat with Mr Dooley. At first, he was rather protective of the solicitor-client confidentiality privilege. However, after some friendly persuasion, he soon put ethics to one side. People often overestimate the powers of MI5 and what we are capable of. I blame TV and the cinema. Overly dramatic and factually inaccurate. But the false impression sometimes comes in handy.'

'If you could hurry this along,' she says tersely, fearing the worst.

'Forgive me. I'll cut to the chase. You'll be pleased to know Tiffany Butler is alive and kicking.'

'How do you know she's alive?'

'Because very recently, Tiffany Butler instructed her solicitor to transfer the deeds of her house into your name—a gift.'

Her expression of outright shock and confusion would win her an Oscar nomination. 'What!'

Magnus studies her intently, his narrow slits searching for the merest hint of artifice. For once in his life, he fails to read a suspect.

'I take it you haven't received any documentation in the post?'

'No, of course I haven't. I'd have reported it immediately to my superiors if I had. This is a set-up. From wherever

Tiffany is, she's playing twisted games, attempting to ruin my career and besmirch my character.'

'Hmm... that was my initial thought. And strangely enough, on Wednesday morning, just two days ago, Mr Dooley was instructed by Miss Butler to rip up the contract and delete any correspondence relating to it. Miss Butler gave no reason for her sudden change of mind. Through my contacts at HQ, we were able to retrieve her last email. Unfortunately, she uses a VPN, which masks the server address. However, we were able to narrow down the location somewhat.'

Prisha has a rising sense of panic. 'You've found out where she is?'

His face creases as his head wobbles from side to side. 'Not exactly. We believe she's in South America somewhere.'

A mild sense of relief washes over her. 'It's a big place.'

'It certainly is, but as a hunch, I'd suggest she's living in Argentina.'

'Why?'

'Because the extradition treaty between Argentina and the United Kingdom is inactive.'

'Inactive?'

'Yes, since the Falkland's war and the ongoing dispute about the sovereignty of the island. It would be the perfect place for her to hide.'

'You're clutching at straws, Mr Crawley. There are many countries in South America without extradition treaties: Bolivia; Venezuela; Ecuador, to name but a few.'

'True,' he acknowledges, annoyed he's gone off track. 'But none of it bodes well for you. The fact you forgot the crucial name, Dolores Fernandez, and now this matter of Miss Butler's house deeds.'

'I've done nothing wrong, and I have nothing to hide.'

'Indeed. However, wherever there's smoke, people assume there's fire. Not that anyone knows of this apart from me and you. I can keep this quiet if you answer me one question truthfully. Did you help Tiffany Butler evade capture?'

'No.'

The cold-blooded smile returns. 'Good. Your word is good enough for me. I can now focus on my primary targets; Butler and Kira Volkov. Right, it's time for my evening stroll, then a spot of supper and an early night. I have requested a meeting on Monday morning with Superintendent Banks and DCI Finnegan. Nothing for you to worry about. It's merely to update them on my progress.' He turns to leave but stops. 'Oh, one last thing, a very minor detail.'

Prisha's mind is turning to mush. She needs fresh air. 'What?'

He still has his back to her. 'Sixth of September, nearly two years ago was the night you and Tiffany were briefly held prisoner in the old lighthouse near Hawsker... am I correct?'

'Yes, you know you are if you've read all the reports.'

He turns, slowly. 'And the other day, Tuesday, I think it was, our little chat in Superintendent Banks' office...'

'What about it?'

'You said after the incident at the lighthouse you saw a doctor at the station. Then DCI Finnegan drove you back to your flat.'

'Yes.'

'And it was late. Roughly around midnight. Maybe a tad later. You had a shower, took some painkillers and a mild sedative, then went to bed. You didn't leave the house until the next day, which would have been the seventh of September.'

'Could you get to the point? You're becoming tiresome.'

'Sorry, my dear. But I need to be certain.' He extracts his phone from his pocket and pulls up a photograph. 'Maybe you can explain this then,' he says, handing her the phone.

'What is it?' she replies, gingerly accepting the mobile. Her heart sinks as she stares at the transaction. It doesn't show the account name, but the date is damning.

'It's a photo of your credit card statement. It details a charge recorded to a local taxi company. You'll note the date—sixth of September. The day you were chased all over the Yorkshire Moors by the Russians, before being rescued at the lighthouse. I checked with the taxi firm, and they have a log of the fare. The driver picked up a woman from your address at approximately 9:15 pm and drove her to Manchester Airport, Terminal Two, international departures. The journey took two hours and forty minutes, arriving just before midnight. The question is, how could you have taken a taxi ride at 9:15 pm when you were still at the station being assessed by the doctor?'

'I...' For once, she is lost for words.

'Come, come, inspector. What have you got to say for yourself?' he demands sternly.

Eyes glaze over as her whole world comes crashing down. 'I'm fucked,' she whispers softly.

A satisfying smirk engulfs Crawley's twisted features. 'Indeed you are, my dear. Well and truly fucked.'

35

Outside, the world continues its nightly routine. Holidaymakers stroll the promenade. Families, couples, friends marvel at the old-world charm of Whitby, a town cloaked in many layers of bygone eras. People seek out food and drink; pubs, restaurants, fish and chip shops. Children nag parents for money to spend in amusement arcades. Riverside kiosks do a brisk trade in candy floss, rock, fresh seafood, doughnuts. For the more adventurous or gullible, some will have their palm read.

Inside the police station, on the second floor, it's a more sombre tale that plays out.

One woman, a good, true, strong woman, stares into the abyss from which there's no escape. Her death sentence encapsulated on a credit card statement. Prisha feels like Ann Boleyn.

One man, a bad, manipulative, vainglorious man, is smug and yet... he attempts to hide his overwhelming sense of superiority with a grave expression. Nevertheless, behind the facade, Magnus Crawley feels like Henry VIII on the prowl for a new concubine.

As the dizziness and shock dissipate, Prisha calms herself. She fully realises the ramifications of her past actions, as she always has. But now it is fact. Known. Undeniable. For a brief second, she tries to conjure up a plausible explanation in her mind, but immediately gives up. Belittled, beaten, humiliated, she has a shred of empathy for the perpetrators she's extracted confessions from over the years. How deflated they must have felt when they realised the game was up.

As ever, she regroups. She'll go down with a quiet dignity and neither implicate, nor embroil, anyone else. Not even Tiffany. It's her mess and her mess alone.

Deep breath, shoulders back, she engages with her accuser. 'For the record, I never did this for monetary gain.'

Magnus offers her a warm, sympathetic smile. 'I realise that.'

'And also, you obtained my credit card statements fraudulently. You would have required a warrant to obtain my bank details.'

His eyes widen in innocence. 'To obtain a warrant would have involved informing your superiors of my suspicions, and the many discrepancies in your story. I did it for your benefit.'

'You're all heart.'

'You are being facetious and understandably so. Take a seat. I'll get you a glass of water. You look washed-out.'

Prisha slumps into a chair and drops her head into her hands. 'Shit and fuck,' she murmurs, desperately trying to hold back the tears.

He returns and hands her the glass, all sympathy. 'Care to give me the full story, although I think I have it all worked out.'

She takes a sip and places the glass down. 'We formed a bond during our pursuit by those crazy fucking murderers—the Russians. Tiffany and I went to hell and back. She saved my life on at least two occasions. I knew she masterminded the kidnapping and ransom of the girls; she admitted as much. But it would have been impossible to prove. The CPS would have never taken it to court. Tiffany wasn't bad, evil. She simply wanted a get-rich-quick scheme. After Maxim was dead, and Kira was nowhere to be seen, I handed her the key to my flat. Told her I had an unused credit card at the back of my knicker drawer. I also knew she had another false passport to assist in her escape.'

'Dolores Fernandez?'

'Yes.' She lifts her head and gazes at him. 'No one can possibly know what they would do in that situation. I did the wrong thing, but for the right reason.'

'Which was?'

'Save someone...'

'Go on?'

'Someone I care for. Someone I grew to... love.'

His eyes widen for a second. 'And have you seen or heard from her since that night?'

Something in his tone puts Prisha on guard. 'No. Never.'

His first mistake. He believes her. 'It's a tough one. I appreciate the friendship that was melded in the heat of battle. Sisters in arms. Evading predators. Understandable.'

'I will go home and type up my resignation letter, along with a full account of the facts. Will you at least allow me that dignity?'

Magnus smiles benignly. 'Of course. You're an officer of the highest calibre, who already at such a tender age has made a name for yourself. Highly respected.'

'Thanks.' A tear drips onto her cheek.

Magnus deftly pulls out a pristine white handkerchief and dabs it away.

'Of course... it doesn't have to be like this,' he says softly, making his play, the script he's been working on since the first day he was smitten.

Her eyelashes flutter, unsure what he means. 'Sorry. I don't understand?' she murmurs, sniffling.

'The last thing I want is to bring down one of my own. After all, we are both on the same side. Different teams—granted; but still united against a common enemy.'

'What are you implying?'

He touches her on the shoulder, fatherly. 'I don't care about your indiscretion, my dear. I don't really care about Tiffany Butler. My main concern is Kira Volkov and what she may know about state secrets. You and Tiffany are but flotsam and jetsam on the shore of my pursuit. Why ruin a brilliant career?'

Prisha wipes the snot from her nose. 'You mean... you won't take your findings to my superiors?'

He chortles. 'I didn't say that. But I'm sure we can find a compromise?'

Her spider senses tingle. 'Compromise?'

'As I've alluded to, I'm quite bewitched with this area of the country. Do you know, until I was handed this assignment, I'd never been further north than Nottingham? I do believe I've fallen in love with the place; North Yorkshire, Cumbria, and specifically... Whitby. I shall endeavour to spend more time in this magnificent location.'

Prisha is not stupid. But she is tired, worn down. 'And?'

Magnus studies her. Removes his hand from his pockets. 'You are an exquisite beauty. I am a man. My proposal is this: three, maybe four times a year I shall have long weekends in Whitby. Friday to Monday. Hotels are nice, but a little soulless. I propose that I stop at your flat for my jaunts. We can maybe go for long walks together and have nice meals in the evenings.'

It all becomes crushingly clear to Prisha. 'That's not possible. I only have the one bedroom.'

'Precisely.'

'You're blackmailing me for sex?'

He tut tuts. 'No, no, no! Blackmail is a dirty word. Think of it as mutual favours. What's the phrase the younger generation have coined to describe such relationships?' He pauses. 'That's right, friends with benefits. After all, consider the alternative: perverting the course of justice; accessory after the fact; misconduct in public office; aiding and abetting with your convenient memory loss about Dolores Fernandez. The list goes on. It would be an instant dismissal without notice and no doubt the courts would make an example of you to deter others. What do you reckon, eight to ten years in prison?' He shudders. 'Imagine that. A bent copper in a women's prison. You'd have to become the prison bitch to some stout, lesbian top-dog just to survive. A pariah to your colleagues. Shame and humiliation for your family and friends. A brilliant career cut short and because of what? A silly little mistake trying to help someone you felt beholden to, someone you had feelings for. Would you risk suffering that nightmare compared to accommodating me a few times a year?'

The very thought of sleeping with him makes her want to retch. 'How long would this arrangement last?'

'Oh, hard to say. Once your looks begin to fade, I dare say I'd move onto pastures new. What are you now? Early thirties? Maybe ten years... at a push.'

'Not much of a choice, is it? Either way, I'm facing a prison sentence.'

He creeps a step closer, his gaze a predatory waltz. Oozing false charm, his voice lowers. 'Now, don't be like that, Prisha. Am I that repugnant? I am a very considerate lover, my dear.'

Prisha rises and takes a sideways step.

He reaches out and touches her breast.

The lightning jab is instant, clocking him hard on the side of the mouth.

He yelps and stumbles back, crashing into a table. A moment of anger radiates across his features, then fades.

'Try that again and I'll break your fucking nose,' she spits.

Dabs at his mouth with the handkerchief and inspects the crimson stain, then grins. 'Fiery. I like that in my women. It makes it more fun.'

He pulls a small object from his pocket and holds it aloft. Prisha gazes at it. A small, plastic, black and white football, no bigger than a plum, is attached to a short chain, beneath which hangs a memory stick. It looks odd, out of place, almost childish.

'Take a good look at this, my dear. This tiny object represents your freedom, or your incarceration. Your choice. On here, I've consolidated all the facts; a detailed report of my investigation; an audio recording of my chat with the solicitor, along with a transcript. I also have digital scans of your bank records, the incriminating credit card statement, and a photocopy of the driver's licence belonging to Dolores Fernandez.' He edges towards her. 'The damning information only exists in three places.' He points to the side of his head. 'In here.' He reaches out and gently taps Prisha on the forehead. 'In here.' She slaps his hand away as he mockingly waggles the USB drive in front of her eyes. 'And in here.'

'Not only have you illegally hacked my bank records, but you've also illegally recorded the solicitor. That evidence wouldn't be admissible in a court of law.'

'Correct. But it would convince your superiors of your guilt and pave the way for a fresh investigation into you. They'd probably hand it over to officers from another force, and of course, I'd be more than willing to assist them in their endeavours. You also seem to be forgetting some key fundamentals. The secret service is not as hamstrung by ethics and probity as the police are. We play dirty because our enemies play dirty. We are not here to serve the public. We are here to serve the state. A much higher call of duty.'

'I'd have thought the secret service would have been a bit more high-tech than to keep their evidence on a humble USB drive.'

His laugh is patronising. 'I'm old-school. You see, I trust no one. Not my colleagues below me and certainly not those above me. Internet connections, secure encrypted protocols, messaging apps, phone records; all can be and have been, hacked. I only work on my personal laptop. Nothing flash. A bog standard Dell. Everything is saved to this drive. And while working, I disconnect from the wi-Fi. I am inoculated from outside interference. The USB can only be opened with my fingerprint. It may seem archaic to you, but believe me, it is one hundred per cent secure. If you agree to my compromise, I shall hand the drive over to you. I realise it's a token gesture, as we cannot go back in time to eradicate the evidence. But it will be a symbol of my honour, and of our pact.' His demeanour instantly changes, becoming businesslike. 'You have until 9:30 am Monday morning to consider my very generous proposal. Otherwise, my brief meeting with Superintendent Banks and DCI Finnegan may drag on for quite a while. And by the way, I will not enter into any further discussion on this matter. There'll be no bartering, begging, or further debate.' He pulls the collar up on his long overcoat and stuffs his hands into the pockets. A cheery smile splashes across his face. 'I think I'll take in some fresh sea air. Hmm... yes. A walk along the beach to work up an appetite. Then I really must try the famous Whitby fish and chips people have been recommending. Enjoy the rest of your evening and weekend, inspector.'

He turns and heads out of the door as Zac enters.

Oblivious to proceedings, he's in a chipper mood as he throws the food down onto the table.

'Sushi! Tuna, prawn, avocado and crab. Take your pick.'

Prisha slides into her seat and stares at her knees, hands clasped. 'I'm not hungry,' she mutters.

Zac shakes his head in disbelief. 'Strike a light! What do you mean, you're not hungry? Fifteen minutes ago, you were ravenous. You're just like my missus. She can change with the weather. Oh, well, more for me,' he adds, taking a mouthful of the food. He chews and eyeballs her, then swallows as he realises something's amiss.

'What's happened?'

36

Prisha's not the only one whose appetite has vanished. Zac closes the lid on the sushi pack and pushes it away, trying to comprehend what she's just told him. He reaches out and cups her hand.

'We'll find a way out of this, promise,' he whispers in his soft Scottish brogue.

She sniffs, holding back the tears. 'There is no way out. I always feared this would come back to bite me.'

'Listen, let's get Frank down here and tell him everything. He'll have your back. Three heads are better than one.'

Alarmed, she says, 'Absolutely not. There's nothing he can do even if he wanted to. I couldn't bear to witness his disappointed face. That credit card statement and taxi fare are my death warrant. Everything else is unsubstantiated fluff that can be explained away. But not the taxi ride to Manchester Airport. It's either prison, or...' She cannot finish the sentence, the grisly thought too odious to articulate.

'No, please god, you're not actually considering that sleazy, oil-slicked, stick insect's proposal, are you?'

'It's either that or the end of my career and prison. Choices, eh?' she says with a half laugh.

'No, listen, I have an idea. Go to his hotel room tonight and get him to repeat his proposition and secretly record it on your phone. That way, you have one over on him. Then on Monday, when he arrives, you can play him the recording. It will be a stalemate. Sexual blackmail would end his career. He'd have no other choice than to drop the matter.'

She shakes her head. 'He's not stupid. There's no way he'd fall for that. He made it very clear he'd not enter into any further discussion about the matter. If I show up at his hotel room, he'd smell a rat.'

Zac pushes back in his seat. 'Okay, then let's kill him,' he says matter-of-factly.

Prisha shakes her head in dismay. 'Don't talk bloody stupid.' She rises and picks up her jacket.

'Where are you going?'

'Home.'

'I'll give you a lift.'

'Thanks, but I prefer to walk. I need some air and thinking time alone.'

———◆———

Prisha gently closes the door to her flat, trudges into the front room, and drops her bag onto the couch. She enters the kitchen and pulls a bottle of Tesco's own-brand white wine from the fridge. Filling a very generous sized wine glass, she knocks it back in three thirsty gulps. The icy liquid causes a moment of excruciating brain freeze. Hunched over, her arms propping her up on the counter, she pants rapidly, then refills the glass. She takes a packet of Jacob's Cream Crackers from the bread bin and nibbles at one without enthusiasm.

As she mulls over the devastating facts, a shoot of an idea sprouts. Pulling open a cupboard door, she stands on tiptoes and reaches for a metal container that reads FLOUR. She lifts the lid and takes out the burner phone Tiffany gave her. Taps at the only number on the phone, lets it ring three times, then ends the call. Waiting a few seconds, she presses the call button again. It's answered almost immediately.

'Who is this?' a voice with a Spanish inflection demands.

'It's me.'

The voice changes. 'Aha! Prisha. You called. To be honest, I didn't think you would. What's happening, girlfriend?'

'Where are you?' she asks solemnly.

'I'm here, there and everywhere, enjoying life. It's the only way. I've spent the day indulging in a little shopping therapy and I've just enjoyed an exquisite evening meal at a swanky restaurant. For the appetiser I had seared foie gras with a balsamic reduction. For the main I went with wild-caught salmon with a dill and caper sauce, and to finish it off I had blackberry and macadamia mille-feuille. It was to die for. Heavenly! All washed down with a couple of glasses of sauvignon blanc from the Loire Valley. Oh, and I flirted outrageously with the drop-dead gorgeous sommelier. Unfortunately, the Red Baron is flying low over the gates of Buckingham Palace, so I couldn't take it any further. Just my luck.' Her effervescent laugh echoes through the ether. 'What about you?'

Prisha takes another nibble of the dry cracker and stares disconsolately at the Tesco wine bottle.

'Oh, me? Just wonderful.'

'You're being sarcastic, aren't you? What's the matter; tough day at the office?'

'You could say that.'

'Is Adam with you?'

'No. He'll be over later. Now, shut up and listen.'

Prisha finally comes to the end of explaining the horrendous series of events, each one igniting the next like a conflagration. Tiffany's response is swift.

'Prisha, listen to me; you cannot sleep with that nefarious, conniving, gargoyle. You'll never forgive yourself. There must be another way. What about bribery? Everyone has their price.'

'I have eight thousand in the bank; I hardly think that's going to sway him.'

'Not a problem. Find out his price and I can transfer the money across.'

'NO! Don't you dare. You've already caused enough trouble. That's just adding more fuel to the fire. Another link between us. And anyway, you don't understand him. He's not driven by money. That's not what floats his boat. He's a narcissist, who has a dominance personality disorder. He gets his kicks from controlling and manipulating others. I don't think he's particularly bothered about the sex. It's the control he's after. He must win at all costs. If he were to accept a bribe, he'd relinquish control. I'd have taken the upper hand. I've been on training courses about this shit and dealt with countless criminals over the years who displayed similar traits.'

A moments silence. 'Then I don't know what to suggest, but you know I'll help you in any way I can.'

'There is one thing you could do,' Prisha says in a hushed tone.

'Name it. Anything.'

'You can hand yourself in to the police. Confess everything; the kidnapping, the ransom, instructing your solicitor to sign the deed of your house over to me. And this is the most important part; the night at Hawsker lighthouse, during our fight with the Russian, Maxim, you say I lost my keys. You picked them up and escaped. You went to my flat and found my credit card and booked a taxi. You tell them that you knew my address because I'd mentioned it when we were on the run together.'

Silence.

'Tiffany, are you still there?'

'Yes. I'm here.'

'Well?'

'I'll go to prison.'

'And so you bloody well should! You did the wrong thing, and you should pay the price. Instead, I'll end up paying the price for you. Either I'll end up in prison or I'll have to sleep with that scaly skink for the next decade. And what about Adam? I'll have to end my relationship with him. I couldn't betray him.' Her exasperation fades as tiredness moves in. 'Please, Tiffany, will you do it for me? I'm begging you.'

'I can't. I'm sorry.'

Anger rises. 'No. I thought not. So much for love. Bye, Tiffany.'

She ends the call, prises the back off the phone and removes the sim card. Taking the lid off the blender, she drops the card inside, returns the lid and flicks it on. A few seconds pass. Removing the lid, she rinses the debris out in the sink and sobs as the liquid drains away. She drops to the floor and pulls her knees into her chest, tears trickling down her cheeks.

'I'm alone. I have no one,' she weeps, as tiredness steps aside to usher in despair.

She hears the latch on the front door click.

'Yoo-hoo! It's me, Prisha. I have the takeaway curry,' Adam's voice booms out.

She quickly dries her tears, stands, and straightens herself out.

He enters the gloomy kitchen and deposits the plastic bag on the table. 'Ah, now you're a sight for sore eyes. I've been looking forward to this moment since I woke up. Here, give me a hug.' He drapes his muscular arms around her and pulls her close. 'How was your day? Hope it was better than mine?'

'Yep. Fine.'

Snuggling into his chest, a realisation dawns on her.

She does have someone.

Adam.

In that perfect, ghastly moment, love arrives like a belated party guest.

Unfortunately, the party has ended.

37

His arms rest at the side of Prisha's head as his buttocks move rhythmically up and down. She stares, not into his eyes, but at a spot on the ceiling, near the light-fitting. It only has one coat of paint, and it definitely doesn't match the rest of the ceiling.

The painter did a shitty job.

Adam throws the towel in and rolls off her, emitting a huff.

'What's the matter?' she asks, concerned the lovemaking has ended so soon, but also thankful the lovemaking has ended so soon.

'Christ, Prisha. If you're not into it, just say. I don't want sex. I want to make love to my girlfriend. It's a two-way street. If it was just sex I was after I could pay a prostitute. I want a connection, and a bit of fun and passion.'

'Sorry.'

'Now you've made me feel bad.'

'Sorry.'

'Stop saying bloody sorry! Instead, tell me what's going on inside that head of yours. You're a closed book. You never tell me anything about your day, how you feel, what's troubling you. I thought it was us men who were supposed to be cut off from our emotions.'

'I'm being...' She pauses. '... silly. I don't talk about my day because it's confidential. And yes, I wasn't in the mood tonight, but I was doing what a lot of women do.'

'Which is?'

'Putting out for their partner.'

'Well, don't in future. I'd rather go without.'

She curls up at the side of him, resting her head on his chest as she drags her fingers over his abdomen.

'Tell me about your day.'

He sighs. 'The tractor broke down again. At some point I'm going to have to bite the bullet and get shut of it and find the money for a new one, or at least a good second-hand one. I'm throwing good money after bad with the bloody thing.'

'No. I didn't mean about the nuts and bolts. Tell me about the weather, the views. The sounds you hear and the smells. What thoughts are in your head.'

He frowns. 'Are you tapped or what?'

'Come on. I want to hear it.'

'I don't really notice what goes on.'

'Come on, try. Close your eyes and imagine you're walking out of the door at five this morning. Transport yourself back there.'

There's silence for a moment as he struggles with the concept and his mild embarrassment.

'When I walk outside, the first thing I notice is the weather. It's always the weather. Today, it was one of those typical summer days up there, not particularly warm, a bit of a chill in the air. The sky was a dull grey, with a few patches of blue fighting to break through. I could feel the moisture in the air, like a fine mist that clings to your skin. The grass was damp with dew, making my boots wet.'

'As I walked towards the barn, I could hear the sheep bleating in the distance, their calls echoing across the valley. The birds were starting their morning chorus, a mix of chirps and songs that blend together. The crows were the loudest, their harsh caws drowning out the softer melodies of the smaller birds. It's a sound I've grown to love, like nature's alarm clock.'

'I could smell the earth, damp and rich, mixed with the faint scent of hay and manure. It's a smell that's hard to describe, but it's comforting, like the smell of home. There was a hint of wildflowers too, sweet and subtle, carried on a light breeze. The air up there is always clean and crisp. It's like breathing in purity itself.'

'When I got to the barn, the steers were already in a holding pen, awaiting a visit from the vet. Their low moos greeted me as I got near them. The warmth from their bodies was a contrast to the cool morning air. I could hear them shifting and moving, the soft rustle of straw under their hooves. I always take a moment to pat Bullseye on the head. He's my favourite. He's black but has these big white circles around his eyes, like spectacles. He's got a right personality. A bit of a cheeky bugger. Sounds daft, but he seems to understand more than you'd think a steer could. I'll be sad to see him go to market when the time comes.'

'For lunch, I had a simple sandwich—cheese and pickle, nothing fancy. I sat on the old stone wall overlooking the fields behind the barn, the landscape stretching out in front of me as I drank a cup of hot tea from my thermos. The fields were a patchwork of greens and yellows, the hay-grass swaying in the breeze. I could see the hedgerows teeming with life, rabbits darting in and out, and the occasional fox slinking along the underbrush. It's a sight that never gets old.'

Adam's soft voice walks through his day, as Prisha's eyes flutter and close, her own harsh future rising up like a giant raven blanking out all daylight. The choice is stark; prison, and humiliation for her family and friends, or a decade of being a concubine for that evil, twisted, Dickensian extra.

Either way, she will have to let Adam go. She'll never learn to share his love of the farm, or witness the months slip by as they change from winter to spring, summer to autumn. The veil of sleep drapes over her like a sedative as Adam continues his journey.

'As the day went on, I could feel the sun breaking through the clouds, warming my back as I worked. The tractor breaking down was a right pain, but it gave me a chance to pause and really take in my surroundings. Sometimes, I think we get so caught up in the tasks at hand that we forget to appreciate the beauty around us.'

'In those moments, when I'm forced to stop, I can hear the gentle hum of the bees buzzing around the flowers, the distant sound of the river flowing over the rocks, the hiss of the wind amongst the trees. The land is alive, breathing and moving to its own beat. It's in those peaceful moments I feel most connected to the place, like I'm a part of it, and it's a part of me.'

'I think about the generations of farmers who've worked the land before me, their hands touching the same soil, their eyes seeing the same views. It's a humbling thought, knowing that I'm just a small part of a much larger story.'

'By the time evening rolls around, the sky starts to change, the blue giving way to shades of pink and orange as the sun sets. The temperature drops again, and I can feel the chill seeping back in. The sounds of the farm start to hush, the animals settling in for the night, and the bird song becomes more tuneful, especially the blackbirds.'

'Lying here with you now, I can still hear the distant calls of the owls, their hoots echoing across the fields. The smell of the earth and the hay linger on my clothes, a constant reminder of the day's work. And despite the aches and the frustrations, there's a deep sense of satisfaction, knowing that I'm doing what I love, living a life that's connected to nature and the changing seasons. That's what goes on in my head, love. That's my day.'

Prisha's gentle snoring makes him smile as he removes her arm and gently kisses her on the forehead. She flips onto her side and curls up in the foetal position as he switches off the bedside lamp. His hand brushes against wetness on his chest.

He realises she's been silently weeping.

38

The view from North Terrace car park on West Cliff is stunning. To the east, the harbour hemmed in by the iconic piers of Whitby. To the west, the rugged headland of Sandsend and Lythe. Directly ahead, the North Sea. It's late, but the daylight is reluctant to retire, painting the sky in a glorious reddish hue which is reflected over rippling waves.

Magnus stares through the windscreen for a moment before unravelling the butcher's paper wrapped around the fish and chips, allowing himself a smug smile for a job well done. While the prospect of undressing Prisha sparks his ardour, it's a fleeting temptress compared to the exhilarating rush of his masterful manipulation. Desires of the flesh are easy to satisfy. However, the exquisite dance of control and deceit are much longer lasting pleasures, firing a cerebral ecstasy that has no equal.

He pops a chip into his mouth and instantly winces as the salt and vinegar infiltrate the cut to his lip. His tongue darts out and licks the slight wound. Chuckling, he emits a satisfying sigh as he attacks his meal. As far as he's concerned, it's a fait accompli. Prisha has only one credible choice. He reflects that, while she's a smart copper and a rising star, she's still a tyro compared to him. An absolute beginner. He lets his mind bask in its own shining glory as he quickly devours the food.

Scrunching the paper into a ball, he drops it into a plastic bag, ties the handles and lobs it onto the back seat of the car, then relaxes for a moment and breathes in the vista. Removing the memory drive from his jacket, he spins the plastic football around and around in his fingers, smirking.

'No plan is ever perfect, but goddamn it, this one almost is.' His inflated ego is in danger of self-combusting.

Something flits across his peripheral vision as he slides the memory stick back into his jacket.

He glances out of the side window as a figure approaches. Watching, scrutinising intently, he assesses the situation.

'This could be interesting,' he mutters, his sexual desire rekindled.

The woman nears as his window rolls down.

'How are you tonight?' she enquires in perfect English cloaked a husky foreign accent.

'I'm very well, thank you for asking,' he replies, staring into her large sunglasses which mask her face. 'And how are you?' His gaze now falls onto her ample, firm bosom.

'I am well. Are you looking for business?'

'Possibly. Remove your shades and let me see you.'

He stares into the green eyes of a natural beauty. The blonde hair is probably a wig, and she's wearing make-up. But she's youngish and has a vigour and vitality about her.

'Do you like what you see?'

'Indeed I do. How much?'

'That depends on what you want.'

'Oral.'

'One hundred... for you, ninety.'

He grimaces. 'That's a little steep for my tastes. In London I can get...'

She cuts him off. 'You are not in London,' she states, a slight impatience in her tone. Her tongue salaciously rolls around her glossy red lips in a provocative manner.

Magnus swallows hard. 'Okay. Get in.'

The woman saunters around to the passenger side, pulls open the door, and slides into the seat. Her perfume is fresh with a hint of citrus, nicely understated.

'Money first,' she states in a businesslike fashion.

Magnus pulls his wallet out of his jacket and peels off the notes. 'Here you go. Ninety pounds.'

She quickly slides the money into a small purse. 'You will not be disappointed.'

'I should hope not at that price.'

'Not here. It is too risky. Police cars patrol this area. I know a quiet spot not far from here. It is private. We will not be disturbed there.'

'How far?' Magnus asks as he fires the engine, already experiencing a rapid hardening down below.

'Five minutes, max.'

'Okay. Direct the way. Oh, one more thing, my dear. Before the main act, I liked to be kissed.'

'Not a problem.'

'Passionately, with tongue,' he adds, wetting his lips.

The woman winks at him. 'You are a very sexy man. I'm looking forward to our little tryst. Maybe you will become a regular?'

'Maybe I will.'

Magnus Crawley is on top of the world.

39

Saturday 15th July

In the murky light of dawn, a Mercedes-Benz maintenance truck from the Revenue Protection Team rolls to a stop. Its familiar yellow and white livery revealing it as a vehicle from the local electricity supplier—Northern Lights Distribution. The two occupants wearily exit the vehicle and spark up cigarettes.

'We've been on this case for three days now,' Jez says, puffing out smoke into the cool summer air.

'Aye. It's a tough one all right,' Danny replies. He draws on his cigarette and stares down the valley, his eyes taking in the rugged beauty of the North Yorkshire Moors and the cut-back swathe of the maintenance access track. 'Mind you, there are worse places to be. And look on the bright side – it's a Saturday morning, which means time-and-a-half. A bit extra in the pay packet at the end of the month is always welcome.'

'I'd rather be at home with the wife and kids. Anyway, it has me baffled. The illegal draw averages around 10,000 kWh per day. That's a sign of a large-scale operation. Control has identified this five-mile stretch as the source of the illegal draw, and yet...'

'There's absolutely nothing here. No farms, no agri-business. Nothing.'

'Could be an anomaly with the software back at HQ?' Jez suggests.

'Nah. Not these days, especially since they did the upgrade. All state-of-the-art. And it's way too big for leakage.' He drops his cigarette onto the track and grinds it in with the toe of his boot. 'Must give up one day. Filthy habit. Okay, Jez, your turn in the bucket lift. Isolate the next section.'

As the hydraulics whirr into action, the aerial work platform rises into the air like a sluggish giraffe.

———◇———

Danny pulls the mobile close to his ear. 'We've found it, boss. It's pole H1072 on the Boundary Brooke track about two miles north of the Hamer Bank turn off.'

'Sophisticated?'

'I wouldn't call it sophisticated, but it's effective. They've used insulation piercing connectors to tap into the power. Two cables come down the pole into a new junction box, then disappear underground. I'd say the underground cable must have already been in-situ, as there's no sign of ground disturbance.'

'That's odd. We have no record of any properties in that neck of the woods.'

'Do you want us to disconnect?'

'No. The power consumption patterns match with what we'd expect from a large-scale operation. This isn't a pensioner trying to lower his monthly electric bill. It has to be industrial.'

Danny gazes out at the beautiful, but barren countryside. 'Boss, it's in the middle of the moors. National Park. There are no industrial units out here.'

'What about farms?'

'No. Not to the naked eye. We really are out in the wilderness.'

'Hmm... well, the only other thing I can think of is a drugs lab. Possibly a cannabis farm. They require high-intensity lights twenty-four-seven, HVAC systems, and irrigation setups. If we disconnect, it will alert them. Then they'll either fly the coop or send someone out to investigate the interruption. It's not our job to confront drug gangs. They don't take prisoners. Use the cable avoidance scanner to trace the underground cable to its end location. Get a GPS position and take plenty of photos. Then we'll hand it over to the coppers. And if you see any activity, get the hell out of there ASAP.'

'Okay, boss,' he says, removing his hard-hat and scratching his head as he surveys the terrain. 'It must be an underground operation.'

'Possibly. If it is a drugs lab, they'll need a ventilation shaft. Okay, stay in touch and good luck.'

Danny drops his mobile into his pocket. 'Right, Jez, get the handheld cable scanner. We need to trace the cable to its destination, get a GPS marker, then head back to HQ.'

'Righto.'

Jez gazes at the screen of the scanner.

'Good signal?' Danny asks.

'Yes. It's strong. Got a good reading.'

'Good. Come on, let's take a walk.'

After an hour's rather tedious stroll, the two men come to a halt.

Jez walks forward a few paces. 'Lost the signal.' He takes four steps back. 'Got it again. X marks the spot,' he states. 'This must be the entry point right beneath our feet. I'll be buggered if I know where the cable goes from here, though.'

Danny scrunches his face up. 'It doesn't make sense. There's nothing here. Anyway, we've done our job.' He pulls out a pair of binoculars and scans the horizon. 'Well, I'll be.'

'What is it?' Jez asks.

'If I'm not mistaken, there's a small metal chimney stack sticking out of the ground about a half-mile ahead. Here, take a look.'

Jez takes the binoculars and adjusts the focus. 'Aye, you're right. It's only protruding twelve inches or so, but it's definitely some sort of ventilation pipe. What now?'

'You head back to the truck and pack up the gear. I'll continue ahead and get an exact positioning on the chimney, and some photos. Then it's time to bugger off home.'

'I have a bad feeling about this,' Jez mumbles.

'Yeah, me too. We're like fish in a bloody barrel stuck out here.'

Alone in the vast landscape, Danny realises his vulnerability as he nears the flue sprouting from the heather. He drops to his stomach and crawls along, commando fashion.

'This is above my bloody paygrade,' he grumbles, edging closer. He pulls out his mobile and places a marker on his GPS, then takes some photos. 'Right, that will do.' As he twists like a snake and slithers away, he abruptly freezes as the crack of gunshot ricochets through the air, way too close for comfort.

'What the?'

Voices drift to him on a lazy breeze. For some reason he squints, as if it will help him hear better. The voices come again. But they're odd, indecipherable. Raising his head, he looks around.

He spots them about fifty feet away, walking along the top of a gully.

Two people. A tall woman. A mountain of a man.

They both have hunting rifles slung over their shoulders.

'Shite. Am I bloody blessed, or what?' he whispers, chin buried in heather that tickles his nose.

The Goliath suddenly stops and with expert precision aims his rifle and fires a shot. A rabbit somersaults in the air.

Laughter.

The man says something, again, incomprehensible.

Danny has seen enough. Their very demeanour fills him with dread.

'Fuck this for a game of bow and arrows. I'm asking for a desk job!'

He half crouches and scurries away.

40

As the assortment of officers troop into the incident room, Frank and Zac peer out of the office window.

'Looks like the team is ready for the brief,' Frank notes, rising from behind his desk.

'Frank, did you consider my request for a firearm?' Zac probes, hopefully.

He throws him a disparaging glance. 'Aye, I did. For all of about two seconds.'

'I take it that's a no, then?'

'Too bloody right it is. You have a touch of the Edward Woodward's about you.'

'Edward who?' Zac asks as they saunter from the office.

'The Equaliser?' Zac's blank expression says it all. 'Never mind. It would have ended in tears, and curtailed a glittering career.'

Zac chuckles. 'I can't say I'm not disappointed, but thanks for the compliment.'

'I wasn't talking about your glittering career. I was talking about mine. Letting you loose with a gun would be like handing Rambo a bazooka in a nightclub full of Mexican drug lords. And the buck would have stopped with me. Right, come on, look lively. You operate the interactive whiteboard. I've still not mastered the bloody thing.'

'You have trouble switching your phone on,' Zac replies drily as both men meander to the middle of the room.

Frank claps his hands together to end the amiable chatter between the officers. 'Okay, team, listen up. I know you've all been kept in the dark about this little operation, but loose lips sink ships. In a nutshell, we believe a cannabis farm is operating on the moors a few miles east of Rosedale Abbey, in the back of beyond. The cover for their activities is a mushroom farm. We've run a check on Companies House and the business, Moor Top Mushroom Farm, appears legitimate. The directors are Eamon, Cillian, and Fergus Murphy. None have any form.'

'They even have a very professional-looking website,' Zac adds, pulling it up on the whiteboard. 'They sell wholesale and directly to the public, and distribute all over the North of England. They even offer schools guided tours of the farm for educational purposes. Take a look at these smiling beauties,' he says, tapping at the About Us page. Three mugshots of Eamon, Cillian and Fergus Murphy stare out at the officers.

'Bonny buggers,' Frank says. 'Apart from that, we don't have much intel. We'll be going in blind. We don't know how many individuals are involved and we don't know if they're armed. Zac, pull the brief up,' he adds as the officers move in closer to the whiteboard. There's a collective groan as the name of the operation pops up on the board in large letters.

'Christ, Frank, is that one of yours?' asks Arnie Jenkins, lead officer from the Armed Response Unit.

Frank appears mortally wounded. 'Aye. What's wrong with it, Arnie?'

'Operation Fun Guy. Give me a break.'

The small convoy pulls up in a lay-by a mile before the turnoff to the mushroom farm. A single car carries Frank, Zac and Dinkel. Two transit vans contain five uniformed officers and five officers from the Armed Response Unit. The last vehicle, a smaller van, contains two K9 officers and a pair of sniffer dogs.

Frank and Zac exit the car and have a quick word with each driver, ensuring everyone is aware of their duties but also offering words of encouragement. Raiding a suspected cannabis farm is a risky business. Anything could happen.

Frank pokes his head inside the driver's window and smiles.

'All right lads, you'll soon be back in the canteen with your feet up watching the cricket. Everyone okay?'

He's greeted with a volley of good-natured replies.

'Aye, all good here, Frank.'

'Piece of cake, boss.'

'Hey, Frank, who do you fancy in the cricket?'

He considers the conundrum for a moment. 'You'd have to wager England at home, wouldn't you? Although, the opposition has some talent in their batting line-up. They bat deep. Test cricket has a way of throwing up surprises. Right, we'll have a debrief back at the station once we have these scallywags safely under lock and key.'

All officers appear relaxed but are acutely aware of the inherent dangers.

Zac pops a Polo mint into his mouth and offers one to Frank. 'Mint?'

'Nah. Had enough mints to last me a lifetime when I was giving up the smokes. Some sort of bad connection was made. All I fancy now when I have a mint is a ciggy. Good to go?'

Zac chuckles. 'Raring to go.'

Frank can well remember when he was Zac's age. All testosterone and reckless abandon. Searching for excitement and the thrill of a good punch up. He's a little wiser, and more circumspect these days.

He pats him on the shoulder. 'Just watch yourself, lad. The best result is this ends with a whimper, not a bang. Don't go looking for trouble when there's none there. Understand?'

'Of course, Frank. I'll be a pillar of restraint.'

'Hmm... more like a pillock,' he replies, unconvinced, as he jumps into the front passenger seat.

Zac positions himself behind the steering wheel and cheerily turns to Dinkel sitting in the back. 'Dinks, my little cock Womble, looking forward to it?'

His washed-out demeanour speaks louder than any words. 'Erm, not really.'

Zac pulls a set of leather gloves from the door pocket and slides them over his large hands, stretching his fingers as he does so. 'That's better,' he whispers to himself as he cracks his knuckles.

'Bit warm for gloves, isn't it?' Dinkel innocently enquires.

Frank and Zac exchange glances. 'To protect the knuckles, sunshine. Teeth can leave nasty incisions.'

Dinkel swallows hard. 'Oh,' he murmurs.

Frank picks up the radio. 'All units, this is Sierra One. Final check-in before we proceed. Report status, over.'

Unit One, Armed Response Unit: 'Sierra Two, ready and in position, over.'

Unit Two, K9 Unit: 'Sierra Three, ready and in position, over.'

Unit Three, Uniformed Officers: 'Sierra Four, ready and in position, over.'

Frank nods. 'Copy that. All units proceed as planned. Unit One to advance first and secure location. Sierra One, over.'

The unmarked ARU van pulls onto the main road and leads the way as the other vehicles fall in behind.

'Ah, it's days like these I feel good to be alive,' Zac declares, brimming with excitement and vitality.

As the lead van traverses down the narrow winding track towards the gates of the compound, the other vehicles follow, leaving a bit of distance between the ARU team.

Frank zooms in with his binoculars. 'All quiet on the Western Front,' he murmurs. 'Can't see a bloody dicky bird. The gates are locked. I can see a chain and padlock.'

'Don't worry, the lads from ARU will bust that open with the van.'

Frank lowers the binoculars and stares at him. 'You've never had to manage a police budget, have you? Bust those gates down with the van and there's going to be smashed headlights, a crumpled bonnet, possibly a paggered radiator, and we'll be responsible for fixing up the gates. Do you know how much that little lot would cost to put right? That's before the mountain of paperwork. I've informed the lads to use a pair of bolt cutters if needs be.'

Zac curls his mouth up in distaste. 'You're no fun anymore, Frank.'

'Aye. And you've been watching too many Guy Ritchie films. Right, come on, let's get on with it.'

The three vehicles traverse the bumpy gravel track as the ARU van comes to a sedate halt outside the gates. An officer alights with a pair of formidable looking bolt cutters. He gives the gate and chain a quick once over then snips them open with ease and motions the van forward as he opens the gates. The transit screeches through, kicking up a spray of dirt and dust, then comes to a skidding stop as four officers pile out, brandishing their weapons.

Zac, looking for action, accelerates the car alarmingly, circles the van and hits the brakes hard.

'Daft bugger,' Frank grumbles as he's thrown around inside. He picks up the megaphone and exits the vehicle, as officers fan out around the compound. He takes up position behind the car with Zac and Dinkel.

'This is the police!' The tinny sound from the bullhorn ricochets off the metal panels of the large sheds. 'I want everyone to make themselves known. Come out slowly, hands above your heads and lay down on the ground.'

An eerie silence pervades the calm, warm day as unseen birds lazily sing from perches. A rattling noise disrupts the peace as a roller door on the biggest shed rises. Two ARU officers take up the firearms stance behind the cover of the van, their guns trained on the door.

Two men walk forward, arms raised.

'Lay face down on the ground and place your hands behind your back!' Frank bellows. 'Is there anyone else on this site?'

The older of the two men shakes his head as he ungainly crouches, then lies on the ground. 'No, officer. Just the two of us today,' he replies in a lilting Irish twang.

With the two men laid prone on the ground, two ARU officers approach and roughly clamp handcuffs around their wrists.

'Clear!'

Frank thrusts the megaphone onto Dinkel and saunters forward with Zac.

'Names?' Frank barks, although he already recognises them from the website photos.

'The name's Eamon Murphy, sir. And this is my lad, Fergus,' the older man says, staring at dirt. 'If you don't mind, can I stand up, please? I'm in my Sunday best, and I am in my sixties. My old bones aren't up to this sort of malarkey these days.'

Frank nods at an ARU officer who bends and assists Eamon Murphy to his feet. His son attempts to do the same, unaided, but Zac drops his boot onto his backside and pushes him back down.

'Not you, sunshine,' he snarls.

Frank and Eamon Murphy eyeball each other as Frank pulls out the search warrant.

'I'm DCI Finnegan, and we believe you're operating a cannabis farm under the cover of growing mushrooms. Would you care to assist and save us all a lot of time?'

Murphy smiles, chuckling. 'Mr Finnegan, you seem to be under some misapprehension. I'm an honest man and I have nothing to hide. The only thing we grow here is mushrooms.'

'Aye, of course you do. Save your Irish blarney for another day.'

'It's true Mr Finnegan. It's all legit. I have all my permits and authorisations from the various government and council agencies. Planning permission, insurance, health and safety, and labelling compliance, environmental permits... not that I use chemicals. Nasty stuff.'

Frank eyeballs him suspiciously. 'And you'd be able to show me all the paperwork, would you?'

'Indeed I would, sir. If you'd care to step into my office,' he says, nodding towards a portable workers' cabin at the far end of the yard.

'Who do you sell to?'

'We have contracts with a lot of the smaller supermarket chains. Independent greengrocers, restaurants, market stall holders, even the public.'

'Hmm... I'll inspect your paperwork once I've had a look around. Dinkel, escort Mr Murphy and his son to the cabin and keep an eye on them.'

Murphy appears perturbed. 'Inspector, if you wish to inspect the spawning and incubation rooms, then I really must insist you wear the correct protective gear, not only for your officers' welfare but also for the integrity of the mushrooms. If pseudomonas tolaasii was to get inside the growing sheds, it could decimate my crops.'

'Come again?'

'Pseudomonas tolaasii—bacterial blotch, as it's commonly known.'

'What sort of protective gear?'

'Not dissimilar to the type you'd wear at a crime scene. We have a special room where we disinfect before, and after, entering the rooms. If you were to take the cuffs off, I could assist you.'

———◦———

The inside of the large shed is dim, a musty atmosphere pervading the space. A few thin beams of natural light pierce the eaves, casting long shadows across the floor. Twelve shipping containers line the walls in two neat rows, their industrial steel forms contrasting sharply with the organic growth inside them.

After searching for thirty minutes, Frank and Zac enter the last shipping container, which is empty.

'Nothing to see in here,' Frank says as he turns around and exits. 'Let's get out of this gear.'

Zac stares at the double doors to the rear of the steel container. His eyes move to the floor. Something niggles him, but as there's not even a single leaf of cannabis in sight, he follows Frank outside.

After exiting the disinfecting room and removing their safety gear, they stand with hands in pockets, expressions of bewilderment etched across their faces. The earthy smell of damp soil and mushrooms fills the air, adding to the surreal ambience.

Frank's brow furrows as he rubs a hand over his grey hair and surveys the scene, his mind racing to make sense of it all. Beside him, Zac's mouth is slightly agape, the usually unflappable detective as puzzled as his boss.

The rest of the shed is eerily silent, the only sounds being the faint scratching as the sniffer dogs and their handlers complete yet another circuit. An occasional drip of water echoes inside the cavernous space.

'What a bloody balls up,' Frank mutters. 'Poor intel.'

'It doesn't make sense,' Zac replies. 'I saw an Asian guy throw a bag of something over the fence with my own eyes. It had to be weed. Bo-Bo didn't drive all the way out here late at night to retrieve a bag of washing.'

'Let's take a quick walk around the compound. You check out the rear of the shed. I'll circumnavigate the boundary fence.'

After completing a circuit, Frank spies Zac beckoning him over. He saunters to the back of the shed. The rear panels are close to a rocky bluff, with a narrow gap running the full width. It's overgrown with brambles and long grass.

'What is it?' he asks.

Zac points at a pipe rising out of the ground. About four inches in diameter, it's sealed shut with a removable cap, which is padlocked to a small eyelet welded onto the side of the pipe.

Zac kneels and drags his middle finger over the surface of the cap and holds it up. 'Pretty certain it's diesel.'

Frank bends and dabs a finger on top of the pipe, then sniffs the residue. 'Aye, that's diesel all right. Possibly an underground holding tank. Not unusual to find diesel tanks on a farm, though.'

Both men pull out handkerchiefs and wipe their fingers. 'Should we quiz Murphy about it?'

Frank considers the question carefully. 'No, let's keep our powder dry. The magistrate won't issue us with another search warrant for cannabis, but they would for stolen diesel.'

'Yeah, good point.'

'Time to eat humble pie. Come on.'

They make their way to the small cabin located on the opposite side of the compound where the two Murphys are patiently waiting, chaperoned by Dinkel.

They knock and enter.

'Ah, Mr Finnegan, how'd you go, sir?' Eamon says, rising from a chair, all smiles and humility.

'Ahem, you're clean.'

'Now, didn't I tell you so? And your boy here,' he nods at Dinkel, 'has gone over all my paperwork, haven't you lad?'

'That's right, boss,' he says, glancing nervously at Frank. 'All present, correct and up to date.'

'I see. I apologise for wasting your time, Mr Murphy. These things happen, occasionally,' he adds, throwing Zac a dirty look.

'Don't apologise, Mr Finnegan. You have a job to do. Wires must have got crossed somewhere.'

'Yes, it appears that way. Right, we won't take up any more of your time.' Frank turns to leave, but not before he takes in the layout of the cabin, his eyes searching like a hawk. He stares at Fergus, sitting at the far end in the small kitchenette. 'Doesn't say much, your lad, does he?'

Eamon shoots his son a glance. 'No, not my Fergus. Always been a quiet boy.'

'Good day, Mr Murphy, and once again apologies for the misunderstanding.'

'Not a worry, inspector, not a worry.'

Frank and Dinkel descend the steps and head across the yard as Zac sidles up to Eamon Murphy.

Towering over him, he lowers his head and whispers, 'I know you're up to no good, Murphy. You're on my radar.'

Murphy tries to smile, but it ends in more of a grimace as Zac leaps down and jogs across the yard, catching up with the others.

'They're up to something, Frank.'

'Aye, I know, but what?'

Dinkel is unsure. 'His paperwork was all legitimate and if the sniffer dogs didn't detect cannabis, then maybe they are innocent.'

Frank stops and turns to him. 'Under normal circumstances, your naturally trusting nature would be a charming personality trait, constable.'

'Thank you, sir,' he says, beaming.

'But you're a police officer, and there are *no* normal circumstances in our line of work. Your inherent belief in the good of people, always giving them the benefit of the doubt, is a serious chink in your armour. It's a chink you need to iron out, and fast, lad. Did you notice anything odd inside the cabin?'

He pulls a frown. 'Not really. It was grubby, unkempt with a lot of dirty pots.'

'You didn't spot the condiments and food stuff?'

He touches his face. 'Condiments?'

'Aye. Soy sauce, fish sauce, rice wine vinegar, bags of dried noodles, tins of coconut milk, an empty bowl with remnants of rice in it. Not the usual fare for good old-fashioned Irish folk. They like their tatties and cabbage.'

'Maybe they fancied a change.'

Frank loses patience and walks on. 'You're on the money, Zac. The conniving toerags are up to mischief. But if they are growing cannabis, they're not growing it here.'

41

Prisha raps hard on the glass door of Prescott and Hill Domestic Electrical, with DC Kylie Pembroke at her side. Behind them in a van are two forensics officers, waiting for the okay.

'It is Saturday morning,' Kylie says. 'He may not be at work.'

'That's okay. If he's not in, I'll call a locksmith. We have the warrants we need.'

Kylie studies her for a moment. 'Are you okay?'

'Yes. Why?'

'It's just...'

'Just what?'

'I don't know. You seem a little preoccupied.'

'I'm fine,' Prisha replies curtly, as she bangs on the door again and tries the handle. 'Locked.'

The sound of a diesel engine has them spinning around. They appear to be in luck as a white utility truck pulls up on the forecourt. Nick Prescott clambers out, his face a mixture of weary surprise.

'Ah, inspector, back again so soon?'

She's in no mood for pleasantries, brandishing the warrant, she declares, 'Mr Prescott, I have a search warrant for your workshop. If you could open up, please.'

He groans. 'You've got to be kidding me. What the hell's going on here?'

Prisha has no intention of divulging her suspicions backed up by Jake Hill's phone records and video security footage. 'The door, if you don't mind. It's the weekend and, quite frankly, I have better things to do. The sooner we get this over and done with, the better.'

He pulls a jangle of keys from his pocket, fumbles one into the lock and pushes the door open.

'What exactly are you looking for? And don't say my business partner because he's not here. I don't suppose you've found Jake?'

As Prisha enters, she turns back to the road and nods her head towards the two forensic officers in the van. 'No, Mr Prescott, we have not found Jake Hill, but I suspect you already know that don't you?'

Nick Prescott is feeling confident. He's sitting in his office, feet on a desk, happily smoking a cigarette as Prisha, gloves on, meticulously pulls open drawers, filing cabinets and searches in boxes.

An hour has passed since they first entered the workshop, and no incriminating evidence has been discovered.

'Come on, love, get a wriggle on. I'm playing darts at one o'clock and I want to go home and get washed and changed. In fact, if you tell me what it is you're after, maybe I could help?' he says, taking another drag on his ciggy, voice dripping in sarcasm.

His cockiness infuriates Prisha. *You smug bastard.*

Kylie enters the office and stands behind Prescott. She surreptitiously shakes her head, indicating "no" they haven't unearthed anything.

Prisha glares at Prescott. 'Thank you for your cooperation, Mr Prescott. Our investigation into the disappearance of your partner is ongoing.'

'Aye, good luck with it,' he replies, lazily rising from his chair, unconcerned.

Prisha and Kylie walk out into the storage area as the two forensic officers are busy at the far end of the building inspecting a chest freezer.

Prisha stops and gazes upwards. The workshop is a basic shed, with metal rafters and horizontal purlins supporting the roof.

She points at the dozens of orange plastic piping resting on the purlins. 'What are those?'

Prescott follows her gaze. 'Conduit, love. For underground cables.'

She turns to Kylie. 'Did you check them?'

Appearing embarrassed, she replies, 'No, I didn't.'

Prisha scans the room and spots a set of steps. 'Ladders, please.'

Kylie quickly grabs the ladders and splays them out, fixing the safety catches in place. 'You want me to go up?'

'Yes. Use a torch and look inside each one. I'm going to have one last look around.' Half glancing at Prescott, she notes his cocky demeanour has subsided, somewhat.

He's nervous.

Wandering over to the forensics officers, she notes by their body language that something has piqued their interest.

'What have you found?' she asks.

One officer lifts the lid on the large freezer. Prisha is instantly accosted by the overpowering smell of bleach and disinfectant. 'The inside is clean. I've sprayed it with luminol, which reacts with iron in haemoglobin, causing a blue luminescence that is visible in the dark. But nothing showed up.'

'And?' Prisha prompts.

The officer points at the rubber seals on the lid and top edges, then switches on her UV, or black light, shining it into one corner.

'You see the very faint luminescence? Blood doesn't fluoresce under UV light, but certain substances mixed with it can cause a reaction visible under UV.'

'Other substances?'

'Sweat, urine, semen, saliva,' the officer elaborates.

'Hmm... okay. Get a swab and I want it fast-tracked for DNA analysis.'

'It's the weekend, ma'am. And I'd need a higher authority to...'

'I don't care if it's the King's birthday, I want it fast-tracked. If necessary, I'll get Chief Constable Overland to authorise it. Understood?'

'Yes, ma'am. I'll see what I can do.'

'Thank you.'

Prisha returns to the ladders and stares up as Kylie painstakingly shines the torch into each pipe of conduit.

'Nothing so far,' she calls down.

Prisha notes that Prescott has another smoke in his mouth, but this time he doesn't appear to be enjoying it as much. She looks up, studying the plastic tubing, and one pipe in particular catches her eye.

'That one on top, the one with a cap on the end—untwist the cap and take a look inside.'

Kylie dutifully obliges. Her face scrunches, as she leans forward. Delicately, she places her hand inside the tube, grabs something and pulls it out, holding it aloft.

'Looks like the pipe is packed with the stuff, ma'am,' she exclaims, beaming.

Prisha smiles as she turns to Prescott. 'Mr Prescott, would you like to tell me why the plastic pipe is packed with wads of fifty-pound notes?'

He takes a long, slow drag on his cigarette, puffs out a plume of blue smoke into the air, and replies, 'No idea. Nowt to do with me, love.'

42

Prisha enters the incident room as Zac emerges from the kitchenette, sipping on a coffee.

She performs a neck stretch, which emits a satisfying crack. 'I heard Operation Fun Guy was under-cooked. Maybe your intel was shiitake?'

Zac scowls. 'Ha, ha. You need to work on your delivery. And for the record, we may not have found any cannabis, but there was a fuel pipe sticking out of the ground. It had diesel residue on it.'

'The hijackers?'

'Possibly. But it is a registered farm.' He looks around and lowers his voice. 'How are you holding up with this Creepy Crawley thing hanging over you? It must be a nightmare.'

She swallows hard. 'I'm good at compartmentalising. At the moment, my brain is occupied with work. I won't allow that sleaze to put me off my game. It's a battle, Zac. A mind-game war zone. The winner will be the one with the strongest willpower.'

He chortles and pats her on the shoulder. 'Poor old Crawley. I don't fancy his chances.'

She spots Dinkel in the corner of the room, opposite Kylie, diligently beavering away. 'What's he working on?'

Zac considers him with an air of impatience. 'The missing persons investigation. I told him it was a window-dressing exercise, so we could issue a press release to appease the relatives and media, but the little sheep worrier won't let it go. Got a bee in his bonnet about something. It's keeping him busy, which means he's not hassling me. How did you go with Prescott?'

'He's in custody. We've collated a lot of evidence against him, thanks to some good work from Kylie during the week. I'll leave him in the cells to stew overnight and interview him early tomorrow. How's Frank's mood after the unsuccessful raid?'

'He's like a pan of water slowly simmering on the stove.' Zac looks over Prisha's shoulder. 'Eh, up, here's the old bulldog now.'

Frank closes his office door and marches into the room, clapping his hands in an urgent manner.

'Everyone gather round. Let's have a debrief on all the cases we've been working on, then call it a day. I've better things to do on my Saturday afternoons. I have an allotment in need of my attention. By the way, Dinkel?'

'Sir?'

'I have a job for you first thing Monday morning. Just had a call from a supervisor, Mark Ruskin, at Northern Lights Electricity Distribution. They've identified an illegal tap on one of their overhead power lines. Looks like someone's sucking a lot of juice out of their system. Details are sketchy, but the illegal draw is somewhere on the moors. Seems to be a bloody hot-spot of illegal activity at the moment.'

'I could look into it this afternoon, sir.'

Frank eyes him warily. 'Have you not got a home to go to, lad?'

'Yes. I live on...'

'Doesn't matter. Right, Prisha, you do the honours.'

'What?' she asks, her mind digesting Frank's last statement.

'The debrief,' he shouts.

'Oh, sorry, yes.'

Dinkel and Kylie join Frank and Zac in front of the whiteboard as Prisha pulls up a bullet-point brief and proceeds to read the list.

'As you can see from the board, last week we had four *apparently* separate cases to deal with. Number one. Last Friday night a tanker carrying a full load of diesel was hijacked and stolen, leaving the driver Gareth Atkin in hospital with a fractured skull and out of a job. I spoke with Gareth's wife earlier and she said Gareth's now stable and doing well and his appetite has returned. So, that bodes well.'

'Number two. Last Saturday night one of Zac's informants, Declan Hughes, was waiting for his weed supplier to turn up, a man named Bo-Bo, at a car park in Runswick Bay. Bo-Bo never showed, but three other gentlemen did. Declan said he witnessed the men remove a tarpaulin out of the back of their car, carry it to the beach and put it into a motorised rubber dinghy and head out to sea. He believed there was a body in the tarp.'

'Number three. On Monday morning a human leg was uncovered on Tate Hill Sands, later identified as belonging to Jake Hill, an electrician from Guisborough, partner in a firm called Prescott and Hill Domestic Electrical. His business partner is a man named Nick Prescott who is now in custody. We believe Prescott has either murdered Jake Hill or had a hand in his murder and subsequent disappearance.'

'Number four. After staking out a drop off from Declan's supplier, Bo-Bo, Zac and I followed him to Top Moor Mushroom Farm a few miles east of Rosedale Abbey. A very isolated spot. We suspect he received a plastic bag containing two kilos of weed. Earlier today, the farm was raided on the suspicion of being a front for a cannabis operation. Unfortunately, not a trace was found.'

'Okay, things to consider. The oil tanker hijacking; Gareth Atkin said his attackers had Southern Irish accents. Declan Hughes, who thinks he saw a body wrapped in a tarp, said two of the men spoke and both had Southern Irish accents. And lastly, the mushroom farm is owned and run by Eamon Murphy and his two sons, Cillian and Fergus, and surprise, surprise... they have Southern Irish accents.'

Zac leans back on a table and folds his arms. 'The Irish accents could be circumstantial. They do suggest a connection but are not conclusive on their own.'

Frank nods in agreement. 'Correct. There are plenty of Irish folk around this neck of the woods, so let's not rush to conclusions. Just bear it in mind.'

'I totally agree,' Prisha says. 'But there were three men at Runswick Bay. Gareth Atkin said there were two hijackers, but possibly a third was driving a transit van. And there are three people involved with the mushroom farm. So, let me play devil's advocate for a moment. Let's suppose the Murphys are involved in the tanker incident, the body in the tarp, and are growing weed somewhere. It raises these questions: what did the Murphy's want with forty-thousand litres of diesel; who was in the tarpaulin—was it Jake Hill or someone else; and if it was Jake Hill, then what is the Murphys connection with Nick Prescott?'

Frank huffs and straightens. 'Excellent. Plenty of food for thought. Well done everyone. Okay, let's wrap this up for today.'

Dinkel raises his hand in the air. 'Mr Finnegan, sir?' he asks expectantly.

'What is it lad?'

'I have an update on the missing persons investigation.'

Frank glances at Zac, who merely shrugs. 'Okay, lad, let's hear it, but keep it brief.'

Dinkel takes command of the whiteboard and pulls up a large ordnance survey map of the North Yorkshire Moors. Superimposed over the top are a number of coloured circles with interconnecting lines.

Nervously, Dinkel points at the map with a ruler. 'I've been indulging in a spot of amateur geo-profiling, sir.'

'Have you by-gum. You want to be careful you don't do yourself a mischief.'

'Sorry?'

'Forget it. Carry on.'

'The green circles represent the departure point for our three missing men—the villages where they lived. The red circles signify the intended destination. I drew a straight line from each man's departure point to their intended destination.'

Frank nods. 'I can see that. What's the orange circle in the middle?'

'It's the point where all three lines roughly intersect. It's not a perfect hit, but it's within a mile or two.'

'And what does it signify?'

He shuffles awkwardly, embarrassed. 'Well... I'm not certain, yet. But it was something Zac said the other day that got me thinking.'

'Don't drag me into this,' Zac says. 'You're on your own, sunshine.'

'He mentioned an army could disappear on the moors because they're so vast and desolate. And of all the possible dangers; potholes, caves, old mineshafts, bogs. What if somewhere near the epicentre of the connecting lines there's a hidden danger that is unknown about, and all three men stumbled upon it?'

Frank juts his chin out. 'Highly unlikely. Ordnance survey maps are meticulous at detailing natural and man-made features. If there was a hidden shaft or a quagmire out there, then I'm sure it would be on the map.' He notices Dinkel's crestfallen face. 'But, well done lad. You may be onto something. Ten out of ten for initiative. Right, everyone...'

'One more thing, sir?' Dinkel says, interrupting.

Frank's patience is at breaking point, but he does well to mask it. 'Go on?'

'If you take a closer look at the epicentre...'

Frank takes a step forward and squints at the map. 'What am I looking for, exactly?'

'The epicentre is roughly four miles east of Rosedale Abbey.'

'I can see that. And?'

'And roughly one mile east of the Murphys' farm.'

A faint smile brushes across Frank's lips. 'I'll go to the foot of our stairs. You're right, Dinkel!'

43

Sunday 16th July

Prisha and an excited Kylie Pembroke march toward Interview Room Two in the custody suite.

'How are we going to play it?' Kylie asks, her verve obvious. 'I've interviewed lots of low-level offenders before; drunks, pushers, kids who have nicked things, but this is my first murder suspect.'

Prisha, with a heavy cloud hanging over her, is abrupt. 'He's not a suspect. The bastard has done it. And we're going to nail him.' As they stop outside the door, Prisha relaxes, and reflects for a moment, noting her junior partner's masked apprehension. 'I'll lead. You keep quiet and take notes. It unnerves them. If you spot something which doesn't add up, tap your finger twice on the table, subtly, and I'll shut up as you put forth your concerns. Mainly, watch the body language for any telltale signs of what upsets him.'

Kylie hits the record button and reads out the obligatory caution, reminding Nick Prescott of his rights. She resumes her seat as the duty solicitor carefully adjusts his pen and notepad on the table.

Prisha flicks her manilla folder open. 'Mr Prescott, did you kill your business partner, Jake Hill?'

———◦———

The interview drags on for over an hour.

Prisha is tired and stressed, but at least this form of tedium prevents her from focusing on the bigger worry—Magnus Crawley.

Deliberately holding back the most damning evidence until last, she feels Prescott is now suitably relaxed and confident... over-confident. Now's the time to make his world come tumbling down.

'Okay, Nick, let's go over it again. Fifty thousand pounds in used notes was found in an electrical conduit tube in your workshop. You said you know nothing about the money, yet your fingerprints have been found on many of the notes. Can you explain that?'

His assured, thin smile says it all. 'Listen, love, if you went and rounded up all the fifty-pound-notes in North Yorkshire I'm certain your fingerprints would be on some of them. Money changes hands. Simple as that.'

'And you can't explain why the money came to be in your workshop?'

'As I've said, time and again, I know nothing about it.' He leans forward and clasps his hands together. 'Look, all I can assume is it must have been Jake's little stash. I'll admit that sometimes we'll knock the VAT off customers' bills if they pay us in cash. I've done it myself, many times. The customer pays less—they're happy. I don't have to declare it to the tax office, so I save on my tax bill at the end of the year—I'm happy. It's just a little bonus. It's a win win. It's hurting no one.'

'It's tax evasion and VAT fraud, Mr Prescott.'

He holds his arms out in front of him. 'None of your business, though, is it?'

'No, but I'm sure my colleagues in the Fraud Squad would be interested, and of course, our friends at HM Revenue and Customs.'

'I'm sure they would... if they could prove the money was mine, which they can't. So, I'm in the clear.'

She'd like to reach across the table and punch him on the nose but remains poker-faced.

Pulling a photo from the folder, she slides it across the table. 'Exhibit A. For the recording, a photograph of a large chest freezer located in Mr Prescott's workshop. Can you tell me about the chest freezer?'

He tenses ever so slightly. 'What about it?'

'Where did you get it from?'

A scratch of the chin. 'We rewired a butcher's shop a few years back. Can't remember exactly when, or who the customer was. The butcher had the freezer in the back yard. It was still in good condition, but he was getting rid of it. We paid him twenty quid to take it off his hands. We thought we'd keep it in case one of our customers ever needed one. Small business is tight, love. You need to make a few extra quid where you can.'

'It was exceptionally clean inside. Smelled of bleach and pine disinfectant. Had you cleaned it recently?'

'Had a bit of a spring clean a fortnight ago.'

'It's the height of summer, Mr Prescott. Little late for a spring clean.'

'You know what I mean.'

'Forensics took swabs. A small amount of blood was detected in the rubber seals on the lid.'

Shrugs again. 'What can I tell you? It belonged to a butcher. Probably animal blood.'

'You're right, it was animal blood. The animal in question being human. Not only human, but the DNA profile matches that of Jake Hill, your business partner. Can you explain that?'

'No, I can't. Maybe Jake had a cut or scratch at some point.'

'We've checked Jake's phone records and banking details. The last transaction he made was on Tuesday June sixth at 4:43 pm; some shopping from Tesco. The last telephone call he *received* was also on Tuesday June sixth, at 7:38 pm. Since then, there have been no further calls or banking transactions.'

'As I said, he told me he was going to New Zealand because his lad was in hospital after being involved in a cycling accident.'

'I spoke with the New Zealand Police, who located his ex-wife Zoe. Jake's son is called Harry. He is alive and well.'

'Glad to hear it.'

'Harry was never involved in an accident.'

'Really?'

'Yes, really. Also, when we visited your workshop last Tuesday, you said you'd last spoken, or at least received a text message from Jake, five weeks prior.'

'That's right.'

'Which would have roughly been June sixth—the same date as his last call and bank transaction.'

'So?'

Prisha leans forward. 'Do you remember you showed me the text message you'd received from Jake?'

'What about it?'

'The message was date-stamped as Monday July third, 11:30 pm, which is four weeks later than you indicated.'

He stretches his neck and adjusts his seating position. 'Are you sure? To be honest, I do get mixed up with my dates and times.'

'You also said that Jake's son, Harry, had been in a cycling accident. The text message did mention his son had been involved in an accident, but there was no mention of a bicycle.'

He sits upright and folds his arms. 'I just assumed that's what it was. Jake was always telling me how his lad liked to go off cycling. I must have put two and two together.'

'I see. So just to be perfectly clear; Jake's phone and bank accounts had no activity since June sixth. Then suddenly, on July third, he sends you a text message, which you somehow thought was from a month earlier. It's all a bit iffy, isn't it?'

'I got confused with my dates, that's all. June, July, they sound similar.'

'Yes, easily done I suppose.' She pulls a sheet of paper from her folder and slides it across the desk. She taps at the sheet with her finger. 'This telephone number here. Can you confirm it's yours?'

He studies it briefly. 'You know it's mine. What about it?'

'You remember me talking about the last voice call Jake received was on Tuesday June sixth, at 7:38 pm?'

'Yes.'

'It was from your mobile phone. What was the call about?'

He coughs, straightens his arms, then folds them over his chest again. 'We, erm, I thought someone was trying to break into the workshop, so I called Jake to tell him to meet me there. Didn't fancy tackling the buggers alone.'

'Why didn't you call the police?'

He scoffs. 'Yeah, right. Waste of bloody time. You might have got there a day or two later.'

Kylie taps the table with her finger. Prisha gives her a slight nod.

'Mr Prescott,' Kylie begins, 'you said your workshop was being broken into and you rang Jake to ask him to meet you there, correct?'

'Aye, that's right.'

'And where were you when you made the call?'

'Where was I?'

'Yes.'

'I was, ahem, in the workshop. Working late doing the books.'

'Let me get this right. You're working late, alone. Your vehicle would have been outside, and you thought you heard intruders. You didn't want to confront them single-handedly, so you called Jake. Is that correct?'

'Yes.'

'And did Jake arrive?'

'Yes. Within ten minutes or so.'

'And the intruders?'

'False alarm, or possibly kids climbing the back fence to retrieve a ball or something.'

'Then what happened?'

'We locked up and went our separate ways.'

'And that was the last time you saw Jake in the flesh?'

'Yes.'

'You drove home and Jake returned to his home?'

'I went home, yes. Can't vouch for what Jake did.'

As Prescott picks at imaginary fluff on his jumper, Prisha gives Kylie a slight wink and mouths the words—now.

Kylie lifts the lid on the laptop and positions it so Prescott and his solicitor can see it. 'Did you know Jake had a security camera at his house?'

Utter shock rips across his face. 'No, he didn't. He'd talked about installing a system but he'd never got around to it.'

'Not true. Sunday June fourth, two days before the suspected break-in at your workshop, he installed a doorbell camera. We spoke with his neighbours who witnessed him doing it. I'm about to play you footage from the night of Tuesday, June sixth. There's a date and time stamp in the bottom left corner. The time reads 8:25 pm.' She hits the play button.

Prescott sticks one hand under his armpit and clasps his face with the fingers of his other hand.

'Hell,' he whispers.

44

Prisha finishes going over the facts with Nick Prescott. Even his solicitor looks convinced. Prescott, face hardened, arms folded tightly, stares into the middle-distance, avoiding eye contact. The sterile breeze-block room, painted white, is about as welcoming as cold, lumpy gravy served up for breakfast.

'I already have more than enough evidence to charge you with murder, Mr Prescott. Why don't you tell me the truth?'

'No comment.'

'You made a call to Jake Hill on that Tuesday night. It was the last call he ever received. You urged him to come to your shared workshop on the pretence of an attempted break-in. Jake Hill has not been seen since. You were captured on his own doorbell video camera, dropping his work van off in his driveway at 8:25 pm on the evening of June sixth. So, what happened to Jake, and what did you do with the body?'

'No comment.'

Prisha leans back in her chair and idly spins a pen around in her fingers. 'What I haven't figured out yet is the motive. I've a good idea what happened. You called Jake to the workshop where you killed him and stashed him in the freezer. At some point, weeks later, you disposed of his body at sea, probably weighted down. For whatever reason, the body floated to the surface and was hit by a boat propeller, severing the leg, which then washed ashore. But the motive still eludes me. You said you weren't friends, but that's no reason to kill someone. We've looked into your bank accounts, and you certainly aren't struggling financially. So why? That's the question.'

'No comment.'

'Of course, then there's the money. Fifty thousand pounds. Quite a haul. Especially to keep in a plastic tube in your shed. You say it must be Jake's, as it isn't yours. But you've lied about everything else and people follow predictable patterns, so I assume the money *is* yours.'

'No comment.'

'We've had some of the notes tested by forensics.'

For the first time, his eyes dart onto her for a brief second. 'No comment.'

'It wasn't a question, Mr Prescott.' She flicks her hair back. 'It was a random selection of notes, but every single one contained micro traces of cannabis. Are you a dealer,

Mr Prescott? A low-level pusher, supplementing your income selling a bit of weed?'

'No comment.'

She purses her lips and shakes her head. 'No, I don't think you are. You run a profitable business with a large client base. You wouldn't risk it all by selling drugs. So, where did the money come from?'

'No comment.'

'A one-off payment perhaps, for services rendered?'

He pushes back in his chair, creating a grating squeal. 'No comment.'

'But what services could you provide to warrant such a large pay-off?'

'No comment.'

'Maybe electricity theft. An illegal tap. Is that why Jake Hill was murdered? He found out about your illicit deal and wasn't happy about it. You were worried he'd go to the police, so you made sure he couldn't. Is that it?'

'No comment.'

'We're closing in, you know. On your associates, if they are associates. Just a matter of time.'

'No comment.'

Changing tack, she leans across the table, palms upturned. 'Look Nick,' she says, her voice gentle and caring, 'as it stands, you're going down for murder, premeditated murder. After all, you did lure Jake to the workshop. But something has been niggling away at me. I don't think you are a killer. For whatever reason, you became mixed up with some bad people. Are you going to sacrifice twenty years of your life for them? Do you think they'd do the same for you if they were in your shoes?' She snorts and leans back. 'No, of course they wouldn't. You're on your own now, Nick. No one's going to come to your rescue. The only person who can help you is yourself.' She pauses for a moment. 'Nick, look at me.'

His eyes swivel to meet hers. 'What?'

'I won't lie to you. You'll do time. Not sure yet what the charges would be; accessory to murder, perhaps. I'm sure there are mitigating circumstances in your defence. You've never been in trouble with the law before. Judges and jurors take these things into account. You may be looking at five to ten years. Half that for good behaviour. It's a damn sight more attractive than a twenty stretch with a minimum of eighteen. Remember what I said, the only person who's going to fight your corner is you. Do yourself a favour. What do you say? Shall we go over it again, from the beginning and actually get to the truth?'

He takes a deep breath, then sighs. 'Can you give me thirty minutes alone with my solicitor?'

45

As Nick Prescott takes time out with his solicitor, Prisha and Kylie grab a quick cup of coffee and a cinnamon swirl. They enter the incident room and spot Dinkel poring over a huge sheet of paper spread out over two desks.

The two women glance at each other and shrug.

'Morning, Dinkel,' Prisha says.

'Yes,' he mumbles, completely engrossed in his work.

The door bursts open and Zac strides in. 'Spank my arse! Look at you lot, gaming the system. Pretending you have important case work to attend to on a Sunday. Nothing to do with the overtime, eh?' he says with a chuckle.

Prisha and Kylie smirk. 'We're just about to get the truth out of Nick Prescott,' Kylie replies.

'Ah, I see,' he says, walking to his desk. 'Got him on the ropes, have you?'

Prisha shakes her head. 'He's not on the ropes. He's on the canvas and the ref is counting. What are you doing here, anyway?'

Zac unplugs his phone charger and holds it aloft. 'Forgot this. These things are like rocking horse shit in our house. The kids and missus are forever misplacing them.' Freezing, he peers over at Dinkel. 'What's Mr Bean up to?'

They both twitch and pull faces. 'Ask him?'

'Not on your Nelly. It's my day off and I want to enjoy it. Whatever he's doing, it's keeping him quiet, which can only be a good thing.'

'Zac, have you got a minute?' Dinkel calls out, finally pulling his eyes away from the sprawl of paper.

'Shite,' Zac whispers. 'Ahem, no actually, I don't have a minute,' he says, hurriedly striding towards the exit.

'It could be important. It's about the electricity theft. Yesterday I drove out to Northern Lights main power plant and spoke with...'

'Really?' he replies sarcastically. 'I'm sure it can wait until tomorrow.'

'But I have a plan.'

'To quote Robbie Burns; the best laid plans of mice and men often go awry.'

'Not that sort of plan. It's a layout of an...'

'Tomorrow, Dinkel, tomorrow.'

'But...'

'Tomorrow!' he yells as the door slams behind him.

Dinkel turns to the women. 'Prisha...'

'No. Not interested at the moment. Me and Kylie need a few minutes R and R to gather our thoughts. We could be on the cusp of a full confession.' Prisha looks at her watch. 'Actually, we better get down there. The thirty minutes he wanted with his solicitor are nearly up. Always best to strike while the iron is hot. Give him too much time and he may change his mind.'

As Prisha and Kylie depart, Dinkel purses his lips, annoyed, then turns his attention back to the plan laid out in front of him.

'I'll show them. Damn rotters.'

———◦———

Nick Prescott's cocky demeanour has vanished. The deep creases etched into his weathered face have always been there, but now appear more ingrained.

'Let's start from the beginning, Mr Prescott,' Prisha says.

He expels air and places his palms on the table. 'It started with a telephone call about six months back. Some guy rang and said he had a big job and was I interested. I asked him what sort of job, but he wouldn't discuss it over the phone. Said he'd make it worth my while. We arranged a meeting in a pub, out on the moors.'

'What was this man's name?'

'He didn't say.'

Prisha groans. 'Oh, come off it, Nick. A guy rings you up and arranges to meet you at a pub and he doesn't have a name?'

'I swear. When I asked him, he said it was best for all concerned that he remained anonymous.'

'Describe him?'

'White. Early sixties. Tall, lean, Southern Irish accent.'

Prisha and Kylie exchange glances

'And what was the pub called?'

'The Lion Inn, Blakey Ridge,' he replies wearily.

Kylie leans in. 'Near Rosedale Abbey?'

'Yes.'

Prisha jots something down in her notebook. 'And what happened at the pub?'

'He bought me a pint, then told me the job was illegal, but didn't specify what it was. It would be worth fifty thousand in cash. Twenty-five upfront, the rest when the job was completed. I told him I'd think about it. At first, I wasn't interested, but then as the days passed, I thought what have I to lose by at least seeing what the job was. We met at the same pub again. This time, he had two other guys with him, a lot younger. They told me I'd need to wear a blindfold. Said it was in my interest not to know where I was going. I was apprehensive, thinking they might be dodgy, and that they were going to drive me somewhere remote and put a bullet through my head. Then I told myself not to be so ridiculous. I didn't know them from a bar of soap. They drove for about forty minutes, then took me out of the car and took the blindfold off. It was in the middle of the wilds. An access track, you know, for maintenance crews to check on overhead power lines. I used to work for Northern Lights, the power distribution company, many moons ago, in the field. I had an inkling straight away what they were up to. We walked to this one pole and he, the old fella, said he wanted to tap into the power. They'd provide a cherry picker and pay for any tools or equipment I needed. Then I noticed there was an old distribution board on the back of the pole. I realised that at some point in the past, there must have been an electrical connection in place. The board was knackered, and I told them it would need replacing. But all up, I knew the job was quite easy. Maybe a half-day's work. For fifty grand it was like all my birthdays had come at once.'

'Surely it would have been extremely dangerous connecting an illegal tap when the lines were energised?'

'Working with electricity is always dangerous. But if you know what you're doing, and take adequate precautions, then you're reasonably safe. You're dealing with physics, science. There's no unpredictability involved.'

'Did you ask where the power source went to?'

'I did, yes. They said I didn't need to know. The strange thing was, there was not a building or farm as far as the eye could see. We did the job late one night about three weeks later. They had all the gear; a generator, lights, cherry picker. I replaced the distribution board, then made the tap to the power lines. Tested it all, and that was it, job done. Easy money, although I realise now they were paying for my silence more than my work.'

'Did your partner, Jake Hill, know of it?'

He shakes his head. 'No. Not at first. Jake is...' he pauses, downcast. 'Jake *was* pretty straight. He'd never do anything dodgy. Fifty thousand quid is a lot of money to hide. I knew I couldn't put it in the bank. And I couldn't take it home in case the missus found it. She'd have wanted to know where it came from. She's another one who plays it down the line. So, I stashed it in the conduit at the workshop until I figured somewhere better to hide it.'

'And Jake came across it?' Prisha prompts.

He rubs a hand across his cheek. 'Aye, about six weeks back. Wanted to know where I got it. I told him about the illegal tap and he blew his top. Said that if the police found out, then he'd be tarred with the same brush. Really flipped his lid. He told me to go to the police and confess all, otherwise he would.'

'And that's when you decided to kill him?'

Shock ripples across his features. 'What? No, it wasn't like that at all. I might come across as tough, but I've never hurt a soul in my life. I panicked and rang the Irishman, explained my dilemma. He was quite calm. Said that Jake just needed an attitude adjustment, and that he and his boys would take care of it. We picked a date, and that's when I called Jake and told him about the break-in and asked him to come to the workshop. The three Irishmen were already there, waiting for him. The older guy warned Jake that he better keep his mouth shut, otherwise.'

'Otherwise, what?'

'At that point, I assumed they meant they'd give him a beating.'

'How did Jake react?'

'Not good. He wasn't intimidated at all. He could be a hard-nosed bugger at times. He got angry and told them he was going straight to the police. One of the younger ones pulled a knife on him. They wrestled, fell, and the knife went into Jake's chest. He was dead within seconds.'

'And how did you react?'

'I was horrified. The old guy took charge of the situation. He said if we all kept mum, then no one would ever know. We put the body in the chest freezer, on ice, to dispose of at a later date. I knew Jake was a real loner so he wouldn't be missed for a few weeks, and we also wanted to buy a bit of time because of the security cameras.'

'Security cameras?'

'Yes. The old guy told me to drive Jake's van back to his house. I told him Jake's neighbours might have cameras installed and it would capture me dropping his van off. Then I thought about it. I have security cameras at home. The footage is stored in the cloud, and after thirty days, it's wiped automatically by my service provider. I said if we kept Jake's body in the freezer for five weeks before disposing of it, then we should be right.'

Prisha raises her hand, appearing a bit confused. 'Hold on, let me make sure I understand this. You figured that because Jake was a loner, no one would notice he was missing for at least a month. So, you preserved his corpse in the freezer for five weeks, thinking that by then, any neighbours with security cameras would have had their footage from the previous month automatically overwritten or deleted?'

'Yes.'

'And you weren't aware Jake had installed a door-cam, and his service provider keeps the footage for sixty days?'

'No.'

'I see. Okay, back to the night in the workshop. What happened next?'

'We cleaned up the blood, and the Irishman said after five weeks they'd dispose of the body at sea, weighted down and it'd be never found. And without a body, then you can't be charged with murder.'

'That's a common misnomer, Mr Prescott.'

'Is it?'

'Yes. So, you drove Jake's van back to his home and left it there to avoid suspicion, to make it look like he'd gone on holiday?'

'Something like that.'

'And the cryptic text message about his son and the bicycle accident?'

'I still had Jake's phone, and one night I got pissed. I was brooding about everything. I thought if I sent a text message, it would look like it came from Jake. God knows how I forgot to mention the bike accident. It was a ploy to muddy the waters if the police came calling.'

'But surely, at some point, you would have had to contact the police regarding the disappearance of Jake? He ran a business. He'd have an accountant, and tax returns to file. You couldn't have possibly hoped that no one would miss him?'

'I was going to leave it about ten weeks, then raise my concerns with the police. If that bloody leg hadn't washed up on the beach, then no one would be any the wiser.'

'You seem more concerned with your failed plan than the life of Jake Hill, an innocent man who was murdered and his body disposed of in the most callous of fashions.'

'Hang on, I've explained. It wasn't murder. It was an accident.'

'Luring a man to his death is not an accident. Pulling a knife on someone and getting into a fight is not an accident. Dumping a body at sea is not an accident. Trying to cover your tracks with a false text message is not an accident. You may not have intended to kill Jake that night, but everything you did following his death was premeditated. You may not have been Jake's executioner, but you signed his death warrant. For the recording, I'm suspending the interview for a thirty-minute recess.'

———◦———

As the two officers reach the top of the stairs, Kylie stops and looks at Prisha.

'Is this how it always feels?'

'You were expecting elation and a sense of triumph, weren't you?'

'Yes.'

'But instead, you feel sad, angry, empty, haunted.'

'Yes.'

'Once the initial euphoria dissipates, it's the way you'll feel when you get a confession to murder. Welcome to my world.'

46

Monday 17th July

The clock on the wall is toying with Prisha. Occasionally, when glancing at it, the second hand appears reluctant to move, like a sleepy dog on a warm day, lazing on a patio. When she next looks, the minute hand has jumped forward a quarter of an hour as if in a rush to get somewhere.

Her eyes swivel from the clock to the investigation board. Her excitement from yesterday, after the Prescott confession, and the way the four different cases were moving into alignment, orbiting the same satellite, is now a forlorn memory. She slept badly, forever waking in a clammy sweat, hoping, praying it was all a hellish nightmare, until reality slapped her in the face.

Zac sidles up to her. 'So, you're going to let the snivelling bawbag get away with it?' he says in a forced whisper.

'I don't have any bloody choice, do I? This is my decision. It's my life on the line.'

'I want to wring his skinny, bloody neck. The simpering streak of putrid, parrot piss.'

'Keep your feelings under control. There's nothing anyone can do. At least by agreeing to his demand, I can buy some time. Quiet, here's Frank.'

Frank emerges from his office and studies the investigation board, beaming. He looks at Zac and Prisha, then beckons them over.

'Well done, gang. Things are moving along nicely. Keep on top of it.'

'Boss,' they reply in unison.

He stares at Prisha. 'You feeling all right, lass?'

'Yes. Fine. It's just a little warm and stuffy in here.'

'You look like you've been dunked in a bucket of bleach. Any problems?'

'No. All good.'

His eyes narrow. 'You wouldn't be keeping anything from me, would you?'

A nervous laugh. 'As if.'

He switches his attention to Zac. 'And you look like you've fallen into a barrel of tits and come out sucking your thumb. You've got a face as long as the Humber Bridge.'

'I'm fine.'

'I see. You're both fine?'

They nod. 'Yep,' Zac says. 'You?'

Frank's eyes flit suspiciously between his two officers. 'Aye, fair to middling. But you two buggers know more than you're letting on, like the monkey who drank the tea.'

That particular saying is a new one, even to Zac, who is well versed in Frank's cryptic Yorkshire proverbs. They both offer a sheepish smile and say nothing.

'Well, I can't hang around here all day with you two chewing my ear off. The superintendent should be here any minute. Got a meeting with her and that Crawley fella.' He grimaces and checks his wristwatch. 'Actually, they both should have been here a few minutes ago. Hmm... anyway, I'll make the Super aware of your steady progress on the cases. She may even bestow her gratitude upon you, but then again, don't hold your breath. If she had a mouthful of gumboils, she wouldn't offer you one.' He turns on his heels and heads back to his office.

Prisha shoots Zac a glance. 'The monkey who drank the tea?'

He shrugs, as confused as her. 'I swear to god, I don't have a bloody clue.'

She gazes around the office. 'Where's Dinkel, by the way?'

'He's gone over to Catterick Garrison.'

'Why?'

'Not sure. He's sulking again. But he says he's going to reveal all very shortly. I can barely contain my excitement.'

She reflects. 'I think we've been a bit mean to him lately. We've all been so preoccupied. I haven't deliberately shunned him.'

'I have.'

'Stop it. That's cruel.'

He laughs. 'Cruel to be kind.'

'What do you mean?'

'I've wet-nursed him long enough. He needs to be weaned off the titty at some point.'

'What a delightful expression.'

'And it's working. He's now nutting things out for himself and taking the initiative. So, you see, what you perceive as my callous indifference towards him is, in fact, the opposite. I'm helping the little turnip groper become a proper detective.'

Prisha's eyes nearly pop out of her head. 'Damn,' she hisses. 'Superintendent Banks has just walked in.'

Prisha keeps her head down as Banks strides towards Frank's office and closes the door behind her.

Zac checks the time. 'What's Crawley's game? It's 9:40. I thought he said he'd be here by 9:30?'

'He did. Probably all part of his play. The puppeteer, pulling the strings, messing with my head.'

'I'd like to mess with his head with a sledgehammer. Twat!'

'Zac, if you really want to help me, then let go of the anger. It's not helping. I have no one else to lean on or confide in. I need you to be here for me, a safe harbour. Your anger is making me even more anxious.'

He nods, contrite. 'Okay. Sorry. It's just...'

'I know. What's the old saying? Don't get angry, get even.'

'Christ, you're turning into Frank.'

They share a brief laugh, which, for a few seconds, alleviates the tension.

Prisha pretends to get her head stuck into a report, but it's merely a ruse as she awaits the arrival of her tormentor. It's impossible for her to focus on anything else apart from her impending appointment with horror.

Almost an hour passes before she notices a flurry of movement from Frank's office.

He sticks his head out from the doorway. 'Anyone seen Magnus Crawley this morning?' he shouts. He receives a muted response and a lot of head shaking. 'Bloody odd.' He disappears back inside.

Prisha feels physically sick. She's eaten barely anything since Friday night. She sees Frank staring at his mobile before he emerges from his office accompanied by the superintendent.

'It's not important, Frank,' Superintendent Banks says. 'Magnus said it was a brief catch up to let us know how he was progressing on the case. I can speak to him later by phone.'

'Nevertheless, Anne, it's a bit bloody rude not to let you know where he is.'

'It doesn't matter, really. He could be chasing up a lead. Right, I must head off. I have a working lunch over in Scarborough with some bigwigs from the Met.'

'Sounds like fun.'

'It's a presentation on how they're tackling knife crime in London.'

'Ah, I see.' They offer each other their farewells and Banks departs.

Frank turns to Prisha. 'Oi, Prisha, give Crawley's hotel a ring and see if they've seen him this morning. If not, pop over there and check his room, make sure he hasn't choked to death in his sleep.'

'Really?' she says, appalled at the thought of entering his lair. 'Can't you just ring his mobile?'

'I have. It's switched off.'

'Can't Zac go?'

'If I'd wanted Zac to go, I'd have asked him, wouldn't I? Now come on, chop, chop, look lively.'

47

Prisha pushes at the revolving doors of The Royal Hotel and enters the reception area, which is decked out in plush blue carpet. Taking a deep breath, she marches up to the desk and addresses a young woman behind the counter, flashing her warrant card as she does so.

'Good morning, I'm DI Kumar from CID. I rang earlier regarding a colleague who's staying here, a Mr Magnus Crawley?'

'Ah, yes. It was me you spoke with,' the woman replies with a friendly smile.

'Still no sign of him?'

'No. I called his room and sent the porter to knock on his door, but he received no reply. He entered the room, but Mr Crawley wasn't there. I also checked the security system to see when his card was last used to access the room. His card hasn't been used since Friday afternoon.'

'That's odd.'

'I was on reception on Friday and exchanged a few words with Mr Crawley as he left the bar area and entered the lift.'

'What time was that?'

'Late afternoon, around four-thirty.'

'I see. And how long is he booked in for?'

'Another week, but he did indicate he may extend his stay, without being definite.'

'Hmm... can you let me into his room?'

'Certainly. If you'd like to take a seat, I'll call a porter.'

The lift pings as the doors swoosh open. Prisha follows the porter down the corridor. He pushes a card into the door lock. There's a click, and he opens it for Prisha to enter.

'Thank you. If you could give me five minutes. I want to have a quick look around to see if he's left any message or indication of his whereabouts.'

'Certainly, madam.'

As the door clunks shut, she experiences a flutter of butterflies in her stomach. She turns her nose up and squirms.

The room is impeccably tidy. Not a stitch out of place, as she anticipated. She enters the bathroom and gazes around. Toothbrush, aftershave, deodorant, razor. He certainly intends coming back, she thinks. Throwing one last disgusted glance at the toothbrush, she allows herself a wry chuckle.

'One toothbrush for sale; careful owner, barely used.'

Having poked around in the wardrobe and bedside tables, she sees nothing untoward.

'The slimy prick probably stayed somewhere else over the weekend. Maybe on his quest to find Tiffany or Kira, it led him further afield, or possibly he went back down to London.'

Noticing the writing desk tucked away in a corner, she ambles over and opens the top drawer.

'The Dell laptop.'

She pulls a pair of latex gloves from her inside jacket pocket, slips them on, then removes the laptop, noticing a manilla folder underneath. Intrigued, she places it on the desk and opens it.

Flicking through, she realises it's the official case notes and reports from the Tiffany Butler—Kira Volkov case. She stares at a photo of Tiffany for a moment, then a shot of Kira. Placing the images back, she rifles to the end of the file. 'Bastard,' she hisses as she picks up her own bank statements, paying particular attention to the one item on her credit card, circled with a green highlighter—the cost of the taxi fare. 'You got these illegally, so I am rightfully taking back what is mine.'

Folding the sheets, she slips them into the back pocket of her pants. She realises it changes nothing. If she doesn't agree to Crawley's demand, his theories, and evidence will be enough to convince her superiors to launch an investigation. But still, it gives her a modicum of satisfaction to think she's wandering around, with impunity, inside his warped, little, think tank. How he'd hate that.

Walking over to the bed, she drops to her knees, peers underneath and spots a slim flight case. She pulls it out, unfastens the latches, and lifts the lid. Another laptop, this one matte black and very heavy. There are no manufacturer logos to be seen.

'Hmm... this must be his official work laptop,' she muses. She places it back under the bed.

After a thorough search, she fails to locate the memory stick he held up as a threat on Friday evening. But then again, if he never returned to his room that night, then obviously the USB drive must still be on his person.

Puzzlement and her natural inquisitiveness returns. 'What's your game, Creepy Crawley?'

With nothing else to glean, she exits the room.

Prisha steps from the revolving doors of the hotel and emerges into bright sunshine. She's in desperate need of a shower. The miasma of Crawley's personality clings to her like stale cigarette smoke.

She lingers on the pavement, pulls her phone out, and rings Frank.

'Prisha, anything?'

'No. His keycard hasn't been used since last Friday afternoon.'

'No diary or notes to indicate where he was going?'

'Nothing. Have you checked with his office back in London?'

'Yes. He hasn't been in touch since he left last Monday. If this is a wild goose chase, I'll kick his bloody arse when he surfaces. We've got enough on our plates without coddling the secret bloody service. Why is there always trouble when they show up?'

'Not sure. Listen, Frank, I'm going to take an early lunch. I need some fresh air. Is that okay?'

'Aye, course it is. I said you were looking a little peaky. Speak soon.'

She slips the phone away, saunters up the road, and turns left onto North Terrace. As people go about their day, she experiences a feeling of envy mixed with melancholy. Walkers with backpacks saunter along without a care in the world. A gaggle of children disembark from a coach amidst a cacophony of shrieks and laughter. An open-topped bus offering Whitby town tours glides by, packed with smiling tourists. An elderly couple walk a dog in a haphazard fashion, back and forth. Cars, vans, taxis trundle by. All she sees is grey. All she hears is an amorphous hum.

Anguish is always private.

Without realising it, she finds herself on the walking track above West Beach, ambling past the iconic beach huts. They stand in a cheerful line, each one painted in a different vibrant colour; red, yellow, blue, green, before the pattern repeats. Prisha barely notices them, seeing nothing but monochrome.

She spots an elderly man, sitting on a chair outside one of the huts, scrutinising the canvas on an easel.

Stopping, she admires his painting. 'You're very good. You've really captured the sea and the horizon. It's beautiful and yet, you've also managed to encapsulate the potent danger that always lurks within the water.'

The man offers her a creased smile. 'You're humouring an old man,' he replies with a throaty chuckle.

'No, I mean it. How long have you been painting?'

'Coming up for five years. Took it up after the wife passed on. I grieved long enough. At some point, you just have to get on with it. There's no other option, is there?'

'I suppose not. I'm sorry to hear about your wife. How long were you together?'

'Fifty-nine years, and twenty-six days.'

'You must miss her terribly.'

'Aye, I do that, lass. In life, as in painting, we're given the colours on our palette. It's how you blend them that matters.' He makes a small, deft touch with the tip of his brush to the landscape, then sighs heavily. 'She never felt sorry for herself. That wasn't her way. She always said that if you see yourself as a victim, then you give away your control. And my missus liked to be in control,' he adds with a wry laugh. 'Even when she was having treatment for her illness, she chose to be the strongest version of herself she could be, focusing on the joy of the moment, not the pain. To her, it was a choice. She knew she couldn't win the war, but she won some bloody hard battles along the way.' He lays his brush on the palette and gazes at her. 'So, what's it to be?'

She frowns. 'Sorry, what do you mean?'

'It's plastered all over that face of yours, as plain as day. Are you going to play the victim or are you going to take back control?'

A sudden flashback plays in her mind; the night she and Tiffany were captives in the Hawsker Lighthouse. The ogre, Maxim, was about to rape then murder her. But she took back control. If she could win that battle, she could win this. A gentle wave of euphoria and confidence builds inside her.

With fierce determination, she replies, 'I'm going to take back control.'

His smile is deep and warm. 'Good lass. Yer'll be reet, mark my words. Remember what they say, the darkest hour is the one before dawn.'

Her eyes fall on the beach huts behind him. They are ablaze in all their dazzling, multi-coloured glory.

Her appetite has returned with a vengeance. Climbing the steps at the station, she bites into her second Cornish pasty and washes it down with a slurp of strong black coffee. On hearing the rush of feet on concrete coming down the stairwell, she looks up, surprised, and stands to one side as Zac and Dinkel hurry towards her.

'What's happening?' she asks.

Zac appears distinctly unhappy. 'A car in the river.'

'Whereabouts, exactly?'

'Near the wooden sculpture, next to the site of Fishburn Shipyard.'

'Any other intel? Are there any bodies in it?'

'Possibly. Frank asked me and Dinkel to attend.'

She now understands his grumpiness. 'I see. Don't get sidetracked. We've got enough to do already with the other investigations.'

His reply is curt. 'Yep.'

'Oh, Zac,' she calls out as they hit the ground floor, 'any sign of Crawley?'

'No.' His voice echoes coldly off the harsh walls.

48

Zac exits the car, and waves to Charlene Marsden. She's already kitted out in protective gear behind the chequered police barrier tape. She waves back and saunters over.

'We must stop meeting like this, Charlene,' Zac says. 'People are beginning to talk.'

Laughter lines mingle with her wrinkles. 'I'm old enough to be your mother.'

'No way. Older sister, maybe, but not mother.'

'Charmer.'

He carefully retrieves the protective shoe coverings and awkwardly slips them onto his feet. 'What's the go?'

Charlene points at a tow truck which is reversing towards the river. 'We're about to pull the car out now. Then we'll make a start.'

'Body?'

'Yes. It's been confirmed by one of the divers.'

'Male or female?'

'Not certain yet. The river is very murky and the diver couldn't be definite.'

'Any tyre marks?'

'None noticeable. If the car had gone over the edge, there would have been tread marks.' She turns and points. 'You can't see it because of the truck, but there's a slipway into the river. First guess is that's where the vehicle entered the water. We've taken extensive photographs and video footage of the area, so we'll be able to zoom in and confirm the entry point.'

'Possible suicide?'

She waggles her head from side to side, signifying doubt. 'It's possible, but drowning is rare, even more so when trapped inside a vehicle. Drowning accounts for less than four per cent of fatalities.'

'Medical episode?'

'Again, possible, but unlikely.' A weak grin curls the corners of her mouth. 'Are you worried about your workload, Zac?'

He rolls his eyes. 'Too bloody right. I blame Frank, myself. Ever since he returned to work, it's gone ballistic. What's the make of the car?'

'A Vauxhall Corsa.'

A flurry of voices drift in the wind from the SOCO team, followed by a hand signal to the driver of the truck.

'Here we go,' Zac says, pulling on latex gloves.

Charlene turns and ambles off. 'I'll let you know when we're ready for you. Probably in about a half hour,' she calls back.

Dinkel exits the passenger seat and stretches, groaning. 'Ooh, ah.'

Wearily, Zac gazes at him. 'What's your problem?'

'Aches and pains. I signed up for a boot camp. It started last night. I was put through my paces and now I'm feeling the consequences,' he explains as he launches into a series of less than enthusiastic star-jumps.

'Stop that, you moron. You're at a possible crime scene. Someone has lost their life. The last thing we need is a picture of you splashed across the front page of the Whitby Gazette doing your Jane Fonda workout as a body is pulled from the river.'

'Sorry.'

'Thirty minutes before we can have a butchers.'

'What?'

'I said... never mind. How did you go at Catterick?'

He sticks his nose in the air and turns away. 'You'll find out soon enough.'

They focus on the tow truck as the whirring of the hydraulic winch starts up. Zac ambles to the left to obtain a better view as the car slowly emerges from the depths. A police diver raises his arm and the tow truck moves forward, dragging the car carefully up the ramp until it rests on the level. Another signal from the diver and the truck reverses a few feet to release the tension on the cable.

There's a flurry of activity and the truck drives off to the side, allowing Zac a bird's-eye view of the scene.

'Dinkel, run the number plate through the PNC and get an ID on the registered owner.'

'Wilko, Roger Daltrey that, sergeant.'

'Shut it.'

'Right. Got that.'

Dinkel slips back into the passenger seat as Zac watches on.

'Christ, what am I doing here? I have enough to focus on, plus Prisha's nightmare. I don't need this,' he grumbles.

A few minutes tick by before Dinkel emerges from the car, rubbing the back of his head

Zac barely turns to him. 'Well?' he enquires.

'Well what?'

'The CAR! Who is it registered to?'

'Erm... the car isn't registered to an individual.' He pauses.

'Go on.'

'It's registered to a leasing company.'

'And?'

'It's a pool car for an organisation.'

Zac has no other choice than to turn his head and peer down upon Dinkel. 'What is this? A game of twenty-fucking-questions? Which organisation is leasing the vehicle?' He rubs at his face, agitated. 'It shouldnae be this hard,' he laments softly.

'Ahem, I called them, but they wouldn't say. Client confidentiality.'

'Did you tell them who you were, and you're investigating a suspicious death?'

'Yes.'

'Did you breathe fire and fury down the line and make it clear in no uncertain terms that obstructing a police investigation is a criminal offence?'

Dinkel kicks at the ground. 'I did say, please,' he mumbles.

Gobsmacked, Zac blinks rapidly and waggles his pinky finger in his ear. 'Say that again. I think I may have misheard you.'

'I did say...'

'I heard you the first time,' he snarls. 'There's a time for, please, and there's a time for veiled threats and intimidation. Guess which option you should have used?'

'Veiled threats and intimidation?'

'Correct. You need to learn some street smarts and quickly, Dinkel, for all our sakes.'

Zac ducks under the barrier tape and trots up to the vehicle.

Charlene frowns at him. 'Bit eager, sergeant.'

'I have an uneasy feeling about this.'

'Why?'

'The car's leased to some organisation.'

'So?'

'The lease hire company is reluctant to divulge who the organisation is.'

'Oh, I see. All hush hush.'

'Possibly. I need to see the occupant.'

'Okay. Stand back a little, otherwise you'll end up with wet feet.'

The diver pulls open the front door of the car as a flood of water gushes onto the ground. As it recedes and flows down the slipway into the river, Zac edges forward.

He stoops and peers inside.

'Christ,' he murmurs.

His eyes move from the face of the victim to the seat, then to the footwell.

'Fuck!' He jumps back as if zapped by electricity and tries to quell the urge to vomit.

49

The atmosphere in Frank's office is tense.

Jaws cannot literally drop to the floor. And yet, the chins of Prisha and Frank are in serious danger of incurring carpet burns.

'You're shitting me?' Frank whispers.

'I shit ye not,' Zac replies.

Prisha's mind is a kaleidoscope of swirling thoughts. She collapses into a chair and stares blankly at the carpet. 'I... I...'

The sentence is aborted before birth.

Frank drags his palm back and forth over his stubble. 'Are you a hundred per cent certain?'

Zac pulls his phone out and shows him the photo. 'You can't forget a mug like that in a hurry.'

Frank emits a muted groan as he notices Superintendent Banks pull up in the car park, exit her vehicle, and stride towards the entrance of the station.

'Incoming ballistic missile,' he warns as the others follow his gaze. 'Dinkel, put the kettle on and make everyone a cup of tea. I think we're all in need of sustenance.'

'Sir.'

'And try not to break anything.'

By the time everyone is nursing their brew, Superintendent Banks enters the incident room and marches straight into Frank's office, a pocket battleship ready for action.

'I dropped everything as soon as I read your text message, Frank. Are you certain of this?'

'Positive, Anne.' He nods at Zac. 'I'll let you explain.'

'Me and DC Dinkel were the first investigating officers on the scene once a body had been spotted in the vehicle. Earlier, uniform attended the site after a member of the public reported a submerged car in the river. The vehicle was towed out of the river via a slipway; a black Vauxhall Corsa. Dinkel ran the number plate through the PNC. It was registered to a leasing company who wouldn't divulge their client's name. I then inspected the car and instantly recognised the occupant.' He gulps and licks his lips. 'Then I saw the *thing* in the footwell, between his feet.'

'The thing?'

'Yes, ma'am. The tongue. According to Charlene, she *thinks* it was bitten off. Something to do with the ragged edges and possible teeth marks.'

'Good grief,' she replies, stunned, as she takes a seat. 'Could he have bitten it off himself as he panicked?'

'Possible, ma'am. The body was removed and is now at the mortuary, awaiting Dr Whipple's attention. I dare say he'll be able to tell us more about the tongue after his examination.'

'Anything else?'

'Yes. A small metal wedge was inserted in the seat belt locking mechanism.'

'Meaning he wouldn't be able to release the belt?'

'Yes, ma'am. Whoever was in his car, they'd planned it out in advance.'

'And we're assuming that after the tongue was bitten off, the assailant or assailants pushed the car down the slipway into the river?'

'It looks that way. The back windows were fully wound down, ensuring the car would sink quickly. Speculation, but I'm assuming with the flow of the river, and the ebb and flow of the tides, the car would have been shunted back and forth. We're not exactly sure where the original deposition site was. Uniform are performing house to house at the moment.'

'Can people still scream when they've had their tongue bitten off?'

'I posed the very same question to Charlene, ma'am. Apparently, it's possible. But they wouldn't be able to articulate, meaning it would be guttural. She said the mouth would quickly fill with blood, making it harder to scream and, of course, the natural instinct would be to open the mouth to get rid of the blood.'

'Meaning as he entered the water, he probably had his mouth open.'

'More than likely. A clever, if barbaric, tactic to ensure a quick drowning.'

Banks closes her eyes and shakes her head at the horror before focusing. 'It beggars belief. How did he not notice the killer fouling up the locking mechanism on his seat belt? Any defensive wounds on his hands or arms?'

'Not to the naked eye, although I only saw his hands.'

'It appears he put up no resistance. Which would indicate he may have already been unconscious. But then why sabotage his seat belt?'

'That one's a mystery at the moment. I dare say we'll know more after the post-mortem and toxicology report. And a couple more oddities; his seat was fully reclined.'

'As you would when taking a power-nap?'

'Well... yes.'

'Bizarre.' She hesitates for a moment, cogitating the information. 'And the second oddity?'

Zac shuffles uncomfortably. 'Ahem... his fly was undone.'

'His fly?'

'Yes, ma'am. It's the zipper on...'

'I know what a damn fly is, sergeant,' she snaps. 'What are you suggesting?'

He grimaces and glances at Frank, who nods his approval. 'Ma'am, it would suggest to me he may have been playing solitaire, you know, paying a visit to Sister Palmer and her five lovely daughters, on the sly, and he was caught unawares. Or possibly he was in the company of another person who was burping the worm for him—so to speak.'

Anne Banks frowns. 'I didn't get any of that, sergeant,' she states, turning to Frank for an explanation.

He throws Zac a disapproving glance. 'I think what Zac was trying to allude to, in his cack-handed, gormless way, is that he may have been masturbating alone, or indulging in sexual activities in the company of another person, ma'am.'

She pouts. 'Why didn't he bloody-well say that instead of speaking gibberish?' she snaps, scowling. 'Do we know his sexuality? Was he gay? Could he have been compromised by a rent boy?'

Prisha raises her head. 'Oh, he was not gay.' She instantly regrets her remarks.

Banks stares at her. 'And how did you form that impression?'

'Just a feeling, ma'am.'

'A feeling? Did he make advances towards you, inspector?'

'Not advances, as such. But he made crude remarks dressed in ambiguity. I'm sure you've encountered such individuals during your time on the force.'

'Hmm... yes. I know what you mean.' She returns her focus to Zac. 'Any forensics?'

'Too early yet, ma'am. Charlene and her team are still at the scene.'

'Are you totally sure about this? Was he checked for ID?'

'Yes, ma'am. His wallet contained a driver's license and counter-intelligence ID. It's definitely Magnus Crawley.'

The expression on the face of Anne Banks is one of confusion. 'It doesn't add up. Why would a man of Crawley's considerable experience, a former field operative, highly revered for his analytical skills and weeding out corruption, make so many mistakes?'

Frank takes a sip of lukewarm tea, then glowers at Dinkel. 'Christ, lad. That tastes like witch's water. I like builders' tea. Thick enough to stand a spoon up in it.'

'Sorry, sir. Would you like me to make you another?'

'No. I would not.' He shuffles papers on his desk. 'Now, where were we? I'm not sure whether I'm Arthur or Martha since I got back.'

'The death of Magnus Crawley,' Zac prompts.

'Aye. Magnus Crawley.'

Anne purses her lips. 'Frank, what was the latest update Magnus gave to you?'

He shrugs. 'He hadn't given me an update. As you know, he was supposed to be here this morning to brief the both of us.'

Banks turns to the others. 'When was the last time any of you saw or spoke with Crawley?'

Dinkel lifts his hand in the air, an annoying trait to everyone. 'I have never spoken to him, ma'am.'

'Zac?' she says, turning sideways.

He shuffles awkwardly. 'I briefly bumped into him on Friday evening as I entered the incident room,' he explains. 'I nipped out to get some food for me and Prisha. I saw him on the way out, and when I returned, he was leaving.'

'How long were you gone?'

'Ten, fifteen minutes, max.'

'And who else was in the incident room?'

He attempts to mask his rising compunction. 'Ahem, only Prisha... Inspector Kumar, ma'am.'

Anne fixes Prisha with a blank stare. 'Well, inspector, as you may well have been the last person to see him alive, apart from his killer, did he say anything illuminating?'

'Nothing of any note.'

'He didn't update you on the Tiffany Butler, Kira Volkov investigation?'

'No. I formed the impression he was a man who liked to keep things close to his chest.'

'He must have said something. Why was he in the office? I thought he liked to conduct his investigative work from his hotel room?'

She shrugs. 'To be honest, ma'am, we've been up to our eyeballs with the other investigations. I really didn't pay much attention to his coming and going. I visited his hotel this morning. The last time he accessed his room was Friday afternoon.'

Frank, suspecting something is not quite right, intervenes. 'The spot where his car was retrieved from the river is secluded on a night. It has all the hallmarks of a rendezvous. Maybe he was meeting an informant or someone who had a tip-off for him.'

His remark distracts the Super from her line of questioning. 'Yes, you could be right.' She rises and brushes down her jacket. 'Right, so where are we at? Have you informed MI5 yet, Frank?'

'No. Zac and Dinkel only just got back from the crime scene not long before you arrived. I suggest you liaise with MI5.'

She nods. 'Yes. Leave it to me. And what about his belongings, his laptop, paperwork?'

'Still in his hotel room.'

'Okay, send someone to seize everything from his room and wear protective gear. We don't want cross contamination. Then hand his laptop and any other devices over to digital forensics and see what they can find.'

'I think we need to take a step back for a moment, Anne. Fools rush in, and all that.'

The frown is instant. 'What does that mean? This is a murder investigation, Frank. We need to act fast to ensure the integrity of potential evidence.'

'Under normal circumstances, I'd agree. But he was an operative for the secret service. Who knows what state secrets he has on his laptop, phone, or anything else. I'm not sure the bigwigs at MI5 would be too pleased if we accessed classified documents pertaining to national security before they did.'

Always attuned to the complexities of politics, she puckers her lips and hesitates. 'Hmm... fair point. Seize his belongings and store them in a safe location until I've had a chance to discuss the matter with the deputy director of MI5. I'll be in my office if you need me.' As she makes her way to the door, she stops and gazes back at them. 'I may as well tell you all while you're here. You'll find out soon enough. I threw my hat into the ring for the vacant position of deputy chief constable. I was informed an hour ago I'd been unsuccessful.'

Frank groans in genuine dismay. 'Oh, I'm sorry to hear that, Anne. Did they give a reason?'

'They used weasel words and skirted around the issue, but reading between the lines, they think I'm too old. Ironic really, considering the outgoing chief constable, Gordon Critchley, turned seventy a few weeks back. I'm ten years his junior. They said they wanted to skip a generation and have someone who was more in tune with the younger members of the force.'

'Did they say who?'

'No. An announcement will be made at 3 pm.' She pulls at the door. 'I've booked next week off, Frank, to consider my future. Good work, everyone.'

They watch on in silence as she makes her way across the incident room towards the exit.

There's a moment of embarrassed silence as each person considers the implications.

Frank rises from his seat as his mind returns to the job at hand and the unusual behaviour of his best officers, Prisha and Zac.

'Right, Dinkel, back to work,' he grizzles.

'Sir.'

He waits until Dinkel has departed the office, then glares at Zac and Prisha. 'As for you two—I want a quiet word.'

50

Prisha glances at the photo hanging on the back wall of Frank's office. It pictures him as a young man in his prime, bedecked in boxing gear, post-fight, holding a championship belt above his head. He sports a massive lump above his right eye swollen to nothing more than a slit. His muscular frame glistens in sweat as he sports a wide, handsome beam, only slightly marred by the white mouthguard. As Zac takes a seat beside her, she surreptitiously throws him a sideways glance, shakes her head, and mouths the word—no. In return, he grimaces, as if pleading. Prisha's eyes widen, indicating—*definitely*, no.

Frank flops into his seat and gazes back and forth between them.

'Okay. Cut the crap. What's going on?' he demands in a stern, fatherly tone.

'Nothing's going on, Frank,' Zac states, as innocently as he can muster.

'Prisha?' Frank's eyes fall onto her.

'I don't know what you mean, Frank.'

His voice hardens. 'Do I look like I was born on the back of a bloody bus? You two are hiding something, and I want to know what it is. What's been going on?'

Their mouths momentarily dip, betraying a flicker of deceit.

Prisha innocuously brushes her cheek. 'Really, Frank, nothing has been going on, has it Zac?' she explains, turning to him.

'No. Nothing apart from hard bloody work and sleepless nights.'

Frank's flinty stare feels like a lifetime. Finally, he harrumphs. 'I see. Like that is it. Bonnie and Clyde. Fine. Have it your way.' Their sense of relief is evident, but it's short-lived as Frank leans across his desk. 'But remember this,' he whispers. 'If the shit hits the fan and blindsides me, then there's nothing I can do to help you out.' He pushes back in his seat. 'Right, go on, get on with it, and catch me some lowlife. But first of all, I want both of you to go to The Royal Hotel and collect Crawley's belongings. Wear gloves. Then get it recorded, tagged and stored in a secure location. And take plenty of photos of the room. I don't want the MI5 mob thinking we're country bumpkins.'

'Yes, Frank,' Zac replies.

As they exit, a slight smirk flits across his face. 'Thick as bloody thieves. It's not a bad thing, I suppose.'

In the incident room, Zac is less enamoured of the situation as he coaxes Prisha to the far end of the office, away from prying ears.

'Don't ever ask me to lie to Frank again. Got it?' he hisses.

Prisha is taken aback by the venom in his delivery but takes it on the chin.

'Understood. It won't happen again.'

'Good,' he says, relaxing.

She touches him on the arm, gently. 'Thanks, Zac. I'm not sure I'd have coped without you to confide in. Sharing something horrible seems to diminish its power.'

Instantly, he regrets his anger as self-revulsion swamps him. He offers her a sad smile. 'No worries. And what about you? One minute you're in the dungeon with the jailer about to slam the door shut, then he keels over and you're free to walk away.'

Her expression exhibits the opposite of his sentiments. 'Not quite. The memory stick. Crawley said he'd documented everything onto it. And he had a photo on his phone of my credit statement showing the taxi fare.'

'Forensics emptied, and bagged everything on his person, and from the car, and there was no USB stick and no phone. I was right there. The only thing they took from the car was a plastic carrier bag which contained rolled up fish and chip paper.'

A stab of hope shoots through her. 'Are you certain?'

'Positive.'

She studies the floor for a moment, thinking hard. 'The phone's not that important. The photo of the credit card statement didn't show the account details. All it showed was a transaction. It's the memory stick that's crucial. What happened to it? He had it in his hand on Friday night. He taunted me with it. He didn't return to the hotel so it can't be there, and I checked his room earlier.'

'Who knows? If it had a plastic football attached, maybe it floated from the car when the water rushed in. It could be on its way to Norway by now. Anyway, I'm certain seawater would make the phone and memory stick unreadable.'

'Not always. I worked on cases in the past where digital forensics were able to retrieve data from phones immersed in water. It's unusual, but it can happen.' Another worrisome thought bubbles to the surface. 'A more plausible explanation would be the killer took it.'

'You're becoming paranoid.'

'Maybe. And who is the killer?'

'I imagine Magnus Crawley made many enemies over the years. There could be a cast of hundreds who'd gladly see him dead. And you know what? Good riddance to bad baggage. I, for one, won't be losing any sleep over the sleaze-ball, and I certainly won't be busting a gut to find his killer if we handle the investigation. Although, knowing MI5's track record, they'll keep it in-house. If I were in your shoes, I'd draw a line under it. It's over.'

Prisha doesn't share his conviction. 'Yeah, I guess.'

Zac sports a mischievous grin. 'And promise me one thing, have nothing to do with that conniving bitch ever again.'

'Tiffany?'

'Who else.'

'I have no control over what that woman does. She's a law unto herself. But she did promise she'd never return to these shores again.'

'And you trust her?'

She laughs. 'As Frank would say, do I look like I was born on the back of a bus? I spoke to her on Friday night. Asked her to hand herself in and confess everything.'

'We can expect her to walk into the station any moment now, then?'

'Smart arse. She said no.'

'Of course she did. There's only one person in Tiffany's life and that's Tiffany.' Puzzlement creeps over his face. 'What time did you speak to her on Friday night?'

'When I got home, about seven. Why?'

'Did you tell her about Crawley's sexual blackmail?'

'Yes.'

'You don't suspect she could be...'

Prisha laughs. 'Definitely not. She's a lot of things, but she's not a killer.'

'She stabbed Maxim in the back of the neck with a knife.'

'At my behest and under extreme duress.'

'Where was she when you spoke to her?'

'London... well...' Pausing, she reflects. 'I assumed she was in London,' she adds as doubt surfaces.

'But she didn't specify?'

'No, she didn't.' She considers the possibility for a second before snuffing it out. 'Zac, you're being ridiculous. There's no way Tiffany would be capable of such an atrocity.'

'She's good at making problems go away, though, isn't she?'

'Hmm... she does seem to have a knack for it. Let's drop the subject. It wasn't her. It's not her style.'

'Fair enough. Shall we get back to work?'

A flicker of a smile. 'Yes. Let's do what we do best.'

From his office window, Frank withdraws his thick fingers from the Venetian blinds as the interaction between Prisha and Zac concludes.

'I bloody knew it,' he mutters, his mind swirling with imagined transgressions. 'Body language speaks louder than words.' His phone buzzes and as he sits back down, he gazes at the picture of Meera that fills the screen. 'Hell, today was her appointment with the specialist.' Barely daring to answer, he taps the button and tries to sound cheery.

'Meera, love. How'd you go?'

He closes his eyes and lets out a deep sigh as she replies.

———◇———

Prisha gazes around the hotel room, feeling decidedly icky. 'God, I hate this place. I can feel his presence.'

Zac drops the large cardboard box on the bed, then pushes open a window to let in fresh air. 'You're imagining it. But hardly surprising, considering what he put you through.'

'Can you do his clothes? I don't want to touch them. Oh, and his toiletries.'

'Aye, leave it to me. Why don't you have a wee nap on the bed whilst I do all the heavy lifting,' he says, grinning.

She stares disdainfully at the bed, her mouth downturned. 'Thanks for the offer, but I'll pass.' Kneeling on the floor, she pulls the flight case from under the bed. 'I think this is his official work laptop,' she says, placing it into the box as Zac hurriedly zips up a suitcase and throws it onto the bed.

'He travelled light,' he says, entering the bathroom carrying a toiletry bag.

Prisha pulls open the drawer of the writing desk and removes the personal laptop and manilla folder as Zac returns.

'The slime-ball had been here for a full week and the only intel he had in this folder was to do with me.'

Zac takes it from her and opens it. 'Did you check it earlier?'

'Yes.'

'And you removed anything incriminating?'

'Yes. All he had was the bank statements.'

'Good lass.' He pulls out a Swiss Army knife and flips the laptop onto its lid.

'Zac, what are you doing?'

He quickly begins to remove screws from the underside. 'I'm taking the hard drive. Crawley may have told you he collated all his evidence onto a USB drive, but let's make certain. I'll take the laptop home and dispose of it later at a recycling station. As for the hard drive, well, I'm treating my boys to a chartered fishing trip on Sunday.'

'And?'

He removes a panel and swiftly unscrews the tiny hard drive and holds it aloft. 'And this little beauty will be taking a well-earned rest at the bottom of the North Sea.'

Prisha is anxious. 'What if...'

'What if—nothing. MI5 won't know about his personal laptop, and even if they do, so what? It's missing. Maybe it was in the car with him and was washed away. No one will be any the wiser.' He tosses the laptop into the box on the bed. 'We'll carry it out in the box so it won't be seen on CCTV. I'll remove it when we're safely in the car well away from here. Right, all done. Let's get out of this place. You're right. It is creepy.'

As Prisha turns, she catches sight of a glass tumbler perched on the windowsill, a coaster neatly capping it like a makeshift lid. She holds the glass up, and stares at the tiny prisoner—a fly, belly up, legs splayed in the air in its final surrender.

51

Tuesday 18th July

DC Dinkel carefully affixes the large A1 sized sheet to the front of the whiteboard as everyone gathers round, a murmur of anticipation rippling around the office.

He's kept things close to his chest for two reasons. One, he wanted to do this alone to prove his worth; and two, he triple checked the facts to reduce the chance of making a complete tool of himself. Now it's his big moment. He turns and faces his colleagues, the weight of expectation bearing down on him. Consumed with a mixture of excitement and profound fear, he fidgets nervously, hoping he won't become hamstrung by anxiety.

Frank detects the young constable's barely contained panic. He places a firm hand on Dinkel's shoulder and whispers. 'I have faith in you, lad.' He winks and smiles. 'Take a deep breath and grasp the nettle.'

'Sir.'

Frank takes up a seat and makes himself comfortable. 'Come on then, lad, what have you got for us?'

Dinkel clears his throat, picks up a ruler, and stands side-on to the board. 'Before we dive into the details of the map, let me give you some background. On Saturday, workers from Northern Lights Power discovered an unauthorised connection on one of their overhead power lines. They first noticed some minor anomalies about six months ago, but the losses were small and were initially attributed to technical issues like earth leakage or insulation problems. However, in the last three months, the losses have gradually increased, which triggered a full investigation.'

'Northern Lights reported that last month alone, they lost about 300,000 kWh due to electricity theft from a specific section of their line. To put that in perspective, that's equivalent to the *annual* usage of around thirty domestic properties housing two adults and two children. If this trend continues, the losses could amount to a substantial figure annually, indicating a significant sustained theft operation.'

'The maintenance crew didn't disconnect the illegal connection—instead, they traced the line using ground penetrating radar. The trace led them across the moors for a good mile, where the line suddenly disappeared deep underground. They managed to get a GPS marker on the location before reporting it to us.'

Prisha lifts her finger up. 'During his confession, Nick Prescott said he was paid fifty grand to carry out an illegal tap about six months ago. And it was on the moors somewhere. More than a coincidence, I'd suggest. Sorry, carry on, Dinkel.'

'I visited Northern Lights HQ on Saturday afternoon and spoke with their Maintenance Supervisor to get more details. That's when I started putting the pieces together, which brings us onto Rosedale Nuclear Bunker,' he adds tapping at the floorplan with the ruler.

'This is the original plan of Rosedale bunker. It's a Cold War installation, once owned by the Ministry of Defence, located five miles east of Rosedale Abbey, right in the middle of the North Yorkshire Moors. I obtained a copy of the map from the archives of Northern Lights. The original wiring for the bunker was handled by the Central Electricity Generating Board, which was responsible for the national grid back then. I visited Catterick Barracks and spoke with the Military Archivist from the Historical Archives Department, who deals with the old military records. That's where I obtained the rundown on this place—when it was built, when it was decommissioned, and who bought it.'

'The main entrance is here,' he explains, touching the location with a finger. 'This opens into a tunnel, which runs under the moors for about a mile. The tunnel wasn't just a simple passageway—it was serviced by a light-rail system, which was used to transport food, water, personnel, and supplies directly into the heart of the bunker, which is located here,' he adds, indicating with the ruler. 'This entrance is hidden within the natural landscape, inside what was once known as St Hilda's Cave. According to the archivist from Catterick, this cave was deliberately removed from official Ordnance Survey maps in the late 1950s to keep it off the radar. No walkers, no caving enthusiasts, no accidental discoveries. They erected robust fencing around the cave entrance with warning signs about rockfalls to deter people entering.'

He moves the ruler along the map, highlighting the structure of the bunker. 'The bunker was built to house fifty people, with a total area of around 40,000 square feet. It has thirty individual bedrooms, two large ablution blocks, and a spacious, open-plan kitchen and communal dining area.'

He points to other sections on the map. 'The infrastructure inside is comprehensive. Originally, the bunker's power supply came from a legal connection to an overhead power cable. This fed into the power control room, the nerve centre of the bunker's electrical system.

Additionally, there's a generator room that housed four diesel back-up generators to ensure the bunker would keep running if the main power was cut off. There are also four bulk fuel storage tanks to hold the diesel, with a capacity of forty-thousand litres, per tank.'

Zac shoots a glance at Frank. 'The fuel pipe at the mushroom farm? And forty-thousand litres is around the standard volume for an oil tanker.'

Frank nods, thoughtfully.

Dinkel continues, pointing out other key areas on the map. 'The electrical switchgear room for managing all the circuits, a massive walk-in freezer and adjoining cool room, capable of storing months' worth of food, and a potable water storage area for drinking water. For recreation, they had a games room, a reading room, and a small gymnasium. There are also several large meeting rooms, and a medical centre, as well as many Ops rooms housing communications, maps, etcetera.'

He steps back, looking over the plan once more. 'What we have here is a self-sufficient underground facility, well-hidden under the moors. The fact they went to such lengths—removing St Hilda's Cave from maps, fencing it off, posting warnings—suggests they were serious about keeping this place secret. After it was decommissioned in the early 90s, it was sold off to a private company for £50,000. And here's where it becomes interesting—guess who bought it? One Eamon Murphy from Top Moor Mushroom Farm. And the tunnel entrance?' He leans forward and sticks a pin on the map. 'It's situated right here where their farm is located. The bunker would be the perfect place to run an illegal cannabis farm. And remember the geo-profiling I did the other day, where the three lines of the missing hikers intersected?'

'Aye. I remember,' Frank says.

'It's within spitting distance of St Hilda's cave, on the moors.'

Prisha nods thoughtfully. 'If our missing walkers were snooping around the cave, or even went inside and saw the entrance to the bunker, that could have put Murphy's whole operation in jeopardy. Once the news got out, there'd be film crews and YouTubers all over the place.'

'It's more than enough reason for murder,' Zac adds.

Prisha nods in agreement. 'And, as per Nick Prescott's confession, the Murphys aren't afraid of murder or disposing of bodies. Not that Prescott knew their names, but I'm more than convinced it's them.'

Frank rises and takes a step forward, studying the map, hands on hips. 'It all adds up. The Murphys buy a decommissioned nuclear bunker for a steal. Put up shedding and a security fence in front of the bunker entrance and engage in a legitimate farming business, which would also be handy for laundering money.

They knock-off diesel tankers every so often to fuel the generators. They run them at night as they can't risk using them in the daytime as they'd need an exhaust flue for the fumes, and I dare say, even underground, they may emit some noise. Any passing hikers would be curious. So, during the day they use electricity from the illegal tap. And from the increase in usage, I'd say they're scaling their operation up. And anyone who does come snooping around, they get rid of them. In a way, you've got to admire their ingenuity.' He turns to Dinkel and smiles. 'Well done, Dinkel. I told you we'd make a copper out of you one day. This is good old-fashioned police work.' He claps his hands together as the others join in the applause and offer their congratulations.

Dinkel flushes red, and visibly squirms with embarrassment, but can't control the wide, toothy grin.

'Thank you, sir.'

Zac sidles up to him and pats him on the shoulder. 'I'm proud of you, Dinks.'

'Ha, ha, very funny. Go on, where's the put down?'

Zac stares at him. 'No, I'm serious. This is bloody outstanding police work. Well done. I mean it.'

'Really?'

As Zac turns away, he says, 'Stop fishing for more compliments. Quit while you're ahead.'

Frank addresses his team. 'All right, gang, we have work to do. Tomorrow we're going to bring the Murphys to justice. It's going to take some planning, but plenty of hours left in the day. Prisha, Zac, you start drawing up a plan of who and what's required. We'll obviously need the armed response guys, K9 attack dogs, paramedics on back-up. Oh, and liaise with the drone unit. Tell them to get some shots of St Hilda's cave today. Let's have a look at the layout and terrain.'

'Where are you going?' Zac asks as Frank slips into his jacket.

'Unfortunately, I have an appointment with Dr Whipple at the mortuary. The autopsy of Magnus Crawley. Unless I have any takers for the job?' He's greeted with blank stares. 'Thought not.'

Zac cannot hide a smile. 'While you're there, Frank, ask Raspberry if he managed to get his back sorted out.'

'His back?'

'Yes. He's been suffering from lower back pain. I told him to pay a visit to Mandy's Massage Parlour.'

'You bugger. You didn't?'

Prisha chuckles. 'He did.'

Frank shakes his head. 'One day, Zac, that sense of humour of yours is going to come back and bite you on the arse.'

'Aw, come on, Frank. You've got to have a laugh now and again,' he replies, sporting a wicked grin.

52

As Dr Bennet Whipple places the liver onto the scales, Frank desperately tries to distract himself.

'What did toxicology have to say, Bennet?'

'Preliminary toxicology results indicate the absence of any significant central nervous system depressants, such as sedatives, opioids, or anaesthetic. There are no traces of substances that would likely cause immobilisation or unconsciousness. The victim's toxicity screen is essentially negative for anything that would have rendered him incapacitated before his tumultuous passing from this world.'

Frank ponders the response. 'I see. So, the poor bugger was presumably alive when he had his tongue removed and went into the water?'

'My job is not to paddle in the shallow pond of conjecture, or presumption, chief inspector. As you are well aware, I deal only in facts. I'll leave quantum leaps in reality, or illusion, to you.'

'Fair enough.' The slushy squish of the liver has Frank swallowing hard as he desperately searches for another topic of interest. Not an easy ask when speaking to Dr Whipple. 'Ahem... I heard on the grapevine you've become a part owner in a thoroughbred racehorse, Bennet?' he mumbles behind his face mask.

Whipple throws him a dismissive glance, his eyes doing all the work, as he slides his spectacles down to read the scales.

'Indeed, I have.'

'Wouldn't have picked you to be into the nags.'

'The nags, inspector, the nags!' His bass timbre ricochets off the hard surfaces of the pathology lab. 'My horse is not a nag. I can assure you of that.'

Frank shuffles uncomfortably. 'Keep your wig on, Bennet. No need to shout.' He pauses, then says, 'So, tell me about your horse.'

Whipple notes the weight of the liver, then lifts it out of the receptacle. It makes a sucking noise as it temporarily adheres to the stainless-steel tray.

Frank winces and wishes desperately he was somewhere else, as the doctor's eyes mist over, staring into space.

'The equine, in its majestic and resplendent glory, represents the pinnacle of terrestrial vertebrate evolution. These noble creatures, with their muscular conformation and aristocratic bearing, are a veritable embodiment of strength and grace. Their fluid locomotion and lithe carriage are not merely utilitarian attributes but are the very apotheosis of nature's artistry. To be part owner of such a thoroughbred, a paragon of excellence, is to be custodian of a legacy that transcends the mundane and ascends into the ethereal realm of the sublime.'

Frank scratches at his chin through his face mask. 'I see. And what's the name of this noble steed, if you don't mind me asking?'

Whipple's huge chest puffs out. 'A name which is befitting of its royal lineage—to wit—Ineptus Calceus.'

'You'll have to forgive me, Bennet, but I'm a bit hazy on ancient Greek?'

'That, Detective Chief Inspector Finnegan, is Latin, not ancient Greek!'

'Okay, okay, take a chill-pill.' Frank pulls the zip down a fraction on his protective suit and loosens his tie. 'Ahem, and the name translates to?'

'Clumsy Shoe.'

He takes a deep intake of breath. '*Christ.* I hope it's not a steeplechaser. Is it a he or a she?'

Whipple is whisked away to some Nirvana. 'Ineptus Calceus is a stallion, a creature of unparalleled vigour and robustness. This magnificent beast embodies the very essence of virility and noble spirit. With a mane like the finest silk and a gaze as penetrating as the morning sun, he stands as a paragon of hoofed fortitude. His gait, a harmonious symphony of power and grace, speaks to a lineage of unequalled pedigree and purity.'

Frank scratches his noggin. 'Hellfire, you are smitten, aren't you? Although, stallions can be hard to handle if they have a nasty temperament.'

Balancing the liver in one giant hand, he waves him away with a dismissive air. 'I can assure you, Ineptus Calceus is as calm as the serene waters of a still lake at dawn. His disposition as placid as a summer's breeze over an undisturbed meadow.'

'I see. So how did he go in his maiden run?'

'He distinguished himself in unique style,' Whipple replies, sticking his chin in the air. 'He finished fifth.'

Frank shrugs and waggles his head from side to side. 'Not too bad for his first outing, I guess. Big field, was it?'

'He competed with dignity and honour against four other aspirants.'

'You mean he came last?'

Whipple bristles. 'Ineptus Calceus deliberately ran within himself. He was almost laughing at the other contenders, a rag-tag bunch of chancers. He's young and naïve, inspector. Given time, he will not be embarrassed by his superior, indomitable strength, and spirit.' He places the liver in a transparent medical bag, seals it, then carefully replaces it into the body cavity of the cadaver. Having completed his gruesome task, which he is oblivious to, he stares sadly into space.

'Alas, my foray into the equine world has not been without calamitous rumblings,' he laments.

Frank is intrigued. 'Why's that?'

Whipple appears troubled, downcast. 'The wedded harmony in the marital abode has, of late, been somewhat... strained. In a moment of sentimental folly, I secured a lock from the mane of Ineptus Calceus, a token of esteem, you might say. This relic, I ensconced beneath my pillow, as a talisman of sorts.' He expels a rush of air, his face mask inflating violently. 'Alas, Mrs Whipple construed this gesture as an act of overzealous affection, a transference of, shall we say, more amorous energies typically reserved for marital confines. Her accusations, thinly veiled in metaphor, suggested I have an unnatural fondness for the beast, a devotion crossing the boundaries of decency, and I suggest—the law.'

'She's jealous?'

His eyebrows arch in surprise. 'You are very perceptive, inspector. Are you married?'

'I am. Very happily.'

Whipple moves closer and lowers his voice. 'Inspector, if I may be candid?' he whispers, as if being watched.

'Of course. Get it off your chest, doctor. Better out than in, as they say.'

'At present, I find myself navigating an enigmatic labyrinth when it comes to the fairer sex. In my empirical observations, women, splendid as they are, often exhibit a temperament not bound by the linear constraints of logical progression. Their thoughts and discourse, akin to a butterfly's flight pattern, seem to flutter capriciously from one blossom to another, seldom pausing to elucidate the intricacies of each stop. This spontaneous mode of perambulation, while undoubtedly charming, renders them a conundrum to my analytical mind. I confess, their reasoning often eludes my grasp.'

'Aye, they can be a bloody mystery,' Frank says, scratching the tip of his nose.

'In my matrimonial duties, I've endeavoured to be the quintessence of a provider—financially, intellectually, and, dare I say, carnally. Mrs Whipple and I engage in what I consider exhilarating traditional diversions; card and board games of a bygone era; Titicaca, bridge, occasionally, even tiddlywinks.' He sighs deeply. 'And yet, perplexingly, Mrs Whipple sometimes deems these pursuits somewhat... mundane. Despite my customary abstinence, we occasionally even partake of a modest libation, a low-alcohol vinous beverage, to add a frisson of excitement to our interplay. Yet, there are moments when Mrs Whipple exhibits a visage of dissatisfaction, a conundrum that vexes me profoundly, despite my manifold perfections.' He shakes his head in dismay, then fixes Frank with a puppy-dog stare. 'Inspector, with your more base, crude, grounded sensibilities, how do you decipher such cryptic feminine codes?'

'You're in the doghouse, pal. Maybe liven things up a bit. Take her to the cinema, a meal out, or buy takeaway fish and chips and find a nice spot on the promenade and relax, as the stars twinkle overhead, and the moon rises. But most of all—listen. It doesn't matter what they're talking about—just listen. I know it can feel like your life is ebbing away sometimes, but everyone needs someone to listen to them. Even if you're feigning. It's not hard to do. Ten, fifteen minutes a day and it will work wonders for your marriage and mental health. I dare say women find men as unfathomable as we find them.' He frowns for a moment as he contemplates his own words. 'Then again, maybe not. I think they have us sussed. Food, sex, sport, and we're happy bunnies. But if you take one thing away from this, Bennet, it's—listen.'

'Listen,' he repeats as if he's been handed the blueprint for perpetual motion. He threads a needle and begins to stitch up the cavity with a casualness that unnerves Frank, his hands working like a bespoke tailor.

As Frank watches on, he offers one more piece of advice; advice he realises he should employ more often, himself

'On your way home tonight, stop off and buy a bunch of roses and an expensive bottle of champagne. When you enter the house, whisk Mrs Whipple off her feet, spin her around, and plant a big smackeroony on her lips. Then take her out for a meal, anywhere she fancies. When you arrive back home, make unbridled love to her. And tell her you love her.'

Ceasing his surgical choreography, Whipple regards him with a blend of suspicion, incredulity, and disdain—a hard triad to achieve in one look.

'The guidance you initially proffered bore the weight of practical wisdom, inspector, yet this subsequent suggestion borders on the fantastical.'

Frank offers a nonchalant shrug, admiring the doctor's flawless suturing. 'Oh, well. Your funeral, not mine. By the way, what's your professional opinion on the tongue? Did Crawley accidentally bite it off himself, or was it someone else?'

'Ah, yes, the lingual organ, a most unacknowledged servant of the body.'

'Pardon?'

'The tongue, inspector, the tongue. It's in the kidney bowl on the table if you'd care to look.'

Frank does not care to look. 'No need. Seen one tongue, you've seen them all. If you give me a brief synopsis, in layman's terms, that will suffice.'

Much to Frank's annoyance, Whipple breaks off from his stitching and gathers the kidney bowl and places it under Frank's nose.

'Take a look, inspector. It is a marvel of muscular architecture! Composed of a complex symphony of intrinsic muscles that deftly alters its shape, and extrinsic muscles that propel it in myriad directions. It serves not only as the maestro of mastication and taste but also as an eloquent architect of speech and a subtle aide in respiration.'

'You don't say.'

'The glossal structure is securely tethered to the hyoid bone, mandible, and pharynx, among other anchors, and is divided by the sulcus terminalis into two distinct regions...'

Frank has no choice but to interrupt. 'Riveting stuff, Bennet, but if you could skip ahead to the main act, I would appreciate it.'

'Very well. The tongue in question provided quite the anatomical conundrum, at first. The victim did not bite off his own appendage in a paroxysm of terror. The bite marks are unequivocally those of a feminine set of dentitions.' Whipple pulls out a wooden paddle and prods and pokes at the tongue, then lifts it up in front of Frank's eyes. 'Observe the curvature, the delicate yet precise indentations, the spacing of the teeth—these are the hallmarks of a smaller, more refined mandible, indicative of the fairer sex. The angle and depth of the bite suggest considerable force, yet also a certain... finesse, one that a male jaw, with its brute strength, would lack. Hence, it is with utmost certainty that I posit our victim's tongue was severed by a woman's bite.'

Frank tries to laugh. 'Ha, ha. Quite literally the kiss of death.'

Whipple arches one eyebrow, clearly unimpressed. 'Au contraire, inspector. It wasn't the savage severing of the tongue that killed the victim. As I explained earlier, it was—'

'It was a joke, Bennet.'

Whipple places the kidney dish down with exaggerated care and returns to the body, his tone stern. 'Hmm... a pathology lab is no place for levity, inspector, especially when one is engaged in the solemn study of the lingual organ and its fatal disunion.'

'Pardon me for breathing,' Frank mutters under his breath.

The esteemed doctor finishes stitching up the cavity and sighs heavily as he gazes upon the inert form of Magnus Crawley.

'Peculiar,' he whispers.

Frank notices the change in demeanour. 'What's peculiar?'

A shadow crosses Whipple's usually impassive features. 'In my extensive career, it is rare that I have encountered a sensation so profoundly unsettling.'

'Sensation?'

'Yes,' Whipple continues, his tone laced with a mix of fascination and repulsion. 'This lifeless vessel before us exudes a palpable aura of malevolence, defying all rational scientific explanations. My acquaintance with him does not extend beyond these four walls, and yet...' His voice dwindles into silence, contemplative.

'And yet?' Frank encourages.

Whipple fixes his eyes on Crawley once more, concluding with a weighted certainty, 'And yet, it is unmistakable that his soul harboured intentions most foul. This man had a thread of evil wrapped around his blackened heart.'

Frank nods. 'Hmm... he wasn't my first choice to be stuck in a lift with. Oh, by the way, Bennet, Sergeant Stoker was enquiring about your bad back. Did you manage to get a massage?'

Whipple freezes, then shoots Frank a sideways glance. 'You can inform Sergeant Stoker his recommendation was ill-judged in the extreme, leading to a calamitous debacle. A fractious and lamentable interaction ensued with the owner of the establishment, riddled with degradations I dare not recount. I was subjected to a most unseemly display of pernicious vulgarity, which has left an indelible scar on my refined sensibilities. The entire episode was a harrowing affront to my dignity, and I am still reeling from the psychological repercussions. Suffice to say, I have buried the memory in the darkest recesses of my mind. I shall never speak of the abhorrent experience again.'

'No relief then?'

Whipple's voice booms off the walls. 'No, inspector! Indeed, there was no relief.'

'Right, I best make tracks.' As he heads towards the door, Frank remembers his primary reason for attending the post-mortem in the first place. 'By the way Doc, estimated time of death?'

53

Frank's office is not particularly big, and with seven officers gathered, there's standing room only. Superintendent Banks is in Frank's favourite spot, observing the view through the window, hands clasped behind her back. Prisha and Zac huddle in the corner near the door, alongside Dinkel and Kylie Pembroke. Inspector Arnie Jenkins, the supervising officer of the armed response unit, is standing opposite Frank, arms folded. A giant of a man, with a formidable sized head, he's not the sort of guy you'd wish to meet down a dark alley on a rainy night.

Frank flips his notebook open. 'Tomorrow at 11 am we raid the underground bunker. It will be a two-pronged attack, made up of two teams—Red Team and Blue Team. The main assault by Red Team will be on the mushroom farm and the entrance to the tunnel. That will be led by me and Prisha, with Arnie and his team of six armed officers at the vanguard, plus four K9 patrol dogs.'

Frank picks up a set of aerial photographs recently captured by the drone unit and hands them out.

'As you can see, the farm is situated at the bottom of a hill. The road is a dead end, so there's only one way in and out. We can park the convoy on the south side of the hill so we won't be seen from the farm. There's a small lake near the farm, not far to the north, and a rocky bluff to the east which abuts onto the farm compound. We believe the bunker is under this bluff.'

'Do we have an exact pinpoint on where the entrance to the bunker is, Frank?' Jenkins asks.

'Not exact, no. But we suspect an empty shipping container in the growing shed is merely a ruse hiding the entrance to the bunker.'

Zac leans forward. 'That's right. When we raided the place on Saturday, I knew there was something odd about it. It had two sets of doors. The ones at the rear opened inwards, which is unusual.'

'How do you know?' Jenkins asks.

'Two sweeping scuff marks on the floor.'

Frank continues. 'The Blue Team will be led by Zac and Dinkel, and four armed officers from ARU. You'll cover the moor entrance but you are not to enter the cave. We'll flush them out and no doubt they'll try to escape via the cave onto the moors where you'll be waiting for them.'

Jenkins juts his bulldog jaw forward. 'Frank, how are Blue Team going to get to the cave? Looking at the map, it's a good twelve mile yomp from the nearest road, and the weather forecast isn't looking promising with heavy thunderstorms predicted?'

Frank smiles. 'I've thought of that. I've been in touch with National Police Air Service, and they will transport Blue Team by helicopter to a location two miles from the cave.'

Jenkins nods. 'Good.'

Without turning around, Superintendent Banks says, 'What about pre-operation intel, Frank?'

'Sorry, Ma'am?'

'We need someone to go in undercover first to do a head count and make sure there are no members of the public on site.'

Frank scratches his chin. 'Aye, good point.'

Kylie raises her hand. 'I could go, boss.'

Banks turns sharply. 'Out of the question. You're inexperienced and you're on secondment from uniform.' Her eyes flit onto Prisha. 'What about you? You're unknown to the Murphys at this stage.'

'Yeah, sure. I can do it.'

Frank scribbles in his notepad. 'Good. That's sorted. Communications will be via the Airwave Network, so it will be secure.' He looks at Zac. 'However, once we enter the tunnel, the transmission may be patchy at best. Zac, your team may be out of range, so you'll just have to sit tight.'

'Gotcha.'

He turns his attention to Prisha. 'When you show up for the pre-op intel, I suggest you already be on a call to me via mobile phone. If they spot a police radio or a wire on you, then your cover will be blown.'

'Okay. Got it.'

'And you'll need a believable cover story. The Murphys will probably be on their guard due to our raid the other day.'

'I'll say I'm moving to the area soon and plan to open a high-end restaurant in Whitby, and I've heard from fellow restaurateurs that Top Moor Mushrooms have an excellent reputation. I'll be there to find out about their wholesale prices and deliverability.'

'Nice. I like it.' The smile fades from his lips, replaced by a grim frown. 'The best-case scenario is the Murphys come quietly, and we gain access to the bunker.'

'And worst-case scenario?' Banks prompts.

'If they scarper into the tunnel and bolt the door, then we're going to have our work cut out—quite literally. If it's still the original door to the bunker, it will be designed to withstand the blast from an atomic bomb.'

'And then what?'

Frank sighs and puffs out his cheeks. 'It will be a waiting game. A siege. Not sure what their set-up is like inside, but

I'm sure they'll have supplies of food and water for many a week.'

Banks isn't overly impressed. 'Let's hope it doesn't come to that. This operation is costly enough already.'

'Right, another thing. We think they may have workers inside the bunker. Zac saw an Asian gentleman last week toss a package over the fence to a drug dealer.'

'That's right,' Zac says. 'I got a good look at him, and he was definitely Southeast Asian. Vietnam, Thailand, that area.'

'We can't be sure how many workers are in there, if any, or what the arrangements are. But it's not unusual for drug gangs to use illegal immigrants in their operations and pay them a pittance or nothing at all. We need to tread carefully. I don't want any fatalities or injuries. Right, any questions?' The room remains silent. 'Good. Let's go over it again and see if we can isolate any weaknesses in the plan.'

54

Wednesday 19th July - 10 am

Kira Volkov is going stir-crazy.

Sitting in the canteen of the underground nuclear bunker, she gazes around the gloomy, smoke-filled space.

The Irish brothers, Cillian and Fergus Murphy, are at one end of the room, glued to a television screen that's wired up to an old VHS video recorder playing a Die Hard film featuring Bruce Willis. They are sprawled out on moth-eaten armchairs, legs hanging over the chair arms, chain-smoking.

Her compatriot, Viktor, is on the opposite side of the table to her, eating sardines in tomato sauce. Occasionally, he dips a fork into a jar of sauerkraut to accompany the seafood delight.

She glares at him with menace. 'Viktor! Can you please eat that somewhere else? The fish stinks.'

Viktor looks up, surprised, but follows her command. 'Sorry, Kira,' he replies in his deep timbre as he rises and moves his unconventional breakfast into the kitchen area where Eamon Murphy is making tea and toast.

Kira studies Eamon as he moves slowly towards her.

'How old are you, Eamon?' she asks as he takes a seat at the table.

'Sixty. Why?'

'You move like a man twenty years older.'

He shrugs his shoulders. 'That would be my arthritis and my harsh start to life. Can't be helped, I'm afraid,' he replies with a chuckle as he picks up a slice of toast and bites into it.

'Have you made a succession plan?'

His brow creases as he slowly chews. 'Succession plan?'

'Yes. A succession plan for the business. *This* business.'

Still confused, he nods over at his sons. 'I'm not intending going anywhere soon, but when I do, then Cillian will take over the operation and Fergus will be his sergeant at arms.'

She glances over at them with barely concealed contempt. 'I hate to say it, Eamon, but you spawned imbeciles.'

The comment takes him aback. He tries a smile but fails. 'And what do you mean by that?'

'Look at them. They are not men. They are boys. Cillian is a hot-headed fool and Fergus is weak. He has no spine. Not good attributes for running an operation of this scale.'

He carefully places his toast back on the plate and rubs his fingers together. 'Like I said, I aint going anywhere soon.'

She huffs and changes the subject. 'Me and Viktor have business to take care of tomorrow. Once that is accomplished, Viktor will return here.'

'And you?'

'My transport back to the Balkans arrives on Saturday. That is when I depart.'

'And when will you return?'

'Not sure. You will see me when you see me.'

Eamon shoots a glance at Viktor. 'And what is Viktor's purpose for staying here?'

'He will help pave the way for the next phase of our expansion.'

'I didn't know there was a next phase... or an expansion.'

She rises, pushing her seat back with a squeal. 'There's always a next phase, Eamon.' She scowls. 'I need air and sunlight on my face. We'll discuss business in the cabin at the farm. I cannot stand it in here any longer. It is unnatural and the cigarette smoke is in my hair, on my clothes, my skin, and filling my lungs.'

'Do you want the lads there?'

She puckers her lips, staring over at them. 'If truth be told—no. But as they are the next in line to the throne, then regrettably, yes, they need to be there.'

———◦———

The small gauge electric train clatters along the narrow tracks, rhythmic clanks echoing around the dimly lit tunnel. As it nears the entrance, the train slows, the screech of metal against metal reverberating off the walls. Kira, crouched on the edge of one of the flatbed trolleys, springs to the ground with ease, her boots landing softly on the gravel-strewn ground.

Without hesitation, she darts toward the imposing steel door embedded in rock, its surface pitted by years of grime and rust. Gripping the massive wheel at its centre, she tries to turn it, her muscles straining against the resistance.

The wheel is reluctant to budge even a millimetre.

Cillian and Fergus appear next to her.

'You won't budge that, love,' Cillian says, grinning cockily. 'Needs to be energised. It works on hydraulics.' He taps a button at the side of it.

The heavy locks and bolts hidden within the mechanism groan with the sudden injection of power. A series of deep thuds resonate as the hydraulics shift the immense weight of the door, a barrier designed to withstand the force of an atomic shock wave

As the door inches open, revealing a sliver of daylight between the bunker and the back of the shed, Kira sighs in relief.

The air is humid but at least it's fresh, a welcome change from the recycled fetid air inside.

She steps into the shipping container, followed by the others. They move swiftly across the floor of the growing shed towards the main entrance. Eamon hits a large red button affixed to the wall. A rumbling, creaking noise breaks the silence as the roller shutter rises.

'We need to get some fresh air in here. It's stifling,' Eamon mutters to himself.

They bob under the door into twinkling daylight.

Kira throws her head back, closes her eyes, and performs a series of deep breathing exercises accompanied by overhead arm stretches.

'That feels so good,' she purrs, her positivity a rare visitor.

Cillian and Fergus ogle her, leering lasciviously as her chest pushes forward.

Eamon shakes his head in mock disgust and heads to the portable cabin.

'Come on boys, keep your mind on the job.'

55

Wednesday - 10:02 am

The rhythmic thump of helicopter blades cuts the morning air. A large black Eurocopter swoops down like a giant pterodactyl into a clearing amidst the vast expanse of the Yorkshire Moors.

The six officers, dressed in everyday hiking clothes, disembark quickly, heads bowed, and scurry for cover. The chopper's engines roar as the craft rises. It veers violently to the left and soars away.

Zac, grinning, turns to Dinkel and slaps him on the back. 'Ah! This is the life, eh? Gets the blood pumping, no?'

Dinkel is not enjoying the Boy's Own adventure one little bit. 'It gets something pumping. I can feel a migraine coming on.'

Zac shakes his head in disgust as he pulls out a GPS tracking device and stares at it. 'Exactly two miles northwest to the cave.' He checks his watch. 'Just gone ten. A brisk walk should take about forty minutes, maybe less.'

The four ARU officers remove large packs from their back and pull out weapons. They check their Glock pistols, then safely stash them in concealment holsters inside their lightweight jackets.

The lead officer, Sergeant Toby Morris, nods at Zac. 'Ready when you are, sir.'

Zac is slightly puzzled. 'You only have pistols?'

He grins. 'No sir. We have assault rivals dismantled in the backpacks. Don't want to assemble them yet. It may look conspicuous. Not a typical accessory for a hiker.'

'Fair point. Okay, let's make a start.'

They begin their trek across the moors, the landscape stretching out before them, a patchwork of purple heather, grass, and peat bogs. In the distance, rocky outcroppings jut from the earth.

'You've got to admit, it's bloody beautiful out here,' Sergeant Morris says, trailing Zac.

'It is that. But never underestimate it. Watch your step. These bogs can be treacherous.'

The group marches on, their banter mixing with the melodic warbling of curlews and the distant bleating of sheep.

'Hard to believe there's a massive drug operation hidden out here underground,' Morris states.

'Perfect place for it,' Zac replies. 'The ingenuity of criminals never fails to amaze me. If they actually used their brains for the better good, they'd do just fine.'

'It's the lure of easy money.'

'Aye. The path of least resistance, or so they think.' He halts and pulls a bottle of water from his backpack and unscrews the lid. 'What's the time, Dinkel?'

'Ten-twenty. Forty minutes until the farm raid.'

Morris surveys the landscape with a pair of binoculars. 'There it is,' he says, pointing. 'I can see the cave entrance and the surrounding fence. Perfect vantage point for us. We can position ourselves above the entrance and sit tight until the prey is flushed out. A piece of cake.'

As they approach their destination, the wind picks up, carrying with it the scent of rain. Dark clouds congregate on the horizon.

Zac stares up at the sky. 'Right on cue. Weather's turning to shite.'

They take a wide detour to the West, making sure they cannot be seen from the cave, then circle back around to the East and come to a halt on the grass covered top of the cave.

As the ARU officers do a quick reconnaissance of the terrain, discussing the best vantage points, Zac reaches into his backpack and takes out a sandwich, then flops onto the springy grass. Dinkel sits down beside him and takes an apple from his pocket.

A low rumble of thunder rolls across the moors.

The first fat droplets of rain fall from the heavens, pattering against rocks, and waterproof jackets.

'How're you going, Dinks?' Zac asks, biting into his Tuna-mayo sandwich.

'I've got a bad feeling about this,' he replies sullenly.

Zac laughs and shakes his head. 'You're a real Cheerful Charlie, aren't you? What could possibly go wrong?'

As the rain intensifies, another clap of thunder growls across the land like a prowler searching for a victim.

With his appetite snuffed out, Dinkel tosses the half-eaten apple over his shoulder.

56

Wednesday – 10:20 am

Seated around a small grubby table, Eamon sloshes whisky into four small tumblers. He and his boys take the shots of whisky and knock them back, emitting gasps and wheezes.

Kira stares disdainfully at the amber liquid. 'You drink this early? That is madness.'

Eamon cackles. 'I always like a wee drop before discussing future business plans. It makes me lucid.'

Kira pulls a weary look. 'Alcohol dulls the brain.'

Eamon winks at her. 'Not this brain, lassie. As sharp as a tack.' He shuffles in his seat and leans across the table, becoming serious. 'Right then, what's this next phase you were talking about?'

Kira relaxes. 'I have been studying the layout of the bunker. Currently, you have five rooms used for crop production. You have another fifteen empty rooms. The next phase will be to double yearly production by utilising an extra five rooms for propagation. There will be additional costs, of course; irrigation, heat lights, grow bags, transport, and labour. But the labour cost will be a one-off payment to the people smugglers. After that, it's all profit, apart from their food. We must keep the workers well-nourished and generally happy... or as happy as one can be as a slave. Contented workers are productive. The grow bags—we need. But they are cheap. You now have two sources of energy supply, the diesel generators for nighttime, and your free source of electrical power for daytime. You are missing a great opportunity to expand.'

Eamon, Cillian and Fergus are silent but exchange unconvinced glances as Eamon refills the whisky glasses.

Cillian is the first to speak. 'You make it all sound so easy, Kira.'

'It is easy.'

He laughs and slugs the whisky back. 'Easy for you to say, taking a twenty per cent cut and not putting your neck on the line or doing any of the hard graft. Your suggestion is pure shite.'

'We financed your operation. If it wasn't for me and Sergei, then you'd be back on your Emerald Isle picking potatoes.'

Cillian stiffens. 'Don't fucking speak to me like that. You've got too much off your chest, woman.'

Fergus sniggers. 'Aye, but it is a very nice chest, all the same,' he says in a sing-song Irish brogue.

Kira ignores the smut.

'Boys, boys,' Eamon chastises. 'Show the lady some respect.'

Cillian rounds on his father. 'Since she arrived, she's done nothing but criticise and look down her long Russian nose at us. She thinks we're a bunch of yokels. We've more than paid back what the upfront costs were. I say it's time to cut the Russkies loose. Why should we feather their nest forever?'

Eamon attempts to placate his son. 'It's not forever, Cillian. And a deal is a deal.'

'You need to grow a pair, da, and not be pushed about by a bloody woman.'

Eamon leaps up and slaps his son hard across the cheek. 'Watch your mouth, boy. Don't ever speak to me like that again, especially in front of guests. I run this family and don't you forget it.'

Cillian's anger bubbles, then subsides like boiling milk in a pan as the gas is turned off. 'Sorry, da.'

'Good. Okay, forgotten.'

He resumes his seat as Kira watches on impassively, already noting a division in the family that may well be exploited at a later date.

She turns to Cillian. 'You are entitled to your views. I respect that. But please explain why you think my suggestion is not good?'

'Growing the plants is the easy part. Getting the additional labour is more difficult, but doable. The hard, and risky bit, is distribution. The more we distribute, the more we risk getting caught. We've got a nice little crack going on here. Why risk it all by upping production? Let's not get greedy.'

'If you'd let me explain, then maybe you'll understand.'

Cillian looks like he's about to snap again, but Eamon raises two fingers in the air. 'Hear her out, son. Hear her out.'

'Thank you,' she says. 'I take it you've heard of the Kelmendi family?'

Eamon frowns. 'The Albanian crime syndicate down south?'

'Yes. They supply cannabis to a quarter of London. They have a big farm operation near Salisbury.'

His frown deepens. 'Now, hang on Kira, I've heard stories about that mob. We're not shy about taking care of business ourselves. After all, you have to do what you have to do to protect assets. But the Kelmendi clan are on a different level, altogether. We don't want to be mixed up with them. We could all end up dead.'

Kira laughs and picks up the bottle of whisky. 'Maybe I will take a little snifter, as you English say.'

'Irish!' Cillian snaps. 'We're Irish, not English. Do you know nothing?'

She nods in deference as she pours a drink. 'Apologies. My mistake. I feel the same way about the Chechens.' She reflects for a moment. 'Although, Viktor is Chechen... but a Russian Chechen. Now where was I?'

Eamon prompts her. 'The Kelmendis.'

'Ah, yes. In six months, you will have paid off your debt to Sergei. Then I propose a fifty-fifty deal. You grow, we distribute.'

'We?' Cillian questions.

'We—the Russians. That is why Viktor is here. You see, once we have the other rooms in production, and are nearing our first harvest, there will be a very large fire at the Kelmendi's plantation. Everything will be wiped out. Crops, infrastructure, possibly people. The police will investigate. The Kelmendis will be finished, kaput. It leaves a vacuum that will need to be filled quickly. A vacuum we will fill. So, there is no risk for you. You can distribute to your established markets up north, and we will handle distribution down south. What do you say?'

The three men exchange glances, quickly warming to the proposition.

'What do you think, boys?' Eamon asks.

They grin and nod. 'I'm liking the idea, but I need more details,' Cillian retorts.

Kira throws the whisky back without flinching. 'Very well. Let's delve deeper into the details.'

As they continue discussing logistics, Kira's gaze occasionally drifts towards the cabin window. A lone vehicle catches her eye as it appears at the top of the hill. She watches its descent, barely giving it a second thought, while she continues explaining the expansion plan.

Eamon notices her gaze and turns. 'Oh, looks like a customer. Fergus, can you do the honours?'

'Sure thing, da.'

57

Wednesday – 10:25 am

Prisha is dressed in a lightweight, pale brown suit. The jacket sits above a short-sleeved summer blouse. Her mobile phone juts out of the shallow jacket pocket.

'Starting the descent, Frank,' she says, navigating the car down the track towards the mushroom farm.

'Good. What can you see?'

'Not much. Looks very quiet. A couple of cars, a truck, and a forklift parked outside the main shed. Can't see any people.'

'Okay. The line's not good, you keep breaking up. Don't overstay your welcome. A quick… rec… and… out… possible.'

'Sorry missed the last bit of that,' she says, frowning. 'You're breaking up.'

The vehicle winds its way down the gravel road and enters past the large steel gates. She spins the car round in the compound so it's facing the entrance in case a quick getaway is required.

'I'm here, Frank. A guy has emerged from a cabin and is walking towards me. Pretty sure it's Fergus Murphy. I'm about to get out of the car, so hit your mute button.'

'Aye, Roger that.'

Leaving the keys in the ignition, she steps from the car and offers Fergus a warm smile.

'It's very humid,' she states, pulling at the collar of her blouse.

Fergus grins. 'So it is. I heard a rumble of thunder earlier. I think we could cop a downpour.'

'Yes. At least it will freshen things up.'

'So, what can I do for you?'

Prisha holds her hand out. 'My name is Anita Sharma.'

'Nice to meet you. Fergus Murphy,' he replies as they shake hands.

'I'm moving to Whitby in a few months and I'm opening a restaurant in town. I've been talking with local restaurateurs, and they speak very highly of your produce. I suppose you could say this is a scouting mission. I wonder if I could see your set-up and maybe get a few samples of your mushrooms.'

Fergus beams. 'Of course, come this way into the growing shed.'

———◇———

Eamon picks up his pen again, and a fresh napkin. 'Kira, let's go over quantities and expected demand again, as I haven't quite got my head around the figures.'

Kira, already long tired of the men's inability to comprehend simple calculations, hides her displeasure.

'Okay, Eamon. One more time.'

As she reiterates quantities, costs, schedules, distribution logistics, her attention drifts to the compound and the woman Fergus is leading towards the shed.

'And of course, another factor to take into account is that immediately the Kelmendis farming operation is toast, the price for cannabis will increase dramatically.'

'By how much?' Cillian asks, helping himself to another generous glass of firewater.

'Hard to say, but a rough estimate would be...'

Her voice tails off as she focuses on the woman again.

Mouth agape, almost in a state of shock, she whispers, 'Sparrow.'

Eamon and Cillian are puzzled by her demeanour.

'Sorry?' Eamon asks.

'Sparrow.'

His gaze follows Kira's out into the compound and the new arrival.

'Do you know the lady?'

She grins. 'Oh, yes. I know her very well.'

'Who is she?'

'An old acquaintance.'

'Friend or foe?'

'Foe. We have unfinished business.'

Cillian grins. 'Oh, I'm going to enjoy this. I love a good catfight between two attractive ladies.'

'Watch your mouth,' Eamon chastises. He refocuses on Kira. 'Do you want me and the boys to give her the hard word and send her on her way?'

Kira rises slowly, watching the scene outside. 'Thank you for your offer, Eamon, but I have waited a long time for this moment. I will handle it in my own way.'

———◦———

As Prisha follows Fergus towards the shed, she does a little probing. 'Do you employ many people, Fergus?'

'Not really. It's a family run affair, just my da and my brother. Occasionally we'll hire casual labour.'

'Are you purely wholesale or are you open to the public as well?'

'We're open to everyone, but ninety per cent is wholesale. Direct to markets, greengrocers, smaller supermarket chains. We deliver all over the North of England. That's my brother's job—distribution. I handle the actual growing, and da does the accounts, quality assurance, all the boring stuff.'

Prisha scans the yards and still cannot see another soul. 'I suppose you won't get many of the public out here. A bit out of the way.'

He laughs. 'We have a few drop by, mainly on the weekend, but none today.' He leads her into the shed. 'Here we go.'

As she steps into the gloomy and musty atmosphere, she is acutely aware of how vulnerable she is. Swallowing hard, she steels herself. A harsh bell rings out, giving her a start.

Fergus pulls his phone out and answers it. 'Da?' He stares at the concrete floor covered in a thick layer of dust and grime. He lifts his head and eyeballs Prisha. 'Is that so? I see. Yeah, no worries.' He ends the call.

'Problem?' she asks.

He stares at her impassively before breaking out into a grin. 'No. Why would there be a problem? We'll start at the far end of the shed, in the cool room.'

Something tells her that's not a good idea. 'Actually, can you give me a moment? I left the keys in the car, and I think I may have left the air-conditioning running.'

Turning, she almost stumbles straight into Eamon Murphy. She lets out a little yelp.

'Sorry, there missus. Didn't mean to scare you. I'm Eamon Murphy.' He nods towards Fergus. 'I hope my son is taking care of you?'

'Yes, he is, I was just about to...'

'This is Anita Sharma, da. She's setting up a new restaurant in Whitby.'

'Is that so? Welcome, Miss Sharma. Always good to meet a potential customer,' he says, shaking her hand. 'Are you a chef?'

'Yes, I am.' *Christ, why did I say that?*

He takes her by the arm and gently spins her around and walks her deeper into the shed. 'And where did you train as a chef?'

'Ahem, oh, I trained in London, under... Chef Marcus Wareing.'

He appears troubled. 'Can't say I've heard of him. And whereabouts in Whitby will this new restaurant be?'

'We're looking at a few possible locations.'

'We?'

'Yes. Me and my partner.' *This is turning to shit.* 'I was just saying to Fergus that I've left the keys in the ignition, and it's in the on position. I'm worried about my battery,' she explains, glancing nervously at her car a good twenty metres away. She spots another man she recognises as Cillian Murphy, heading towards the gates.

Eamon completely ignores her as his grip tightens on her arm. 'What kind of cuisine will you be offering?'

'Erm... cuisine?'

'Yes. You know; French, Italian, or will it be classic local fare?'

'French,' she replies, her heart sinking as Cillian starts to close the gates. 'No, wait!' she shouts. 'I've still got my car inside.'

Eamon throws a sideways glance at Cillian. 'Don't worry about that. We can open up again.'

'Actually, you know what, I've just remembered I have an urgent appointment.' She breaks free from his grip. 'Maybe we could do this another day.'

'Aye, maybe we could. Then again...'

A voice, soft, yet menacing, whispers from behind. 'Hello, Sparrow. How have you been?'

Prisha freezes.

Blood turns to ice.

Sweat prickles down her spine.

Reluctantly, she turns, dread pooling in her stomach.

Their eyes lock in the suffocating silence.

'Kira Volkov,' she breathes.

58

Wednesday – 10:40 am

Frank glances at his watch for the umpteenth time. 'Where is she? It's now 10:40. She was supposed to be in and out in five minutes. What was the last thing you heard? My hearing's not as good as it used to be,' he asks, turning to Kylie seated behind the driving wheel.

'Something about cuisine. Then she shouted, wait.'

'What did she mean—wait? Was it an instruction for us to wait?'

'Not sure, sir.'

'Maybe she's spotted members of the public, or possibly children on site for some reason. Their website did say they offered schools guided tours of the farm.'

'I think all the schools around here are on holiday, sir.'

'Oh, aye. Good point.'

'What are you going to do?'

Frank puffs his cheeks out, then sighs. 'I'm loathe to change an operation at the last minute. In my experience, that usually ends up in a right balls up. The power company is killing the power from the illegal tap at 11 am on the dot. If we go in before, the Murphys could see us coming down the hill and scarper back inside the bunker. If they lock the bunker door, we could be in for a very long wait. Days, if not weeks.'

'But if they've rumbled Prisha, then the longer we wait, the more danger she'll be in.'

'Aye. I'm aware of that.'

Kylie turns, worry splashed across her face. 'They wouldn't harm a police officer, would they?'

'We're dealing with shady criminals, Kylie. According to Nick Prescott's confession—killers. They're not known for their critical thinking. If they feel cornered, trapped, then all bets are off. Anything could happen.' He grabs the police radio. 'Zac, state your position, over.'

Static crackles through the ether. 'In position now, Frank. On top of the cave sitting tight, over.'

'We have a slight problem here. Prisha has been gone for over fifteen minutes and we've lost contact with her, over.'

'Any changes to the plan, boss, over.'

Frank pauses before answering. 'No. Not at this stage. Our side of the operation will commence at 11 am, as discussed, over.'

'Roger that, over.'

As Frank steps from the car, he turns to Kylie. 'Right, lass, time to put on our ballistic vests.'

Kylie follows him to the rear of the vehicle, desperately trying to swallow her fear.

59

Wednesday - 10:41 am

Kira ambles forward with an exaggerated, relaxed gait, grinning. 'We meet again, Prisha.'

Her brain has turned to slush. She's hoping and praying Frank can hear her and is already speeding up the hill with the convoy of armed officers.

She decides to brazen it out. It's her only choice. 'What are you doing here?'

'I came to buy some mushrooms... like you.'

The Murphys are enjoying the confrontation.

Eamon addresses Kira. 'How did you two fall out? A miscommunication? A bad business transaction?'

Prisha takes the initiative. It's the last throw of the dice for her. 'I'm a police officer. That's how we met. And I'm here to arrest you all.'

The Murphy men all gawp at one another in horror.

'Cillian, search her,' Eamon barks. He turns to Kira. 'Please tell me it isn't true, that she's a police officer?'

She smiles and pulls a knife from a sheath attached to her belt. 'It's true,' she replies as Cillian fishes out Prisha's warrant card from her jacket pocket.

'Fuck, da. She's right. Detective Inspector Kumar. North Yorkshire Police.'

Eamon shakes with anger. 'You stupid Slovak bitch! You've gone and done it now. Why didn't you say she was a copper?'

Kira tut tuts and places the tip of the knife at Eamon's throat. 'Respect, Eamon, respect. Call me that again and I slice your tongue off.'

Cillian pulls a gun and aims it at Kira's head.

The ominous sound of a shotgun barrel being snapped shut has the Murphys spinning around.

Viktor marches forward with the weapon. 'I think everyone needs to calm down.'

Cillian lowers his weapon, and nods, accepting the situation. 'He's right. Why are we fucking arguing over a copper? She's here now. We can't let her go. So there's only one thing for it.'

Eamon pulls his son aside and whispers angrily in his ear. 'Killing random hikers is one thing. A police officer is another.'

'I don't see why,' Kira says, lapping up every second as she circles Prisha.

Cillian pushes his father away and places the barrel of the gun on Prisha's temple. 'Why are you here, copper?'

'We had a tip-off you were employing illegal migrant workers?'

'Is that it? Is that all?'

'Yes.'

Kira smirks. 'She lies. Someone in your organisation has talked, Eamon.'

'This is madness,' Eamon exclaims. 'She turned up on a routine visit about illegal migrants and now we're in a shootout at the OK Corral. This is all your fault,' he snarls at Kira. 'You could have ruined everything.'

'Calm down, old man. If she was part of a raid, her colleagues would have been here by now. She's acting alone. The solution is simple. After I've finished with her and got the truth, I'll kill her. The boys can bury her body on the moors, never to be found. Take her phone and destroy it and also her car.'

All three Murphys glance at each other as Victor lowers the shotgun.

'Okay,' Eamon says. 'Fergus, take her car and get rid of it in the lake.'

Prisha tries one last attempt to mimic authority. 'Mr Murphy, at the moment you're looking at charges of owning illegal weapons and threatening a police officer. You'll get time, I won't lie. But kill a police officer and you'll die in prison and your sons will be very old men when they're released. Don't listen to Kira. She's a certified psychopath.'

For a moment, Eamon hesitates.

Kira steps forward. 'It is already too late, Eamon. The die has been cast. There is no going back.'

Ruefully, he nods in agreement. 'Get the rozzer inside and down to the bunker. Fergus—car and phone. And when you get back, lock the gates and the bunker door. Let's ride this one out.'

60

Wednesday – 10:54 am

The noose is slack, as all nooses are until a heavy weight is applied to the rope.

Kira circles Prisha in the dim light of the empty room. 'Viktor, bring six bags of ice from the freezer room,' she demands in a joyful tone.

Viktor is puzzled. 'But why, Kira?'

Glaring at him, she says, 'Because I said so. Now do it!' As he leaves, she twirls the hunting knife around and around in front of Prisha. 'I've yearned for this day for a long time. There is no question about it; today you die. How you die is your choice. So, Sparrow, answer my questions truthfully and I will hang you quickly. Lie and I'll hand you over to Viktor, which will not be pleasant, then I will hang you slowly. So, the truth; why are you here?'

The cable ties binding her wrists behind her back dig into her skin. 'I told you before; we received information the farm was employing illegal immigrants. I was on a scouting mission. That's the truth.'

Viktor returns with six, kilo bags of ice. 'What should I do with them?'

Kira motions to the floor beneath Prisha's feet. 'Stack them in twos on top of each other to create a platform and take her shoes off.'

As he drops the bags on the floor and builds the platform, Kira pulls at the thick hemp rope slung over a pulley attached to the concrete roof. Prisha is hauled into the air, her face contorting in agony, feet and legs kicking wildly. She dangles like a stricken marionette until Viktor's task is done. He tosses her shoes into a corner as Kira releases the tension on the rope and Prisha falls in a gasping heap on the floor.

'Pick her up and stand her on the ice,' she commands.

Viktor roughly drags Prisha up by the hair. 'On the ice, now!' he bellows, as she yelps in agony.

Kira laughs. 'How rude of me. I forgot introductions. Prisha, this is Viktor. Viktor, this is Prisha, the woman who killed your brother, Maxim.'

Prisha groans in disbelief. 'Not my lucky day, is it?'

Worryingly, Viktor fumbles in his pocket and pulls out a pair of nutcrackers. He places them on a small side-table next to a pair of secateurs and a bowl of walnuts. Grabbing one nut, he places it between the crease of his elbow and biceps. Flexing his forearm, the nut splinters, and cracks.

The message is obvious—if he doesn't need a nutcracker to crack nuts, then what is it for?

Kira tensions the rope and ties it off to a metal bar bolted into the wall. 'Okay, let's try one more time. Why are you here?'

'Are you deaf, or just stupid?' Prisha spits.

Kira's face reddens. Striding forward, she slaps Prisha hard across the cheek, drawing blood from her lip.

'Do not play games with me.'

Prisha mentally calculates the time. *How long before eleven? Five minutes? Ten?* 'What do you want me to say? I can say anything you want to hear, but it doesn't change the truth. I'm here about illegal migrants.'

Kira holds the tip of the knife to Prisha's neck. 'Very well,' she drawls. 'I will hand you over to Viktor for a few minutes. Maybe when he's finished with you, your memory will have improved.'

'They do say people mellow with age, but my god, you're still a psycho bitch,' Prisha snarls as Viktor picks up the nutcrackers and secateurs.

He moves towards her. 'First, I shatter your fingers one by one. Then I remove them,' he says, holding the pruning scissors in the air. 'Then your eyelids, the tip of the nose, and lastly…' He drags the flat blade of the shears across her nipples, grinning. 'I will enjoy it, avenging my brother's death.'

'Viktor, listen to me—I did not kill your brother, she did.'

Momentarily, he's confused. 'You lie.'

'It's the truth, Viktor. Maxim fell down the steps of the lighthouse. He took a heavy fall, but he wasn't dead. When I came down the steps, he was still alive. Then Sadie Nutjob, over there, appeared at the entrance, took out her hunting knife and threw it at me, except she missed. The knife embedded itself in Maxim's forehead up to the hilt, splitting him open like a ripe melon. She killed him, not me.'

Viktor stares into Prisha's eyes, then turns to face Kira. 'Is this true, Kira?'

'Do not listen to her!' she yells. 'Of course it's not true.'

'I swear on my grandmother's life, Viktor, it's the truth. And she treated Maxim like she does you. Like you're nothing, worthless. She had utter contempt for him.'

'Viktor, she knows she's going to die. She'll say anything,' Kira states, a little unnerved.

He nods. 'Okay.' He walks around the back of Prisha, grabs her thumb and places it in the nutcracker.

Kira grins as she walks to the door. 'Call me when you are done, Viktor. I will collect our things. Change of plan.

I think it's time for us to depart early. Call it a safety precaution.'

The nutcrackers tighten around the knuckle of the thumb. 'Wait! Okay, I'll tell you the truth,' Prisha yells.

Kira turns and chuckles. 'Funny how the intense fear of pain can sharpen the mind. Please continue, Sparrow.'

It's desperation, but it's all Prisha has left. If the name is meaningless to Kira, then she's going to experience a gruesome and terrifying death.

'Magnus Crawley.'

The smile slides from Kira's face.

61

Wednesday – 10:59 am

A flicker of suspicion darkens Kira's gaze as she stalks forward. 'What do you know of Magnus Crawley?'

Prisha hesitates before replying, buying time. 'Did you kill him?'

'Yes, I killed the odious little toad. He was getting too close for comfort.' Prisha sniggers, which infuriates Kira even more. 'What is so funny?' she screams.

'You. That's what's funny. You unwittingly saved me from a fate worse than death.'

'What are you talking about?' she says, increasingly agitated.

'He was sexually blackmailing me. He was going to end my career, which would have sent me to prison, or I had to sleep with him indefinitely. You, my nemesis, got me out of a right pickle. I can't thank you enough. How does that make you feel?'

Kira's eyes flash with anger. 'Viktor, hand me the secateurs. I will do the job myself.'

A faint click and the dim overhead light fades, engulfing the room in darkness.

Confused shouting emanates from outside the room.

'What is happening?' Viktor asks, clearly alarmed.

'Calm down and stay still,' Kira replies. 'A temporary power cut. The lights will return.' She staggers blindly to the door and yanks it open as flashlight beams bounce off walls. 'Eamon! Eamon! What is happening?' A series of distant booms are followed by the unmistakable sound of barking dogs echoing from the tunnel. 'Eamon, talk to me.'

A figure staggers forward. Eamon Murphy, visibly shaking and holding a shotgun and torch, gasps, 'Coppers! It's a raid. They've cut the power.'

'How in Stalin's name did they get past the blast door?'

'Fergus panicked and didn't have time to lock it.'

'Imbeciles,' she cries, outraged. 'How many police?'

'Hard to say, seven, eight, maybe more. It's the armed response unit, and they have dogs.'

'Why have you not started the generators?'

'I prefer to take my chances in the dark, and it will slow the coppers down. We'll have to leave by the exit onto the moors.'

'What if the police are waiting there?'

'I don't think so. No sensors triggered before they killed the electrics. They may not even know about it. I suggest we get out ASAP, and once on the moors, we split up. By the time the police have covered every inch of this place, we'll have a huge head start on them. It's a long shot, but it's the only chance we have. Every man for himself now.'

More lights approach, accompanied by panicked Irish voices, cursing. Cillian and Fergus, out of breath, come into view.

Cillian sticks the torch between his teeth and unzips a backpack. Urgently, he scrabbles around inside before pulling out a pistol. 'Here, take this,' he says, thrusting the gun onto Kira. 'If the cops are waiting at the cave entrance, we can shoot our way out. We've still got time. It will take the ARU at least fifteen minutes to make their way along the tunnel.'

The angry barking from the dogs grows louder by the second.

'And what about the dogs? Do you know how fast a dog can run? Up to thirty miles an hour, some of them. They could be here within minutes.'

Eamon tries to regain command. 'Enough talking. The sooner we get out of here, the better.'

Viktor stumbles through the door. 'Aren't you forgetting something?'

'What?'

'The doors are opened by hydraulics. Without power, the hydraulics are useless.'

Eamon grimaces and clutches his chest. 'There's an override crank handle mechanism. It takes a few minutes, but it can be done. Come on, follow me. I know this layout better than anyone.'

The Murphys set off gingerly along the labyrinth of corridors. Even with torchlight, one wrong turn could lead them down a dead end and cost them precious time.

Viktor stares back into the room. 'What about Sparrow?'

'Time to end it now. Unfortunately, our fun has been cut short.' Kira steps into the room of complete darkness and fires off two shots. She hears a groan. Turning on her heels, she follows the disappearing lights down the passageway, with Viktor right behind her.

62

Kira and Viktor hurriedly catch up to Fergus, who is trailing behind his father and brother.

'Fergus, Fergus,' she whispers.

'What?'

'Wait for us. We do not have torches.'

Fergus slides to a halt. 'Hurry up. Those dogs are getting bloody louder.'

'You go at the back,' Kira suggests. 'Shine the light ahead.'

'Okay but get a move on.'

Kira and Viktor pass him and continue along the passageway, desperately trying to catch up with Eamon and Cillian.

The lights disappear for a moment as Kira aids her navigation with one hand flat against the cool concrete of the wall. Her hand flaps into thin air, then she picks up the torch beams again.

'It's a corner,' she says to Viktor.

Eamon's voice echoes out, bouncing off the hard surfaces. 'Next left and the door ahead opens into the airlock chamber and the blast door.'

They scurry on like sewer rats.

'What's that?' Fergus shouts, his voice full of dread. He comes to a dead stop and spins around as Kira and Viktor turn to look at him.

'What is it?' Viktor asks.

'A clicking noise,' he replies, his voice rising in pitch.

Kira instantly senses danger. She grabs Viktor's sleeve and pulls at him. 'Keep going. Hand on the side wall,' she murmurs.

'But what is that noise?'

'Dog claws on tiles. At last, Fergus may be good for something. He'll distract the dogs for a few seconds.'

They stumble on in near darkness until a piercing scream mingles with a gunshot and the menacing roar of savage dogs attacking their prey.

They turn the corner and rush forward until they hit an obstruction.

'It must be the chamber door.'

The rhythmic clicks return, gathering in pace and volume.

'Quick, Kira, find the handle. The dogs are nearly on us.'

She fumbles, desperate, berating the incompetent fools she must work with.

A deep growl from behind.

Locating the handle, she pushes it down and pulls.

It opens and they rush through, yanking the door shut.

The hounds thump into the door and jump up, scratching and howling, to no avail.

Catching their breath, they watch Cillian struggle with the giant crank handle.

'Where's Fergus?' Eamon demands.

'He didn't make it,' Kira replies. 'The dogs got him.'

'And you just left him?' he screams, incredulous.

'As you said, Eamon, it's every man and *woman* for themselves.'

He lurches towards the door. 'I'll go fetch him myself.'

'Don't be stupid, da!' Cillian cries. 'The dogs will be on you. It's too late for Fergus. It's his fault we're in this position in the first place.'

Kira frowns at Cillian's pathetic effort. 'It will take hours to open the door at this rate. Stand aside. Viktor, time for your brawn.'

The giant lumbers forward and takes the handle. His biceps bulge, blue veins popping up with the strain, but the large crank wheel begins to turn, and the huge blast door cracks open a fraction.

———◦———

Her feet are numb, the ice sucking heat from her body.

The cubes in the bag are melting rapidly.

As each minute passes, the noose tightens around her throat.

Her balance, precarious.

One slip and she'll be swinging by her neck.

The occasional drop of blood hits the hard, unforgiving floor with a dull splat.

Time... is not on her side.

63

Frank marches along the tunnel with Kylie at his side, six uniformed officers behind, and one armed ARU officer in front, chaperoning the group. Frank clicks at his radio.

'Inspector Jenkins, what's the latest, over?'

The response is instant. 'Frank, we're making good progress. One suspect in cuffs. Fergus Murphy. Two German Shepherds had him pinned to the floor, over.'

'Good. Any sign of Inspector Kumar, over?'

'Not yet. We're going as fast as we can, clearing each room and every corridor, but it's a bloody maze, over.'

'Other suspects? Over.'

'Yes. According to Fergus, there's Eamon and Cillian Murphy. And two Russians. One by the name of Viktor, last name unknown. And a woman called Kira Volkov. All armed. And three Vietnamese illegal immigrant workers who are unarmed, over.'

Frank comes to a dead halt as he immediately fears the worst. 'Kira Volkov,' he murmurs to himself.

'That's bad, isn't it sir?' Kylie asks, her excitement of the chase tempered with grave concern for her mentor and friend.

'Aye, lass. That's bad.' He stabs at his radio again. 'We're approaching the end of the tunnel now. We need to get the generators started and get some bloody lights on quick sharp. Have you spotted the generator room, over?'

'Yes. One of my officers is in there now. He's no expert but reckons he's a bit of a handyman, over.'

'DS Stoker, Zac, did you get all that, over?'

A pause followed by a crackle. 'Aye, Frank. What do you want us to do, over?'

'Stick to the plan. The situation is fluid, but if I were in their shoes, I'd be making my escape across the moors. And remember—they're all armed, over.'

'Righto. The situation is fluid out here as well. It's bucketing it down, over.'

The armed officer in front holds his arm aloft. 'End of the tunnel, sir. We're now entering the bunker.'

Frank turns to the troops. 'Listen up, team. We're entering the bunker. I want all rooms searched thoroughly. Let's find inspector Kumar and the immigrant workers. But remember, keep well back from the advance party until it's been declared clear. Understood?'

'Yes, boss,' they all reply.

He turns to Kylie. 'Enjoying your first major drugs raid as part of CID?'

'Not really. I'm worried about Prisha.'

'Aye, lass. Me too,' he replies, voice drenched with concern.

A distant hum is accompanied a moment later by the flicker of fluorescent lights.

'Thank God,' Frank yells. 'Okay, team spread out. Let's check each room thoroughly.'

As they advance, Frank is increasingly worried about Prisha's plight.

Why hasn't the armed response team stumbled upon her yet?

A sudden thought occurs to him.

They may have taken her as a hostage. It would make sense.

Although everyone is well-trained and knows their role, the scene is one of pandemonium. The constant yelling of gruff male voices shouting 'clear.' Dogs barking, howling, and now the overpowering smell of weed. Obviously, one of the team has entered a cultivation room, the change in air pressure sucking out the pungent aromas into the corridors.

Frank enters a large room which is a kitchen, dining and living area. He allows himself a moment to marvel at the sophistication of it all. All mod cons, even a television, and a video paused on what appears to be a Bruce Willis film.

He taps at his radio. 'Jenkins, where's Fergus Murphy, over?'

'An officer is about to escort him back to the farm now, sir, over.'

'Before you do, bring him into the kitchen. I want a word with the scrote, over.'

'Roger.'

A moment later, Fergus, handcuffed and with an officer prodding him forward, enters the kitchen.

'Thanks, constable,' Frank says. 'If you could give me a moment,' he adds, nodding at the door.

'I'm not sure I can...'

'Thirty seconds. That's all I need.' The words are polite, but his expression tells a different story.

'Right, sir. I'll be outside.'

'Good lad.'

Murphy averts eye contact, staring at the grey carpet.

'Where is she?' he growls.

'Who?'

'My officer. Inspector Kumar. The woman who turned up at the farm before the raid began.'

'I don't know what you're talking about?'

The punch is swift and hard. It hits Murphy in the solar plexus, knocking the wind out of him. He drops to his knees, struggling to breathe.

'I'll ask you one more time; where is my officer?'

He coughs and splutters. 'You can't do this. It's not allowed. It's not the fucking 1980s.'

'Funny you should mention that, because I'm always being accused of being stuck in the past.'

Frank grabs Murphy's ear, and in a classic moved used by schoolteachers from a bygone era, twists it violently.

The scream is deafening.

Kylie hurries into the room, assesses the situation, then departs again. 'I'll, erm, be outside, sir.'

'Good idea. Right, Fergus, do you want me to do the other one?'

'No, no. She's in a small room opposite the workers' sleeping quarters.'

'As I'm new around here, you'll have to be a bit more precise.'

'Out of this door, turn left. End of the corridor, last door on the right.'

'Thank you. That wasn't so hard, was it? Constable, he's all yours,' he bellows.

The ARU officer re-enters and stares at Murphy, who is still on his knees, bowed.

'I think he may be Muslim, constable. A call to prayers. Although if my geography's correct, I believe Mecca is behind him. Kylie!'

She bustles into the room. 'Sir?'

'Come with me.'

They leave the dining area, hang left, and race along the corridor.

'Prisha!' Kylie yells.

No response.

They arrive at the door. Frank pushes it open and holds an arm out, blocking Kylie.

'Maybe best to wait outside a moment,' he suggests.

'No way, sir. I'm going in,' she states, determination plastered over her face.

'Okay.'

They step inside, and for a split second, cannot comprehend what they are looking at.

Prisha is desperately trying to stand on her tiptoes, but keeps losing purchase, and momentarily swings back and forth before regaining her footing.

Frank rushes forward and grabs her by the legs, lifting her up. 'Release the rope!' he bellows.

Kylie tugs at the knot wrapped around the bar on the wall. It gives, and Frank gently lowers Prisha to the ground. Pulling out a penknife, he swiftly cuts the cable ties, releasing her hands.

'Christ, she's barely breathing,' he says, sliding the noose from her neck. He positions her carefully on her back, then clamps a finger and thumb over her nostrils. 'I'll have to give her mouth-to-mouth.'

Prisha's arm flicks up and knocks his hand away. 'Over my dead body,' she says, coughing and spluttering. 'Anyway, what took you so long? I've been hanging around here for ages,' she croaks.

Frank gazes up at Kylie, smiling. 'She's going to be just fine.'

64

With each cyclical turn of the crank wheel, the door moves imperceptibly.

Viktor has now entered groaning mode. Teeth gritted, face contorted in agony, the sweat pours off him.

Kira, being tall but the slimmest, tries to squeeze through the opening. 'Just three or four more turns, Viktor, and you've done it.'

He pauses momentarily to take a breath and gazes at the skinny gap. 'For you, maybe. Not for me. At least another ten revolutions.' He bends his back and continues, his biceps and forearms now resembling grotesque caricatures of a bodybuilder.

Eamon turns and stares at the chamber door. 'Did you hear that?' he asks in a whisper.

'No, what?' Cillian replies.

'I heard voices. The coppers are nearly on us.'

'Calm down,' Kira says. 'Voices carry in the corridors. They still have many rooms to check. Each one taking at least a few minutes. We'll still have a good start on them.'

He flinches. 'I'm not so sure about that.'

With a superhuman effort, Viktor lifts his pace. 'For some reason, the wheel is becoming easier to turn,' he says, grinning for the first time.

Kira tries again to slip past the gap. Turning her head sideways, she manages to navigate past the edge of the door and emerge into the gloomy cave. The first thing she senses is the violent thunderstorm raging outside, and the sound of angry water echoing up from the pothole twenty feet away, covered by sturdy steel meshing.

Cillian is next to emerge from the bunker, followed by Eamon brandishing the shotgun.

Clearly struggling with the exertion, he turns to Kira. 'What now?' he pants, struggling for breath.

She shrugs, nonchalantly, as her eyes drift to the grating again. 'I don't know. Maybe you should ask your Succession Plan.'

His stare tightens, as if trying to read her. 'Cillian?'

'Leave it to me, da. I'll go outside and assess the situation. You wait here in the cave. If the coast is clear, I'll call you.'

'Good lad.'

There's a loud groan as Viktor manages to force his huge frame past the door.

Cillian is already making his way to the narrow passage that leads to the cave's entrance, followed by his father. As they both laboriously scramble over boulders, Cillian pulls the pistol from his jacket.

'You be careful, son,' Eamon shouts as Cillian vanishes from view.

Kira stands rooted to the spot as Eamon follows his son into the grotto and waits on a large rock, panting hard.

'Should we not follow them, Kira?'

She puckers her lips. 'Not just yet. Let's see how it plays out. While we're waiting, let's remove the grating from the pothole.'

Viktor stares at it in disbelief. 'Why? You cannot be seriously considering going down there? The drop alone would kill you. And it's raining. I can hear it.'

She shakes her head in disgust. 'Always have a back-up plan, Viktor. Come.'

As they both scamper towards the grating, a distant cry of, 'Police! Drop your weapon and lie face down on the ground,' reverberates from outside.

A second later...

A single shot, followed instantly by a volley of shots, accompanied by a strident scream—then silence.

'No, no, not my boy!' Eamon yells. He labours forward, cocking the shotgun. His face writhes in pain as he grips at his chest. The shotgun falls to the ground as he slumps onto a boulder.

Viktor gazes at the scene. 'Should we not help him?'

'I think not. We need to help ourselves first. We cannot go out of the cave, and we cannot go back into the bunker. And time is running out. Viktor, summon your strength.'

Already fatigued, he manfully pushes two heavy boulders aside that rest on the edge of the grating, weighing it down. He places his fingers between the railings and attempts to pull it back.

Spent, exhausted, he gives up. 'It is too heavy, Kira. Even I cannot move it.'

She rounds on him 'You weak Chechen dog! Now is not the time to succumb. Summon your inner strength.'

'I cannot,' he wails.

She walks up to him and slaps him hard across the face. 'Listen to me carefully, Viktor, and let me point out your options; spend the rest of your life in a British jail eating their disgusting food; do nothing until the police arrive and kill you in cold blood; or shift the grating and take our chance in the water. I know which I prefer.'

His eyes bore into her very soul, and for the first time, Kira Volkov can feel the hatred.

She realises he could strangle her with one giant hand.

Lifting the pistol, she places it against his forehead.

'You heard me... move the grating now, otherwise I will save the police a job.'

Stooping, he grips the bars again, bends at the knees, leans back and uses all the power of his muscular legs to push backwards.

The grating shifts as debris disappears into the black hole, taking an age before a splash is heard.

He drops the grate to the ground, panting hard, his clothes wet with exertion.

'I cannot go down there. I am not a strong swimmer.'

Kira tosses the pistol into a far recess of the cave. 'You won't need to swim. The current will carry you along. All you need to do is keep taking deep breaths. It will help you float.'

He peers into the cavity, the roar of water increasing by the second. 'It must be a thirty-foot drop.'

'Nonsense. Ten at most.'

'I would not survive the fall.'

Kira bends at the hips and leans over. 'Look, I can see whitewater. It is not that far. See?' she says, pointing.

Viktor leans over. 'I think you are wrong.'

She skips behind him and pushes him forcefully.

His arms rotate violently as he tries to keep his balance.

A rush of movement from the bunker.

'Police! Drop your weapons. Hands in the air. Lay face down on the ground, hands behind your backs.'

Viktor loses the battle with gravity and falls into the abyss. A rumbling bellow echoes around the cavern.

'Aaaaaaaah!'

Kira holds her hands aloft. 'I am unarmed. My friend is in trouble. He needs your help.' Another deep booming yell thunders up from the pothole. Kira bends, and calls down, 'Viktor, did you survive the fall?'

'Yes, but the current is taking me...' His voice dies away.

Sergeant Jenkins repeats his command as he's joined by two more armed officers who train their weapons on Kira.

'I said, down on the ground and hands behind your back. Do it, now!'

Kira smiles at him. 'I don't think so. Do svidaniya.'

She pinches her nose and steps into the hole.

65

Frank is animated in his delivery, explaining every detail of the raid on the bunker. Opposite him, noticeably less animated, is Superintendent Anne Banks sitting impassively in a chair. Next to her is Zac, who listens patiently, occasionally gazing out of the window at the brilliant sunshine reflecting off the River Esk.

Frank finally ends the debrief and reclines back into his seat, quietly pleased with himself.

'So, you see, Anne, all in all, a satisfying outcome.'

Anne's eyebrows arch alarmingly. 'A satisfying outcome?' Her tone is incredulous. 'One suspect dead, another in a critical condition on life support in hospital after a massive heart-attack. The two Russians evaded capture and are presumed drowned in the pothole. And one of my officers, who was shot and nearly hanged to death, is in hospital with a gunshot wound and severe rope-burns to her neck. It's certainly an *outcome*, Frank, but how you can summon up the word—*satisfying*—beggars belief.'

'Prisha's injuries are superficial. The bullet grazed her thigh. She may be left with a very small scar, and the rope marks around her neck are already fading. They're keeping her in for observation tonight, but all being well, she'll be released tomorrow morning. Apparently, she's going to spend a few days with her boyfriend, Adam, up on the farm.'

'Superficial or not, any officer injured whilst on duty triggers an internal review and health and safety assessment. You know the amount of time and paperwork involved in that.'

'A box-ticking exercise, Anne.'

'Prisha will have to undergo a series of medical assessments and psychological counselling before she can return to work.'

'Aye, good luck getting her to counselling. Prisha is like a willow tree. She has the ability to bend in the storm but never snap. She's as tough as old boots, that lass. It's like water off a duck's arse... ahem, back,' he adds, with a wry chuckle.

Anne glowers at him. 'It's a clusterfuck, Frank. A gigantic cock-up. And I have to say, I find your attitude cavalier. Do you know how close we came to losing an officer? It's like you don't care. What if the bullet had hit Prisha in the heart?'

Frank's jowls harden as he stares back at her. 'I care deeply for all my officers, ma'am. And I have a special soft spot for Prisha. I no longer beat myself up with what-ifs, or what might have been. All I'm bothered about is reality. I may seem upbeat, and that's because I am. The fact is, we *didn't* lose an officer. And another thing, no one had any inkling Kira Volkov was mixed up with the Murphys. She was a known unknown.'

'Oh please, save me the Donald Rumsfeld's, Frank.'

'It's true. Why the hell wasn't MI5 aware of her involvement? Or maybe they were and just forgot to mention it to us. Whenever we have anything to do with that mob, it ends up in trouble. They are a law unto themselves.'

'We're not here to discuss the inner workings of the secret service. But we are here to discuss costs.' She lifts a report off her lap. Pulling spectacles from her pocket, she daintily puts them on her nose and scans the sheet. 'An estimated damage bill of thirty thousand pounds. Prisha's vehicle is a write off after being dumped in the lake. And another eight thousand pounds damage to the ARUs transit van.'

'I can explain. The gates to the farm compound were locked, so I gave the order to crash through them. You can't be fannying around with bolt cutters in a life and death situation, ma'am.' He throws Zac a sheepish glance. Zac reciprocates with a "really" look, then grins.

Anne removes her glasses and rubs at her forehead. 'The cost of this operation will run into the tens of thousands,' she murmurs to herself. 'That's before we even factor in the cost of the divers' search and recovery mission for the bodies of the Russians.'

'You can't make an omelette without breaking eggs, Anne,' Frank states, instantly regretting the remark.

'If egg breaking was an Olympic event, you'd be a five-time gold medallist.'

'Very droll.'

'The chief constable is not going to be happy, not happy at all.'

Zac leans forward. 'We have taken down a very sophisticated drug operation, ma'am. That's a lot of cannabis off the streets.'

'Yes. For a few months until some opportunist fills the gap. I sometimes wonder why we bother. We should decriminalise the whole shooting match.'

Frank takes his opportunity. 'And on another positive, ma'am, Fergus Murphy has been very cooperative. He's confessed that his brother killed the three missing hikers and buried their bodies in a peat bog. We'll be taking him to the moors tomorrow to try to identify the spot. Hopefully, we'll find the bodies and return them to their families. It will bring some closure for the grieving relatives. He also said his brother killed Jake Hill during a struggle, and he and Cillian dumped the body at sea, which tallies with Nick Prescott's confession. That's four murders solved.'

'And he confessed to a string of hijackings on diesel tankers,' Zac adds.

Anne sighs and slumps back in her chair. 'Yes, I suppose that is one positive to come out of all this, especially for the families. And what about the three illegal workers?'

'Vietnamese, ma'am.' Frank says. 'They're terrified and aren't speaking.'

'Do we know their story?'

'Not really. They have no papers on them. I'm assuming they were brought into the country by people smugglers paid for by the Murphys, then had to work to pay off the debt. Unfortunately, it's a common enough occurrence these days, drug gangs preying on the vulnerable. We brought in an interpreter. He said they'd been at the bunker two years and had one more year to go before they were free. Poor buggers. The only positive is that they're all in rude health. They were well fed and let outside occasionally for exercise and fresh air. An official from the Vietnamese Embassy arrives tomorrow. We'll hand them over to border security, and I'm guessing they'll be deported back home.'

Anne leans forward in her chair. 'You attended the autopsy of Magnus Crawley yesterday. What did Doctor Whipple conclude?'

'Crawley drowned. No drugs were found in his system.'

'Meaning he was conscious during the ordeal?'

'Yes. And according to Prisha, Kira Volkov admitted to his killing. Whipple put the estimated time of death at some point last Friday evening to early Saturday morning.'

'Which ties in with Crawley's last known movements, ma'am,' Zac adds.

She frowns. 'I still can't believe an officer of his experience could be lured into such a simple trap.'

Frank nods and sighs. 'Crawley was cocksure of himself, Anne. But this time, he flew a bit too close to the sun. No one is infallible.'

'Possibly. I've spoken with MI5 and they're sending up two officers tomorrow to seize his belongings and digital devices. Make sure you're here to greet them, Frank. They're setting up a special task force led by the National Crime Agency, with MI5 providing intelligence support and background information. Our role will be to provide reports of the crime scene and answer any questions they may have regarding Crawley's time here.'

'Did they say anything else?'

Sighing heavily, she replies, 'Like getting blood out of a stone. From what was inferred, Crawley was a maverick.

Kept himself to himself. Liked to work alone, off-grid. They gave him a long leash, as he always got results. As your surmised, his manner of death suggests he got lazy.' She rises and heads to the door. 'I want a full report about the operation on my desk by midday tomorrow, Frank. Then I'll have to front the media and put a positive spin on it all. And by the way, I've just heard from Fergus Murphy's solicitor.'

'Oh, aye?'

'Fergus has lodged a formal complaint of police brutality and forceful coercion.'

Frank is aghast. 'The lying mongrel. I can assure you, Anne, no member of my team would ever stoop to such tactics. It would be more than their job's worth. That behaviour is unacceptable and belongs in the past.'

'The complaint is against you, Frank.'

'Me?' he yells in all innocence. 'Has he any witnesses?'

Anne pouts and pulls at the door. 'I think you already know the answer to that. Goodnight, gentlemen.'

Frank and Zac watch her mope across the incident room, her usual officious goosestep replaced by a shuffling gait.

'No pleasing some buggers,' Frank grumbles, as he lifts his jacket off the hatstand and slips it on. 'That woman can suck the joy out of any situation. Just once it would be nice to receive congratulations and a pat on the back, not for me, but for my team.'

'I think she's still nursing a bruised ego from missing out on the deputy chief constable's job.'

'Aye. You have a point. Right lad, it's a nice sunny evening and The White House beckons. I need to slake a thirst. And it's a double celebration.'

'Why's that?'

'A successful operation, despite what Mrs Starchy Knickers thinks, and even better news—something I didn't tell you about. Meera was given the all-clear a couple of days ago. She had a biopsy on a small lump in her breast. The tests came back positive, initially. A bit of a mix up at the lab but all sorted now. She's in the clear.'

'Hell, Frank, you kept that one a secret.'

'It's not the sort of thing you shout from the rooftops. Right, you up for a few jars?'

Zac leaps to his feet. 'Does Dolly Parton sleep on her back?'

66

Saturday 22nd July

Frank pats his niece on the head with affection. 'Okay, Emily, I think it's time we packed up. Your Aunty Meera said she was serving up tea at five. We best get our skates on.'

'Aw! Just one more throw, please, Uncle Frank.'

As Frank winds his own fishing line in, he relents and smiles at her. 'Go on, then. One more cast but make it a quick one.'

'Yay!' The young girl winds in her line, checks the bait is still intact, then with a deftness she's silently proud of, casts hook, line, and sinker into the middle reaches of the River Esk.

Frank dismantles his rod, and packs away the flask and sandwich box into a backpack, then checks his watch as the distant echo of a pleasure boat throbs along the riverbank. He glances up to see the vessel approaching from upstream.

'You best reel in, lass, otherwise you could lose the lot in the boat's propeller.'

'Okay,' she replies, sounding deflated. 'Can we go fishing again tomorrow?'

Frank chuckles. 'Aye. Why not. I know a grand little spot down the coast where we can fish from the rocks close to a sandy little beach.'

'Will we catch anything?'

'Probably. Crabs for one thing, but if we time it right for the incoming tide, then we may snaffle some mackerel, maybe a flounder.'

As her line glistens in the water, droplets cascading from it, she spies something which piques her curiosity. 'Eh up, Uncle Frank, look at that,' she says, pointing at the object bobbing about in the ripples.

Frank stares at it. 'Well, I'll be. A little plastic football. Looks like there's something dangling below it.'

'I'm going to see if I can hook it.'

'You best be quick. That speedboat is nearly on you.'

Emily turns the spindle on the reel as fast as she can, but the plastic football bobs on by. 'Missed it!'

Frank takes her rod, clips the hook onto an eyelet, then picks up the backpack.

'You grab the tackle box. Make sure the lid is secure. Oh, and here.' He pulls a paper bag of jelly babies from his jacket and hands it to her. 'Don't tell your Aunty Meera, though. She'll have my guts for garters if she finds out.'

'Thanks Unc!'

As they turn to head away, the speedboat cruises past, the propeller making silent contact with the tiny plastic football. Fragments surface as the memory stick sinks slowly downwards, settling on the riverbed before a slurry of mud washes over it.

———◦———

The sign pings and lights up, informing passengers they can remove their seat belts. She unclips the lap sash and gazes out of the window as the British Airways Boeing 777 climbs through the clouds. A sense of melancholy washes over her as the land mass of England slowly fades from view.

A flight attendant pushes the drinks trolley along the narrow aisle of First Class.

'Champagne, Miss Gervais?' the attendant queries, snapping Tiffany from her thoughts.

She smiles sweetly. 'Yes, thank you. What have you got?'

The attendant holds a bottle for her to inspect. 'We have Dom Pérignon, Laurent-Perrier Grand Siècle, or Krug Grande Cuvée.'

'I'll have a glass of the Krug Grande Cuvée, thank you.'

As the champagne fizzes into the glass, Tiffany reclines back in her seat and rests her eyes.

'Can I take your meal order yet, Miss Gervaise?' the attendant asks, passing her the flute of bubbly.

Tiffany takes a delicate slip. 'Yes. I'll have the seared fillet of Hereford beef with truffle mashed potatoes, glazed root vegetables, and the red wine jus. Oh, and a bottle of red. The Château Margaux, I think.'

'Excellent choice. And how do you like your steak?'

'Medium rare.'

'Very good, ma'am.'

As the hostess moves away, Tiffany sighs, and thinks of Prisha.

———◦———

Prisha removes the casserole dish from the oven and places it on a heat pad at the centre of the dining room table. She prepares cutlery, napkins, then cracks open a bottle of Merlot and fills two wine glasses. Opening the farmhouse door, she spots Adam in the barn tinkering with a tractor.

'Dinner's nearly ready, Adam,' she calls out.

He stops and grins at her. 'Be right there.'

'Make sure you take your boots off, then wash your hands.'

'Will do.'

She re-enters the house and silently walks from room to room, soaking up the peaceful ambience. The warmth of summer has infused the air with an intoxicating, earthy aroma. In the sunroom she stares out at the vast landscape of open pastures and the verdant hills in the distance. To her right, even the normally dull North Sea is bathed in aqua blue as the fading summer sunlight shimmies across the water. She can just make out the ruins of Whitby Abbey high on East Cliff. Re-entering the kitchen, she speaks to the cylindrical speaker on the counter.

'Hi Alexa, play Cat Stevens.'

As the opening bars of "Where Do the Children Play" drift from the speaker, she hums to herself and sips on the wine. The tranquillity is an elixir she cannot ever remember experiencing. The sound of Adam washing his hands in the bathroom pulls her from the dreamlike state. She taps the homemade bread to make sure it's cooled, then cuts off four slices, butters them and places it on a plate on the table.

She takes a seat as Adam enters the room. He leans in and kisses her on the lips.

'I could get used to this. A hot meal waiting for me at the end of the day.'

'You're not the only one. Although, I'd have preferred a salad on a day like today.'

'Nah, I need something substantial after a hard day's graft. How's your leg?'

'It's fine. Please stop asking about it.'

He sits down as Prisha dons the oven gloves and lifts the lid from the casserole dish.

'Thanks for your help today around the farm,' he says.

She laughs. 'I wasn't much use.'

'That's not true. Another pair of hands is always welcome. I'll make a drystone-waller out of you yet. Anyway, it's not just that. I enjoy your company. You're fun to be around.'

With a large wooden spoon, she scoops out a healthy portion onto his plate and hands him the bread. 'I've been accused of a lot of things in my time, but fun has never been one of them.'

Serving herself, she lifts her wine glass and reaches out to clink his. 'Hope you enjoy it. It's Boeuf Bourguignon.'

'Eh?'

'Beef stew in red wine.'

'Ah.' He lifts a fork, then places it back down 'Actually, before we start, I have something for you. I was going to save it until later, but what the hell.'

As he departs the room, Prisha's puzzlement is obvious. He returns in a jiffy and hands her the small, gift-wrapped box.

Her heart skips a beat, instinctively recognising the proportions. Tentatively, she unwraps the paper, pops open the lid, and gazes upon the diamond encrusted ring.

'Adam...' she whispers.

He falls onto one knee, takes her hand and says, 'Prisha, will you be my wife?'

———⋅◇⋅———

The bow of the small trawler dips with graceful determination, slicing through the salty waves like a pen etching poetry onto a watery canvas. With each rise, it ascends to kiss the horizon, momentarily flirting with the sky before gently sinking back into the bosom of the sea's rhythmic embrace.

The woman holds the railings and gazes at the undulating waves, her mind lost in a whirlpool of emotions. Anger, humiliation, and hatred all fight with one determined, overriding passion—vengeance.

The thrum of the engine dwindles to an idle, the slap of the waves tickling the hull.

The captain emerges from his cabin and nods at a small modern cabin-cruiser anchored forty feet away. He shouts an order to a crew member who begins to lower a rigid hulled inflatable into the sea. The woman at the stern spins around, pulls an envelope from her jacket pocket, and hands it to the captain.

'It's all there, as agreed. Thank you.'

'My pleasure, love,' he replies in a broad Yorkshire accent, slipping the money into his coat pocket as he gazes at the cuts and scratches on the woman's face.

As she heads towards the side of the boat where the dinghy is being prepared, she turns to him. 'This *must* remain secret,' she hisses.

'You have my word. I don't care where you've been, what you've done, or where you're going. It pays to mind one's own business around these parts. There's an old Yorkshire saying, sweetheart; see all, hear all, say nowt.'

Her eyes harden with unmistakable intensity, reading him like a book. 'Hmm... I hope for your sake that is true. My country also has a saying; do not dig a grave for others or you may end up in it yourself... sweetheart.'

The captain removes his woolly hat and scratches his head.

The deckhand calls out as the outboard motor roars into life. She descends the rope ladder and takes a seat.

The boat bounces across the waves until it reaches the cruiser.

As she clambers aboard, the dinghy speeds off back to the trawler. She gazes upon the headland, now nothing more than a distant blur.

A tall, muscular man dressed in paramilitary black saunters up to her, smiling.

'Welcome aboard, Kira. Time to go home and lick your wounds, no?'

As the old trawler veers sharply to starboard and heads back to port, she scowls, then nods towards the mainland. 'Yes. I am finished with this grubby little island. Until next time.'

'And how is Viktor?'

She shrugs, unconcerned. 'Who knows? The last time I saw him, his huge Chechen head was wedged between two boulders as a torrent of water rushed over him.'

The man nods grimly, his brow furrowing deeper as he unzips his jacket with deliberate care. Kira remains unmoved, her gaze fixed on the mainland as it slips into the distance, her expression unreadable.

'Sergei is very upset with you, Kira.'

'Sergei can kiss my arse.'

'He asked me to give you something.'

Removing a pistol from his jacket, he places the barrel to the back of her head.

Keep In Touch

Your thoughts and feedback are incredibly important. If you enjoyed the book, please consider leaving a review on Amazon or Goodreads, or a review/recommendation on Facebook. Such reviews are not only deeply appreciated, but they also help fellow crime fiction enthusiasts discover and enjoy the DCI Finnegan series. Or even better, why not tell someone you know about the book? Word of mouth is still the best recommendation.

I thank you for giving me your time, a very precious and finite commodity.

In case you've missed any of the books, take a quick look at the **Also By Ely North** page.

All the best,
Ely North – October 2024

Ely North Newsletter

Why not sign up to my entertaining newsletter where I write about all things crime—fact and fiction. It's packed with news, reviews, and my top ten Unsolved Mysteries, as well as new releases, and any discounts or promotions I'm running. I'll also send you a free copy of the prequel novella to Black Nab, **Aquaphobia – The Body In The River**

QR code below.

Also By Ely North – DCI Finnegan Series

Book 1: **Black Nab**

Book 2: **Jawbone Walk**

Book 3: **Vertigo Alley**

Book 4: **Whitby Toll**

Book 5: **House Arrest**

Book 6: **Gothic Fog**

Book 7: **Happy Camp**

Book 8: **Harbour Secrets**

Book 9: **Murder Mystery** – Pre-order (Dec 2024)

DCI Finnegan Series Boxset #1: **Books 1 – 3**

DCI Finnegan Series Boxset #2: **Books 4 – 6**

Prequel: **Aquaphobia** (Free ebook for newsletter subscribers)

*Note: All books are available from Amazon in ebook, paperback, and in **Kindle Unlimited** (excluding Aquaphobia). Paperbacks can be ordered from all good bookshops. **Boxset print editions are one book compiled from three books. They do not come in a box. *** Pre-orders only apply to ebooks.

Contact

Contact: ely@elynorthcrimefiction.com

Website: https://elynorthcrimefiction.com

Follow me on Facebook for the latest
https://facebook.com/elynorthcrimefictionUK

Sign up to my newsletter for all the latest news, releases, and discounts.

Printed in Great Britain
by Amazon